#1 *New York Times* Bestselling Author

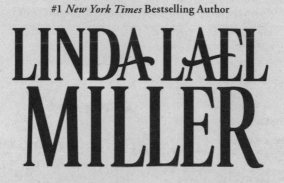

LINDA LAEL MILLER

USED-TO-BE
Lovers

D0249906

⬡ HARLEQUIN® BESTSELLING AUTHOR COLLECTION

ISBN-13: 978-0-373-01025-7

Used-to-Be Lovers
Copyright © 2015 by Harlequin Books S.A.

The publisher acknowledges the copyright holders of the individual works as follows:

Used-to-Be Lovers
Copyright © 1988 by Linda Lael Miller

Into His Private Domain
Copyright © 2012 by Janice Maynard

Recycling programs for this product may not exist in your area.

This edition published by arrangement with Harlequin Books S.A.

For questions and comments about the quality of this book, please contact us at CustomerService@Harlequin.com.

® and TM are trademarks of Harlequin Enterprises Limited or its corporate affiliates. Trademarks indicated with ® are registered in the United States Patent and Trademark Office, the Canadian Intellectual Property Office and in other countries.

Printed in U.S.A.

www.Harlequin.com

Praise for #1 *New York Times* bestselling author Linda Lael Miller

"[Linda Lael] Miller tugs at the heartstrings as few authors can."

—*Publishers Weekly*

"[Miller] is one of the finest American writers in the genre."

—*RT Book Reviews*

"Fans of Linda Lael Miller will fall in love with *The Marriage Pact,* and without a doubt be waiting for the next installments."

—*Fresh Fiction*

Praise for *USA TODAY* bestselling author Janice Maynard

"For those fans who love a decisive (and Stetson-wearing) hero who knows what he wants and goes after it, this one is for you. Here, Maynard proves that she is at the top of her game."

—*RT Book Reviews* on *Beneath the Stetson*

"A wounded warrior, a fragile woman and the kind of passion that starts forest fires yanks the reader deep into this dark read."

—*RT Book Reviews* on *Into His Private Domain*

The daughter of a town marshal, **Linda Lael Miller** is a *New York Times* bestselling author of more than one hundred historical and contemporary novels. Linda's books have hit #1 on the *New York Times* bestseller list seven times. Raised in Northport, Washington, she now lives in Spokane, Washington.

Janice Maynard is a *USA TODAY* bestselling author who lives in beautiful east Tennessee with her husband. She holds a BA from Emory and Henry College and an MA from East Tennessee State University. In 2002 Janice left a fifteen-year career as an elementary school teacher to pursue writing full-time. Now her first love is creating sexy, character-driven contemporary romance stories.

Janice loves to travel and enjoys using those experiences as settings for books. Hearing from readers is one of the best perks of the job! Visit her website, janicemaynard.com, and follow her on Facebook and Twitter.

CONTENTS

Also available from

LINDA·LAEL MILLER

and HQN Books

Visit the Author Profile page at Harlequin.com
for more titles.

USED-TO-BE LOVERS

Linda Lael Miller

For Jean and Ron Barrington,
living proof that romance is alive and well

Chapter 1

Trying hard to concentrate on her work, Sharon Morelli squinted as she placed a wispy chiffon peignoir exactly one inch from the next garment on the rack. This was a standard antiboredom procedure reserved for days when almost no customers wandered into her lingerie shop, Teddy Bares. She was so absorbed in the task that she jumped when two dark brown eyes looked at her over the bar and a deep voice said, "Business must be slow."

Sharon put one hand to her pounding heart, drawing in a deep breath and letting it out again. Clearly, Tony hadn't lost his gift for catching her at a disadvantage, despite the fact that their divorce had been final for months. "Business is just fine," she snapped, hurrying behind the counter and trying to look busy with a stack of old receipts that had already been checked, rechecked and entered into the ledgers.

Without looking up she was aware that Tony had

followed her, that he was standing very close. She also knew he was wearing battered jeans and a blue cambric work shirt open halfway down his chest, though she would never have admitted noticing such details.

"Sharon," he said, with the same quiet authority that made him so effective as the head of a thriving construction company and as a father to their two children.

She made herself meet his gaze, her hazel eyes linking with his brown ones, and jutted out her chin a little way. "What?" she snapped, feeling defensive. It was her turn to live in the house with Briana and Matt, and she would fight for that right if Tony had any ideas to the contrary.

He rolled his expressive eyes and folded his arms. "Relax," he said, and suddenly the shop seemed too small to contain his blatant masculinity. "We've got a project a couple of miles from here, so I stopped by to tell you that Matt is grounded for the week and Briana's with Mama—the orthodontist tightened her braces yesterday and her teeth are sore."

Sharon sighed and closed her eyes for a moment. She'd worked hard at overcoming her resentment toward Tony's mother, but there were times when it snuck up on her. Like now. Damn, even after all this time it hurt that Briana was Carmen's child and not her own.

Beautiful, perfect Carmen, much mourned by the senior Mrs. Morelli. Eleven years after her tragic death in an automobile accident, Carmen was still a regular topic of lament in Tony's extended family.

To Sharon's surprise, a strong, sun-browned hand reached out to cup her chin. "Hey," Tony said in a gentle undertone, "what did I say?"

It was a reasonable question, but Sharon couldn't answer. Not without looking and feeling like a complete fool. She turned from his touch and tried to compose herself to face him again. If there was one thing she didn't want to deal with, it was Maria Morelli's polite disapproval. "I'd appreciate it if you'd pick Bri up and bring her by the house after you're through work for the day," she said in a small voice.

Tony's hesitation was eloquent. He didn't understand Sharon's reluctance to spend any more time than absolutely necessary with his mother, and he never had. "All right," he finally conceded with a raspy sigh, and when Sharon looked around he was gone.

She missed him sorely.

It was with relief that Sharon closed the shop four hours later. After putting down the top on her yellow roadster, she drove out of the mall parking lot. There were precious few days of summer left; it was time to take the kids on the annual shopping safari in search of school clothes.

Sharon drew in a deep breath of fresh air and felt better. She passed by shops with quaint facades, a couple of restaurants, a combination drugstore and post office. Port Webster, nestled on Washington's Puget Sound, was a small, picturesque place, and it was growing steadily.

On the way to the house she and Tony had designed and planned to share forever, she went by a harborful of boats with colorful sails bobbing on the blue water, but she didn't notice the view.

Her mind was on the craziness of their situation. She really hated moving back and forth between her apartment and that splendid Tudor structure on Tamarack Drive, but the divorce mediators had suggested the plan as a way of giving the children a measure of emotional security. Therefore, she lived in the house three days out of each week for one month, four days the next, alternating with Tony.

Sharon suspected that the arrangement made everyone else feel just as disjointed and confused as she did, though no one had confessed to that. It was hard to remember who was supposed to be where and when, but she knew she was going to have to learn to live with the assorted hassles. The only alternative would be a long, bitter custody battle, and she had no legal rights where Briana was concerned. Tony could simply refuse to allow her to see the child, and that would be like having a part of her soul torn from her.

Of course he hadn't mentioned any such thing, but when it came to divorces, anything could happen.

When she reached the house, which stood alone at the end of a long road and was flanked on three sides by towering pine trees, Matt was on his skateboard in the driveway. With his dark hair and eyes, he was, at seven, a miniature version of Tony.

At the sight of Sharon, his face lighted up and he flipped the skateboard expertly into one hand.

"I hear you're grounded," she said, after she'd gotten out of the car and an energetic hug had been exchanged.

Matt nodded, his expression glum at the reminder. "Yeah," he admitted. "It isn't fair, neither."

Sharon ruffled his hair as they walked up the stone steps to the massive front doors. "I'll be the judge of that," she teased. "Exactly what did you do?"

They were in the entryway, and Sharon tossed her purse onto a gleaming wooden table brought to America by some ancestor of Tony's. She would carry her overnight bag in from the trunk of the roadster later.

"Well?" she prompted, when Matt hesitated.

"I put Briana's goldfish in the pool," he confessed

dismally. He gave Sharon a look of grudging chagrin. "How was I supposed to know the chlorine would hurt them?"

Sharon sighed. "Your dad was right to ground you." She went on to do her admittedly bad imitation of an old-time gangster, talking out of one side of her mouth. "You know the rules, kid—we don't mess with other people's stuff around here."

Before Matt could respond to that, Mrs. Harry, the housekeeper, pushed the vacuum across the living room carpet and then switched off the machine to greet Sharon with a big smile. "Welcome home, Mrs. Morelli," she said.

Sharon's throat felt thick, but she returned the older woman's hello before excusing herself to go upstairs.

Walking into the bedroom she had once shared with Tony was no easier than it had been the first night of their separation. There were so many memories.

Resolutely, Sharon shed the pearls, panty hose and silk dress she'd worn to Teddy Bares and put them neatly away. Then she pulled jeans, a Seahawks T-shirt and crew socks from her bureau and shimmied into them.

As she dressed, she took a mental inventory of herself. Her golden-brown hair, slender figure and wide hazel eyes got short shrift. The person Sharon visualized in her mind was short—five foot one—and sported a pair of thighs that might have been a shade thinner. With a sigh, Sharon knelt to search the floor of the closet for her favorite pair of sneakers. Her mind was focused wholly on the job.

A masculine chuckle made her draw back and swing her head around. Tony was standing just inside the bedroom doorway, beaming.

Sharon was instantly self-conscious. "Do you get

some kind of sick kick out of startling me, Morelli?"
she demanded.

Her ex-husband sat down on the end of the bed and
assumed an expression of pained innocence. He even
laid one hand to his heart. "Here I was," he began dramatically, "congratulating myself on overcoming my
entire heritage as an Italian male by not pinching you,
and you wound me with a question like that."

Sharon went back to looking for her sneakers, and
when she found them, she sat down on the floor to
wrench them onto her feet. "Where are the kids?" she
asked to change the subject.

"Why do you ask?" he countered immediately.

Tony had showered and exchanged his work clothes
for shorts and a T-shirt, and he looked good. So good
that memories flooded Sharon's mind and, blushing,
she had to look away.

He laughed, reading her thoughts as easily as he had
in the early days of their marriage when things had
been less complex.

Sharon shrugged and went to stand in front of the
vanity table, busily brushing her hair. Heat coursed
through her as she recalled some of the times she and
Tony had made love in that room at the end of the work-
day....

And then he was standing behind her, his strong
hands light on her shoulders, turning her into his embrace. Her head tilted back as his mouth descended toward hers, and a familiar jolt sparked her senses when
he kissed her. At the same time, Tony molded her close.
Dear God, it would be all too easy to shut and lock the
door and surrender to him. He was so very skillful at
arousing her.

After a fierce battle with her own desires, Sharon

withdrew, wide-eyed and breathless. This was wrong; she and Tony were divorced, and she was never going to be able to get on with her life if she allowed him to make love to her. "We can't," she said, and even though the words had been meant to sound light, they throbbed with despair.

Tony was still standing entirely too close, making Sharon aware of every muscle in his powerful body. His voice was low and practically hypnotic, and his hands rested on the bare skin of her upper arms. "Why not?" he asked.

For the life of her, Sharon couldn't answer. She was saved by Briana's appearance in the doorway.

At twelve, Briana was already beautiful. Her thick mahogany hair trailed down her back in a rich, tumbling cascade, and her brown eyes were flecked with tiny sparks of gold. Only the petulant expression on her face and the wires on her teeth kept her from looking like an angel in a Renaissance painting.

Sharon loved the child as if she were her own. "Hi, sweetie," she said sympathetically, able now to step out of Tony's embrace. She laid a motherly hand to the girl's forehead. "How do you feel?"

"Lousy," the girl responded. "Every tooth in my head hurts, and did Dad tell you what Matt did to my goldfish?" Before Sharon could answer, she complained, "You should have seen it, Mom. It was mass murder."

"We'll get you more fish," Sharon said, putting one arm around Bri's shoulders.

"*Matt* will get her more fish," Tony corrected, and there was an impatient set to his jaw as he passed Briana and Sharon to leave the room. "See you at the next changing of the guard," he added in a clipped tone, and then he was gone.

A familiar bereft feeling came over Sharon, but she battled it by throwing herself into motherhood.

"Is anybody hungry?" she asked minutes later in the enormous kitchen. As a general rule, Tony was more at home in this room than she was, but for the next three days—or was it four?—the kids' meals would be her responsibility.

"Let's go out for pizza!" Matt suggested exuberantly. He was standing on the raised hearth of the double fireplace that served both the kitchen and dining room, and Sharon suspected that he'd been going back and forth through the opening—a forbidden pursuit.

"What a rotten idea," Bri whined, turning imploring eyes to Sharon. "Mom, I'm a person in pain!"

Matt opened his mouth to comment, and Sharon held up both hands in a demand for silence. "Enough, both of you," she said. "We're not going anywhere—not tonight, anyway. We're eating right here."

With that, Sharon went to the cupboard and ferreted out the supply of canned pasta she'd stashed at the back. There was spaghetti, ravioli and lasagna to choose from.

"Gramma would have a heart attack if she knew you were feeding us that stuff," Bri remarked, gravitating toward another cupboard for plates.

Sharon sniffed as she took silverware from the proper drawer and set three places at the table. "What she doesn't know won't hurt her," she said.

There were assorted vegetables in the refrigerator, and she assuaged her conscience a little by chopping enough of them to constitute a salad.

After supper, when the plates and silverware had been rinsed and put into the dishwasher and all evidence of canned pasta destroyed in the trash compactor, the subject of school came up. Summer was nearly over; D day was fast approaching.

Matt would be in the third grade, Briana in the seventh.

"What do you say we go shopping for school clothes tomorrow?" Sharon said. Helen, the one and only employee Teddy Bares boasted, would be looking after the shop.

"We already did that with Gramma," Matt said, even as Bri glared at him.

Obviously, a secret had been divulged.

Sharon was wounded. She'd been looking forward to the expedition for weeks; she and the kids always made an event of it, driving to one of the big malls in Seattle, having lunch in a special restaurant and seeing a movie in the evening. She sat down at the trestle table in the middle of the kitchen and demanded, "When was this?"

Matt looked bewildered. He didn't understand a lot of what had been going on since the divorce.

"It was last weekend," Briana confessed. Her expression was apologetic and entirely too adult. "Gramma said you'd been under a lot of strain lately—"

"A lot of strain?" Sharon echoed, rising from the bench like a rocket in a slow-motion scene from a movie.

"With the shop and everything," Briana hastened to say.

"Quarterly taxes," Matt supplied.

"And credit card billings," added Briana.

Sharon sagged back to the bench. "I don't need you two to list everything I've done in the past two months," she said. Her disappointment was out of proportion to the situation; she realized that. Still, she felt like crying.

When Matt and Bri went off to watch television,

she debated calling Tony for a few moments and then marched over to the wall phone and punched out his home number. He answered on the third ring.

Relief dulled Sharon's anger. Tony wasn't out on a date; that knowledge offered some comfort. Of course, it was early....

"This is Sharon," she said firmly. "And before you panic, let me say that this is not an emergency call."

"That's good. What kind of call is it?" Tony sounded distracted; Sharon could visualize his actions so vividly—he was cooking—that she might as well have been standing in the small, efficient kitchen of his condo, watching him. Assuming, that is, that the kitchen was small and efficient. She'd never been there.

Sharon bit down on her lower lip and tears welled in her eyes. It was a moment before she could speak. "You're going to think it's silly," she said, after drawing a few deep and shaky breaths, "but I don't care. Tony, I was planning to take the kids shopping for their school clothes myself, like I always do. It was important to me."

There was a pause, and then Tony replied evenly, "Mama thought she was doing you a favor."

Dear Mama, with a forest of photographs growing on top of her mantel. Photographs of Tony and Carmen. Sharon dragged a stool over from the breakfast bar with a practiced motion of one foot and slumped onto it. "I am not incompetent," she said, shoving the fingers of one hand through her hair.

"Nobody said you were," Tony immediately replied, and even though there was nothing in either his words or his tone to feed Sharon's anger, it flared like a fire doused with lighter fluid.

She was so angry, in fact, that she didn't trust herself to speak.

"Talk to me, Sharon," Tony said gently.

If she didn't do as he asked, Tony would get worried and come to the house, and Sharon wasn't sure she could face him just now. "Maybe I don't do everything perfectly," she managed to say, "but I can look after Briana and Matt. Nobody has to step in and take over for me as though I were some kind of idiot."

Tony gave a ragged sigh. "Sharon—"

"Damn you, Tony, don't patronize me!" Sharon interrupted in a fierce whisper, that might have been a shout if two children hadn't been in the next room watching television.

He was the soul of patience. Sharon knew he was being understanding just to make her look bad. "Sweetheart, will you listen to me?"

Sharon wiped away tears with the heel of her palm. Until then she hadn't even realized that she was crying. "Don't call me that," she protested lamely. "We're divorced."

"God, if you aren't the stubbornest woman I've ever known—"

Sharon hung up with a polite click and wasn't at all surprised when the telephone immediately rang.

"Don't you ever do that again!" Tony raged.

He wasn't so perfect, after all. Sharon smiled. "I'm sorry," she lied in dulcet tones.

It was after she'd extracted herself from the conversation and hung up that Sharon decided to take the kids to the island house in the morning. Maybe a few days spent combing the beaches on Vashon would restore her perspective.

She called Helen, her employee, to explain the change in plans, and then made the announcement.

The kids loved visiting the A-frame, and they were so pleased at the prospect that they went to bed on time without any arguments.

Sharon read until she was sleepy, then went upstairs and took a shower in the master bathroom. When she came out, wrapped in a towel, the kiss she and Tony had indulged in earlier replayed itself in her mind. She felt all the attendant sensations and longings and knew that it was going to be one of those nights.

Glumly, she put on blue silk pajamas, gathered a lightweight comforter and a pillow into her arms and went downstairs. It certainly wasn't the first night she'd been driven out of the bedroom by memories, and it probably wouldn't be the last.

In the den Sharon made up the sofa bed, tossed the comforter over the yellow top sheet and plumped her pillow. Then she crawled under the covers, reaching out for the remote control for the TV.

A channel specializing in old movies filled the screen. There were Joseph Cotten and Ginger Rogers, gazing into each other's eyes as they danced. "Does Fred Astaire know about this?" Sharon muttered.

If there was one thing she wasn't in the mood for, it was romance. She flipped to the shopping network and watched without interest as a glamorous woman in a safari suit offered a complete set of cutlery at a bargain price.

Sharon turned off the television, then the lamp on the end table beside her, and shimmied down under the covers. She yawned repeatedly, tossed and turned and punched her pillow, but sleep eluded her.

A deep breath told her why. The sheets were tinged

with the faintest trace of Tony's after-shave. There was no escaping thoughts of that man.

In the morning Sharon was grumpy and distracted. She made sure the kids had packed adequate clothes for the visit to the island and was dishing up dry cereal when Tony rapped at the back door and then entered.

"Well," Sharon said dryly, "come on in."

He had the good grace to look sheepish. "I was in the neighborhood," he said, as Briana and Matt flung themselves at him with shouts of joy. A person would have thought they hadn't seen him in months.

"We're going to the island!" Matt crowed.

"For three whole days!" added Briana.

Tony gave Sharon a questioning look over their heads. "Great," he said with a rigid smile. When the kids rushed off to put their duffel bags in the van, the car reserved for excursions involving kids or groceries, Sharon poured coffee into his favorite mug and shoved it at him.

"I was going to tell you," she said.

He took a leisurely sip of the coffee before replying, "When? After you'd gotten back?"

Sharon hadn't had a good night, and now she wasn't having a good morning. Her eyes were puffy and her hair was pinned up into a haphazard knot at the back of her head. She hadn't taken the time to put on makeup, and she was wearing the oldest pair of jeans she owned, along with a T-shirt she thought she remembered using to wash the roadster. She picked up her own cup and gulped with the enthusiastic desperation of a drunk taking the hair of the dog. "You're making an awfully big deal out of this, aren't you?" she hedged.

Tony shrugged. "If you're taking the kids out of town," he said, "I'd like to know about it."

"Okay," Sharon replied, enunciating clearly. "Tony, I am taking the kids out of town."

His eyes were snapping. "Thanks," he said, and then he headed right for the den. The man had an absolute genius for finding out things Sharon didn't want him to know.

He came out with a rolled-up blueprint under one arm, looking puzzled. "You slept downstairs?"

Sharon took a moment to regret not making up the hide-a-bed, and then answered, "I was watching a movie. Joseph Cotten and Ginger Rogers."

Tony leaned back against the counter. "The TV in our room doesn't work?"

Sharon put her hands on her hips. "What is this, an audit? I felt like sleeping downstairs, all right?"

His grin was gentle and a little sad, and for a moment he looked though he was about to confide something. In the end he finished his coffee, set the mug in the sink and went out to talk to the kids without saying another word to Sharon.

She hurried upstairs and hastily packed a bag of her own. A glance in the vanity mirror made her regret not putting on her makeup.

When she came downstairs again, the kids had finished their cereal and Tony was gone. Sharon felt both relief and disappointment. She'd gotten off to a bad start, but she was determined to salvage the rest of the day.

The Fates didn't seem to be on Sharon's side. The cash machine at the bank nearly ate her card, the grocery store was crowded and, on the way to the ferry dock, she had a flat tire.

It was midafternoon and clouds were gathering in the sky by the time she drove the van aboard the ferry connecting Port Webster with Vashon Island and points beyond. Briana and Matt bought cinnamon rolls at the snack bar and went outside onto the upper deck to feed the gulls. Sharon watched them through the window, thinking what beautiful children they were, and smiled.

Briana had been a baby when her bewildered, young father had married Sharon. Sharon had changed Bri's diapers, walked the floor with her when she had colic, kissed skinned knees and elbows to make them better. She had made angel costumes for Christmas pageants, trudged from house to house while Briana sold cookies for her Brownie troop and ridden shotgun on trick-or-treat expeditions.

She had earned her stripes as a mother.

The ferry whistle droned, and Sharon started in surprise. The short ride was over, and the future was waiting to happen.

She herded the kids below decks to the car, and they drove down the noisy metal ramp just as the heavy gray skies gave way to a thunderous rain.

Chapter 2

Holding a bag of groceries in one arm, Sharon struggled with the sticky lock on the A-frame's back door.

"Mom, I'm getting wet!" Briana complained from behind her.

Sharon sunk her teeth into her lower lip and gave the key a furious jiggle just as a lightning bolt sliced through the sky and then danced, crackling, on the choppy waters of the sound.

"Whatever you do, wire-mouth," Matt told his sister, gesturing toward the gray clouds overhead, "don't smile. You're a human lightning rod."

"Shut up, Matthew," Sharon and Briana responded in chorus, just as the lock finally gave way.

Sharon's ears were immediately met by an ominous hissing roar. She set the groceries down on the kitchen counter and flipped on the lights as Bri and Matt both rushed inside in search of the noise.

"Oh, ick!" Bri wailed, when they'd gone down the three steps leading from the kitchen to the dining and living room area. "The carpet's all wet!"

Matt's response was a whoop of delight. His feet made a loud squishing sound as he stomped around the table.

"Don't touch any of the light switches," Sharon warned, dashing past them and following the river of water upstream to the bathroom. The source of the torrent proved to be a broken pipe under the sink; she knelt to turn the valve and shut off the flow. "Now what do I do?" she whispered, resting her forehead against the sink cabinet. Instantly, her sneakers and the lower part of her jeans were sodden.

The telephone rang just as she was getting back to her feet, and Matt's voice carried through the shadowy interior of the summer place she and Tony had bought after his family's company had landed a particularly lucrative contract three years before. "Yeah, we got here okay, if you don't count the flat tire. It's real neat, Dad—a pipe must have broke or something because there's water everywhere and the floor's like mush—"

Sharon drew in a deep breath, let it out again and marched into the living room, where she summarily snatched the receiver from her son's hand. "'Neat' is not the word I would choose," she told her ex-husband sourly, giving Matt a look.

Tony asked a few pertinent questions and Sharon answered them. Yes, she'd found the source of the leak, yes, she'd turned off the valve, yes, the place was practically submerged.

"So who do I call?" she wanted to know.

"Nobody," Tony answered flatly. "I'll be there on the next ferry."

Sharon needed a little distance; that was one of the reasons she'd decided to visit the island in the first place. "I don't think that would be a good idea…" she began, only to hear a click. "Tony?"

A steady hum sounded in her ear.

Hastily, she dialed his number; she got his message. Sharon told it, in no uncertain terms, what she thought of its high-handed owner and hung up with a crash.

Both Bri and Matt were looking at her with wide eyes, their hair and jackets soaking from the rain. Maternal guilt swept over Sharon; she started to explain why she was frustrated with Tony and gave up in midstream, spreading her hands out wide and then slapping her thighs in defeat. "What can I say?" she muttered. "Take off your shoes and coats and get up on the sofa."

Rain was thrumming against the windows, and the room was cold. Sharon went resolutely to the fireplace and laid crumpled newspaper and kindling in the grate, then struck a match. A cheery blaze caught as she adjusted the damper, took one of the paper-wrapped supermarket logs from the old copper caldron nearby and tossed it into the fire.

When she turned from that, Bri and Matt were both settled on the couch.

"Is Daddy coming?" Briana asked in a small voice.

Sharon sighed, feeling patently inadequate, and then nodded. "Yes."

"How come you got so mad at him?" Matt wanted to know. "He just wants to help, doesn't he?"

Sharon pretended she hadn't heard the question and trudged back toward the kitchen, a golden oasis in the gloom. "Who wants hot chocolate?" she called, trying to sound lighthearted.

Both Bri and Matt allowed that cocoa would taste

good right about then, but their voices sounded a little thin.

Sharon put water on to heat for instant coffee and took cocoa from the cupboard and milk and sugar from the bag of groceries she'd left on the counter. Outside the wind howled, and huge droplets of rain flung themselves at the windows and the roof. "I kind of like a good storm once in a while," Sharon remarked cheerfully.

"What happens when we run out of logs?" Briana wanted to know. "We'll freeze to death!"

Matt gave a gleeful howl at this. "Nobody freezes to death in August, blitz-brain."

Sharon closed her eyes and counted to ten before saying, "Let's just cease and desist, okay? We're all going to have to take a positive approach here." The moment the words were out of her mouth, the power went off.

Resigned to heeding her own advice, Sharon carried cups of lukewarm cocoa to the kids, then poured herself a mugful of equally unappealing coffee. Back in the living room, she threw another log on the fire, then peeled off her wet sneakers and socks and curled up in an easy chair.

"Isn't this nice?" she asked.

Briana rolled her eyes. "Yeah, Mom. This is great."

"Terrific," agreed Matt, glaring into the fire.

"Maybe we could play a game," Sharon suggested, determined.

"What?" scoffed Bri, stretching out both hands in a groping gesture. "Blindman's bluff?"

It *was* a little dark. With a sigh, Sharon tilted her head back and closed her eyes. Memories greeted her within an instant.

She and Tony had escaped to the island often that

first summer after they bought the A-frame, bringing wine, romantic music and very little else. They'd walked on the rocky beaches for hours, hand in hand, having so much to say to each other that the words just tumbled out, never needing to be weighed and measured first.

And later, when the sun had gone and a fire had been snapping on the hearth, they'd listened to music in the dark and made love with that tender violence peculiar to those who find each other fascinating.

Sharon opened her eyes, grateful for the shadows that hid the tears glimmering on her lashes. *When did it change, Tony?* she asked in silent despair. *When did we stop making love on the floor, in the dark, with music swelling around us?*

It was several moments before Sharon could compose herself. She shifted in her chair and peered toward Bri and Matthew.

They'd fallen asleep at separate ends of the long couch and, smiling, Sharon got up and tiptoed across the wet carpet to the stairs. At the top was an enormous loft divided into three bedrooms and a bath, and she entered the largest chamber, pausing for a moment at the floor-to-ceiling windows overlooking the sound.

In the distance Sharon saw the lights of an approaching ferry and, in spite of her earlier annoyance, her spirits were lifted by the sight. Being careful not to look at the large brass bed she and Tony had once shared—Lord knew, the living room memories were painful enough— she took two woolen blankets from the cedar chest at its foot and carried them back downstairs.

After covering the children, Sharon put the last store-bought log on the fire and then made her way back to the chair where she rested her head on one arm and sighed, her mind sliding back into the past again, her gaze fixed on the flames.

There had been problems from the first, but the trouble between Tony and herself had started gaining real momentum two years before, when Matt had entered kindergarten. Bored, wanting to accomplish something on her own, Sharon had immediately opened Teddy Bares, and things had gone downhill from that day forward. The cracks in the marriage had become chasms.

She closed her eyes with a yawn and sighed again. The next thing she knew, there was a thumping noise and a bright light flared beyond her lids.

Sharon awakened to see Tony crouched on the hearth, putting dry wood on the fire. His dark hair was wet and curling slightly at the nape of his neck, and she had a compulsion to kiss him there. At one time, she would have done it without thinking.

"Hello, handsome," she said.

He looked back at her over one broad, leather-jacketed shoulder and favored her with the same soul-wrenching grin that had won her heart more than ten years before, when he'd walked into the bookstore where she was working and promptly asked her out. "Hi," he replied in a low, rumbling whisper.

"Have you been here long?"

Tony shook his head, and the fire highlighted his ebony hair with shades of crimson. "Ten minutes, maybe." She wondered if those shadows in his brown eyes were memories of other, happier visits to the island house.

She felt a need to make conversation. Mundane conversation unrelated to flickering firelight, thunderstorms, music and love. "Is the power out on the mainland, too?"

Again, Tony shook his head. There was a solemn set to his face, and although Sharon couldn't read his expression now, she sensed that his thoughts were similar to hers. When he extended his hand, she automatically offered her own.

"I'm hungry," complained a sleepy voice.

Tony grinned and let go of Sharon's hand to ruffle his son's hair. "So what else is new?"

"Dad, is that you?" The relief in the little boy's voice made Sharon wonder if she'd handled things so badly that only Tony could make them better.

Tony's chuckle was warm and reassuring, even to Sharon, who hadn't thought she needed reassuring. "One and the same. You were right about the floor—it is like mush."

Bri stirred at this, yawning, and then flung her arms around Tony's neck with a cry of joy. "Can we go home?" she pleaded. "Right now?"

Tony set her gently away. "We can't leave until we've done something about the flood problem—which means we're going to have to rough it." Two small faces fell, and he laughed. "Of course, by that I mean eating supper at the Sea Gull Café."

"They've got lights?" Bri asked enthusiastically.

"And heat?" Matt added. "I'm freezing."

"Nobody freezes in August," Bri immediately quoted back to him. "Blitz-brain."

"I see things are pretty much normal around here," Tony observed in wry tones, his head turned toward Sharon.

She nodded and sat up, reaching for her wet socks and sneakers. "An element of desperation has been added, however," she pointed out. "As Exhibit A, I give

you these two, who have agreed to darken the doorway
of the Sea Gull Café."

"It doesn't have that name for nothing, you know,"
Bri said sagely, getting into her shoes. "Don't anybody
order the fried chicken."

Tony laughed again and the sound, as rich and warm
as it was, made Sharon feel hollow inside, and raw. She
ached for things to be as they had been, but it was too
late for too many reasons. Hoping was a fool's crusade.

Rain was beating at the ground as the four of them
ran toward Tony's car. Plans encased in cardboard tubes
filled the back seat, and the kids, used to their worka-
holic father, simply pushed them out of the way. Sharon, however, felt an old misery swelling in her throat
and avoided Tony's eyes when she got into the car beside him and fastened her seat belt.

She felt, and probably looked, like the proverbial
drowned rat, and she started with surprise when the
back of Tony's hand gently brushed her cheek.

"Smile," he said.

Sharon tried, but the effort faltered. To cover that she
quipped, "How can I, when I'm condemned to a meal
of sea gull, Southern-style?"

Tony didn't laugh. Didn't even grin. The motion of
his hand was too swift and too forceful for the task of
shifting the car into reverse.

Overlooking the angry water, the restaurant was
filled with light and warmth and laughter. Much of the
island's population seemed to have gathered inside to
compare this storm to the ones in '56 or '32 or '77, to
play the jukebox nonstop, and to keep the kitchen staff
and the beaming waitresses hopping.

After a surprisingly short wait, a booth became available and the Morellis were seated.

Anybody would think we were still a family, Sharon thought, looking from one beloved, familiar face to another, and then at her own, reflected in the dark window looming above the table. Her hair was stringy and her makeup was gone. She winced.

When she turned her head, Tony was watching her. There was a sort of sad amusement in his eyes. "You look beautiful," he said quietly.

Matt groaned, embarrassed that such a sloppy sentiment should be displayed in public.

"Kissy, kissy," added Briana, not to be outdone.

"How does Swiss boarding school sound to you two?" Tony asked his children, without cracking a smile. "I see a place high in the Alps, with five nuns to every kid...."

Bri and Matt subsided, giggling, and Sharon felt a stab of envy at the easy way he dealt with them. She was too tired, too hungry, too vulnerable. She purposely thought about the rolled blueprints in the back seat of Tony's car and let the vision fuel her annoyance.

The man never went anywhere or did anything without dragging some aspect of Morelli Construction along with him, and yet he couldn't seem to understand why Teddy Bares meant so much to her.

By the time the cheeseburgers, fries and milk shakes arrived, Sharon was on edge. Tony gave her a curious look, but made no comment.

When they returned to the A-frame, the power was back on. Sharon sent the kids upstairs to bed, and Tony brought a set of tools in from the trunk of his car, along with a special vacuum cleaner and fans.

While Sharon operated the vacuum, drawing gallon after gallon of water out of the rugs, Tony fixed the broken pipe in the bathroom. When that was done, he raised some of the carpet and positioned the fans so that they would dry the floor beneath.

Sharon brewed a fresh pot of coffee and poured a cup for Tony, determined to do better than she had in the restaurant as the modern ex-wife. Whatever that was.

"I appreciate everything you've done," she said with a stiff smile, extending the mug of coffee.

Tony, who was sitting at the dining table by then, a set of the infernal blueprints unrolled before him, gave her an ironic look. "The hell you do," he said. Then, taking the coffee she offered, he added a crisp, "Thanks."

Sharon wrenched back a chair and plopped into it. "Wait one second here," she said when Tony would have let the blueprints absorb his attention again. "Wait one damn second. I *do* appreciate your coming out here."

Tony just looked at her, his eyes conveying his disbelief...and his anger.

"Okay," Sharon said on a long breath. "You heard the message I left on your answering machine, right?"

"Right," he replied, and the word rumbled with a hint of thunder.

"I didn't really mean that part where I called you an officious, overbearing—" Her voice faltered.

"Chauvinistic jerk," Tony supplied graciously.

Sharon bit her lower lip, then confessed, "Maybe I shouldn't have put it in exactly those terms. It was just that—well, I'm never going to know whether or not I can handle a crisis if you rush to the rescue every time I have a little problem—"

"Why are you so damn scared of needing me?" Tony broke in angrily.

Sharon pushed back her chair and went to the kitchen to pour a cup of coffee for herself. When she returned, she felt a bit more composed than she had a few moments before.

She changed the subject. "I was thinking," she said evenly, "about how it used to be with us before your construction company became so big—before Teddy Bares..."

Tony gave a ragged sigh. "Those things are only excuses, Sharon, and you know it."

She glanced toward the fire, thinking of nights filled with love and music. Inside, her heart ached. "I don't understand what you mean," she said woodenly.

"You're a liar," Tony responded with cruel directness, and then he was studying the blueprints again.

"Where are you sleeping tonight?" Sharon asked after a few minutes, trying to sound disinterested, unconcerned, too sophisticated to worry about little things like beds and divorces.

Tony didn't look up. His only reply was a shrug.

Sharon yawned. "Well, I think I'll turn in," she said. "Good night."

"Good night," Tony responded in a bland tone, still immersed in the plans for the next project.

Sharon fought an utterly childish urge to spill her coffee all over his blueprints and left the table. Halfway up the stairs, she looked back and saw that Tony was watching her.

For a moment she froze in the grip of some unnamed emotion passing between them, but her paralysis was broken when Tony dropped his gaze to his work.

Upstairs, Sharon took a quick shower, brushed her teeth, pulled on a cotton nightgown and crawled into the big, lonely bed. Gazing up at the slanted ceilings and blinking back tears of frustration, she wriggled down under the covers and ordered herself to sleep.

But instead of dreaming, Sharon reviewed the events of the evening and wondered why she couldn't talk to Tony anymore. Each time she tried, she ended up baiting him, or sliding some invisible door closed between them, or simply running away.

She was painfully conscious of his nearness and of her need for him, which had not been assuaged by months of telling herself that the relationship was over. She put one hand over her mouth to keep from calling his name.

From downstairs she heard the low but swelling strains of familiar music. Once, the notes had rippled over her like the rays of the sun on a pond, filling her with light. They had flung her high on soaring crescendos, even as she clung to Tony and cried out in passion....

Sharon burrowed beneath the covers and squeezed her eyes shut and, an eternity later, she slept. When she awakened the room was filled with sunlight and the scent of fresh coffee.

After a long, leisurely stretch, Sharon opened her eyes. A dark head rested on the pillow beside hers, and she felt a muscular leg beneath the softness of her thigh.

"Oh, God," she whispered, "we made love and I missed it!"

A hoarse laugh sounded from the pillow. "No such luck," Tony said. "Our making love, I mean. We didn't."

Sharon sat up, dragging the sheets up to cover her bosom even though she was wearing a modest cotton nightgown. She distinctly remembered putting it on, and with a quick motion of her hands, she lifted the sheet just far enough away from her body that she could check. The nightgown was still in evidence.

"What the devil do you think you're doing, Tony Morelli?" she demanded furiously.

He rolled onto his back, not even bothering to open his eyes, and simultaneously pulled the covers up over his face, muttering insensibly all the while.

"You guys made up, huh?" Briana asked from the doorway. She was all smiles and carrying two cups of coffee, hence the delicious aroma.

"No, we didn't," Sharon said primly.

"Not a very diplomatic answer," Tony observed from beneath the covers. "Now, she's going to ask—"

"Then how come you're in bed together?" the child demanded.

"See?" said Tony.

Sharon elbowed him hard, and crimson color flooded her face. "I don't know," she said with staunch conviction.

Briana brought the coffee to the end table on Sharon's side of the bed, and some of it slopped over when she set the cups down. There were tears brimming in her eyes.

"Damn you, Tony," Sharon whispered, as though there were no chance of Bri's not hearing what she said. "Explain this to her—right now!"

With a groan, Tony dramatically fought his way out from under the blankets and sat up. "There's only one bed," he said reasonably, running a hand through his rumpled hair and then yawning again. "The couch is too short for me, so I just crawled in with your mom."

"Oh," Bri said grudgingly, and left the room, shutting the door behind her.

"She didn't understand," Sharon lamented.

Tony reached past her to collect one of the cups of

coffee. "Kids don't need to understand everything," he said.

If the man hadn't been holding a steaming hot cup of coffee, Sharon would have slapped him. As it was, she glared at him and stretched out a hand for her own cup.

After a while Tony got up and wandered into the adjoining bathroom, and Sharon didn't look to see whether or not he was dressed. When he returned, he crawled back into bed with her, rolling over so that one of his legs rested across both of hers.

His mouth descended toward hers, smelling of toothpaste, and he was definitely not dressed.

"Tony, don't—"

The kiss was warm, gentle and insistent. Sharon trembled as all the familiar sensations were awakened, but she also braced both hands against Tony's chest and pushed.

The motion didn't eliminate all intimate contact—Tony had shifted his weight so that he was resting lightly on top of her—but it did make it possible to speak.

"No," Sharon said clearly.

Tony slid downward, kissing her jawline, the length of her neck, her collarbone.

"No," she repeated with less spirit.

His lips trailed across her collarbone and then downward. He nibbled at her breast through the thin fabric of her nightgown.

Her voice was a whimper. "No," she said for the third time.

Tony's mouth came to hers; his tongue traced the outline of her lips. "You don't mean that," he told her.

Sharon was about to admit he was right when there

was a knock at the door and Bri called out in sunny tones, "Breakfast is served!"

Tony was sitting up, both hands buried in his hair, when Briana and Matt entered the room carrying trays.

Chapter 3

The downstairs carpets were far from dry. "Leave the fans on for another day or so," Tony said distantly. Standing beside the dining room table, he rolled up a set of plans and slid it back inside its cardboard cylinder.

A sensation of utter bereftness swept over Sharon, even though she knew it was best that he leave. The divorce was final; it was time for both of them to let go. She managed a smile and an awkward, "Okay—and thanks."

The expression in Tony's eyes was at once angry and forlorn. He started to say something and then stopped himself, turning away to stare out the window at Bri and Matt, who were chasing each other up and down the stony beach. Their laughter rang through the morning sunshine, reminding Sharon that some people still felt joy.

She looked down at the floor for a moment, swallowed hard and then asked, "Tony, are you happy?"

The powerful shoulders tensed beneath the blue cambric of his shirt, then relaxed again. "Are you?" he countered, keeping his back to her.

"No fair," Sharon protested quietly. "I asked first."

Tony turned with a heavy sigh, the cardboard cylinder under his arm. "I used to be," he said. "Now I'm not sure I even know what it means to be happy."

Sharon's heart twisted within her; she was sorry she'd raised the question. She wanted to say something wise and good and comforting, but no words came to her.

Tony rounded the table, caught her chin gently in his hand and asked, "What happened, Sharon? What the hell happened?"

She bit her lip and shook her head.

A few seconds of silent misery passed, and then Tony sighed again, gave Sharon a kiss on the forehead and walked out. Moving to the window, she blinked back tears as she watched him saying goodbye to the kids. His words echoed in her mind and in her heart. *What the hell happened?*

Hugging herself, as though to hold body and soul together, Sharon sniffled and proceeded to the kitchen, where she refilled her coffee cup. She heard Tony's car start and gripped the edge of the counter with one hand, resisting an urge to run outside, to call his name, to beg him to stay.

She only let go of the counter when his tires bit into the gravel of the road.

"Are you all right, Mom?" Bri's voice made Sharon stiffen.

She faced this child of her spirit, if not her body, with a forced smile. "I'm fine," she lied, thinking that Bri looked more like Carmen's photographs with every passing day. She wondered if the resemblance ever grieved Tony and wished that she had the courage to ask him.

"You don't look fine," Briana argued, stepping inside the kitchen and closing the door.

Sharon had to turn away. She pretended to be busy at the sink, dumping out the coffee she'd just poured, rinsing her cup. "What's Matt doing?"

"Turning over rocks and watching the sand crabs scatter," Bri answered. "Are we going fishing?"

The last thing Sharon wanted to do was sit at the end of the dock with her feet dangling, baiting hooks and reeling in rock cod and dogfish, when right now her inclinations ran more toward pounding her pillow and crying. Such indulgences, however, are denied to mothers on active duty. "Absolutely," she said, lifting her chin and straightening her shoulders before turning to offer Bri a smile.

The child looked relieved. "I'll even bait your hooks for you," she offered.

Sharon laughed and hugged her. "You're one kid in a thousand, pumpkin," she said. "How did I get so lucky?"

Carmen's flawless image, smiling her beauty-queen smile, loomed in her mind, and it was as though Tony's first wife answered, "I died, that's how. Where would you be if it weren't for that drunk driver?"

Sharon shuddered, but she was determined to shake off her gray mood. In just two days she would have to give Briana and Matt back to Tony and return to her lonely apartment; she couldn't afford to sit around feeling sorry for herself. The time allowed her was too fleeting, too precious.

She found fishing poles and tackle in a closet, and

Bri rummaged through the freezer for a package of herring, bought months before in a bait shop.

When they joined Matt outside, and the three of them had settled themselves at the end of the dock, Bri was as good as her word. With a deftness she'd learned from Tony, she baited Sharon's hook.

In truth, Sharon wasn't as squeamish about the task as Bri seemed to think, but she didn't want to destroy the child's pleasure in being helpful. "Thanks," she said. "I'm sure glad I didn't have to do that."

"Women," muttered Matt, speaking from a seven-year pinnacle of life experience.

Sharon bit back a smile. "Shall I give my standard lecture on chauvinism?" she asked.

"No," Matt answered succinctly. It was the mark of a modern kid, his mother guessed, knowing what a word like *chauvinism* meant.

Bri looked pensive. "Great-gramma still eats in the kitchen," she remarked. "Like a servant."

Sharon chose her words carefully. Tony's grandmother had grown up in Italy and still spoke almost no English. Maybe she followed the old traditions, but the woman had raised six children to productive adulthood, among other accomplishments, and she deserved respect. "Did you know that she was only sixteen years old when she first came to America? She didn't speak or understand English, and her marriage to your great-grandfather had been arranged for her. Personally, I consider her a very brave woman."

Bri bit her lower lip. "Do you think my mother was brave?"

Questions like that, although they came up periodically, never failed to catch Sharon off guard. She drew in a deep breath and let it out again. "I never met her, sweetheart—you know that. Wouldn't it be better to ask your dad?"

"Do you think he loved her?"

Sharon didn't flinch. She concentrated on keeping her fishing pole steady. "I know he did. Very much."

"Carl says they only got married because my mom was pregnant with me. His mother remembers."

Carl was one of the cast of thousands that made up the Morelli family—specifically, a second or third cousin. And a pain in the backside.

"He doesn't know everything," Sharon said, wondering why these subjects never reared their heads when Tony was around to field them. "And neither does his mother."

Sharon sighed. God knew, Tony was better at things like this—a born diplomat. He and Carmen would have made quite a pair. There probably would have been at least a half dozen more children added to the clan, and it seemed certain that no divorce would have goofed up the entries in the family Bible. Maria Morelli had shown her all those names, reaching far back into the past.

Sharon was getting depressed again. Before Bri could bring up another disquieting question, however, the fish started biting. Bri caught two, Matt reeled in a couple more, and then it was time for lunch.

The telephone rang as Sharon was preparing sandwiches and heating canned soup.

"It's Gramma!" Matt shouted from the front room.

"Tell her your dad isn't here," Sharon replied pleasantly.

"She wants to talk to you."

Sharon pushed the soup to a different burner, wiped her hands on a dish towel and went staunchly to the telephone. "Hello," she said in sunny tones.

"Hello, Sharon," Maria responded, and there was nothing in her voice that should have made her difficult to talk to.

All the same, for Sharon, she was. "Is there something I can help you with?"

"Michael's birthday is next week," Maria said. She was referring to her youngest son; Tony was close to him and so were the kids.

Sharon had forgotten the occasion. "Yes," she agreed heartily.

"We're having a party, as usual," Maria went on. "Of course, Vincent and I would like the children to be there."

Sharon's smile was rigid; her face felt like part of a totem pole. She wondered why she felt called upon to smile when Maria obviously couldn't see her.

A few hasty calculations indicated that Bri and Matt would have been with Tony on Michael's birthday anyway. "No problem," Sharon said generously.

There was a pause, and then Maria asked, "How are you, dear? Vincent and I were just saying that we never see you anymore."

Sharon rubbed her eyes with a thumb and a forefinger, suppressing an urge to sigh. She regarded Vincent as a friend—he was a gentle, easygoing man—but with Maria it seemed so important to say and do the right things. Always. "I-I'm fine, thanks. I've been busy with the shop," she responded at last. "How are you?"

Maria's voice had acquired a cool edge. "Very well, actually. I'll just let you get back to whatever it was that you were doing, Sharon. Might I say hello to Bri, though?"

"Certainly," Sharon replied, relieved to hold the receiver out to the girl, who had been cleaning fish on the back porch. "Your grandmother would like to speak with you, Briana."

Bri hastened to the sink and washed her hands, then reached eagerly for the receiver. The depth of affection this family bore for its members never failed to amaze Sharon, or to remind her that she was an outsider. Even during the happiest years she and Tony had shared, she'd always felt like a Johnny-come-lately.

"Hi, Gramma!" Bri cried, beaming. "I caught two fish and the floors got all flooded and this morning I thought things were okay between Dad and Mom because they slept together...."

Mortified, Sharon turned away to hide her flaming face. *Oh, Bri,* she groaned inwardly, *of all the people you could have said that to, why did it have to be Maria?*

"Right," Briana went on, as her words became clear again. "We're having—" she craned her neck to peer into the pan on the stove "—chicken noodle soup. Yeah, from a can."

Sharon shook her head.

"Listen, Gramma, there's something I need to know."

An awful premonition came over Sharon; she whirled to give Bri a warning look, but it was too late.

"Was my mother pregnant when she married my dad?"

"Oh, God," Sharon moaned, shoving one hand into her hair.

Bri was listening carefully. "Okay, I will," she said at last in perfectly ordinary tones. "I love you, too. Bye."

Sharon searched the beautiful, earnest young face for signs of trauma and found none. "Well," she finally said, as Bri brought in the fish but left the mess on the porch, "what did she say?"

"The same thing you did," Briana responded with a shrug. "I'm supposed to ask Dad."

Sharon allowed her face to reveal nothing, though Tony had long since told her about his tempestuous affair with Carmen and the hasty marriage that had followed. She had always imagined that relationship as a grand passion, romantic and beautiful and, of course, tragic. It was one of those stories that would have been wonderful if it hadn't involved real people with real feelings. She turned back to the soup, ladling it into bowls.

"I guess I could call him."

Sharon closed her eyes for a moment. "Bri, I think this is something that would be better discussed in person, don't you?"

"You *know* something!" the girl accused, coming inside and shutting the door.

"Wash your hands again, please," Sharon hedged.

"Dad told you, didn't he?" Briana asked, though she obediently went to the sink to lather her hands with soap.

Sharon felt cornered, and for a second or two she truly resented Bri, as well as Carmen and Tony. "Will you tell me one thing?" she demanded a little sharply, as Matt crept into the kitchen, his eyes wide. "Why didn't this burning desire to know strike you a few hours ago, when your father was still here?"

Briana was silent, looking down at the floor.

"That's what I thought." Sharon sighed. "Listen, if it's too hard for you to bring this up with your dad, and you feel like you need a little moral support, I'll help. Okay?"

Bri nodded.

That afternoon the clouds rolled back in and the rain

started again. Once more, the power went out. Sharon and the kids played Parcheesi as long as the light held up, then roasted hot dogs in the fireplace. The evening lacked the note of festivity that had marked the one preceding it, despite Sharon's efforts, and she was almost relieved when bedtime came.

Almost, but not quite. The master bedroom, and the bed itself, bore the intangible but distinct impression Tony seemed to leave behind him wherever he went. When Sharon retired after brushing her teeth and washing her face in cold water, she huddled on her side of the bed, miserable.

Sleep was a long time coming, and when it arrived, it was fraught with dreams. Sharon was back at her wedding, wearing the flowing white dress she had bought with her entire savings, her arm linked with Tony's.

"Do you take this man to be your lawful wedded husband?" the minister asked.

Before Sharon could answer, Carmen appeared, also wearing a wedding gown, at Tony's other side. "I do," Carmen responded, and Sharon felt herself fading away like one of TV's high-tech ghosts.

She awakened with a cruel start, the covers bunched in her hands, and sank back to her pillows only after spending several moments groping for reality. It didn't help that the lamp wouldn't work, that rain was beating at the roof and the windows, that she was so very alone.

The following day was better; the storm blew over and the electricity stayed on. Sharon made sure she had a book on hand that night in case her dreams grew uninhabitable.

As it happened, Carmen didn't haunt her sleep again, but neither did Tony. Sharon awakened feeling restless and confused, and it was almost a relief to lock up the A-frame and drive away early that afternoon.

The big Tudor house was empty when they reached it; Mrs. Harry had done her work and gone home, and there was no sign of Tony. The little red light on the answering machine was blinking rapidly.

Sharon was tempted to ignore it, but in the end she pushed the Play button. Tony's voice filled the room. "Hi, babe. I'm glad you're home. According to Mama mia, I need to have a talk with Bri— I'll take care of that after dinner tonight, so don't worry about it. See you later." The message finished, and then another call was playing, this one from her mother. "Sharon, this is Bea. Since you don't answer over at the other place, I figured I'd try and get you here. Call me as soon as you can. Bye."

The other messages were all for Tony, so Sharon dialed her mother's number in Hayesville, a very small town out on the peninsula.

Bea answered right away, and Sharon sank into the chair behind Tony's desk. "Bea, it's me. Is anything wrong?"

"Where are you?" Bea immediately countered.

"At the house," Sharon replied in even tones.

"Crazy arrangement," Bea muttered. She had never approved of Sharon's marriage, Sharon's house or, for that matter, Sharon herself. "In, out, back, forth. I don't know how you stand it. Furthermore, it isn't good for those kids."

"Bea!"

"All right, all right. I just wanted to know if you were still coming over this weekend."

Sharon shoved a hand through her hair. She hated avoiding her own mother, but an encounter with Bea was more than she could face in her present state of mind. "I don't remember telling you that I'd be visiting," she said carefully, feeling her way along.

It turned out that Bea was suffering from a similar lack of enthusiasm. "It isn't like I don't want you to come or anything," she announced in her blunt way, "but Saturday's the big all-day bingo game, and one of the prizes is a car."

Sharon smiled to herself. "I see. Well, I have inventory at the shop, anyway. Call me if you win, okay?"

"Okay," Bea replied, but it was clear from her tone that her attention was already wandering. She was a beautician by trade, with a shop of her own, and an avid bingo player by choice, but motherhood had descended on her by accident. Bea Stanton had never really gotten the knack of it. "Part of the mill burned down," she added as an afterthought.

Sharon's father, who had never troubled to marry Bea, and probably would have been refused if he had proposed, was a member of the Harrison family, which owned the mill in question. Hence Bea's assumption that Sharon would be interested.

"That's too bad," she said. "Was anybody hurt?"

"No," Bea answered distractedly. "There's one of those big televisions, too. At bingo, I mean."

"Good," Sharon answered, as a headache began under her left temple and steadily gained momentum. "If there's nothing else, Bea, I think I'd better hang up. I have to get the kids squared away before I go back to the apartment."

Bea started muttering again. Sharon said a hasty goodbye and hung up, and when she turned in the swivel chair, Tony was standing in the doorway.

She gasped and laid one hand to her heart. "I really wish you wouldn't do that!"

"Do what?" Tony asked innocently, but his eyes were dancing. He left the doorway to stride over and sit on the edge of the desk.

He was wearing dirty work clothes, but Sharon still found him damnably attractive.

"That was my mother," she said, in an effort to distract herself.

Tony's smile was slow, and he was watching Sharon's lips as though their every motion fascinated him. "I hope you gave her my fondest regards."

"You don't hope any such thing," Sharon scoffed, scooting the chair back a few more inches.

Tony stopped its progress by bending over and grasping the arms in his hands. "I've missed you," he said, and his mouth was so close to hers that Sharon could feel his breath whispering against her skin.

"The kids are here," she reminded him.

He touched her lips with his and a sweet jolt went through her. One of his index fingers moved lightly down the buttoned front of her flannel shirt.

"Stop it," she said in anguish.

Tony drew her onto her feet and into his kiss, holding her so close that she ached with the awareness of his masculinity and his strength. She was dazed when, after a long interlude, the contact was broken.

In another minute she was not only going to be unable to resist this man, she could end up taking him by the hand and leading him upstairs to bed. Resolutely, Sharon stepped back out of his embrace. "Why, Tony?" she asked reasonably. "Why, after all these months, has it suddenly become so important to you to seduce me?"

He folded his arms across his chest. "Believe me,"

he said, "it isn't sudden. Has it ever occurred to you, Sharon, that our divorce might have been a mistake?"

"No," Sharon lied.

Tony's expression said he saw through her. "Not even once?" When she shook her head, Tony laughed. The sound was sad, rueful. "I've always said you were stubborn, my love."

Sharon was easing toward the door. "You'll talk to Bri?"

"I said I would," Tony replied quietly, his arms still folded, that broken look lingering in his eyes.

She cleared her throat. "Did your mother tell you what the problem is?"

Tony nodded. He looked baffled now, and watchful, as though he was curious about something. "I'm surprised it didn't come up before this, given the gossip factor. Sharon—"

She felt behind her for the doorknob and held on to it as though it could anchor her somehow. "What?"

"It bothers you, doesn't it? That Carmen was pregnant when I married her."

It would be stupid, and very unmodern, to be bothered by something like that, Sharon reasoned to herself. "Of course it doesn't," she said brightly, throwing in an airy shrug for good measure.

A look of fury clouded Tony's face, and in the next second he brought his fist down hard on the surface of the desk and rasped a swearword.

Sharon's eyes were wide. She opened her mouth and then closed it again as Tony shook his finger at her.

"Don't lie to me," he warned in a low, even voice.

Sharon stepped inside the den and closed the door so that the kids wouldn't hear. "Okay," she whispered angrily, "you win. Yes, it bothers me that Carmen was pregnant! It bothers me that she ever existed! Are you satisfied?"

He was staring at her. "You were jealous of Carmen?" he asked, sounding amazed.

Sharon turned away to hide the tears she wasn't sure she'd be able to hold back, and let her forehead rest against the door. For several seconds she just stood there, breathing deeply and trying to compose herself. When she felt Tony's hands on her shoulders, strong and gentle, she stiffened.

His chin rested against the back of her head; she was aware of the hard, masculine lines of his body in every fiber of her being.

"I didn't understand, babe," he said in a hoarse whisper. "I'm sorry."

Sharon couldn't speak, and when Tony turned her and drew her into his arms, she hid her face in the warm strength of his shoulder. He buried his fingers in her hair.

"I made a lot of mistakes," he told her after a long time.

Sharon nodded, lifting her head but unable to meet Tony's eyes. "So did I," she confessed. "I—I think I'd better go."

His embrace tightened for an instant, as though he didn't want to release her, and then relaxed. Sharon collected her purse, hurried out to the garage and slid behind the wheel of her roadster.

The door rolled open and Sharon backed slowly out into the driveway.

Saying goodbye to Briana and Matt didn't even occur to her.

Chapter 4

Sharon's small garden apartment seemed to have all the ambience of a jail cell when she walked into it late that afternoon, carrying a bag of take-out food in one hand. The walls were nicotine yellow, unadorned by pictures or any other decoration, and the cheap furniture had served a number of previous tenants.

Feeling overwhelmingly lonely, as she always did when she left the house and the kids to return to this place, Sharon flipped on the television set and sank onto the couch to eat fish-and-chips and watch the shopping channel.

She was teetering on the brink of ordering a set of marble-handled screwdrivers when there was a knock at the door. Sharon turned down the volume, crumpled the evidence of her fast-food dinner into a ball and tossed it into the trash as she called, "Who's there?"

"It's me," a feminine voice replied. "Helen."

Sharon crossed the short distance between the kitchenette and the front door and admitted her employee with a smile. In her early thirties, like Sharon, Helen was a beautiful woman with sleek black hair and a trim, petite figure. Her almond-shaped eyes accented her Oriental heritage.

Helen's glance fell on Sharon's overnight bag, which was still sitting on the floor in front of the coat closet. "How were the kids?" she asked.

Sharon looked away. "Fine," she answered, as her friend perched gracefully on the arm of an easy chair.

Helen sighed. "You're awfully quiet. What went wrong?"

Sharon pretended not to hear the question. She went into the kitchenette, took two mugs from the cupboard and asked brightly, "Coffee?"

"Sure," Helen replied, and Sharon jumped because she hadn't heard her friend's approach. It seemed that people were always sneaking up on her.

She filled the mugs with water, thrust them into her small microwave oven and set the time, still avoiding Helen's gaze.

"My, but we're uncommunicative tonight," the younger woman observed. "Did you have some kind of run-in with Tony?"

Sharon swallowed, and her eyes burned for a moment. "Listen," she said in a voice that was too bright and too quick, "I've been thinking that I should do something about this place—you know, paint and get some decent furniture...."

Helen put a hand on Sharon's shoulder. "What happened?" she pressed gently.

Sharon bit into her lower lip and shook her head.

"Nothing dramatic," she answered, after a few seconds had passed.

The timer on the microwave chimed, and Sharon was grateful for the distraction. She took the cups of steaming water out and transferred them to the counter, where she spooned instant coffee into each one.

Helen sighed and followed Sharon into the living room. "I stopped by to borrow your burgundy shoes," she said. "The ones with the snakeskin toes."

Sharon was looking at the television set. The sound was still off, so the man selling crystal cake plates seemed to be miming his routine. "Help yourself," she replied.

Helen went into Sharon's tiny bedroom and came out a short time later with the shoes in one hand and a firm conviction in her eyes. "Why don't you give it up and go home, Sharon?" she asked quietly. "You know you're not happy without Tony."

"It isn't as simple as that," Sharon confessed.

"Is he involved with someone else?"

Sharon shook her head. "I don't think so. The kids would have mentioned it."

"Well?"

"It's too late, Helen. Too much has happened."

Helen sat on the arm of the chair again, lifted her cup from the end table and took a thoughtful sip of coffee. "I see," she said, looking inscrutable.

Sharon assessed the dingy walls of her living room and said with forced good cheer, "It's time I got on with my life. I'm going to start by turning this place into a home."

"Terrific," agreed Helen, her expression still bland. "If you're going to start embroidering samplers, I'm out of here."

Sharon laughed. "You know, that's not a bad idea. I could do some profound motto in cross-stitch—Anybody Who Says Money Doesn't Buy Happiness Has Never Been to Neiman-Marcus."

At last, Helen smiled. "Words to live by," she said, setting aside her coffee and standing up. "Well, I've got a hot date with my husband, so I'd better fly. See you tomorrow at the shop." She held up the burgundy pumps as she opened the door. "Thanks for the loan of the shoes," she finished, and then she was gone.

Sharon was even lonelier than before. Knowing that the only cure for that was action, she put on a jacket, gave her hair a quick brushing and fled the apartment for a nearby discount store.

When she returned, she had several gallons of paint and all the attending equipment, except for a ladder. It seemed silly to buy something like that when there were several in the garage at home; she would stop by the house when she left Teddy Bares the next day and pick one up.

Sharon had never painted before, and it took all her forbearance to keep from plunging into the task that very night before any of the preparations had been made.

She rested her hands on her hips as she considered the changes ahead. She'd chosen a pretty shade of ivory for the living room, the palest blue for the kitchenette and a pastel pink for the bedroom and bath. If it killed her, she was going to give this apartment some pizzazz and personality.

While she was at it, she might as well do the same for the rest of her life. It was time to start meeting new men.

Sharon caught one fingernail between her teeth and

grimaced. "Exactly how does a person go about doing that?" she asked the empty room.

There was no answer, of course.

Sharon took a shower, washed and blow-dried her hair and got into pajamas. She was settled in bed, reading, when the doorbell rang.

She padded out into the dark living room. "Yes?"

"Mom," Bri wailed from the hallway, "I'm a bastard!"

Sharon wrenched open the door, appalled to find the child standing there, alone, at that late hour. "You aren't, either," she argued practically, as she pulled Briana into the apartment.

"Yes, I am," Bri cried, with all the woe and passion a wounded twelve-year-old is capable of feeling. Her face was dirty and tear streaked, and she hadn't bothered to zip her jacket. "My whole life is ruined! I want to join the Foreign Region!"

"That's 'legion,' darling," Sharon said softly, leading her toward a chair, "and I think you have to be older."

"Stupid rules." Bri sniffled, dashing at her tears with the back of one hand.

"The world is full of them," Sharon commiserated, bending to kiss the top of the girl's head. "Does your dad know where you are?"

"No," Bri replied without hesitation, "and I don't care if he worries, either!"

"Well, I do," Sharon answered, reaching for the living room extension and punching out the familiar number. "I take it you had that talk about your conception," she ventured in tones she hoped were diplomatic, as the ringing began at the other end of the line.

Bri was fairly tearing off her jacket, every motion

designed to let Sharon know that she was here to stay.
The child nodded and sniffled loudly.

Sharon turned away to hide her smile when Tony
answered, "Hello?"

"It's ten o'clock," Sharon said warmly. "Do you know
where your daughter is?"

"In bed," Tony replied, sounding puzzled.

"Wrong," Sharon retorted. "I'm sorry, Mr. Morelli,
but you don't win the week's supply of motor oil and the
free trip to Bremerton. Bri is here, and she's very upset."

"How the hell did she manage that?"

Sharon shrugged, even though Tony couldn't see the
gesture. "Maybe she called a cab or took a bus—I don't
know. The point is—"

"The point is that I hate my father!" Bri shouted,
loudly enough for Tony to hear.

He sighed.

"I see everything went very well between the two of
you," Sharon chimed sweetly. Her hackles were rising
now; she was thinking of the danger Bri had been in
and of the pain she was feeling. "Tony, what the devil
did you say to this child?"

"He said," Bri began dramatically, "that he and my
mother were such animals that they couldn't even wait
to be married!"

Sharon turned, one hand over the receiver. "I'd keep
quiet, if I were you," she said in warm, dulcet tones.
Tony, meanwhile, was quietly swearing on the other
end of the line.

"I'll be right over to get her," he announced when
he'd finished.

"And leave Matt alone?" Sharon countered. "I don't
think so."

"Then you can bring her home."

Sharon was angered by his presumption. "Maybe," she began stiffly, "it would be better if Bri spent the night. She's very upset, and—"

"Briana is my daughter, Sharon," Tony interrupted coldly, "and I'll decide how this is going to be handled."

Sharon felt as though he'd slapped her. *Briana is my daughter.* Tony had never hurled those words in Sharon's face before, never pointed out the fact that, in reality, Bri was exclusively his child.

"I'm sorry," he said into the stricken silence.

She couldn't speak.

"Damn it, Sharon, are you there or not?"

She swallowed. "I-I'll bring Briana home in a few minutes," she said.

"I don't want to go back there ever again!" Bri put in.

Tony's sigh was ragged. Again, he swore. "And I thought I was tactful."

Sharon's eyes were full of tears, and her sinuses had closed. "Apparently not," she said brokenly.

"She can stay," Tony conceded.

Sharon shoved a hand through her hair. "That's magnanimous of you," she replied. "Good night, Tony." Then, not trusting herself to say more, she hung up.

During the next few minutes, while Bri was in the bathroom washing her face and putting on a pair of Sharon's pajamas, her stepmother made the sofa out into a bed. Tony's words were still falling on her soul like drops of acid. *Briana is my daughter...I'll decide how this is going to be handled....*

Bri came out of the bathroom, looking sheepish and very childlike. The emotional storm had evidently blown over. "Is Daddy mad at me?"

Sharon shook her head. "I don't think so, sweetie. But you were plenty mad at him, weren't you?"

Bri nodded, biting her lower lip, and sat down on the end of the sofa bed.

Sharon joined her, putting an arm around the child's shoulders. "Want to talk?"

Bri's chin quivered. "I'm a mistake!" she whispered, and tears were brimming in her eyes again.

Sharon hugged her. "Never."

The little girl sniffled. "I was probably conceived in the backseat of a Chevy or something," she despaired.

Sharon couldn't help laughing. "Oh, Bri," she said, pressing her forehead to her stepdaughter's. "I love you so much."

Briana flung her arms around Sharon's neck. "I love you, too, Mom," she answered with weary exuberance. "I wish you could come home and stay there."

Sharon didn't comment on that. Instead, she smoothed Bri's wildly tangled hair with one hand and said, "It's time for you to go to sleep, but first I want to know something. How did you get here?"

Bri drew herself up. "I called a cab. Dad was doing laundry, so he didn't hear me go out."

Sharon sighed. "Sweetheart, what you did was really dangerous. Do I have your word that you won't try this ever again?"

Bri hesitated. "What if I need to talk to you?"

Sharon cupped the lovely face, a replica of Carmen's, in her hands. "Then you just call, and we'll make plans to get together right away," she answered softly. "Do you promise, Briana?"

The child swallowed hard and nodded, and then Sharon tucked her into bed and kissed her good-night just as she had so many times in the past. She'd reached the privacy of her room before her heart cracked into two pieces and the grieving began in earnest.

Tony arrived early the next morning while Sharon was still in the shower, and collected Briana. He left a terse note on the kitchen table, thanking her for "everything."

Sharon crumpled the note and flung it at the wall. "Thank you for everything, too, Morelli," she muttered. "Thanks one hell of a lot!"

She was in a terrible mood by the time she reached the shop. Helen had already arrived, and Teddy Bares was open for business.

Since there were several customers browsing, Sharon made herself smile as she stormed behind the counter and into the small office at the back.

Helen appeared in the doorway after a few minutes had passed. "Are you okay?" she ventured carefully.

"No," Sharon replied.

"Is there anything I can do?"

Sharon shook her head. She was going to have to pull herself together and get on with the day. It was a sure bet that Tony wasn't standing around agonizing over the fact that his family was in pieces. He knew how to set aside his personal life when it was time to concentrate on work.

Sharon drew a deep breath and went out to greet her customers. The morning was a busy one, fortunately, and there wasn't time to think about anything but taking care of business.

It was noon, and Helen had gone to the pizza place at the other end of the mall to get take-out salads, when Tony wandered in. Instead of his usual jeans, work shirt and boots, he was wearing a three-piece suit, beautifully tailored to his build. He approached the counter and inclined his head slightly to one side, his dark eyes seeming to caress Sharon for a moment before he spoke.

"I'm sorry we didn't get a chance to talk this morning," he said.

"I'll bet you are," Sharon scoffed, remembering the brisk note tucked between the salt-and-pepper shakers in the middle of her table. "What's with the fancy clothes?"

"I had a meeting," Tony answered. Then he arched one ebony eyebrow and sighed. "I don't suppose you're free for lunch."

Sharon opened her mouth to say that he was dead right, but Helen arrived before she could get the words out. "Know what?" she chimed. "They were all out of salad. I guess you have no choice but to accept Tony's invitation."

Sharon wasn't buying the no-salad routine—the pizza place made the stuff up by the bushel—and she frowned at Helen, wondering where she'd hidden all that lettuce. "I've got an idea," she told her friend tartly. "Why don't you go to lunch with Tony?"

Like a spectator at a tennis match, Tony turned his head toward Helen, waiting for her to return the ball.

"I have plans," Helen said loftily, and marched around behind the counter, elbowing Sharon aside. "It just so happens that I'm out to build an underwear empire of my own, Ms. Morelli, so watch your back."

Tony laughed and took Sharon's arm and, rather than make a scene, she allowed him to lead her out of the shop and along the mall's crowded concourse. The place was jammed with mothers and children shopping for school clothes.

Sharon jutted out her chin and walked a little faster, ignoring Tony as best she could.

"Where do you want to eat?" he finally asked.

"I don't care," Sharon responded firmly.

"I like a decisive woman," came the taut reply. Tony's grasp on her elbow tightened, and he propelled her toward a sandwich place.

When they were seated at a table in a corner by a window, Sharon's rigid control began to falter a little. "How could you say that?" she demanded in a miserable whisper, avoiding Tony's eyes.

"What?" he asked, in a baffled tone that made Sharon want to clout him over the head with the menu that had just been shoved into her hands.

"What you said last night," Sharon whispered furiously. "About Bri being your daughter!"

"Isn't she?" Tony asked, having the audacity to read the menu while he awaited her answer.

Sharon suppressed an urge to kick him in the shin. She pushed back her chair and would have left the table if he hadn't reached out and caught hold of one of her wrists. "You know that isn't what I mean!" she said.

Tony looked as though he had a headache. *Men,* Sharon thought to herself, *are such babies when it comes to pain.* "We do not seem to be communicating, here," he observed a few moments later.

"That's because one of us is stupid," Sharon said. "And it isn't me, buddy."

Tony sighed. "Maybe I was a little insensitive—"

"A little?" Sharon drew a deep breath and let it out. "My God, Tony, you've got insensitivity down to an art. You don't even know why I'm angry!"

His jaw tightened. "I'm sure after you've tortured me for a few hours," he responded, "you'll tell me!"

A teenage waitress stepped into the breach. "The special today is baked chicken."

"We'll take it," said Tony, his dark, furious gaze never shifting from Sharon's face.

"Right," said the waitress with a shrug, swinging her hips as she walked away.

Tony didn't wait for Sharon to speak. "So help me God," he told her in an ominously low voice, "if you say you don't want the baked chicken, I'll strangle you."

Sharon sniffed. "I had no idea you felt so strongly about poultry," she said.

Tony glared at her. "Sharon," he warned.

She sat back. "Bri is not just your daughter, regardless whose Chevy she was conceived in," she said with dignity. "I raised that child. I love her as much as I love Matthew."

Tony looked bewildered. "Regardless of whose…" His words fell away as an expression of furious revelation dawned in his face. "Last night. You're still mad because of what I said last night on the phone about Bri being my daughter."

Sharon said nothing; she didn't need to, because she knew the look on her face said it all.

"Good Lord," Tony muttered. "I apologized for that."

Sharon was dangerously near tears; she willed herself not to cry. She had a store in this mall; people knew her. She couldn't afford to make a public spectacle of herself. "And you thought that made everything all right, didn't you? You could just say 'I'm sorry' and it would be as though it had never happened."

The baked chicken arrived. When the waitress had gone, Tony demanded, "What else could I have said, Sharon?"

She swallowed and looked down at her food in real despair. Never in a million years was she going to be able to get so much as a bite down her throat. "Bri is mine, too, and I love her," she insisted miserably, and then she got up and walked out of the restaurant with her head held high.

The shop was full of customers when Sharon got back, and she threw herself into waiting on them. All the same, it was a relief when the day ended. Unlike many other shops in the mall, Teddy Bares closed at five-thirty.

"You really ought to think about getting someone in to work until nine," Helen ventured quietly as the two women went through the familiar routine of emptying the cash register, totaling receipts and locking up.

Sharon just shrugged. She felt raw inside and had ever since her encounter with Tony at noon. Going through the motions was the best she could hope to accomplish, for the moment, anyway.

Helen's gaze was sympathetic. "What happened, Sharon?" she asked. At her friend's look, she went on. "I know, it's none of my business, but I've never seen two people more in love than you and Tony. And yet here you are, divorced—unable to have a civilized lunch together."

Sharon remained stubbornly silent, hoping that Helen would let the subject drop.

She wasn't about to be so accommodating. "He loves you, Sharon," she said insistently. "The rest of us see that so clearly—why can't you?"

The numbers on the receipts blurred together. Sharon chose to ignore Helen's remark about Tony's feelings. "You know, my mother warned me that the marriage wouldn't work. Tony was already successful then, and Bea said he was way out of my league—that he'd get tired of me and start running around."

Helen was seething; Sharon didn't even have to look at her friend to know that smoke was practically blow-

ing out of her ears. "Excuse my bluntness, but what the
devil does your mother know? Who is she, Dr. Ruth?"
Helen paused. "Tony didn't cheat on you, did he?"

Sharon shook her head. "No, but he got tired of me.
I'm sure it would only have been a matter of time until
there were other women."

Helen made a sound that resembled a suppressed
scream. "How do you know he got tired of you? Did
he say so?"

"No," Sharon answered in a sad, reflective tone. "He
didn't have to. He worked more and more, harder and
harder, and when we were together, we fought—like
today."

"What did you fight about?" Helen persisted.

Sharon looked around her at the teddies and pei-
gnoirs and robes, all made from shimmering silks and
satins of the highest quality. "Teddy Bares, mostly," she
answered. And then she took up her purse and started
toward the door.

The subject, like the shop, was closed.

Chapter 5

Tony slammed his fist on the hood of a pickup truck marked with the company name, and swore. He'd just fired one of the best foremen in the construction business, and now he was going to have to swallow his pride, go after the man and apologize.

"Tony."

He stiffened at the sound of his father's voice, then turned, reluctantly, to face him. "You heard," he said.

Vincent Morelli was a man of medium height and build, and of quiet dignity. He'd begun his working life as an apprentice carpenter at fifteen and had passed a thriving company on to his sons fifty years later. "Everybody heard," he replied. "What happened, Tonio?"

Tony shoved one hand through his hair. "I'm not sure, Papa," he confessed, shifting his gaze to the line of condominiums under construction a hundred yards away. "I know one thing—I was wrong. I've been wrong a lot lately."

Vincent came to stand beside him, bracing one booted foot against the front bumper of the truck. "I'm listening," he said.

Tony had heard those words often from both his parents since earliest childhood, and he knew Vincent meant them. He was grateful for the solid, sensible upbringing he'd had, and he wanted desperately to give the same gift to his own children. "It's Sharon," he said. "And the kids—it's everything."

Vincent waited, saying nothing.

"I didn't want the divorce," Tony went on after a few moments, aware that he wasn't telling his father anything he didn't already know. Vincent had seen the grief and pain Tony had hidden so carefully from Sharon. "Ever since it happened, I've been trying to find a way to make things right again. Papa, I can't even talk to the woman without making her mad as hell."

His father smiled sadly. He'd always liked Sharon, even defended her desire to strike out on her own. Vincent had insisted that she was only trying to prove herself by starting the shop, while Tony had dismissed the project as silly. And worse.

"In some ways, Tonio," Vincent said, his voice quiet and calm, "you're too much like me."

Tony was taken aback; there was no one he admired more than his father. It was impossible to be too much like him.

"I worked hard building this company for many, many years. But I was also something of a failure as a man and as a father. I didn't know my own sons until they were men, working beside me, and I may never truly know my daughters."

Tony started to protest, but Vincent stopped him with one upraised hand, still callused from years of labor, and went on. "You all grew up to be successful men, you and Michael and Richard, and your sisters are fine women, but you give me too much of the credit. Most of it should go to your mother, Tony, because she taught you all the things that make you strong—confidence in yourself, clear thinking, personal responsibility, integrity."

Tony looked down at his boots.

"I was sixty years old," Vincent continued, "before I had the good sense to appreciate Maria for the woman she is. If you're wise, Tonio, you won't wait that long before you start treating Sharon with the respect she deserves."

"I do respect her," Tony said, his eyes still downcast. "She came into my life at a time when I thought I wanted to die, Papa, and she gave me back my soul. And even though she'd had a rotten childhood herself, she knew how to be a mother to Bri."

Vincent laid a hand on his son's shoulder. "These are pretty words, Tony. Perhaps if you would say them to Sharon, instead of assuming that she knows how you feel, things might get better."

"She won't listen. There are always too many demands—too many distractions—"

"That is simple to fix," Vincent broke in reasonably. "You bring the children to your mother and me and you persuade Sharon to go to the island house for a couple of days. There, you hold her hand and you speak softly, always. You make sure that there is wine and music, and you tell her that you love her. Often."

Tony grinned, feeling a certain tentative hope. "You're quite the ladies' man, Papa," he teased.

Vincent chuckled and slapped his son's shoulder

again. "I did not father three sons and three daughters by accident," he replied.

Just then, the recently fired foreman drove up in a swirl of dust. Scrambling out of his car, the man stormed toward Tony, shaking his finger. "I've got a few more things to say to you, Morelli!" he bellowed.

Tony sighed, gave his father a sheepish look and went to meet his angry ex-employee. "I've got something to say to you, too," he responded evenly. "I was wrong, Charlie, and I'm sorry."

Charlie Petersen stared at him in astonishment. "Say what?" he finally drawled.

"You heard me," Tony said. "There's a foreman's job open if you want it."

Charlie grinned. "I want it," he admitted.

The two men shook hands, and then Charlie strode back toward the framework rising against the sky. "Hey, Merkins," he called out to a member of his crew. "If I see you walking around without your hard hat again, you're out of here, union steward or not!"

Tony laughed and went back to his own work.

Sharon had left the shop early in hopes of getting the stepladder from the garage without encountering Tony. Conversely, she was almost disappointed that she'd succeeded.

"I wish we could come and help you," Matt said, as they gathered in the kitchen to say goodbye, biting forlornly into a cookie, "but we're both grounded."

Bri, perched on one of the stools at the breakfast bar, nodded disconsolately.

Sharon pretended to ponder their offenses, a finger to her chin. "Let's see," she said to Matt, "you're being punished for the wholesale slaughter of goldfish, am I right?"

Matt gave Bri an accusing look, but admitted his guilt with a nod.

"And I'm on the list," Briana supplied glumly, "because Dad says running away isn't cool."

"He's right," Sharon said. "Did the two of you manage to work things out?"

Bri shook her head. "Not yet. We're supposed to talk tonight."

Sharon sighed and laid gentle hands on her stepdaughter's shoulders. "Sometimes your dad isn't the most tactful man on earth. You might try looking past what he says to what he means."

"You could try that, too, Mom," Bri remarked, with the kind of out-of-left-field astuteness children sometimes use to put their elders in their places.

"Touché," Sharon replied, kissing Bri's forehead and then Matt's.

Matt groaned, but spared her his usual, heartfelt "yuck!"

"How are we supposed to get Uncle Michael a birthday present if we're both grounded?" he demanded, when Sharon would have made her exit.

"Gramma already told us the party will have to be postponed because Uncle Michael is going to be out of town and because Daddy has other plans for the weekend," Bri told him in a tone reserved for little brothers and other lower forms of life. "Boy, are you stupid."

Sharon closed her eyes. She didn't want to give a damn that Tony had a special date lined up for the weekend, but she did. Oh, hell, did she ever.

Matt wasn't about to stand for any nonsense from his sister. "Saturday is still Uncle Michael's birthday and we still have to get him a present and you're *still* a royal pain in the rear end, Briana Morelli!"

Reminding herself that the job of worrying about these two little darlings was rightfully Tony's—bless his heart—Sharon backed out of the door, waving. "Bye," she chimed, as the argument escalated into a confrontation that might well require peacekeeping forces.

Mrs. Harry, the housekeeper, would keep them from killing each other before Tony got home.

The stepladder was leaning against the wall of the garage, where Sharon had left it. She put it into the trunk of the roadster along with her oldest pair of jeans from the dresser upstairs and two ancient work shirts that she'd stolen from Tony's side of the closet.

The refurbishing of Sharon Morelli and her surroundings was about to begin.

Two and a half hours later, when Sharon had moved and covered all her furniture and masked off every inch of baseboard, every electrical outlet and every window in her apartment, she was starting to wish she'd been more resistant to change, more of a stick-in-the-mud.

There was a resolute knock at the door—her dinner was about to be delivered, no doubt—and Sharon unwrapped the knob and turned it. Tony was standing in the hallway, paying the kid from the Chinese restaurant. He'd already appropriated her pork-fried rice and sweet-and-sour chicken.

Sharon snatched the white cartons from her ex-husband's possession and went into the kitchen to untape one of the drawers and get out a spoon and fork.

"Oh, are you still here?" she asked pleasantly, when she turned to find Tony standing behind her with his arms folded and his damnably handsome head cocked to one side.

"No," he answered dryly, his eyes smiling at her in a way that melted her pelvic bones. "I'm only an illusion. It's all done with mirrors."

"I wish," Sharon muttered, edging around him to march back into the living room, her feet making a crackling sound on the newspaper covering the carpet. She knew she looked something less than glamorous, wearing a bandana over her hair, those disreputable jeans, dirty sneakers and a shirt that reached to her knees, but one couldn't paint walls and ceilings in a flowing ballgown.

Tony followed her. He was too big for her apartment; he didn't fit.

Sharon wished that he'd leave and at the very same moment was glad he hadn't. "Sit down," she said with a generous gesture. Then, realizing that both chairs were covered, along with the couch, she plunked down on the floor, cross-legged, and Tony joined her.

Sharon opened her food and began to eat. "I'd offer you some," she said through a mouthful of fried rice, "but I'm incredibly greedy."

Tony's eyes left Sharon warm wherever they touched her, which was everywhere, and he let her remark hang unanswered in the air.

She squirmed and speared a chunk of sauce-covered chicken from the carton on the floor in front of her. "Are you here for some specific reason or what?" she asked.

He looked around at all the masking and newspapering she'd done. "I came to help you paint," he said.

Sharon sighed. "Tony—"

He was watching her mouth. Sharon found it very distracting when he did that. "Yes?" The word had a low rumble, like a faraway earthquake.

"I can manage this on my own."

His smile was a little forced, but it was a smile. He was trying; Sharon had to give him credit for that. "I'm sure you can," he answered reasonably. "But I'd like to help." He spread his hands. "Call it a personal quirk."

"I call it a crock," Sharon responded, but she was grinning. She couldn't help herself.

"I love you," Tony said quietly.

Sharon's forkful of fried rice hung suspended between the carton and her mouth. She remembered what the kids had said about the plans he'd made and stiffened her spine. "Are you practicing for your hot date this weekend?" she asked.

"Jealous?" he wanted to know.

"Not in the least," lied Sharon, jamming the fork into her rice as if it were a climber's flag she was planting on a mountain peak.

Tony reached out, took the carton from her hand and set it aside. Then he caught her wrists gently in his hands and pulled until she was straddling his lap. "Just this once," he suggested, breathing the words rather than saying them, his lips brushing against Sharon's, "let's skip the preliminary rounds, okay?"

Sharon's arms were trembling as she draped them around his neck. "Okay," she whispered. She knew that what was about to happen was a mistake, but she couldn't stop it. Tony was a man any woman would want, and Sharon had the added handicap of loving him.

The kiss was long and thorough and so intimate that it left Sharon disoriented. She was surprised to find herself lying on the floor, because she didn't remember moving. And she was frightened by the scope of her feelings.

Tony's hand was unfastening the buttons on her shirt when she stopped him by closing her fingers over his.

"This woman you're seeing this weekend—who is she?" she dared to ask.

He kissed her again, briefly this time, and playfully. "She's you," he answered. "If you don't turn me down, that is."

Sharon withdrew her hand, and the unbuttoning continued, unimpeded. She closed her eyes as he opened the shirt and then removed it. She made a soft sound in her throat when she felt the front catch on her bra give way. "Oh, Tony—"

"Is that a yes or a no?" he asked in a husky voice, and Sharon could feel his breath fanning over her nipple.

"What's the...question?" she countered, gasping and arching her back slightly when she felt the tip of Tony's tongue touch her.

He chuckled and took several moments to enjoy the territory he'd just marked as his own before answering, "We'll talk about it later."

Sharon's fingers had buried themselves, at no conscious order from her, in his hair. She felt an inexplicable happiness founded on nothing of substance. Her eyes were burning, and there was an achy thickness in her throat.

His hand was warm as it cupped her breast, his thumb shaping a nipple still moist and taut from the caresses of his lips and tongue. "Oh, God, I've missed you," he said, and then he kissed her again, hungrily, as though to consume her.

And she wanted to be consumed.

Tony's mouth strayed downward, along the line of her arched neck, over her bare shoulder, midway down her upper arm. When he reclaimed her nipple, Sharon moaned an anguished welcome.

The snap on her jeans gave way to his fingers, closely

followed by the zipper, and still he availed himself of her breasts, first one and then the other. Sharon was like a woman in the throes of an uncontrollable fever; she flung her head from side to side, blinded by the sensations Tony was creating with his hand and mouth, her breath too shallow and too quick. She grasped his T-shirt in her hands and pulled at it; if she'd had the strength, she would have torn it from him.

He finally cooperated, however, allowing Sharon to undress him, to pleasure him in some of the same ways that he had pleasured her.

Their joining, when it happened, was graceful at first, like a ballet. With each flexing of their bodies it became more frenzied, though, culminating in a kind of sweet desperation, a tangling of triumph and surrender that left both Tony and Sharon exhausted.

Tony recovered first and, after giving Sharon a leisurely kiss, sat up and began putting his clothes back on. The newspaper crackled as he moved, and Sharon began to laugh.

"What's funny?" he asked, turning and bracing himself with his hands so that he was poised over her. His eyes were full of love and mischief.

"I probably have newsprint on my backside," Sharon replied.

"Turn over and I'll look," Tony offered generously.

"Thanks, but no thanks," she answered, sliding out from beneath him and reaching for her own clothes.

"'Housing Market Bottoms Out,'" he pretended to read in a ponderous tone when Sharon reached for her panties and jeans.

She laughed and swung at him with the jeans, and that started a bout of wrestling, which ended in Sharon's bed a long time later.

"What were you going to ask me—about the weekend?" Sharon ventured, her cheek resting against Tony's shoulder. It felt good to lie close to him like that again.

Tony rested his chin on top of her head. He seemed to be bracing himself for a rebuff of some sort. "I'd like to go to the island house for a couple of days—just you and me."

Sharon absorbed that in silence. She had planned to take inventory at the shop that weekend, but a woman in business has to be flexible. She sighed contentedly and kissed the bare skin of his shoulder. "Sounds like an indecent proposal to me."

He laughed and his arm tightened around her waist. "Believe me, lady, it is."

Sharon raised her head to squint at the clock on the bedside table. "Oh, Lord. Tony, who's with the kids?"

"Mrs. Harry stayed late. Why? What time is it?"

"Boy, did Mrs. Harry stay late," Sharon agreed. "Tony, it's after midnight."

He swore and threw back the covers, crunching around on the newspaper looking for his clothes, and Sharon laughed.

"Do you realize what that woman gets for overtime?" Tony demanded, bringing his jeans and T-shirt from the living room to put them on.

Sharon was still giggling. "No, but I know how much she hates working late. I'm glad you're the one who has to face Scary Harry, and not me."

"Thanks a lot," Tony replied, snatching his watch from the bedside table. "We're leaving for the island Friday night," he warned, bending over to kiss her once more, "so make sure you have all the bases covered."

Sharon opened her mouth to protest this arbitrary

treatment, then closed it again. She really didn't want to argue, and they could discuss such issues on the island.

"Good night, babe," Tony said from the doorway of her room.

Sharon felt a sudden and infinite sadness because he was leaving. "Bye," she replied, glad that he couldn't see her face.

After she'd heard the door close behind him, she went out to put the chain lock in place. This, she thought, was what it was like to have a lover instead of a husband.

She tried to decide which she preferred while picking up her clothes. Lovers had a way of disappearing, like smoke, but husbands were surely more demanding. Sharon guessed that this was a case of six in one hand and half a dozen in the other.

She also deduced pretty quickly that she wasn't going to be able to crawl back into that bed where she'd just spent hours making love with Tony and fall placidly to sleep. She took a shower, put on her clothes and mixed the first batch of paint.

The new coat of soft ivory revitalized the living room and, coupled with the after effects of Tony's lovemaking, it brightened Sharon's spirits, as well. For the first time in months—the first time since she'd filed for divorce—she felt real hope for the future.

It was 3:00 a.m. when she finished. After cleaning up the mess, Sharon stumbled off to her room and collapsed facedown on the rumpled covers of the bed. She had absolutely no problem sleeping.

She entered Teddy Bares, bright eyed and humming, at precisely nine o'clock the next morning to find Helen reading a romance novel behind the counter.

The cover showed a dashing pirate holding a lushly buxom beauty in his arms. There were eager lights in Helen's eyes as she told Sharon breathlessly, "The woman in this book was given the choice of sleeping in the hold with a lot of soiled doves on their way to Morocco or sharing the captain's bed!"

Sharon took the book and studied the hero on the cover. He was an appealing rake with a terrific body. "Share his bed or languish in the hold, huh? Decisions, decisions."

Helen reclaimed the paperback and put it under the counter with her purse. Her expression was watchful now, and curious. "You look happy," she said suspiciously.

Sharon took her own purse to the back room and dropped it into a drawer of her desk. After settling herself in her chair, she reached for a pad of legal paper and a pencil and began making notes for an ad in the help wanteds. "Thank you," she replied in belated response to Helen's remark. "We won't be taking inventory this weekend, but I'll need you to work on Saturday if you will."

Helen was reading over her shoulder. "You're hiring another clerk? Excuse me, but is there something I should know?"

Sharon stopped writing and smiled up at her friend. "Good heavens, are you asking me if I mean to fire you?"

Helen nodded. "I guess I am," she said, looking worried.

Sharon shook her head. "Absolutely not. But I've decided that you're right—it's time we got someone to work evenings, and I'd like to be able to take more time off. That means we need two people, really. Both part-time."

Out front, the counter bell rang. Helen was forced

to go and wait on a customer, but she returned as soon as she could. Sharon was on the computer by that time, placing her ad.

"With any luck, we'll have applicants by Monday," she said.

Helen's eyes were wide. "I know what's going on here!" she cried in triumph. "It's like that Jimmy Stewart movie where he wishes he'd never been born and *whammie*, this angel fixes him right up. His friends don't recognize him—his own mother doesn't recognize him. His whole life is changed because he realizes how important he really is, and he's so happy—"

Sharon was shaking her head and smiling indulgently. "You can't seriously think that anything like that really happened," she said. "Can you?"

Helen sighed and shook her head. "No, but sometimes I get carried away."

With a nod, Sharon got out the books and began tallying debits and credits.

Chapter 6

"The pictures have to go, Mama," Tony said gently, gesturing toward the photographs of Carmen and himself on top of his parents' mantel.

Maria Morelli looked down at her hands, which were folded in her lap. She was a beautiful woman who always wore her dark hair done up in an impeccable coronet, and her skin was as smooth as Italian porcelain. Although she was the finest cook in all the family, her figure was trim, like those of her daughters. "Carmen's mother was my dearest friend," she finally replied, her voice small and soft. "We might as well have been sisters."

Tony nodded. "I know that, Mama. I'm just trying to make things a little easier for Sharon, that's all."

The flawless, ageless face hardened for the merest fraction of a second. "Sharon divorced you," she reminded him. "She is not your wife."

Tony let out the sigh he had been restraining. "Do you dislike her that much, Mama?" he asked quietly, after a few moments had passed.

"I don't dislike Sharon at all," Maria replied, her dark eyes snapping as she met her eldest son's gaze. "She is my grandson's mother." She paused, probably to allow Tony time to absorb the significance of such a bond.

"The pictures bother her," Tony reasoned. "You can understand that, can't you?"

"Carmen was practically family. You were raised together from the time you were babies—"

"Yes," Tony interjected softly. "And I loved Carmen very much. But she's dead now—"

"All the more reason she should be remembered properly," Maria said, and although her voice was low, it was also passionate. "Have you forgotten that she was Briana's mother, Tonio?"

Tony shook his head. "No, Mama. But Sharon isn't asking any of us to forget."

Maria drew in a long breath, let it out slowly and nodded. Her glance strayed to the assortment of pictures she'd kept for twelve years, lingering fondly on each one in turn. "She was so beautiful, Tonio."

Tony looked at Carmen, smiling happily and holding his arm in their wedding picture, and some of the old feelings came back, if only for a moment. "Yes," he said hoarsely.

"You take the pictures," Maria said, with an abrupt sweep of her hand that didn't fool Tony in the least. "Save them for Briana—someday, she'll want them."

Tony nodded and rose to stack the framed photographs one on top of the other. Maria had left her chair to stand with her back to him. "You still love Sharon, then?" she asked.

"Yes," Tony replied. "Maybe more than before, Mama."

"There were so many problems."

He thought of the hours he'd spent with Sharon during the night just past. Although the sex had been better than ever—and it had always been good, even at the end of their marriage—it was the laughter and the quiet talk that Tony loved to remember. He cherished the images that lingered in his mind. "There isn't anything I want more in all this world than a second chance with Sharon," he told his mother, and then he left the huge house, where every item in every room was familiar.

Tony went to his condo, rather than the house, partly because he needed some time alone and partly because he wanted to give the photographs to Briana at a time when things were better between them. At the moment, his relationship with his daughter was rocky, to say the least.

When he reached the one-bedroom place where he'd been living since the final separation from Sharon, Tony set the photographs of Carmen down and immediately forgot about them. His grandmother, Lucia, made one of her surprise entrances, coming out of the kitchen with her arms extended.

Lucia went wherever she wanted, that being a privilege of age and rank in the Morelli family, and Tony kissed her forehead and greeted her in gentle Italian.

She responded by explaining that his sister, Rosa, had brought her—she knew, as did everyone in the family, where he kept a spare key hidden—and that she wanted to cook for him. Tony adored the old woman, but he wasn't in the mood to eat or to chat amiably.

"Another time," he told Lucia, in her own language. "I can't stay."

Lucia smiled, touched his face with one of her small, veined hands and replied that she would put the food in plastic containers and tuck it into the refrigerator for him to have later.

Tony laughed and shook his head, then bent to kiss her cheek. "Enjoy, Grandmama," he told her, and then he left the condo, got back into his car and drove until he reached the secret place overlooking the sound.

This bit of ground with a view of trees and water was a place to think, a place to hope and hurt and plan. Twice, it had been a place to cry.

Sharon returned from her lunch break with her book tucked away in her purse so that Helen wouldn't see it. What was happening between her and Tony was still too fragile and tentative to discuss, even with her closest friend, and she knew that an Italian cookbook would raise questions.

While Helen was out having her customary salad, Sharon called Tony's sister, Rosa, and enlisted her help. Married two years and pregnant with her first child, Rose was a willing collaborator. She promised to pick up the kids and take them home with her for the evening.

When it came time to close the shop, Sharon rushed through her part of the routine and dashed to the grocery store at the opposite end of the mall. Holding the book two inches from the end of her nose, she studied the list of ingredients needed to make clam spaghetti as she wheeled her cart up and down the aisles. If this dish didn't impress Tony, nothing would.

After leaving the supermarket, Sharon drove to the house on Tamarack Drive and let herself in. In the kitchen, on the big blackboard near the telephone,

Bri had written carefully, "Dear Daddy, we're at Aunt Rose's. I told her we were grounded and she said our sentence had been suspended and you're supposed to go to the condo. Love, Bri."

Beneath this Rose had added a scrawled, "Don't worry about Grandmama—I'm on my way to collect her right now. Ciao, handsome. R."

Smiling, Sharon went to the rack where assorted keys were kept and ran her finger along it until she came to the one that would admit her to Tony's place. She dropped it into the pocket of her skirt and left the house again.

Tony's building stood on a road well out of town; Sharon remembered exactly where it was because he'd been working there overseeing the construction of the place when she'd had him served with divorce papers. The address was burned into her mind, as was the image of Tony storming into Teddy Bares with the papers in his hand, demanding answers Sharon hadn't been able to give.

He lived at the far end of the first row of condos; Bri and Matt had told her that weeks before, after a visit. Sharon pulled into the empty driveway and then sat for several minutes, trying to work up the courage to go in.

Finally, she did, her hand trembling a little as she unlocked the door and stepped inside, her bag of groceries in one arm.

The place was dim and sparsely furnished in the way that homes of divorced men often are, and it was neat to a fault.

A lighted aquarium bubbled on one end of the raised hearth of the fireplace, boasting several brightly colored fish. On the mantel was a framed picture of the kids taken at Disneyland during happier times. Tony's mother, sisters and aunts had supplied him with hand-crocheted pillow covers and afghans, which were discreetly displayed. Sharon knew Tony kept them not because he loved the handiwork, but because he loved the family.

She felt a bittersweet mixture of hope and grief as she switched on a lamp and found her way into the kitchen. Just as she'd expected, it was small and efficient, organized down to the last olive pick. A delicious aroma of tomato sauce and mingling spices filled the air.

Humming, Sharon took the new cookbook from her purse and the groceries from their paper bag. She knew a few moments of chagrin when the telephone rang and Tony's answering machine picked up the call; maybe she shouldn't have let herself in this way without his knowing.

The caller was Tony's youngest brother, Michael. "Get back to me when you can, Tonio," he said with quiet affection. "We landed the contract on that new supermarket, so it's partytime at my place tonight. Bring the blonde."

Sharon's hands froze as Michael's closing words echoed through the condo like something shouted into a cave. She considered gathering up her cookbook and food and leaving, then drew a deep breath and reminded herself that she and Tony were divorced. Certainly, he had a right to date.

On the other hand, it hurt so very much to think of him with someone else....

In the end, Sharon decided to stay. Since she'd come this far, she might as well see this idea through to the last chopped clam and strand of spaghetti.

Sharon soon discovered that she'd forgotten to buy olive oil, and Tony's supply, if he'd ever had one, was gone. "What blonde?" his ex-wife muttered, still a little nettled, as she got down the butter-flavored shortening and plopped some into a skillet.

When she had the meal well underway—she had to admit that it didn't smell like anything Maria Morelli had ever cooked—she decided to switch on some music, touch up her lipstick and make sure that her hair was combed.

The bathroom had to be at the end of the hall next to the front door. Sharon headed that way, but was halted by an eerie glow coming from the single bedroom.

Puzzled, she paused and looked inside, and what she saw made her mouth drop open. The shock wounded her so deeply that she had to grasp the doorjamb in one hand for a moment to steady herself, and just as she found the strength to turn away, she heard Tony coming in.

Still, she stared at the familiar photographs, the ones that had once graced Maria's living room. They were neatly aligned on Tony's dresser, a votive candle flickering in front of them.

Sharon turned away with one hand to her mouth, her eyes scalded with tears, and came up hard against Tony's chest.

He took her upper arms in his hands to steady her, and even though the light was dim in the hallway, Sharon could see the baffled look in his eyes. She broke free of him and stumbled back to the living room, where she grabbed for her purse.

"Sharon, wait a minute," Tony pleaded reasonably. "Don't go—"

She dashed at her tears with the back of one hand and marched into the kitchen to turn off the burner under her clam sauce. "I guess I deserved this," she called, knowing that she probably sounded distracted and hysterical but unable to help herself. When she reached the living room again, Tony was beside the front door, as if to stand guard. "It was presumptuous of me to just walk in, thinking we could pick up where we left off—"

"You're welcome here anytime," Tony hold her. "Day or night."

"The woman Michael refers to as 'the blonde' would probably take issue with that," Sharon said, and the words, intended to be sophisticated and flippant, came out sounding like a pathetic joke. She reached for the doorknob and turned it. "Goodbye, Tony. And I'm sorry for intruding—I really am."

When she opened the door, he caught hold of her arm and pulled her back inside. The stereo was playing a particularly romantic tune, one she and Tony had once liked to listen to together.

"Damn it, Sharon, I'm not going to let you walk out. Not again."

She wrenched her arm free of his grasp. "You can't stop me," she spat, and this time there was no attempt at sounding anything but angry and hurt. She stood with her back to him, trembling, gazing out at the street and seeing nothing.

"You're too upset to drive," Tony reasoned, making no attempt to renew his hold on her arm. "Come in and talk to me. Please."

Sharon lifted one hand to her forehead for a moment. "There's no point in our talking—we should have learned that by now."

He sighed. "Sharon, if it's about the woman, we're divorced—"

"It isn't that," she said in wooden tones. "It's that spooky little shrine in your room." She paused on the doorstep, turning to look up at him. "My attorney will be contacting yours about the joint custody arrangement—our sharing the house and all that. We're going to have to work out some other way."

"Sharon." Tony's voice had taken on a note of hoarse desperation. He reached out cautiously to take her hand, and then he pulled her behind him along the hallway toward his room.

In the doorway, he paused. Sharon saw the muscles in his broad shoulders go rigid beneath the fabric of his shirt. "Oh, my God," he muttered, and didn't even turn around to face her. After giving a raspy sigh, he said, "You'll never believe me, so I'm not even going to try to explain. Not right now." His hand released Sharon's, and hers fell back to her side. "I'll call you later."

"There isn't going to be a 'later,'" Sharon said mildly. "Not for us."

With that, she turned and walked away, and Tony made no move to stop her.

Back at the apartment, she changed into work clothes and began painting with a vengeance. Tears streamed down her face as she worked, but she dared not stand still. She painted the kitchen, the bedroom and the bathroom, and gave the living room a second coat.

When that was done it was so late that there was no sense in going to bed at all. Sharon disposed of all the newspaper, leftover paint, brushes and cans, and then took a shower. As she turned around under the spray of water, she scoured her breasts and hips, all the places where Tony had touched her, hoping to wash away the sensations that still lingered.

"My God," Helen breathed, when she walked into the shop an hour later, "you look terrible!"

Sharon said nothing. She simply marched into the

back room like a marionette on strings that were too
tautly drawn, and sat down at her desk. She scanned
the morning's mail, taking special note of a fashion
show coming up in Paris in a couple of weeks. Maybe
it was time to go on a real buying trip instead of ordering everything from wholesalers. She wondered numbly
whether or not her passport had expired.

She felt almost ready to go out into the main part
of the shop and face the customers by that time, but as
Sharon slid back her chair, she got a surprise.

Michael, Tony's brother, came striding into the little room, looking very earnest, very young and very
angry. Sharon had always liked him tremendously, and
she was injured by the heat she saw burning in his dark
Morelli eyes.

"What did you do to him?" he whispered tightly.

"Shall I call the police?" Helen put in from the doorway.

Sharon shook her head and gestured for Helen to
leave her alone with Michael. "Sit down," she told her
former brother-in-law.

He took the chair beside her desk, still fuming. "I
had a party last night," he said, glaring at her.

Sharon sat down and folded her hands in her lap. "I
know," she replied evenly.

"Tony was there."

By this time, there was a wall of ice around Sharon.
"Good," she answered.

Michael was obviously furious. To his credit, however, he drew a deep breath and tried to speak reasonably. "Sharon, my brother looks like he's been in a train
wreck. He showed up at my place late last night, stink-
ing drunk and carrying on about shrines and blondes
and clam sauce. The only halfway reasonable statement

I could get out of him was that your lawyer was going to call his lawyer." Michael was a little calmer now. "Which brings us back to my original question. What did you do to Tony?"

Sharon was too tired and too broken inside to feel resentment, but she knew that she should. "I didn't do anything to Tony," she replied coolly. "And the problem is between your brother and me, Michael. Forgive me, but none of this is any of your business."

Michael leaned toward her, his eyes shooting fire. "Do you think I give a damn whether or not you consider this my business? Tony is my brother and I love him!"

Sharon closed her eyes for a moment. She had a headache, probably resulting from the combination of this confrontation and the paint fumes at home. She wanted the whole world to go away and leave her alone—yesterday, if not sooner.

"I salute you, Michael." She sighed, rubbing her temple with three fingers. "Tony is a hard man to love—I've given up trying."

Michael shoved a strong, sun-browned hand through his curly hair. "Okay," he said in frustration. "I gave it a shot, I blew it. Tony is going to kill me if he ever finds out I came here and told you about last night."

"He won't hear it from me," Sharon assured the young man. "Congratulations on the new contract, by the way. The one for the supermarket."

Michael looked at her curiously for a moment, then got out of his chair. He ran his palms down his thighs in a nervous gesture. "Thanks. Sharon, I just want to say one more thing, and then I'll get out of here. Tony loves you as much as any man has ever loved a woman, and if the two of you don't find a way to reach each other, it's going to be too late."

"It already is," Sharon said with sad conviction. "We shouldn't even have tried."

At that, Michael shook his head and went out. Helen appeared the moment the shop door had closed behind him.

"Are you all right?" she asked.

Sharon shook her head. "No," she answered, "I'm not. Listen, Helen, I have this wretched headache..." *And this broken heart.* "I'd like to leave for the rest of the day. If you don't want to stay, you don't have to— you can just lock up and go home."

Helen was looking at her as though she'd just suggested launching herself from the roof of the mall in a hang glider. "I'll close the shop at the regular time," she said.

Sharon nodded. "Okay, good. Umm—I'll see you tomorrow...."

"Sure," she said with a determined smile. "No hurry, though. I can handle things alone if I have to."

Sharon put on sunglasses, even though it wasn't a particularly bright day, and walked across the parking lot to the roadster. Because she wanted to feel the wind in her face, she put the canvas top down before pulling out of her customary parking space. With no special destination in mind, she drove onto the highway and headed out of town.

She'd been traveling along the freeway for almost an hour before she became aware that she was, after all, definitely going somewhere. She was on her way to Hayesville, the little town on the peninsula where she'd grown up and where her mother still lived.

As huge drops of rain began to fall, Sharon pulled

over to the side of the road and, smiling grimly to herself, put the car's top back up. After another hour, she stopped at a restaurant along the roadside to have coffee and call Briana and Matt.

"Where are you, Mom?" Briana wailed. "You're supposed to be with us—it's your turn."

Matt was on one of the other phones. "School starts tomorrow, too," he added.

Sharon closed her eyes for a moment, trying hard to collect herself. It wouldn't do to fall apart in a truck stop and have to be carried back to Port Webster in a basket. "You guys aren't alone, are you? Isn't Mrs. Harry there?"

"No," Bri answered. "Dad is. But he's got a headache, so we're supposed to stay out of the den."

Responsible to the end, Sharon made herself say, "One of you go and tell him to pick up the telephone, please. I have to explain why I can't be there."

While Bri rattled on about her favorite rock group, her prospects of surviving seventh grade and what the orthodontist had said about her friend Mary Kate's broken tooth, Matt went off to the den.

After an eternity of adolescent prattle, Tony came on the line. "Hang up, Briana," he said tersely.

Bri started to protest, then obeyed.

Sharon took the plunge. "Tony, listen to me—"

"No, lady," he broke in brusquely, "you listen to me. I don't know where you are or what you're doing, but it's your turn to hold down the fort, so get your shapely little backside over here and look after these kids!"

Sharon sighed, counted mentally and went on. "I can't. I-I'm out of town."

Tony sounded so cold, like a stranger. "Wonderful.

Was your lawyer planning on mentioning that to my lawyer?"

"Don't, Tony," Sharon whispered. "Please, don't be cruel."

"I'm not trying to be. I thought that was the way we were going to be communicating from now on— through our attorneys. God knows, we can't seem to manage a one-to-one conversation."

"That's true, isn't it?" Sharon reflected. "We're like two incompatible chemicals—we just don't mix."

"Where are you?" Tony asked evenly, after a long and volatile silence.

"I'm going to visit my mother." The words came out sounding stiff, even a little challenging, though Sharon hadn't meant them that way.

"Great," Tony replied. "If you catch her between bingo games, you can pour out your soul."

"That was a rotten thing to say, Tony. Did I make remarks about your mother?"

"Often," he answered.

It was just no damned use. Sharon was glad Tony couldn't see the tears brimming in her eyes. "Give my love to the kids, please, and let them know that I'll be home tomorrow. Tell them we'll have supper out to celebrate their first day of school."

Tony was quiet for so long that Sharon began to think he'd laid the receiver down and walked away. Finally, however, he said, "I'll tell them."

"Thanks," Sharon replied, and then she gently hung up the telephone and went back out to her car.

It was raining hard, and Sharon was glad. The weather was a perfect match for her mood.

Chapter 7

It was getting dark when Sharon arrived in Hayesville. She turned down Center Street, passing the bank and the feed-and-grain and the filling station, and took a left on Bedford Road.

Her mother lived in a tiny, rented house at the end. The picket fence needed painting, the top of the mailbox was rusted out and the grass was overgrown. Sharon parked in the empty driveway and got out of her car, bringing her purse with her.

She entered through the tattered screen door on the back porch. As always, the key was hanging on its little hook behind the clothes drier; Sharon retrieved it and let herself into her mother's kitchen.

"Bea?" she called once, tentatively, even though she knew she was alone. No doubt, Tony had been right; Bea was playing bingo at the Grange Hall. She only worked part-time as a beautician these days, having acquired some mysterious source of income, which she refused to discuss.

Predictably, there was no answer. Sharon ran a hand through her hair and wondered why she'd driven all this way when she'd known her mother wouldn't be there for her, even if she happened to be physically present.

She looked at the wall phone, wishing that she could call Tony just to hear his voice, and she was startled when it rang. She blinked and then reached out for the receiver. "Hello?"

"Sharon?" Bea's voice sounded cautious, as though she wanted to make sure she was talking to her daughter and not a burglar.

Sharon smiled in spite of everything. "Yes, it's me," she answered quietly. "I just got here."

"Melba Peterson told me she saw you drive by in that fancy yellow car of yours, but I wasn't sure whether to believe her or not. She said they were going to have a thousand-dollar jackpot at bingo tonight, too, and all they've got is a few cases of motor oil and a free lube job at Roy's Texaco."

Sharon twisted one finger in the phone cord. "Does that mean you're coming home?"

Bea was clearly surprised. "Of course I am. Did you think I was just going to let you sit there all by yourself?"

After a moment, Sharon managed to answer, "Yes—I mean, no—"

"I'll be right there, darlin'," Bea announced cheerfully. "Have you had anything to eat?"

"Well—"

"I didn't think so. I'll stop at the burger place on my way home."

Sharon tried again. "I don't really feel—"

"See you in a few minutes," Bea chimed, as though she and her daughter had always been close.

By the time her mother had arrived, roaring up in her exhaust-belching dragon of a car, Sharon had splashed her face with cold water, brushed her hair and mustered a smile.

Bea dashed up the front walk, a grease-dappled white bag in one hand, her purse in the other. "What did he do to you, that big hoodlum?" she demanded, dashing all Sharon's hopes that she'd managed to look normal.

She sighed, holding the screen door open wide as Bea trotted into the living room. "Tony isn't a hoodlum, and he didn't do anything to me—"

"Sure, he didn't. That's why you're up here in the middle of the week looking like you just lost out on a three-card blackout by one number." She gestured with the paper bag, and Sharon followed her into the kitchen.

Bea was a small woman with artfully coiffed hair dyed an improbable shade of champagne blond, and she wore her standard uniform—double-knit slacks, a colorful floral smock and canvas espadrilles. She slapped the burger bag down in the middle of the table and shook one acrylic fingernail under Sharon's nose.

"It's time you let go of that man and found somebody else," she lectured.

Sharon was annoyed. "You never looked for anybody else," she pointed out, lingering in the doorway as she'd done so often in her teens, her hands gripping the woodwork.

Bea drew back a chair and sat down, plunging eagerly into the burgers and fries, leaving Sharon the choice between joining her or going hungry. "What makes you think I needed to look?" she asked after a few moments.

Sharon sat and reached for a cheeseburger. "You mean you had a romance in your life and I didn't even know it?"

Bea smiled and tapped the tabletop with one of her formidable pink nails. "There was a lot you didn't know, sweetheart," she said smugly. Then she laughed at her daughter's wide-eyed expression.

The two of them sat in companionable silence for several minutes, consuming their suppers. Finally, Sharon blurted out, "I'm still in love with Tony."

"Tell me something I didn't already know," Bea answered with a sigh.

Sharon's throat had closed; she laid down what remained of her cheeseburger and sat staring at it. "I guess you were right when you said it would never work," she said, when she could get the words out.

Bea's hand, glittering with cheap rings, rose hesitantly to cover hers. "I didn't want you to be hurt," she answered gently. "Tony was young, he'd just lost his wife, he had a little baby to raise. I was afraid he was going to use you."

"But you said—"

"I know what I said. I told you that he was out of your league. That he'd get tired of you."

Sharon was watching her mother, unable to speak. This understanding, sympathetic Bea wasn't the woman she remembered; she didn't know how to respond.

"I was hoping to discourage you," Bea confessed, a faraway expression in her eyes. "It was never easy for you and me to talk, was it?"

"No," Sharon said with a shake of her head. "It wasn't."

Bea smiled sadly. "I didn't know how," she said. "We

didn't have Dr. Phil and to tell us things like that when you were a girl."

Sharon turned her hand so that she could grip her mother's. "How's this for talking?" she asked hoarsely. "I can't think anymore, Bea—all I seem to be able to do is feel. And everything hurts."

"That's love, all right," Bea remarked. "Do you have any idea how Tony feels?"

Sharon shook her head. "No. Sometimes I think he loves me, but then something happens and everything goes to hell in the proverbial hand basket."

"What do you mean, 'something happens'?"

Dropping her eyes, Sharon said, "Yesterday I got this bright idea that I was going to surprise Tony with a real Italian dinner. Only I was the one who got the surprise."

Bea squeezed her hand. "Go on."

She related how she'd stumbled upon the pictures of Carmen with the votive candle burning reverently in front of them.

"There was probably an explanation for that," Bea observed. "It doesn't sound like the kind of thing Tony would do, especially after all this time."

Sharon bit into her lower lip for a moment. "I know that now," she whispered miserably.

"You couldn't just go back and apologize? Or call him?"

"Tony has a way of distancing himself from me," Sharon mused with a distracted shake of her head. "It hurts too much."

"It would probably be safe to assume that you've hurt him a time or two," Bea reasoned. "Didn't you tell me once that Tony went into a rage when you divorced him?"

Sharon closed her eyes at the memory, nodding.

She'd never once been afraid of Tony, not until that day when he'd come into Teddy Bares with the divorce papers in his hand, looking as though he could kill without hesitation. She'd stood proudly behind the counter, trembling inside, afraid to tell him why she couldn't remain married to him—and not sure she knew the answer herself.

Bea spoke softly. "You say you love Tony, but it would be my guess that you still don't understand what's going on between the two of you. Well, you were right before, Sharon—you don't dare go back to him until you know what went wrong in the first place."

"What can I do?" Sharon whispered, feeling broken inside. She ached to be held in Tony's arms again, to lie beside him in bed at night, to laugh with him and fight with him.

"Wait," Bea counseled. "Try to give yourself some space so that you'll be able to think a little more clearly. If you love a man, it's next to impossible to be objective when you're too close."

"How did you get so smart?" Sharon asked with a tearful smile.

Bea shrugged, but she looked pleased at the compliment. "By making mistakes, I suppose." She got up to start brewing coffee in her shiny electric percolator.

Sharon gathered up the debris from their casual dinner and tossed it into the trash, then wiped the tabletop clean with a damp sponge.

"Tony's not such a bad man," Bea said in a quiet voice. "I guess I just have a tendency to dislike him because he has so much power to hurt you."

Sharon looked at her mother in silence. Their relationship was a long way from normal, but at least they were both making an effort to open up and be honest about what they thought and felt.

That night she slept in her own familiar room. When she awakened the next morning, she felt a little better, a little stronger.

Sharon found Bea in the kitchen, making breakfast. As Bea fried bacon, she told her daughter all about the new car she intended to win at that day's bingo session. And then the telephone rang.

Pouring two cups of fresh coffee, as well as keeping an eye on the bacon, Sharon listened while her mother answered with a bright hello. "Yes, she's here," she said after a moment of silence. "Just a moment."

Sharon turned, smoothing her skirt with nervous hands, and gave her mother a questioning look.

"It's Mr. Morelli—Vincent," Bea whispered, holding the receiver against her bosom.

Some premonition made Sharon pull back a chair and sit down before speaking to her former father-in-law. "Vincent?" she asked, and her voice shook.

The gentle voice thrummed with sadness and fear. "I have bad news for you, sweetheart," Vincent began, and Sharon groped for Bea's hand. It was there for her to grip, strong and certain. "There was an accident early this morning, and Tony's been hurt. The doctors still don't know how bad it is."

The familiar kitchen seemed to sway and shift. Sharon squeezed her eyes shut for a second in an effort to ground herself. "What happened?" she managed to get out.

Vincent sighed, and the sound conveyed grief, frustration, anger. "Tonio was climbing the framework on one of the sites, and he fell. He wasn't wearing a safety belt."

Sharon swallowed, envisioning the accident all too clearly in her mind. "Are Briana and Matt all right?"

"They're at school," Vincent answered. "They haven't been told. The rest of the family is here at City Hospital."

"I'll be there as soon as I possibly can," Sharon said. "And Vincent? Thank you for calling me."

"Thank heaven the housekeeper knew where you were. Drive carefully, little one—we don't need another accident."

Sharon promised to be cautious, but even as she hung up she was looking around wildly for her purse. She was confused and frantic, and tears were slipping down her cheeks.

Bea forced her to stand still by gripping both of Sharon's hands in her own. "Tell me. One of the children has been hurt?"

Sharon shook her head. "No—it's Tony. He fell—the doctors don't know…" She pulled one hand free of her mother's and raised it to her forehead. "Oh, God, it will take me hours to get there—my purse! Where is my purse?"

Bea took the purse from the top of the dishwasher and opened it without hesitation, taking out Sharon's car keys. "I'm driving—you're too upset," she announced.

Minutes later Bea was at the wheel of the expensive yellow roadster, speeding out of town, her daughter sitting numbly in the passenger seat.

Sharon nearly collided with Michael when she came through the entrance of the hospital; in fact, she would have if her brother-in-law hadn't reached out with both hands to prevent it.

"Tony…?" she choked out, because that was all she

could manage. She knew that her eyes were taking up her whole face and that she was pale.

Michael's expression was tender. "He's going to be all right," he said quickly, eager to reassure her, still supporting her with his hands.

Relief swept over Sharon in a wave that weakened her knees and brought a strangled little cry to her throat. "Thank God," she whispered. And then, in a fever of joy, she threw her arms around Michael's neck.

He held her until she stepped back, sniffling, to ask, "Where is he? I want to see him."

Michael's dark eyes were full of pain. "I don't think that would be a good idea, princess," he said, his voice sounding husky. "Not right now."

"Where is he?" Sharon repeated, this time in a fierce whisper. Her entire body was stiff with determination.

Michael sighed. "Room 229. But, Sharon—"

Sharon was already moving toward the elevator. Bea, still parking the car, would have to find her own way through the maze that was City Hospital.

Room 229 was in a corner, and members of the Morelli family were overflowing into the hallway. Sharon was glad she'd encountered Michael before coming upstairs, or she might have thought that the worst had happened.

News of her arrival buzzed through the group of well-wishers, and they stepped aside to admit her.

Tony was sitting up in bed with a bandage wrapped around his head. His face was bruised and scraped, and his left arm was in a cast. But it was the look in his eyes that stopped Sharon in the middle of the room.

His expression was cold, as though he hated her.

Vincent and Maria, who had been standing on the other side of the room, silently withdrew. Sharon knew without looking around that the other visitors had left, also.

And she was still stuck in the middle of the floor with her heart jammed in her throat. She had to swallow twice before she could speak. "I got here as quickly as I could," she said huskily. "Are—are you all right?"

Tony only nodded, the intensity of his anger plainly visible in his eyes.

A cold wind blew over Sharon's soul. "Tony—"

"Stay away," he said, shifting his gaze, at last, to the window. In the distance the waters of the sound shimmered and sparkled in the afternoon sun. "Please— just stay away."

Sharon couldn't move. She wanted to run to him; at the same time, she needed to escape. "I'm not going anywhere until you tell me what's the matter," she told him. The moment the words were out of her mouth, she wondered if she'd really said them herself, since they sounded so reasonable and poised.

Tony was still looking out the window. "We cause each other too much pain," he said after a long time.

She dared to take a step closer to the bed. Her hands ached to touch Tony, to soothe and lend comfort, but she kept them stiffly at her sides. His words, true though they were, struck her with the aching sting of small pelted stones.

Sharon waited in silence, knowing there was nothing to do but wait and endure until he'd said everything.

"We have to stop living in the past and go on with our lives. Today taught me that, if nothing else."

There were tears burning in Sharon's eyes; she lowered her head to hide them and bit into her lower lip.

"You can have the house," he went on mercilessly. At last Tony looked at Sharon; she could feel his gaze touching her. His voice was a harsh, grinding rasp. "I've never been able to sleep in our room. Did you know that?"

Sharon shook her head; pride forced her to lift it. "I've slept in the den a lot of times myself," she confessed.

The ensuing silence was awful. Unable to bear it, Sharon went boldly to the side of the bed even though she knew she wouldn't be welcome.

"I was so scared," she whispered. Her hand trembled as she reached out to touch the bandage encircling his head. It hid most of his hair and dipped down on one side over his eye, giving him a rakish look.

"No doubt," Tony said with cruel dryness, "you were afraid that Carmen and I had found a way to be together at last."

The gibe was a direct hit. Sharon allowed the pain to rock her, her eyes never shifting from Tony's. Speech, for the moment, was more than she could manage.

"The 'shrine,' as you called it, was my grandmother's doing," Tony went on, with a terrible humor twisting one side of his mouth and flickering in his eyes. "I'd talked Mama into giving up the pictures, since they bothered you so much. I planned on turning them over to Bri later on, when she and I were getting along a little better. In the meantime, Grandmama found them. Evidently, she decided to while away the time by honoring the dead."

Sharon lifted her index finger to his lips in a plea for silence, because she could bear no more. He was right—so right. They were causing each other too much pain.

She grasped at a slightly less volatile subject with the desperation of a drowning woman. "What about Bri? Will I still be able to see her?"

Tony looked at her as though she'd struck him. "You're the only mother she's ever known. I wouldn't hurt her—or you—by keeping the two of you apart."

"Thank you," Sharon said in a shattered whisper. She touched his lips very gently with her own. "Rest now," she told him, just before she turned to walk away.

He grasped her arm to stop her, and when she looked back over one shoulder, she saw that his eyes were bright with tears. "Goodbye," he said.

Sharon put a hand to her mouth in an effort to control her own emotions and ran out of the room. The hallway was empty except for her father-in-law.

Vincent took one look at Sharon and drew her into his arms. "There, there," he said softly. "Everything will be all right now. Tonio will be well and strong."

The sobs Sharon had been holding back came pouring out. She let her forehead rest against Vincent's shoulder and gave way to all her grief and confusion and pain.

"Tell me, little one," he urged gently when the worst was over. "Tell me what hurts you so much."

Sharon looked up at him and tried to smile. Ignoring his request, she said instead, "Tony is so lucky to have a father like you." She stood on tiptoe and kissed Vincent's weathered, sun-browned cheek, and that was her farewell.

Bea, who had been in the waiting room with Maria, came toward Sharon as she pushed the button to summon the elevator. Neither woman spoke until they'd found the roadster in the parking lot and Sharon had slid behind the wheel, holding out her hand to Bea for the keys.

With a shake of her head, Bea got into the car on

the passenger side and surrendered them. "Where are we going now?"

Sharon started the car and then dried her cheeks with the heels of her palms. Before backing out of the parking space, she snapped her seat belt in place. "Home," she replied. "We're going home. Tony just gave me the house."

"He just what?" Bea demanded. "The man is giving away his possessions? Tony's own mother told me, not fifteen minutes ago, that he's going to be fine. They're letting him leave the hospital tomorrow."

Sharon was concentrating on the traffic flow moving past the hospital. If she didn't, she was sure she would fall apart. "The house isn't his 'possession,' Mother. It belonged to both of us."

Sharon had addressed Bea by a term other than her given name for the first time in fifteen years; she knew that had to have some significance, but she was too overwrought to figure out what it was.

"If it's all the same to you," Bea said, when they were moving toward Tamarack Drive, "I'd like to go home tomorrow. I could take the bus."

Sharon only nodded; she would have agreed to almost anything at that point.

The moment the car pulled into the driveway, Bri and Matt came bursting out the front door, still wearing their first-day-of-school clothes. They were closely followed by Rose, who was resting both hands on her protruding stomach

Sharon addressed her former sister-in-law first. "He's all right—you knew that, didn't you?"

Rose nodded. "Papa called. It's you we're worried about."

Bri and Matt were both hugging Sharon, and she

laughed hoarsely as she tried to hold each one at the same time.

"Mom, is Daddy really okay?" Briana demanded, when they were all in the kitchen moments later.

Sharon was careful not to meet the child's eyes. "Yes, babe. He's fine."

"Then why isn't he here?" Matt wanted to know. He was staying closer to her than usual; Sharon understood his need for reassurance because she felt it, too.

"They want to keep him in the hospital overnight, probably just to be on the safe side," Sharon told her son. "He's got a broken arm, a few cuts and scrapes and a bandage on his head. Other than that, he seems to be fine."

"Honest?" Bri pressed.

"Honest," Sharon confirmed. "Now, I want to hear all about your first day of school."

Both children began to talk at once, and Sharon had to intercede with a patient, "One at a time. Who wants to be first?"

Bri generously allowed her brother that consideration, and Matt launched into a moment-by-moment account of his day.

Much later, when dinner was over and both Bri and Matt had gone upstairs to their rooms, Sharon made out the sofa bed in the den for her mother. She was like an automaton, doing everything by rote.

Bea retired immediately.

Wanting a cup of herbal tea before bed, Sharon returned to the kitchen and was surprised to find that Michael had let himself in. He was leaning against a counter, his arms folded, just as Sharon had seen Tony do so many times. As a matter of fact, the resemblance was startling.

"I tried to warn you that Tony was in that kind of mood," Michael said kindly, his eyes full of sympathy and caring. Sharon reflected again that Tony was fortunate—not only did he have Vincent for a father, he had a whole network of people who truly loved him.

"Yes," Sharon replied in a small voice. "You did."

"Whatever he said," Michael persisted, "he didn't mean it."

Sharon longed to be alone. "You weren't there to hear," she answered. And then she turned and went upstairs, hoping that Michael would understand.

She had no more strength left.

Chapter 8

Sharon found her passport in the bottom of a drawer of her desk at home, jammed behind some of Tony's old tax records and canceled checks, which she promptly dropped. Kneeling on the floor and muttering, she began gathering up the scattered papers.

That was when she saw the check made out to her mother. Tony had signed it with a flourish, and the date was only a few weeks in the past.

Frowning, Sharon began to sort through the other checks. She soon deduced that Tony had virtually been supporting Bea for years.

Having forgotten her passport completely by this time, Sharon got to her feet and reached for the telephone. It was early on a Saturday morning and, unless Tony had changed considerably since their divorce, he would be sleeping in.

Sharon had no compunction at all about waking him.

She hadn't seen Tony, except from an upstairs window when he picked up the kids, in nearly two months. She also avoided talking to him on the telephone, although that was harder.

She supposed this was some kind of turning point.

A woman answered the phone, and Sharon closed her eyes for a moment. She hadn't expected to feel that achy hurt deep down inside herself, not after all this time. "Is Tony there, please?"

"Who's calling?" retorted the voice. Sharon wondered if she was speaking to the infamous blonde of Michael's mentioning. She also wondered if the woman had spent the night with Tony.

"I'm Sharon Morelli," she said warmly. "Who are you?"

"My name is Ingrid," came the matter-of-fact response.

Yep, Sharon thought miserably. *It's the blonde. People named Ingrid are always blond.* "I'd like to speak to Tony," she reminded his friend with consummate dignity.

"Right," Ingrid answered. "Hey, Tony—it's your ex-wife."

"Bimbo," Sharon muttered.

"I beg your pardon?" Ingrid responded politely.

Tony came on the line before Sharon had to reply, and he sounded worried. In fact, he didn't even bother to say hello. "Is everything all right?" he wanted to know.

Sharon looked down at the assortment of checks in her hand. "Since when do you support my mother?" she countered.

He sighed. "She told you," he said, sounding resigned.

"Hell no," Sharon swore, her temper flaring. And it

wasn't just the checks; it was Ingrid, and a lot of other problems. "Nobody around here tells me anything!"

"Calm down," Tony told her in reasonable tones. "You don't begrudge Bea the money, do you?"

"Of course not," Sharon said crisply.

"Then what's the problem?"

"You didn't mention it, that's what. I mean a little thing like supporting someone usually comes up in day-to-day husband-and-wife conversation, doesn't it?"

"We aren't husband and wife," Tony pointed out.

"Damn it, we were when you started writing these checks every month. And neither you nor Bea said a word!"

"Sorry. Guess we were just trying to maintain our images, having convinced everybody that we didn't like each other."

Sharon sighed and sagged into a chair. Sometimes it was so frustrating to talk to this man, but in a way it felt good, too. "Are you still sending my mother money every month?" she asked straight-out.

"Yes," Tony answered just as succinctly.

"I want you to stop. If Bea needs financial help, I'll take care of it."

"That's very independent and liberated of you, but the thing is out of your hands. My accountants see to it every month—like the child support."

Sharon drew in a deep breath and let it out again. Then she repeated the exercise. In, out, in, out. She would not let Tony short-circuit her composure; she'd grown beyond that in the past two months. "Bea is not a child," she said.

"That," Tony immediately retorted, "is a matter of opinion. I think we need to talk about this in person."

Sharon was filled with sweet alarm. She'd stayed out

of Tony's range since that day in the hospital, and she wasn't sure she was ready to be in the same room with him. On the other hand, the idea had a certain appeal. "I'm busy," she hedged.

Too late Sharon realized how thin that argument was. In truth, with all the help she'd hired at Teddy Bares, she had more time on her hands than she was used to.

"Doing what?" The question, of course, was inevitable. It was also a measure of Tony Morelli's innate gall.

Sharon's eyes fell on the blue cover of her passport. She smiled as she spoke. "I'm getting ready to go to Paris on a buying trip, actually."

"The kids didn't mention that," Tony said, and the statement had a faint air of complaint to it.

So Bri and Matt were making reports when they visited their dad, just as they did when they came home to Sharon. Well, it figured.

She smiled harder. "They don't tell you everything, I'm sure."

Tony was quiet for a few moments, absorbing that. "What should they be telling me that they aren't?" he finally asked.

Sharon wound her finger in the phone cord, hoping to sound distracted, disinterested. "Oh, this and that," she said. "Nothing important. I know you're busy, so I won't keep you." With that, she summarily hung up.

Twenty-two minutes later, Tony entered the den. Sharon noted, out of the corner of her eye, that he was wearing jeans, a T-shirt and a running jacket. Tony was especially attractive when he was about to work out.

"Hi," he said somewhat sheepishly.

Sharon smiled. She knew he'd just realized that he'd forgotten to come up with an excuse for dropping by. She looked up from the ledgers for Teddy Bares, which she always liked to check before they went to the accountant. "Hi, Tony." There was a cheerful fire crackling in the den's large brick fireplace, and the radio was tuned to an easy-listening station. "I see they took off your cast."

Tony sighed and then nodded, jamming his hands into the pockets of his navy-blue jacket. "Are the kids around?"

Briana and Matt were on the island staying in the A-frame with Tony's sister Gina and her husband. And Tony knew that.

"No," Sharon answered, refraining from pointing up the fact.

Still, he lingered. "Isn't November kind of a rotten time to go to Paris?" he finally asked.

Sharon looked down at her ledgers to hide a grin. "There is no such thing as a 'rotten time to go to Paris,'" she commented.

Tony went into the kitchen and came back with two mugs of coffee—one of which he somewhat grudgingly set down on the surface of Sharon's desk. "We went there on our honeymoon," he said, as if that had some bearing on Sharon's plans.

"I know," she replied dryly.

"The Bahamas would be warmer."

"They're not showing the spring lingerie lines in the Bahamas," was the reasonable reply. Sharon still hadn't looked up into those brown eyes; if she did that, she'd be lost.

Tony went to stand in front of the fire, his broad, powerful back turned to Sharon. "I guess we still haven't learned to talk to each other," he observed.

Sharon hadn't even realized that she'd been playing a game until he spoke. "I thought we'd given up on that," she said, in a soft voice that betrayed some of the sadness she felt.

"I've always found it difficult to do that," Tony remarked somewhat distantly. "Give up, I mean. Are you going to the company party?"

The mention of the celebration Vincent and Maria held every year just before Thanksgiving brought Ingrid to Sharon's mind. "I was invited," she said, avoiding his eyes. With the speed of Matt's hamsters fleeing their cage, her next words got out before she could stop them. "Are you taking Ingrid?"

There was an element of thunder in Tony's silence. "Yes," he answered after a very long time.

I've done it again, Sharon thought to herself. *I've asked a question I didn't want to have answered.* "If I have time, what with my trip to Paris," she told him, putting on a front, "I'll probably drop by."

"Good," Tony answered. His coffee mug made a solid thump sound as he set it down. "I'd better get to the gym, I guess," he added as a taut afterthought.

Sharon pretended a devout interest in the figures in her ledgers, although in reality they had about as much meaning for her as Chinese characters. "Aren't you forgetting something?"

"What?" he challenged in a vaguely belligerent tone. Sharon knew without looking that he'd thrust his hands into his jacket pockets again.

"We didn't discuss your sending money to Bea. I don't like it—it makes me feel obligated." At last she trusted herself to meet his eyes.

Quiet fury altered Tony's expression. "Why the hell should it do that? Have I asked you for anything?"

Sharon shook her head, stunned by the sheer force of his annoyance. "No, but—"

He folded his arms, and his dark eyes were still snapping. "I can afford to help Bea and I want to. That's the end of it," he said flatly.

Sharon sighed. "It isn't your responsibility to look after my mother," she told him gently. "I don't even understand why you feel it's necessary."

"You wouldn't," Tony retorted, his tone clipped, and then he walked out.

The festive feeling that autumn days often fostered in Sharon was gone. She propped both elbows on the surface of her desk and rested her forehead in her palms.

At least he hadn't made her cry this time. She figured that was some sort of progress.

"You've got to go to that party!" Helen said sternly, resting her arms on the counter and leaning toward Sharon with an earnest expression in her eyes. It had been a busy day, and they were getting ready to turn Teddy Bares over to Louise, the middle-aged saleswoman Sharon had hired to work from five-thirty until nine o'clock when the mall closed. "Furthermore, you have to take a date that will set Tony Morelli back on his heels!"

"Where am I going to get someone like that?" Sharon asked, a little annoyed that the dating game was so easy for Tony to play and so difficult for her. She'd been out with exactly four men since the divorce, and all of them were duds.

Helen was thoughtfully tapping her chin as she thought. A moment later her face was shining with revelation. "You could ask Michael to help you."

Sharon frowned, nonplussed. "Tony's brother?"

"He must know a lot of terrific guys, being pretty spectacular himself."

"Yeah," Sharon said wryly. "For instance, he knows

Tony. He'd go straight to big brother and spill his guts. I can hear it now. 'Tonio, Sharon is so desperate that she's after me to fix her up with blind dates.' No way, Helen!"

Helen shrugged. "I'm only trying to help. It's too bad you don't have the kind of business where you might meet more men."

"I wouldn't want one who shopped at Teddy Bares," Sharon remarked with a grin. "He'd either be married or very weird."

Helen made a face. "You are no help at all. I'm going to ask Allen what he can dig up at the gym."

Sharon winced at the thought of Helen's husband approaching strange men and asking them what they were doing on the night of the twenty-second. It could get him punched out, for one thing. "Thanks, but no thanks. I don't like jocks."

"Tony's a jock," Helen pointed out. "Or are those washboard stomach muscles of his an illusion?"

"When," Sharon demanded loftily, holding back a smile, "did you happen to get a look at my ex-husband's stomach, pray tell?"

Helen batted her lashes and tried to look wicked. "Fourth of July picnic, two years ago, on Vashon. Remember the volleyball game?"

Sharon remembered, all right. Tony had been wearing cutoffs and no shirt, and every time he'd jumped for the ball...

She began to feel too warm.

Helen gave her an impish look and went to the back room for their coats and purses. When she came out again, Louise had arrived to take over.

"I'm going to ask Allen to check out the jocks," Helen insisted, as she and Sharon walked out of the mall together.

Sharon lifted her chin a degree. "I might not be back from Paris in time for the party anyway, so don't bother."

"Maybe you'll meet somebody on the plane," Helen speculated.

Sharon rolled her eyes and strode off toward her car. When she got home, a surprise awaited her.

Maria was sitting at the kitchen table, chatting with Bri and Matt. Mrs. Harry had evidently been so charmed that she'd not only stayed late, she was serving tea.

She said a pleasant good-night and left when Sharon came in, and the kids, after collecting their hugs, ran off to watch TV in the den.

Sharon had a suspicion that their disappearance had been prearranged. "Hello, Maria. It's good to see you." She realized with a start that she'd meant those words.

Maria returned Sharon's smile. "I hope I haven't come at a bad time."

"You're always welcome, of course," Sharon replied with quiet sincerity. Mrs. Harry had started dinner— there was a casserole in the oven—so she had nothing to do but take off her coat, hang it up and pour herself a cup of tea.

She sat down at the table with Maria, who looked uncomfortable now, and even a little shy.

"I've come to ask if you were planning to attend our party," the older woman said softly. "Vincent and I are so hoping that you will. We don't see enough of you, Sharon."

Sharon was taken aback. "I'm not sure if I can come or not," she answered. "You see, I'm traveling to Paris that week."

Maria seemed genuinely disappointed. "That's exciting," she said, and she sounded so utterly insincere that Sharon had to smile. Her former mother-in-law smiled, too. Sharon had never noticed before now how sweet it made her look.

Sharon knew her eyes were dancing as she took a sip of her tea. "It's important to you that I come to the party, but I'm not sure why."

Maria looked down at her lap. "I guess I'm trying to make amends—however belatedly. I realize now that I didn't treat you as well as I could have, and I regret it."

Sharon reached out to touch Maria's hand. "I have regrets, too," she said. "I didn't try very hard to understand how you must have loved Carmen."

Maria swallowed and nodded. "She was like my own child, but I should have made you feel more like a part of our family. Forgive me, please, for letting an old grief stand in the way of the friendship we could have had."

Sharon felt tears sting her eyes. "There's nothing to forgive," she replied. After a short interval had passed, she added, "You know, Maria, if I could be the kind of mother to Matt and Briana that you were to your children, I'd count myself a resounding success."

The compliment brought a flush of pleasure to Maria's porcelain-smooth cheeks and a gentle brightness to her eyes. She was of another generation; her life revolved around her husband, children and grandchildren. "What a wonderful thing to say," she whispered. "Thank you."

Sharon leaned forward, her hand still resting on Maria's. "They're all so self-assured and strong, from Tony right down to Michael and Rose. What's your secret?"

Maria looked surprised. "Why, I simply loved them," she answered. "The way you love Briana and Matthew." She paused and smiled mischievously. "And, of course,

I had the good sense to marry Vincent Morelli in the first place. The self-assurance—as you call it—comes from him, I'm sure. And there have been times when I would have used another word for what my children have—brass. They can be obnoxious."

Before Sharon could agree that Tony, at least, had been known to suffer from that condition, there was a brief rap at the back door and he came strolling into the kitchen. He spared his ex-wife a glance, crossed the room and bent to give his mother a kiss on the cheek.

Bri and Matt, having heard his car, came racing into the room, full of joy. Tony was always greeted like a conquering hero, there to save the two of them from a death too horrible to contemplate, and that was a sore spot with Sharon.

"Hi," she said to him, when the hubbub had died down a little.

"Hello," he responded quietly.

Guilt struck Sharon full force. It was getting late, and Mrs. Harry's casserole was probably shriveling in the oven. She left her chair and hurried over to pull it out.

"Won't you stay to dinner, Maria?" she asked. Then, hesitantly, she added, "Tony?"

Both potential guests shook their heads. "Vincent and I are meeting downtown at our favorite restaurant," Maria said. "In fact, if I don't hurry, I'll be late."

With that, she went through a round of farewells including Tony, Briana, Matt, and finally, Sharon. "Don't let him push you around," she whispered to her former daughter-in-law, squeezing her hand.

Sharon grinned and, when Maria was gone, turned her attention to Tony. "Okay, what's your excuse, Morelli? Why can't you stay for dinner?"

"Because I hate Scary Harry's tuna-bean surprise,

that's why," he answered. "Last time I had it, it was worse than a surprise—it was a shock."

Naturally, the kids took up the chorus.

"Tuna-bean surprise?" wailed Bri, with all the pathos of a person asked to eat kitty litter. "Yech!"

"Can't we go out?" Matt added.

"See what you started?" Sharon said, frowning at Tony. "Thanks a lot."

Tony slid his hands into the pockets of his jeans and rocked back on the heels of his boots, looking pleased with himself. "I could always take the three of you out for dinner," he suggested innocently.

Bri and Matt were beside themselves at the prospect. "Please, Mom?" they begged in pitiful unison. "Please?"

Sharon was glaring now. "That was a dirty trick," she said to Tony. "It would serve all of you right if I said no." She paused, glancing down at the concoction Mrs. Harry had left in the oven. It did have a surprising aspect about it.

"She's weakening," Tony told the kids.

Sharon tried for a stern look. "Did you two finish your homework?"

Both Briana and Matt nodded, their eyes bright with eagerness.

She shrugged. "Then what can I possibly say," she began, spreading her hands, "except yes?"

Two minutes later they were all in Tony's car. "Put on your seat belts," he said over one shoulder, and Bri and Matt immediately obeyed.

Sharon wondered how he managed to elicit such ready cooperation. She always had to plead, reason, quote statistics and, finally, threaten in order to achieve what Tony had with a mere five words.

When they'd reached the restaurant and the kids were

occupied with their all-time favorite food, spaghetti, he turned to Sharon and asked, "Are you really going to Paris?"

She looked down at the swirl of pasta on the end of her fork. Maybe it was wrong of her, given the fact that their marriage was over, but she was glad that he cared what she did. "Yes," she answered. Only superhuman effort—and the presence of her children—kept her from countering, *Are you sleeping with Ingrid?*

An awkward silence fell, and Tony was the one who finally broke it.

"Remember when we were there?" he asked quietly.

There was a lump in Sharon's throat. Vincent and Maria had given them the trip as a wedding present, and it had been like something out of a fairy tale. "How could I forget?" she asked in a voice that was barely audible. She hadn't thought, until now, how many bittersweet memories would be there to meet her once she arrived in France.

"Sharon?"

She lifted her eyes and met his gaze questioningly.

"If I said the wrong thing again," he told her, "I'm sorry."

She swallowed and worked up a smile. "You didn't," she answered, marveling at herself because if he'd asked to go along on the trip to Paris, she would have agreed with delight.

Only Tony wasn't going to ask because he had Ingrid now and he'd only been trying to make conversation in the first place. He probably wasn't even interested in Sharon's plans.

She thought of how Tony would react if she told him that she was considering opening a second shop in nearby Tacoma and winced at the memories that came to mind. A fairly modern man in most respects, he'd reverted to the Neanderthal mind-set when Sharon had opened Teddy Bares, and things had gotten progressively worse....

Tony started to reach for her hand, then hesitated. Although he said nothing, his eyes asked her a thousand questions.

She looked at him sadly. If only he'd been proud of her, she reflected, things might have turned out so differently.

Chapter 9

The red-sequined dress was long and slinky with a plunging neckline and a sexy slit up one side, and it looked spectacular on Sharon.

"I can't afford it," she whispered to Helen, who was shopping with her while Louise looked after Teddy Bares. The two women were standing in the special occasions section of the best department store in the mall, gazing at Sharon's reflection in a mirror.

"Tony's going to fall into the punch bowl when he sees you," Helen responded, as though Sharon hadn't said anything.

Sharon squinted and threw her shoulders back. "Do you think it makes me look taller?"

Helen nodded solemnly. "Oh, yes," she answered.

With a sigh, Sharon calculated the purchasing power remaining on her credit card—the margin had narrowed considerably after the divorce, and if she bought this dress, it would take her to her limit. "I haven't even got a date," she reflected aloud, speaking as much to herself as to Helen.

"Have a little faith, will you? Allen's checking out the hunks up at the gym—it's a matter of time, that's all."

"A matter of time until he gets his teeth rearranged, you mean."

Helen shook her head, a half smile on her face. "Stop worrying and buy the dress. If our plans don't work out, you can always return it."

The logic of that was irrefutable. Sharon returned to the dressing room to change back into her clothes and when that was done, she bought the dress. She and Helen parted company then, and Sharon hurried home.

The kids were in the kitchen obediently doing their homework, and something good was baking in the oven. "I've got it," Sharon said, bending to kiss Briana's cheek and then Matt's. "I've been caught in a time warp or something and flung into a rerun of *The Donna Reed Show*, right?"

Bri gave her a look of affectionate disdain. "Mrs. Harry had to leave early—she lost a filling and needed to go to the dentist. She tried to call you at the shop, but you were gone, so—"

"So your dad came over to pinch-hit," Sharon guessed. The prospect of encountering Tony now made her feel a festive sort of despondency. "Where is he?"

As if in answer to that, Tony came out of the den. He was wearing jeans and a dark blue pullover, and his eyes slid over Sharon at their leisure, causing her a delightful discomfort. He strolled casually over to the wall oven and checked on whatever it was that smelled so marvelous. "Been shopping for your trip?" he asked.

Sharon realized that she was still holding the dress

box from her favorite department store and self-consciously set it aside. "Not exactly," she said, with an exuberance that rang false even in her own ears. "How have you been, Tony?"

"Just terrific," he answered, with an ironic note in his voice as he closed the oven door. "Somebody named Sven called. He said Bea gave him your number."

Sven? Sharon searched her memory, but the only Sven she could come up with was a Swedish exchange student who had spent a year in Hayesville long ago when she'd still been in high school. "Did he leave a message?" she asked airily, wanting to let Tony wonder a little.

"He said he'd call back," Tony answered offhandedly. Sharon knew that he was watching her out of the corner of his eye as he took plates from a cupboard. "Your accountant wants a word with you, too."

Sharon was careful not to show the concern that fact caused her. Her accountant never called unless the news was bad.

At some unseen signal from their father, Matt and Bri had put aside their homework, and they were now setting the table. "You're supposed to call her at home," Tony added. He washed his hands at the sink, took some plastic bags of produce from the refrigerator and began tearing lettuce leaves for a salad.

Sharon was really fretting now, though she smiled brightly. She took off her coat and hung it up, then went upstairs with the box under her arm. The moment she reached the sanctity of the bedroom, she lunged for the telephone.

Moments later she was on the line with Susan Fenwick, her accountant. "What do you mean I can't afford to go to Paris?" she whispered in horror. "This is a business trip—"

"I don't care," Susan interrupted firmly. "You've got quarterly taxes coming up, Sharon, and even though you've been gaining some ground financially, you're going to put yourself in serious jeopardy if you make any major expenditures now."

Sharon sighed. She'd told everyone that she was going to Paris—Tony, the kids, Helen and Louise... just everyone. She was going to look like a real fool, backing out now.

"Okay," she said, forcing herself to smile. She'd heard once in a seminar that a businessperson should keep a pleasant expression on her face while talking on the telephone. "Thank you, Susan."

"No problem. I'm sorry about the trip. Maybe in the spring—"

"Right," Sharon said. "Goodbye."

Susan returned the sentiment and then the line was dead.

Sharon hung up and went downstairs, the smile firmly affixed to her face. The kids were already eating and Tony was in the den, gathering up the ever-present blueprints.

"Are those the plans for the new supermarket?" Sharon asked, wanting that most elusive of things—a non-volatile conversation with Tony.

He nodded, and it seemed to Sharon that he was avoiding her eyes. "The kids are having supper," he said. "Don't you want to join them?"

"I'm not hungry," Sharon answered with a slight shake of her head. In truth she was ravenous, but that fabulous, slinky dress didn't leave room for indulgences in Tony's cooking. Once he was gone, she'd have a salad.

Tony's gaze swung toward her, assessing her. "Trying to slim down to Parisian standards?" he asked dryly.

Sharon longed to tell him that the trip was off, that she couldn't afford to go, but her pride wouldn't allow her to make the admission. Her need to make a mark on the world had been a pivotal factor in their divorce, and Sharon didn't want to call attention to the fact that her standard of living had gone down since they'd parted ways. She let Tony's question pass. "Thank you for coming over and taking care of the kids," she said.

"Anytime," he responded quietly. There was a forlorn expression in Tony's eyes even as he smiled that made Sharon want to cross the room and put her arms around that lean, fit waist of his. The desire to close the space between them, both physically and emotionally, was powerful indeed.

Sharon resisted it. "Did Sven leave a number?" she asked in a soft voice, to deflect the sweet, impossible charge she felt coursing back and forth between herself and this man she loved but could not get along with.

Tony looked tired, and his sigh was on the ragged side. His grin, however, was crooked and made of mischief with a pinch of acid thrown in for spice. "It isn't tattooed on your body somewhere?" he countered.

Color throbbing in her face, Sharon ran a hand through her hair and did her best to ignore Tony as she went past him to the desk. A number was scrawled on a pad beside the telephone, along with a notation about Susan's call. Conflicting needs tore at her; she wanted to pound on Tony with her fists, and at the same time she longed to make love to him.

She was startled when he turned her into his embrace

and tilted her chin upward with the curved fingers of his right hand. "I'm sorry," he said huskily.

Sharon forgave him, but not because of any nobility on her part. She couldn't help herself.

She stood on tiptoe, and her lips were just touching Tony's when the doorbell rang.

"One of the kids will get it," he assured her in a whisper, propelling her into a deep kiss when she would have drawn back.

The kiss left Sharon bedazzled and more than a little bewildered, and she was staring mutely up at Tony when Bri bounded into the room and announced, "There's a man here to see you, Mom. He says his name is Sven Svensen."

"Sven Svensen," Tony muttered with a shake of his head. His hands fell away from Sharon's waist and he retreated from her to roll up his blueprints and tuck them back into their cardboard tube.

Sven appeared in the doorway of the den only a second later, tall and blond and spectacular. He was indeed the Sven that Sharon remembered from high school, and his exuberance seemed to fill the room.

"All these years I have dreamed of you," he cried, spreading his hands. But then his eyes strayed to Tony. "This is your husband? This is the father of your children?"

"No to the first question," Sharon answered, keeping her distance, "and yes to the second. Tony and I are divorced."

Sven beamed after taking a moment to figure out the situation, and she introduced the two men to each other properly.

Tony's eyebrows rose when Sven grasped Sharon by the waist and thrust her toward the ceiling with a shout of joyous laughter. "Still you are so beautiful, just like when you were a leadcheerer!"

The altitude was getting to Sharon in a hurry. She smiled down at Sven. "You haven't changed much, either," she said lamely.

He lowered her back to the floor, his happy smile lighting up the whole room. Tony's expression provided an interesting contrast; he looked as though he was ready to clout somebody over the head with his cardboard tube of blueprints.

"What brings you back to America?" Sharon asked her unexpected guest, nervously smoothing her slacks with both hands.

"I am big businessman now," Sven answered expansively. "I travel all over the world."

Sharon was aware that Tony was leaving, but she pretended not to notice. If he felt a little jealous, so be it; she'd certainly done her share of agonizing over the mysterious Ingrid.

It was then that the idea occurred to Sharon. "Will you be in the area for a while, Sven?" she asked, taking his arm. "There's this party on the night of the twenty-second—"

"You talk to him!" Michael raged, flinging his arms wide in exclamation as his father entered the small office trailer parked on the site of the new supermarket. "The man has a head of solid marble—there's no reasoning with him!"

Tony glared at his brother, but said nothing. The argument, beginning that morning, had been escalating all day.

Vincent met Tony's gaze for a moment, then looked at Michael. "I could hear the two of you 'reasoning' with each other on the other side of the lot. Exactly what is the problem?"

Tony was glad Michael launched into an answer first, because he didn't have one prepared. All he knew was that he felt like fighting.

"I'll tell you what the problem is," Michael began furiously, waggling an index finger at his elder brother. "Tony's got trouble with Sharon and he's been taking it out on me ever since he got here this morning!"

Michael's accusation was true, but Tony couldn't bring himself to admit it. He folded his arms and clamped his jaw down tight. He was still in the mood for an all-out brawl, and his brother seemed like a good candidate for an opponent.

Vincent gazed imploringly at the ceiling. "I am retired," he told some invisible entity. "Why don't I have the good sense to go to Florida and lie in the sun like other men my age?"

Tony's mind was wandering; he thought of that Sven character hoisting Sharon up in the air the way he had, and even though his collar was already loose, he felt a need to pull at it with his finger. He wondered if she found that kind of man attractive; some women liked foreign accents and caveman tactics....

"Tonio?" Michael snapped his fingers in front of his brother's eyes. "Do you think you can be a part of this conversation, or shall we just go on without you?"

Vincent chuckled. "Do not torment your brother, Michael," he said. "Can't you see that he's already miserable?"

Michael sighed, but his eyes were still hot with anger. "You were thinking about Sharon when you fell and damn near killed yourself, weren't you, Tony?" he challenged. After an awkward moment during which Tony remained stubbornly silent, he went on. "Now, you seem determined to alienate every craftsman within a fifty-mile radius. How the hell do you expect to bring this project in on time and within budget if we lose every worker we've got?"

Vincent cleared his throat. "Tonio," he said diplomatically, "I was supposed to be at home an hour ago. If I walk out of this trailer, what is my assurance that the two of you will be able to work through this thing without killing each other?"

Tony sighed. "Maybe I have been a little touchy lately—"

"A *little* touchy?" Michael demanded, shaking his finger again.

"Unless you want to eat it," Tony said, "you'd better stop waving that damned finger in my face!"

The sound of the phone dialing broke the furious silence that followed. "Hello, Maria?" Vincent said. "This is the man who fathered your six children calling. If I come home now, I fear you will be left with only four.... Yes, yes, I will tell them. Goodbye, my love."

Michael shoved one hand through his hair as his father hung up. "Tell us what?" he ventured to ask.

"Your mother says that her cousin Earnestine has been very happy as the mother of four children," Vincent answered, reaching for his hat. "My orders are to leave you to work out your differences as you see fit, whether you kill each other or not. Good night, my sons."

Tony and Michael grinned at each other when the door of the trailer closed behind their father.

"Come on," Michael said gruffly. "I'll buy you a beer and we'll talk about these personality problems of yours."

Tony had nothing better to do than go out for a beer,

but he wondered about Michael. "Don't you have a date or something?"

His brother looked at his watch. "Ingrid will understand if I'm a little late," he answered. "She knows you've been having a tough time."

Tony was annoyed. His hands immediately went to his hips, and he was scowling. "Is there anybody in Port Webster you haven't regaled with the grisly saga of Tony Morelli?"

"Yes," Michael answered affably. "Sharon. If you won't tell the woman you're crazy about her, maybe I ought to."

"You do and a certain old lady will be lighting lots of candles in front of your picture," Tony responded with conviction.

Michael shrugged, and the two brothers left the trailer.

Helen's eyes sparkled and she lifted one hand to her mouth to stifle a giggle when Sharon described her visit from Sven Svensen the night before.

"And Tony was there when he arrived?" she whispered in delighted scandal.

Sharon nodded. "Sven has business in Seattle, but he'll be back here on the twenty-second to take me to the company party."

Helen clapped her hands. "Thank heaven Mrs. Morelli invited Allen and me," she crowed. "I wouldn't want to miss this for anything! You'll wear that fantastic dress, of course."

Again, Sharon nodded. But she was a little distracted. "There is one thing I have to tell you about my trip to Paris," she began reluctantly.

Helen leaned forward, one perfectly shaped eyebrow arched in silent question.

"I can't go," Sharon confided with a grimace. "Susan says I absolutely can't afford it."

"Well, there's always next spring," Helen reasoned. "November isn't the greatest time—"

"That isn't the problem," Sharon broke in. "I told Tony all about the trip—I made it sound like a big deal. If I say I can't go because I don't have the money, he'll laugh at me."

"I can't imagine Tony doing that," Helen said solemnly.

"You haven't seen his financial statement," Sharon replied. "He pays more in taxes for a month than I make in six."

"He stepped right into a thriving business," Helen pointed out. "You started your own. Anyway, Morelli Construction is a partnership. Maybe Tony's had a big part in the company's success, but he can't take all the credit for it."

Sharon sighed. A woman was examining the items in the display window, but she didn't look as though she was going to come in and buy anything. It was time for the Christmas rush to begin, if only people would start rushing. "What would you do if you were me?"

Helen drew a deep breath. On the exhalation, she said, "I'd go straight to Tony and tell him that I loved him, and then I'd not only ask him to pay for the trip to Paris, I'd invite him along. Whereupon he would accept graciously and I would kiss his knees in gratitude."

"You're no help at all," Sharon said, giving Helen a look before she walked away to put each half-slip on a rack exactly one inch from the next one.

Sharon sat in front of the lighted mirror in her too-big, too-empty bedroom, carefully applying her makeup.

"I don't understand why you want to go out with that guy, anyway," Bri said, pouting. Curled up on the foot of the bed, she had been watching her stepmother get ready for the big party. "He's not nearly as good-looking as Daddy."

Sharon privately agreed, but she wasn't about to look a gift-Swede in the mouth. Her only other options, after all, were staying home from the party or going without an escort and spending a whole evening watching Tony attend to Ingrid. She shuddered.

"I knew you'd get cold in that dress," Matt observed from the doorway. "I can practically see your belly button."

Sharon gave her son an arch look. "Did your father tell you to say that?" she asked.

"He would if he saw the dress," Bri put in.

"Are you going to marry the Terminator?" Matt demanded to know.

After a smile at the nickname Sven didn't know he had, Sharon tilted her head back and raised one hand dramatically to her brow. "No, no, a thousand times no!" she cried.

"I think she should marry Daddy," Bri commented from her perch on the end of the bed.

Sharon was finished with her makeup and had now turned her attention to her hair. She let her stepdaughter's remark pass unchallenged.

"You could take him to Paris with you," Matt suggested. "Dad, I mean. You guys might decide you like each other and want to get married again."

"Paris is a city for lovers," Briana agreed with rising enthusiasm.

"Your dad and I are not lovers." Sharon felt a twinge of guilt, which she hid by reaching for her brush and sweeping her hair up into a small knot at the back of her head. She hadn't been able to tell the kids that the Paris trip was off, mostly because she knew they would go straight to Tony with the news. It would be too humiliating to have him know that she was having a hard time financially while he was making a success of everything he did.

Her plan was to hide out on the island for a few days and let everyone think that she was in Paris. She didn't look forward to living a lie, but for now, at least, she couldn't bear for Tony to think that she was anything less than a glittering sensation.

"I don't understand why no kids are allowed at this party," Bri complained, biting her lower lip. "It would be fun to wear something shiny."

"To match your grillwork," Matt teased.

Sharon was relieved that the conversation had taken a twist in another direction, away from Paris and lovers and Tony. "Don't start fighting now, you guys. Scary Harry will want double wages for watching you."

Bri had folded her arms and was studiously ignoring her brother. The combined gesture was reminiscent of Tony. "Gramma and Grampa include us kids in everything else," she said. "Why is this party for adults only?"

"You said it yourself," Sharon answered, turning her head from side to side so that she could make sure her hair looked good before spraying it. "Your grandparents include you and your nine hundred cousins in everything else. There has to be one occasion that's just for grown-ups."

"Why?" Bri immediately retorted. "There isn't one that's just for kids."

The doorbell chimed, and Sharon was grateful. "Go

and answer that, please," she said, reaching out for her favorite cologne and giving herself a generous misting.

"It's probably the Terminator," Matt grumbled, but Bri dashed out of the bedroom and down the stairs to answer the door.

Five minutes later Sharon descended the staircase in her glittering red dress to greet a tall and handsome man wearing a tuxedo. Everything would have been perfect if the man had been Tony and not Sven.

The Swede had not been exaggerating when he had described himself as a "big businessman," physical stature aside. Sven was obviously successful; he'd proved it by arriving in a chauffeured limousine.

Sharon's eyes were wide as she settled herself in the leather-upholstered backseat and looked around.

"You like this, no?" Sven asked, with the eagerness of a child displaying a favorite toy.

"I like this, yes," Sharon answered. "I'm impressed. You've done very well for yourself, Sven."

Sven beamed. "You too are doing well with your store selling underwear."

Sharon laughed and squeezed his hand. "Oh, Sven," she said. "You do have a way with words."

"This will be a very interesting evening, I think," Sven replied, his pale eyebrows moving up. "This old husband of yours, the one you do not anymore want—tell me about him."

Sharon sighed, and then related a great many ordinary things about Tony. There must have been something revealing in her tone or her manner, because Sven took her hand and sympathetically patted it with his own as the sleek limo sped toward the first event of the holiday season.

Chapter 10

The banquet room of Port Webster's yacht club shimmered with silvery lights. Even though there were hordes of people, Sharon's gaze locked with Tony's the moment she and Sven walked through the door.

Her heart fishtailed like a car on slick pavement, then righted itself. Tony looked fabulous in his tuxedo, and the woman standing at his side was tall and lithe with blond hair that tumbled like a waterfall to her waist.

Ingrid, no doubt.

Glumly, Sharon resigned herself to being short and perky. *Cute*, God forbid. In high school those attributes had stood her in good stead; in the here and now they seemed absolutely insipid.

"Someone has died?" Sven inquired, with a teasing light in his blue eyes as he bent to look into Sharon's crestfallen face. "The stock market has crashed?"

Sharon forced herself to smile, and it was a good

thing because Tony was making his way toward them, pulling Ingrid along with him.

A waiter arrived at the same moment, and Sven graciously accepted glasses of champagne for himself and his nervous date. Sharon practically did a swan dive into her drink.

Sven stepped gallantly into the conversational breach. "So, we meet again," he said to Tony, but his eyes were on Ingrid.

Tony's jawline clamped down, then relaxed. Ingrid had slipped her arm through his and clasped her hands together.

Sharon wondered why the woman didn't just execute a half nelson and be done with it, but she would have eaten one of the centerpieces before letting either Tony or Ingrid know how ill at ease she felt.

"Are you Sharon?" the blonde demanded pleasantly, extending one hand in greeting before Tony could introduce her. "I've been so eager to meet you!"

I'll just bet you have, Sharon thought sourly, but she kept right on looking cute and perky. "Yes," she answered, "and I presume you're Ingrid?"

The blonde nodded. She really was stunning, and her simple, black cocktail dress did a lot to show off her long, shapely legs. She seemed genuinely pleased to know Sharon, though her gaze had, by this time, strayed to Sven. "Hello," she said in her throaty voice.

Sharon took a hasty sip of her champagne and spilled a little of it when Tony took hold of her elbow, without warning, and pulled her aside. "If I stick that guy with a pin, will he deflate and fly around the room?" he asked, feigning a serious tone.

Sharon glared at her ex-husband. "If you stick Sven

with a pin, I imagine he'll punch you in the mouth," she responded.

Tony looked contemptuously unterrified. He lifted his champagne glass to his mouth, taking a sip as his eyes moved over Sharon's dress. "Where did you buy that—Dolly Parton's last garage sale?"

Sharon refrained from stomping on his instep only because Sven and Ingrid were present. "You don't like it?" she countered sweetly, batting her lashes. "Good."

"We are from the same town in Sweden, Ingrid and I!" Sven exclaimed in that buoyant way of his.

"Would you mind if I borrowed your date for just one dance?" Ingrid asked Sharon. She didn't seem to care what Tony's opinion might be.

"Be my guest," Sharon said magnanimously.

"Michael is going to love this," Tony muttered, as he watched Sven and Ingrid walk away.

Sharon was desperate for a safe topic of conversation, and her former brother-in-law was it. She craned her neck, looking for him. "I'd enjoy a waltz with Michael," she said. "He's the best dancer in the family."

Tony took Sharon's glass out of her hand and set it on a table with his own. "You'll have to settle for me, because my brother isn't here," he said. His fingers closed over hers and she let him lead her toward the crowded dance floor.

To distract herself from the sensations dancing with Tony aroused in various parts of her anatomy, Sharon looked up at him and asked, "Michael, missing a party? I don't believe it."

"Believe it. He's out of town, putting in a bid on a new mall."

Sharon lifted her eyebrows. "Impressive."

"It will make ours the biggest construction operation in this part of the state," Tony replied without any particular enthusiasm.

Sharon thought of her canceled trip to Paris and sighed. "I guess some of us have it and some of us don't," she said softly.

Tony's hand caught under her chin. "What was that supposed to mean?" he asked. His voice was gentle, the look in his eyes receptive.

Sharon nearly told him the truth, but lost her courage at the last millisecond. She couldn't risk opening herself up to an I-told-you-so or, worse yet, a generous helping of indulgent sympathy. "Nothing," she said, forcing a bright smile to her face.

There was a flicker of disappointment in Tony's eyes. "Is it that hard to talk to me?" he asked quietly.

Sharon let the question go unanswered, pretending that she hadn't heard it, and turned her head to watch Sven and Ingrid for a moment. "There's something so damned cheerful about them," she muttered.

Tony chuckled, but there was scant amusement in the sound. Maybe, Sharon reflected with a pang, he was jealous of Ingrid's obvious rapport with Sven. When she looked up into those familiar brown eyes, they were solemn.

Resolved to get through this night with her dignity intact if it killed her, Sharon smiled up at him. "I'm surprised I haven't met Ingrid before this," she said brightly.

Tony shrugged. "If you'd come to any of the family gatherings lately, you would have," he observed, as though it were the most natural thing in the world for a woman to socialize with her ex-husband's girlfriend.

Sharon was inexpressibly wounded to know that Tony cared enough about Ingrid to include her in the mob scenes that were a way of life in the Morelli family. Reminding herself that she and Tony were no longer husband and wife, that she had no real part in his life anymore, did nothing to ease the pain.

The plain and simple truth was that she had been replaced with the simple ease and aplomb she'd always feared she would be. Her smile wavered.

"I've been busy lately," she said, and then, mercifully, the music stopped and Sven and Ingrid were at hand. Sharon pulled free of Tony's embrace and turned blindly into Sven's. "Dance with me," she whispered in desperate tones, as the small orchestra began another waltz.

Sven's expression was full of tenderness and concern. "So much you love this man that your heart is breaking," he said. "Poor little bird—I cannot bear to see you this way."

Sharon let her forehead rest against her friend's strong shoulder, struggling to maintain her composure. It would be disastrous to fall apart in front of all these people. "I'll be fine," she told him, but the words sounded uncertain.

"We will leave this place," Sven responded firmly. "It is not good for you, being here."

Sharon drew a deep breath and let it out again. She couldn't leave, not yet. She wouldn't let the pain of loving and losing Tony bring her to her knees that way. She lifted her chin and, with a slight shake of her head, said, "No. I'm not going to run away."

An expression of gentle respect flickered in Sven's blue eyes. "We will make the best of this situation, then," he said. He looked like the shy, awkward teenager Sharon had known in high school when he went on. "There are other men who want you, little bird," he told her. "I am one of these."

Gently, Sharon touched Sven's handsome, freshly shaven face. A sweet, achy sense of remorse filled her. He'd been so kind to her; she didn't want to hurt him. She started to speak, but Sven silenced her by laying one index finger to her lips.

"Don't speak," he said. "I know you are not ready to let a new man love you. Do you want him back, Sharon—this Tony of yours?"

"I've asked myself that question a million times," Sharon confided. "The truth is, I do, but I know it can never work."

"He betrayed you? He was with other women?"

Sharon shook her head.

"He drank?" Sven persisted, frowning. "He beat you?"

Sharon laughed. Tony liked good wine, but she'd never actually seen him drunk in all the years she'd known him, although there had been that incident Michael had mentioned weeks before. Tony had always been a lover, not a fighter. "No," she answered.

"Then why are you divorced from him?" Sven asked, looking genuinely puzzled.

"There are other reasons for divorce," Sharon replied, as the orchestra paused between numbers.

"Like what?" Sven wanted to know, as he led Sharon off the dance floor. He'd seated her at a table and secured drinks for them both before she answered.

For some reason—perhaps it was the champagne—Sharon found that she could talk to Sven, and the words came pouring out of her. "Tony was married once before when he was very young. His wife was killed in a terrible accident, and he was left with a baby girl to raise. He and I met only a few months after Carmen died."

Sven took her hand. "And?" he prompted.

"I know people say this doesn't happen to real people, but the moment I saw Tony I fell in love with him."

Sven smiled sadly, and his grasp on Sharon's fingers tightened a little. "Tell me how you met your Tony."

Sharon sighed. "I was working in a bookstore here in Port Webster and going to business college at night." She paused, gazing back into the past. "He made his selections, and I was one of them, I guess. We went out that night, and six weeks later we were married."

"You say that as though you were one of the books he bought," Sven observed. "Why is this?"

Sharon shrugged, but her expression was one of quiet sorrow. "There have been times when I felt that he'd chosen me for a purpose, the same way he chose those books. He was lonely, and he needed a mother for his daughter."

"Children can be raised successfully without a mother," Sven put in.

Sharon nodded. "That's true, of course," she conceded. "And heaven knows there are enough kids growing up without a father. But Tony is—well—he's family oriented. It's the most important thing in the world to him." She swallowed. He'd remarried quickly after Carmen, and he was going to do the same thing now. Exit wife number two, enter number three.

"You're going to cry, I think," Sven said. "We can't have that, since he's looking our way, your buyer of books." Rising from his chair, the Swede drew Sharon out of hers, as well. "Trust me when I do this, little bird," he said huskily, and then, with no more warning than that, he swept Sharon into his arms and gave her a kiss that left her feeling as though she'd had her head held under water for five minutes.

She blushed hotly, one hand to her breast, and hissed, "Sven!"

His azure eyes twinkled as he looked down at her. "Now we can leave," he said. "We have given your used-to-be lover something to think about on this cold winter night."

It seemed unlikely that Tony would spend the night thinking—not when he'd have Ingrid lying in bed beside him—but Sharon knew that Sven was right about one thing. She could escape that ghastly party now without looking like the scorned ex-wife.

She felt Tony's gaze touching her as she waited for Sven to return with her coat, but she refused to meet it. It was time to cut her losses.

After saying a few words to Vincent and Maria, and to Helen and her husband, Allen, Sharon left the party with her hand in the crook of Sven's powerful arm and her chin held high. The luxurious interior of the limousine was warm and welcoming.

"You will come to my suite for drinks and more talk of old times, no?" Sven asked.

"No," Sharon confirmed.

Her friend frowned. "You must," he said.

Sharon squirmed a little. Maybe Sven wasn't as understanding as she'd thought. "If I have to jump for it," she warned, "I will."

Sven laughed. "I am more the gentleman than this, little bird. And since I am a man, I know how your Tony is thinking now. He will either telephone or drive past your house at the first opportunity. Do you want to be there, sipping hot cocoa and knitting by the fireside? Of course you don't!"

Sven's theory had its merits, but Sharon wasn't ready for an intimate relationship with a new man, and she had to be sure that her friend understood that. "Promise you won't get me into another lip-lock?" she asked seriously.

Sven gave a shout of amusement. "What is this 'lip-lock'?" he countered.

"I was referring to that kiss back at the party," Sharon said, her arms folded. "Nobody under seventeen should have been allowed to see that unless they were accompanied by a parent."

Sven's eyes, blue as a fjord under a clear sky, danced with mischief. "I wish you could have seen Tony's face, little bird," he said. "You would feel better if you had."

Sharon bit her lip. It seemed just as likely to her that Sven's trick would backfire and propel Tony into some R-rated adventures of his own, but she didn't want to spoil her friend's delight by saying so. "I don't want to talk about Tony anymore," she said. "Tell me about you, Sven."

Since there was no hotel in Port Webster, the limo rolled toward nearby Tacoma, where Sven's company had provided him with a suite. During the drive he told Sharon about his company, which manufactured ski equipment that would soon be sold in the United States. He also mentioned his short and disastrous marriage, which had ended two years before.

As Sven was helping Sharon out of the limo in front of his hotel, she stepped on the hem of her slinky dress and felt the slit move a few inches higher on her thigh. "Oh, great," she muttered.

Sven chuckled. "There is a problem, no?"

"There is a problem, yes, I've torn my dress," Sharon answered. "And I'm not getting the hang of this being single, Sven. I'm not adjusting."

His hand was strong on the small of her back as he ushered her toward the warmth and light of the lobby. "It takes time," he told her. "Much time and not a little pain."

Sharon was glad she was wearing a long coat when they stepped inside that elegant hotel. There were a lot of people milling around, and she didn't want them to see that the sexy slit in her dress had been extended to the area of her tonsils.

"You are hungry?" Sven asked, as they passed a dark restaurant looking out over Commencement Bay.

Except for a few hors d'oeuvres, Sharon had had nothing to eat all evening, and all that champagne was just sloshing around in her stomach, waiting to cause trouble. "I suppose I am," she confessed, "but I don't want to take off my coat."

Sven chuckled. "Little bird, there is only candlelight in there. Who will see that your dress is torn?"

Sharon succumbed to his logic, partly because she'd missed supper and partly because she wanted to delay for as long as possible the moment when she and Sven stepped inside his suite. She loved Tony Morelli with all her heart and soul, but her desires hadn't died with their divorce. Sven's kiss, back at the party, had proved that much to her.

They enjoyed a leisurely dinner, during which they laughed and talked and drank a great deal of champagne. By the time they got to Sven's suite, Sharon's mind was foggy, and she was yawning like a sleepy child.

Sven gave her an innocuous kiss and said, "How I wish that I were the kind of man to take advantage of you, little bird. Just for tonight, I would like to be such a scoundrel."

Sharon sighed and smiled a tipsy smile. By then she was carrying her shoes in one hand and her hair was falling down from its pins. "Know what?" she asked. "I wish I could be different, too. Here I am in a fancy suite with a man who should be featured in one of those hunk-of-the-month calendars, and what do I do with such an opportunity? I waste it, that's what."

Sven grinned, cupping her face with his large, gentle hands. "Always, since I was here for high school, when I think of America, I think of you," he said with a sigh of his own. "Ah, Sharon, Sharon—the way you looked in those jeans of yours made me want to defect and ask for political asylum in this country."

Sharon stood on tiptoe to kiss his cheek. "Nobody defects from Sweden," she reasoned.

Sven put her away with a gentle purposefulness that said a lot about his sense of honor, and looked down at his slender gold watch. "It is time, I believe, to take you home," he said in a gruff voice. "It would seem that my wish to become a scoundrel is beginning to come true."

"Oh." Sharon swallowed and retreated a step. She had removed her coat in the restaurant, but she'd put it on again before they left. Now she held it a little closer around her.

"When next I come to America," Sven went on, his back to Sharon now as he looked out at the bay and the lights that adorned it like diamonds upon velvet, "you may be through loving Tony. For obvious reasons, I want you to remember me kindly if that is the case."

Sharon had had a great deal to drink that evening, but she was sober enough to appreciate Sven's gallantry. "You don't have to worry about that," she said softly. "My having kind thoughts about you, I mean. I'm no sophisticate, but I know that men like you are rare."

When Sven turned to face her, he was once again flashing that dazzling smile of his. It was as reassuring as a beam from a lighthouse on a dark and storm-tossed sea. "What you have yet to learn, little bird," he told her, "is that you also are special. You are fireworks and blue jeans and county fairs—everything that is American."

Sharon shrugged, feeling sheepish and rumpled and very safe. "I'm going to take that as a compliment since I've had too much booze to fight back if it was an insult," she said.

Sven laughed again and went to the telephone to summon the limousine and driver his company had provided for him.

It was 3:00 a.m. exactly when the limo came to a stop in front of the house on Tamarack Drive, and Tony's car was parked in the driveway.

Sven smiled mysteriously, as though some private theory of his had been proven correct. "You would like me to come in with you?" he inquired.

He didn't look surprised when Sharon shook her head. She knew she had nothing to fear from Tony, even if he was in a raving fury, but she wasn't so sure that the same was true of Sven. With her luck the two men would get into a brawl, half kill each other and scar the kids' psyches for life.

"Thanks for everything," she said, reaching for the knob. As she'd expected, the door was unlocked. "And good night."

Sven gave her a brotherly kiss on the forehead and then walked away.

The light was on in the entryway, and there was a lamp burning in the living room. Barefoot, her strappy silver shoes dangling from one hand, Sharon followed the trail Tony had left for her.

He was in the den, lying on the sofa bed and watching the shopping channel. He was wearing battered jeans and a T-shirt, and his feet were bare. He didn't look away when Sharon came to stand beside the bed.

She glanced at the TV screen. A hideously ornate clock with matching candelabras was being offered for an exorbitant price. "Thinking of redecorating?"

Tony sighed, still staring at the screen. "Who do I look like?" he countered. "Herman Munster?"

Sharon tossed her shoes aside and sat down on the edge of the mattress. "What are you doing here?" she asked.

He rubbed his chin with one hand. "I seem to have some kind of homing device implanted in my brain. Every once in a while I forget that I don't live here anymore."

Sharon felt sad and broken. The slit in the dress she hadn't been able to afford went higher with an audible rip when she curled her legs beneath her. She plucked at the blanket with two fingers and kept her eyes down. "Oh," she said.

Tony's voice was like gravel. "Do you know what time it is?" he demanded.

Sharon's sadness was displaced by quiet outrage. "Yes," she answered. "It's 3:05, the party's over and a good time was had by all. You can leave anytime now, Tony."

He reached out with such quick ferocity that Sharon's eyes went wide, and he caught her wrist in one hand. Even though Tony wasn't hurting her, Sharon felt her heart trip into a faster, harder beat, and her breath was trapped in her lungs.

Before she knew what was happening, she was lying on her back, looking up into his face. A muscle flexed along his jawline. He was resting part of his weight on her, and even though she was angry, Sharon welcomed it.

"If you're in love with that Swede," Tony said evenly, "I want to know it. Right now."

Sharon swallowed. "I'm not really sober enough to handle this," she said.

Tony looked as though he might be torn between kissing Sharon and killing her. "Fine. If I have to pour coffee down your throat all night long, I'll do it."

She squeezed her eyes shut. "I really think you should let me go," she said.

"Give me one good reason," Tony replied.

"I'm going to throw up."

He rolled aside. "That's a good reason if I've ever heard one," he conceded, as Sharon leaped off the bed, a hand clasped to her mouth, and ran for the adjoining bathroom.

When she came out some minutes later, Tony was waiting with her favorite chenille bathrobe draped over one arm, and a glass of bicarbonate in his hand.

Sharon drank the seltzer down in a series of gulps and then let Tony divest her of the coat. He did raise an eyebrow when he saw that the slit had advanced to well past her hip, but to his credit he made no comment. He turned her so that he could unzip the dress, and Sharon didn't protest.

Her hair was a mess, her mascara was running and her gown—which she would still be paying for in six months—was totally ruined. She couldn't afford her trip to Paris, and she loved a man she couldn't live with.

It was getting harder and harder to take a positive outlook on things.

Chapter 11

The hangover was there to meet Sharon when she woke up in the morning. Head throbbing, stomach threatening revolt, she groaned and buried her face deep in her pillow when she heard Tony telling the kids to keep the noise down.

Sharon lifted her head slightly and opened one eye. She was in the den.

There was a cheerful blaze snapping and crackling in the fireplace, and Matt was perched on the foot of the hide-a-bed, watching Saturday morning cartoons. Tony was working at the desk, while Briana strutted back and forth with Sharon's ruined dress draped against her front.

"That must have been some party," the child observed, inspecting the ripped seam.

"Coffee," Sharon moaned. "If anyone in this room has a shred of decency in their soul, they'll bring me some right now."

Tony chuckled and got out of his chair. Moments later he was back with a mug of steaming coffee, and the kids had mysteriously vanished. "Here you go, you party animal," he said, as Sharon scrambled to an upright position and reached out for the cup with two trembling hands.

"Thanks," she grumbled.

Tony sat on the edge of the bed. "Want some breakfast?"

"There is no need to be vicious," Sharon muttered. The coffee tasted good, but two sips told her the stuff wasn't welcome in her stomach.

He laughed and kissed her forehead. "You'll feel better later," he said gently. "I promise."

She set the coffee aside and shoved a hand through her rumpled hair. "You're being awfully nice to me," she said suspiciously, squinting at the clock on the mantelpiece. "What time is it, anyway?"

Tony sighed. "It's time you were up and getting ready for your trip to Paris. Your flight leaves Seattle this afternoon, doesn't it?"

Sharon settled herself against the back of the sofa and groaned. She wanted so much to confess that she was really planning to spend the next four days on the island, but she couldn't. She had an image to maintain. "Yes," she said.

"I'd like to drive you to the airport," Tony told her.

Sharon stared at him. Although she wanted to accept, she couldn't because then, of course, Tony would find out that she wasn't really going anywhere. "That won't be necessary," she replied, dropping her eyes.

Never a man to let well enough alone, Tony persisted. "Why not?"

Sharon was trapped. She could either lie or admit

that she was a failure and a fraud. She gnawed at her lower lip for a moment and then blurted out, "Because Sven is seeing me off."

There was a short, deadly silence, then Tony stood. "Great," he said, moving toward the desk, gathering whatever he'd been working on earlier.

Sharon steeled herself against an impulse to offer him frantic assurances that she and Sven weren't involved. After all, Tony wasn't letting any grass grow under his feet, romantically speaking. He had Ingrid. "I knew you'd understand," she hedged, reaching for her chenille bathrobe and hopping out of bed. She was tying the belt when Tony finally turned around to face her again.

"I don't have the right to ask you this," he said, his voice gruff and barely audible over the sounds of muted cartoons and the fire on the hearth. "But I've got to know. Is he—Sven—going to Paris with you?"

Sharon's throat ached with suppressed emotion; she knew what it had cost Tony, in terms of his dignity, to ask that question. She could only shake her head.

Tony nodded, his eyes revealing a misery Sharon didn't know how to assuage, and said, "I'll just take the kids out for a while, if that's okay. Have a good trip."

The guilt Sharon felt was monumental. She loved these people, Tony and Briana and Matt, and she was lying to them, acting out an elaborate charade for the sake of her pride.

"I will," she said. "Thanks."

He gave her a look of wry anguish. "Sure," he answered, and within five minutes Briana and Matt had said goodbye to Sharon and left with Tony.

Woodenly, Sharon trudged upstairs, got out of her robe and the nightgown she had no memory of putting on, and stepped into a hot shower. When she came out, she felt better physically, but her emotions were as tangled as yarn mauled by a kitten.

She put on jeans and a burgundy cable-knit sweater, along with heavy socks and hiking boots. "Just the outfit for jetting off to Paris," she muttered, slumping down on the side of the bed and reaching for the telephone.

Helen answered on the second ring. "Teddy Bares. May I help you?"

Sharon sighed. "I wish someone could. How's business this morning?"

"We're doing pretty well," Helen replied. "Everything is under control. That was some kiss old Sven laid on you at the party last night, my dear."

"I was hoping no one noticed," Sharon said lamely.

"You must know that Tony did. He left five minutes after you and Sven went out the door, and your former in-laws had to take the blonde home because he forgot her."

Sharon's spirits rose a little at the thought of Ingrid slipping Tony's mind like that. She said nothing, sensing that Helen would carry the conversational ball.

"If I ever had any doubt that Tony Morelli is nuts about you, and only you, it's gone now." She paused to draw a deep, philosophical breath. "You're not still going through with this trip-to-Paris thing, are you?"

"I have to," Sharon said, rubbing her temple with three fingers.

"Nonsense."

Sharon didn't have the energy to argue. The shop had been a big part of the reason she and Tony had gotten divorced; he was very old-fashioned in a lot of ways, and she doubted that he understood even now why she wanted the hassles of owning a business. If she didn't succeed, all his misgivings would be justified. "I'll be back the day before Thanksgiving," she said firmly. "If there are any emergencies in the meantime, you know where to call."

Helen sighed. "This is never going to work, you know. The truth will come out."

"Maybe so," Sharon replied, "but it had better not come out of you, my friend. I'll explain this to Tony myself—someday."

"Right," Helen said crisply. "Tell me this—what number are you going to give him to call if one of the kids gets sick or something? He'll expect you to be registered in a hotel...."

"I told Tony several days ago that I'd be checking in with you regularly, so if anything goes wrong, you'll hear from him. All you would have to do then is call me at the A-frame."

"This is stupid, Sharon."

"I don't recall asking for your opinion," Sharon retorted.

"What about postcards?" Helen shot back. "What about souvenirs for the kids? Don't you see that you're not going to be able to pull this off?"

Sharon bit her lip. The deception was indeed a tangled web, and it was getting stickier by the moment, but she was already trapped. "I'll check out that import shop in Seattle or something," she said.

"You're crazy," commented Helen.

"It's nice to know that my friends are solidly behind me," Sharon snapped.

There was a pause, and then Helen said quietly, "I want you to be happy. You do know that, don't you?"

"Yes," Sharon replied distractedly. "Goodbye, Helen. I'll see you when I get back from—Paris."

"Right." Helen sighed, and the conversation was over.

Sharon packed jeans, warm sweaters and flannel nightgowns for the trip, leaving behind the trim suits and dresses she would have taken to Europe. Such things would, of course, be of no use on the island.

She loaded her suitcase into the trunk of her roadster and set out for Seattle and the import shop she had in mind. First things first, she reflected dismally, as she sped along the freeway.

Halfway there, she asked herself, "What am I doing?" right out loud and took the next exit. Within minutes, she was headed back toward Port Webster.

Enough was enough. Surely going through all this was more demeaning than admitting the truth to Tony could ever be.

Sharon drove by his condominium first, but no one answered the door. With a sigh, she got back into the roadster and set out for his parents' house. Reaching that, Sharon almost lost her courage. There were cars everywhere; obviously something was going on. Something big.

Resigned, Sharon found a place for her roadster, got out and walked toward the enormous, noisy house. The very structure seemed to be permeated with love and laughter, and she smiled sadly as she reached out to ring the doorbell. She didn't belong here anymore; maybe she never had.

Vincent opened the door, and his look of delight enveloped Sharon like a warm blanket and drew her in out of the biting November cold. "Come in, come in," he said, taking her hand in his strong grasp. "We're having a celebration."

Sharon lingered in the entryway when Vincent would

have led her into the living room. "A celebration?" she echoed.

Vincent spread his hands and beamed in triumph. "At last, he is getting married, my stubborn son...."

Sharon's first reaction was primitive and instantaneous; her stomach did a flip, and she wanted to turn and flee like a frightened rabbit. A deep breath, however, marked the return of rational thought. Maybe things weren't very good between her and Tony, and maybe they weren't communicating like grown-up people were supposed to do, but she knew he wouldn't get married again without telling her. A man would think to mention something that important.

"Come in and have some wine with us," Vincent said gently. He'd noticed Sharon's nervous manner, but he was far too polite to comment.

She shook her head. "If I could just talk to Tony for a few minutes..."

Vincent shrugged and disappeared, leaving Sharon to stand in the colorful glow of a stained-glass skylight, her hands clasped together.

Tony appeared within seconds, slid his gaze over Sharon's casual clothes and said in a low, bewildered tone, "Hi."

Sharon drew a deep breath, let it out and took the plunge. "I have to talk to you," she said, and she was surprised to feel the sting of tears in her eyes because she hadn't planned to cry.

He took her hand and led her to the foot of the stairway, where they sat down together on the second step. Tony's thumb moved soothingly over her fingers. "I'm listening, babe," he said gently.

With the back of her free hand, Sharon tried to dry her eyes. "I lied," she confessed, the words a blurted whisper. "I'm not going to Paris because I can't afford to—Teddy Bares isn't doing that well."

Tony sighed, and enclosing her hand between both of his, lifted it to his lips. He wasn't looking at her, but at the patch of jeweled sunshine cast onto the oaken floor of the entryway beneath the skylight. "Why did you feel you had to lie?" he asked after a very long time.

Sharon sniffled. "I was ashamed, that's why. I thought you'd laugh if you found out that I couldn't spare the money for a plane ticket."

"Laugh?" The word sounded hollow and raw, and the look in Tony's eyes revealed that she'd hurt him. "You expected me to laugh because you'd been disappointed? My God, Sharon, do you think I'm that much of a bastard?"

Sharon was taken aback by the intensity of Tony's pain; he looked and sounded as though he'd been struck. "I'm sorry," she whispered.

"Hell, that makes all the difference," Tony rasped in a furious undertone, releasing her hand with a suddenness that bordered on violence. "Damn it, you don't even know me, do you? We were married for ten years, and you have no idea who I am."

Sharon needed to reach Tony, to reassure him. "That's not true," she said, stricken.

"It is," he replied, his voice cold and distant as he stood up. "And I sure as hell don't know you."

Grasping the banister beside her, Sharon pulled herself to her feet. "Tony, please listen to me—"

"If you'll excuse me," he interrupted with icy formality, "I have a brother who's celebrating his engagement." He paused and thrust one hand through his hair, and when he looked at Sharon, his eyes were hot with hurt and anger. "I hope to God Michael and Ingrid will do better than we did," he said.

Michael and Ingrid. Michael and Ingrid. The words were like a fist to the stomach for Sharon. She closed her eyes against the impact and hugged herself to keep from flying apart. "Can—can you keep the kids—the way we'd planned?" she managed to ask.

Tony was silent for so long that Sharon was sure he'd left her standing there in the entryway with her eyes squeezed shut and her arms wrapped around her middle, but he finally answered raggedly, "Sure. What do you want me to tell them?"

"That I love them," Sharon said, and then she turned blindly and groped for the doorknob. A larger, stronger hand closed over hers, staying her escape.

"You're in no condition to drive," Tony said flatly, and there wasn't a shred of emotion in his voice. "You're not going anywhere until you pull yourself together."

Sharon couldn't face him. She knew he was right, though; it would be irresponsible to drive in that emotional state. She let her forehead rest against the door, struggling to hold in sobs of sheer heartbreak.

Tentatively, he touched her shoulder. "Sharon," he said, and the name reverberated with hopelessness and grief.

She trembled with the effort to control her runaway feelings, and after a few more moments she had regained her composure. "I'll be on the island if the kids need me," she said.

"Okay," Tony whispered, and he stepped back, allowing her to open the door and walk out.

Sharon drove to the ferry landing and boarded the boat. She didn't get out of the car and go up to the snack bar to drink coffee and look at the view, though. She wasn't interested in scenery.

Once the ferry docked, Sharon's brain began to work again. She set her course for the nearest supermarket and wheeled a cart up and down the aisles, selecting food with all the awareness of a robot.

The A-frame was cold since no one had been there in a while, and Sharon turned up the heat before she began putting her groceries away. Her soul was as numb as her body, but for a different reason.

The warmth wafting up from the vents in the floor would eventually take the chill of a November afternoon from her bones and muscles, but there was no remedy for the wintry ache in her spirit. She went into the living room and collapsed facedown on the sofa. She needed the release weeping would provide, but it eluded her. Evidently, she'd exhausted her supply of tears in the entryway of Vincent and Maria's house.

"How did it all go so wrong?" she asked, turning onto her back and gazing up at the ceiling with dry, swollen eyes.

The telephone jangled at just that moment, a shrill mockery in the silence. Sharon didn't want to answer, but she didn't have much choice. She had two children, and if they needed her, she had to know about it.

She crossed the room, indulged in a deep sniffle and spoke into the receiver in the most normal voice she was able to manage. "Hello?"

"Are you all right?" Tony wanted to know.

Sharon wound her finger in the phone cord. "I'm terrific," she replied. "Just terrific. Is anything wrong?"

"The kids are fine." The words immediately put Sharon's mind at rest.

"Good. Then you won't mind if I hang up. Goodbye, Tony, and enjoy the party."

"Except for that night when we were supposed to paint your apartment and ended up making love instead, I haven't enjoyed anything in eight months," Tony responded. "And don't you dare hang up."

Sharon drew a chair back from the nearby dining table and sank into it. "What am I supposed to say now, Tony? You tell me. That way, maybe I won't step on your toes and you won't step on mine and we can skip the usual fifteen rounds."

When Tony answered, that frosty distance was back in his voice. "Right now I feel like putting both my fists through the nearest wall. How can I be expected to know what either of us is supposed to say?"

"I guess you can't," Sharon replied. "And neither can I. Goodbye, Tony, and give my best to Michael and Ingrid."

"I will," Tony replied sadly, and then he hung up.

Sharon felt as though her whole body and spirit were one giant exposed nerve, throbbing in the cold. She replaced the receiver and went out for a long walk on the beach.

It was nearly dark when she returned to brew herself a cup of instant coffee, slide a frozen dinner into the oven and build a fire in the living room fireplace.

The flames seemed puny, and their warmth couldn't penetrate the chill that lingered around Sharon. She was eating her supper when the telephone rang again.

Again, she was forced to answer.

"Mom?" piped a voice on the other end of the line. "This is Matt."

Sharon smiled for the first time in hours. "I know. How are you, sweetheart?"

"I'm okay." Despite those words, Matt sounded worried. "Bri and I are spending the night with Gramma and Grampa. How come you didn't go to Paris like you said you were going to?"

Sharon clasped the bridge of her nose between her thumb and index finger. "I'll explain about Paris when I get home, honey. Why aren't you and Bri sleeping at your dad's place?"

Before Matt could answer that, Bri joined the conversation on an extension. "Something's really wrong," she said despairingly. "You and Daddy are both acting very weird."

Much as Sharon would have liked to refute that remark, she couldn't. "I guess we are," she admitted softly. "But everything is going to be all right again soon. I promise you that."

She could feel Bri's confusion. "Really?" the girl asked in a small voice, and Sharon wished that she could put her arms around both her children and hold them close.

"Really," Sharon confirmed gently.

There was a quiet exchange on the other end of the line, and then Maria came on. "Sharon? Are you all right, dear?"

Sharon swallowed. "I guess so. Maria, why did Tony leave the children with you and Vincent? I understood him to say that he was going to look after them himself until I got back."

Maria hesitated before answering. "Tonio was upset when he left here," she said cautiously. "Vincent was worried and went after him. I haven't seen either of them since."

Sharon ached. Vincent Morelli was not the kind of father who interfered in his children's lives; if he'd been worried enough to follow Tony, there was real cause for concern.

"Did Tony say anything before he left?"

Sharon realized that Maria was weeping softly. "No," the older woman answered. "I'd feel better if he had. He was just—just hurting."

"I see," Sharon said, keeping her chin high even though there was no one around to know that she was being brave.

"Tonio can be unkind when he is in pain," Maria ventured to say after a few moments of silence. It was obvious that she'd used the interval to work up her courage. "But he loves you, Sharon. He loves you very much."

Sharon nodded. "I love him, too—but sometimes that grand emotion just isn't enough."

"It's the greatest force in the world," Maria countered firmly. "You and Tonio don't understand how it works, that's all."

Sharon was still mulling that over when Maria changed the subject. "You'll be back in town in time for Thanksgiving, won't you?"

"Yes," Sharon answered after a brief hesitation. She hadn't given the holiday much thought since her emotions had been in such turmoil.

"We've missed you," her ex-mother-in-law went on forthrightly. "You are still one of us, no matter what may be happening between you and that hardheaded son of mine, and—well—Vincent and I would be very pleased if you would join us all for dinner on Thursday."

Being invited to a family Thanksgiving at the Morellis' was probably a small thing, but Sharon was deeply moved all the same. Maria could have had her son and her grandchildren around her table on that special day without inviting an erstwhile wife, after all. "Thank you," Sharon said. "That would be nice."

"Of course, your mother is welcome, too," Maria added.

Bea had never made much of holidays, preferring to ignore them until they went away, but Sharon would extend the invitation anyway. "You realize that my presence might be awkward. Tony may not like it at all."

Maria sniffed. "Don't worry about Tonio. He'll behave himself."

In spite of everything that had happened, Sharon chuckled at Maria's motherly words.

"You get some rest," the older woman finished, "and don't worry about the children. I'll take very good care of them."

"Thank you," Sharon replied quietly, and after a few more words the two women said their farewells and hung up.

Sharon went upstairs to take a hot bath, and when that was done she crawled into bed and shivered under the covers. While she waited for sleep to overtake her, she laid plans for the morning.

It was time she stopped acting silly and made some sense of her life. She and Tony were divorced, but they had two children in common, and that meant they had to learn to talk to each other like civilized adults.

The task seemed formidable to Sharon.

Chapter 12

The sound brought Sharon wide awake in an instant. She sat bolt upright in bed, her heart throbbing in her throat as she listened.

There it was again—a distinct thump. A shaky *who's there?* rose in Sharon's throat, but she couldn't get it out. Besides, she reasoned wildly, maybe it wasn't smart to let the prowler know she was there. If she kept quiet, he might steal what he wanted and leave without bothering her.

On the other hand, Sharon reflected, tossing back the covers and creeping out of bed as the noise reverberated through the A-frame again, her car was parked outside—a clear indication that someone was at home. If she just sat there with her lower lip caught between her teeth, she might end up like one of those women in the opening scenes of a horror movie.

She crept out of the bedroom and across the hall

to Matt's room, where she found his baseball bat with only minimal groping. Thus armed, Sharon started cautiously down the stairs.

She'd reached the bottom when a shadow moved in the darkness. Sharon screamed and swung the bat, and something made of glass shattered.

A familiar voice rasped a swearword, and then the living room was flooded with light.

Tony was standing with his hand on the switch, looking at Sharon in weary bafflement. The mock-Tiffany lamp she'd bought at a swap meet was lying on the floor in jagged, kaleidoscope pieces.

Slowly, Sharon lowered the bat to her side. "You could have knocked," she observed lamely. Her heart was still hammering against her rib cage, and she laid one hand to her chest in an effort to calm it.

Tony was frowning. "Why would I do that when I have a key?" he asked, pulling off his jacket and tossing it onto the sofa. "Go put some shoes on, Babe Ruth," he said. "I'll get the broom."

Sharon went upstairs without argument, baseball bat in hand, wanting a chance to put her thoughts into some kind of order. When she came down minutes later, she was wearing jeans, sneakers and a heavy sweater. Tony was sweeping up the last of the broken glass.

"What are you doing here?" she asked, lingering on the stairs, one hand resting on the banister.

Tony sighed. "It was Papa's idea," he said.

Sharon rolled her eyes and put her hands on her hips, mildly insulted. "Now that's romantic," she observed.

Her ex-husband disappeared with the broom and the dustpan full of glass, and when he came back there was a sheepish look about him. He went to the hearth without a word, and began building a fire.

Sharon watched him for a few moments, then went into the kitchen to heat water for coffee. Hope was pounding inside her in a strange, rising rhythm, like the beat of jungle drums. Her feelings were odd, she thought, given the number of times she and Tony had tried to find common ground and failed.

She filled the teakettle at the sink, set it on the stove and turned up the flame beneath it. She'd just taken mugs and a jar of coffee down from the cupboard when she sensed Tony's presence and turned to see him standing in the doorway.

"I'm not going to leave," he announced with quiet resolve, "until you and I come to some kind of understanding."

Sharon sighed. "That might take a while," she answered.

He shrugged, but the expression in his eyes was anything but dispassionate. "Frankly, I've reached the point where I don't give a damn if supplies have to be airlifted in. I'm here for the duration."

The teakettle began to whistle, and Sharon took it from the heat, pouring steaming water into cups. "That's a pretty staunch position to take, considering that it was your father's idea for you to…drop in."

Tony sighed and took the cups from Sharon's hands, standing close. He set the coffee aside, and his quiet masculinity awakened all her sleepy senses. "Sharon," he said in a low voice, "I love you, and I'm pretty sure you feel the same way about me. Can't we hold on to that until we get our bearings?"

Sharon swallowed. "There are so many problems—"

"Everybody has them," he countered hoarsely. And then he took her hand in his and led her into the living room. They sat down together on the couch in front of the fireplace. Sharon, for her part, felt like a shy teenager.

"Why did you let me believe that you and Ingrid were involved?" she dared to ask. A sidelong look at Tony revealed that he was gazing into the fire.

His fingers tightened around Sharon's. The hint of a grin, rueful and brief, touched his mouth. "The answer to that should be obvious. I wanted you to be jealous."

Sharon bit her lower lip, then replied, "It worked."

Tony turned toward her then; with his free hand, he cupped her chin. "When that Swede kissed you at the party last night, I almost came out of my skin. So maybe we're even."

"Maybe," Sharon agreed with a tentative smile. She had a scary, excited feeling, as though she were setting out to cross deep waters hidden under a thin layer of ice. She was putting everything at risk, but with ever so much to be gained should she make it to the other side.

Cautiously, Tony kissed her. The fire crackled on the hearth and, in the distance, a ferry whistle made a mournful sound. After long moments of sweet anguish, he released her mouth to brush his lips along the length of her neck.

"Did your father tell you to do this, too?" Sharon asked, her voice trembling.

Tony chuckled and went right on driving her crazy. "He did suggest wine and music. I suppose he figured I could come up with the rest on my own."

Sharon closed her eyes, filled with achy yearnings. She was facing Tony now, her arms resting lightly around his neck. "Remember," she whispered, "how it used to be? When Bri was little?"

He had returned to her mouth, and sharp desire stabbed through her as he teased and tasted her.

"Um-hmm. We made love on the living room floor with the stereo playing."

"Tony." The word sounded breathless and uncertain. "What?"

"I don't see how we're going to settle anything by doing this."

She felt his smile against her lips; its warmth seemed to reach into the very depths of her being. "Let me state my position on this issue," he whispered. "I love you. I want you. And I'm not going to be able to concentrate on anything until I've had you."

Sharon trembled. "You've got your priorities in order, Morelli—I'll say that for you."

He drew her sweater up over her head and tossed it away, then unfastened her bra. Sharon drew in a sharp breath when he took both her breasts into his hands, gently chafing the nipples with the sides of his thumbs. "I'm so glad you approve," he teased gruffly, bending his head to taste her.

Sharon muffled a groan of pure pleasure and buried her fingers in his hair as he indulged. "I think—I see where we—went wrong," she managed to say. "We should never have—gotten out of bed."

Tony's chuckle felt as good against her nipple as his tongue. "Sharon?"

"What?"

"Shut up."

She moaned, arching her neck as he pressed her down onto her back and unsnapped her jeans. He left her to turn out the lights and press a button on the stereo. The room was filled with music and the gracious glow of the fire, and Tony knelt beside the sofa to caress her.

A tender delirium possessed Sharon as Tony reminded her that he knew her body almost as well as she did. There was an interval during which he drew ever greater, ever more primitive responses from her, and then he stood and lifted her into his arms. She worked the buttons on his shirt as he carried her up the stairs and into the bedroom.

The light of a November moon streamed over Tony's muscular chest and caught the tousled ebony of his hair as Sharon undressed him. In those moments she prayed to love Tony less because what she felt was too fierce and too beautiful to be endured.

He tensed as she touched one taut masculine nipple with the tip of her tongue, and she knew that the anticipation he felt was almost beyond his ability to bear. The words that fell from his lips as she pleasured him belonged not to earth but to a world that love had created, and while Sharon couldn't have defined a single one, she understood them in her heart.

When Tony had reached the limits of his control, he used gentle force to subdue Sharon; after lowering her to the bed, he clasped her wrists in his hands and stretched her arms above her head. His body, as lean and dynamic as a panther's, was poised over hers. In the icy, silver light of the moon, Sharon saw in his face both the tenderness of a lover and the hunger of a predator.

She lifted her head to kiss the curve of his collarbone. Tony could no longer restrain himself; his mouth fell to Sharon's as if he would consume her. A few hoarse, intimate words passed between them, and then, with a grace born of mutual desperation, they were joined.

Tony's and Sharon's bodies seemed to war with each other even as their souls struggled to fuse into one spirit. The skirmish began on earth and ended square in the center of heaven, and the lovers clung to each other as they drifted back to the plane where mortals belong.

When Tony collapsed beside her, still breathing hard, Sharon rolled over to look down into his face, one of her legs resting across his. She kissed the almost imperceptible cleft in his chin.

"I think my toes have melted," she confided with a contented sigh.

Tony put his arms around her, positioning her so that she lay on top of him. "Promise me something," he said, when his breathing had returned to normal. "The next time I make you mad, remember that I'm the same man who melts your toes, will you?"

Sharon kissed him. "I'll try," she said, snuggling down to lie beside Tony and wishing that this accord they'd reached would last forever. Unfortunately, they couldn't spend the rest of their lives in bed.

"What are you thinking?" Tony asked when a long time had passed. He'd turned onto his side to look into Sharon's face, and he brushed her hair away from her cheek with a gentle motion of one hand.

"That I love you. Tony, I want to make this relationship work, but I don't know how."

He sat up and reached out to turn on the lamp on the bedside table. "I've got a few theories about that."

Wriggling to an upright position, Sharon folded her arms and braced herself. She had a pretty good idea what he was going to say—that she was spreading herself too thin, that their marriage would have lasted if she hadn't insisted on opening Teddy Bares....

Tony laughed and caught her chin in his hand. "Wait a minute. I can tell by the storm clouds gathering in your eyes that you're expecting my old me-Tarzan-you-Jane routine—and I wasn't planning to do that."

Sharon gave him a suspicious look. "Okay, so what's your theory, Morelli?"

He sighed. "That we don't fight fair. We sort of collide like bumper cars at a carnival—and then bounce off each other. I try to hurt you and you try to hurt me, and nothing ever gets settled because we're both so busy retaliating or making up that we never talk about what's really wrong."

"That makes a scary kind of sense," Sharon admitted in a small voice. She couldn't look at Tony, so she concentrated on chipping the polish off the nail of her right index finger. "Where do we start?"

"With Carmen, I think," he said quietly.

Even after ten years as Tony's wife, after bearing one of his children and raising the other as her own, Carmen's name made Sharon feel defensive and angry. "I hate her," she confessed.

"I know," Tony replied.

Sharon made herself meet his gaze. "That's really stupid, isn't it?"

His broad, naked shoulders moved in a shrug. "I don't know if I'd go so far as to say that. It's certainly futile."

"You loved her."

"I never denied that."

Sharon drew in a deep, shaky breath. "Even after you married me," she said, "I was a replacement for Carmen at first, wasn't I?"

He shoved a hand through his hair and, for a fraction of a second, his eyes snapped and the line of his jaw went hard. At the last moment he stopped himself from bouncing off of her like one of those carnival bumper cars he'd mentioned earlier. "It's true that I didn't take the time to work through my grief like I should have," he admitted after a long time. "The loneliness—I don't know if I can explain what it was like. It tore at me. I couldn't stand being by myself, but hanging around my family was even worse because they all seemed to have some kind of handle on their lives and I didn't."

Tentatively, Sharon reached out and took Tony's hand in hers. "Go on."

"There isn't much else to say, Sharon. I did want a wife, and I wanted a mother for Briana—but I wouldn't have had to look beyond Mama's Christmas card list for a woman to fill those roles. Mama, my aunts and sisters and female cousins—they all had prospects in mind. I married you because I wanted you."

Sharon was watching Tony's face. "You wanted me? Is that all?"

Tony sighed and tilted back his head, gazing forlornly up at the ceiling. "No. I loved you, but I didn't realize it at the time. I was using you."

This honesty business hurt. "You—you wanted out, I suppose."

His arm moved around her shoulders, and he drew her close. "Never," he answered. "Do you know when I figured out that I loved you as much as I'd ever loved Carmen? It was at that Fourth of July picnic when you climbed fifteen feet up a damned pine tree to get some kid's toy plane and broke your arm taking a shortcut down."

Sharon was amazed. Her predominant memory of that first Independence Day after their marriage had been that she'd missed out on the fireworks and her share of cold watermelon because she'd spent most of the afternoon and evening in the hospital getting X rays and having a cast put on. "That made you fall in love with me? You're a hard man to please, Morelli."

He turned his head to kiss her temple. "You're not

listening. I said I realized that day that what I'd felt for you all along was love."

They were silent for a few minutes, both of them lost in their own thoughts, but Sharon finally said, "I didn't grow up in a family like yours, Tony. I didn't— and don't—have your self-confidence. My insecurities have caused a lot of problems—I can see that now." She paused and sighed sadly. "And then there's Teddy Bares. How do you really feel about my business?"

"I hate it," he answered politely. "But that's my problem, not yours." Tony scooted down far enough to give Sharon a mischievous kiss. "I'll work through it."

Sharon felt a quiet happiness steal through her. "Are you saying that you want to try again?"

He cupped her breast with his hand. "Yes," he answered bluntly. "Will you give me a second chance?"

"At marriage, or our favorite nighttime activity?" Sharon teased.

Tony began to caress her. "Marriage. If I can dissolve your toes, lady, it would seem that I've got a handle on the rest."

Sharon laughed, then gave a little crooning groan as his hand moved downward to make tantalizing circles on her stomach. "It would—seem so," she agreed.

He slid beneath the covers, and his tongue encircled one of Sharon's nipples. "Marry me," he said. "Please?"

She gasped as Tony began to work his private magic. "Maybe—maybe we should live together first," she managed to say. "Until we learn to fight correctly."

"Fine," Tony agreed, preoccupied. "You explain it to Matt and Bri. And my grandmother. And—"

"I'll marry you," Sharon broke in. She pretty much knew when she was beaten. "But there will probably be a lot of fights. We'll both have to make a great many adjustments...."

"Um-hmm," Tony replied, sounding downright disinterested now. "Probably."

He was doing such delicious things to her that it was hard to speak normally. "Sometimes I'll win, and sometimes you will."

Tony flung back the covers and reached out to turn off the lamp. "I'm pretty sure you'll still be talking," he said, gathering her close to him.

He was wrong. Sharon was through talking.

When Sharon awakened the next morning, Tony wasn't in bed. She was worried for a moment until she heard him running up the stairs.

He burst into the bedroom, wearing running shorts and a tank top and dripping sweat. He gave Sharon a grin and disappeared into the bathroom to take his shower.

She waited until she heard the water come on, then went to join him.

That day was magical. They walked along the beach, hand in hand, talking, saying what they really felt, dreaming aloud and deciding how to interweave their separate hopes. They even argued at odd intervals.

It was late that night, when they were eating a complicated pasta concoction that Tony had whipped up, that the first real test of their resolve to be truthful came up.

Sharon had been talking about the opportunity she'd missed because she hadn't been able to go to Paris, and Tony said, "If you needed money, you should have asked me."

Curled up in the easy chair in front of the hearth,

Sharon lowered her fork back to her plate and said quietly, "I couldn't."

Tony qualified her statement. "Because of your damned pride."

"As if you didn't have any."

A tempest was brewing in those dark, spirited eyes, but it ebbed away as fast as it had arisen, and Tony smiled, albeit sheepishly. "Okay. Back to our corners— no kidney punches and no hitting below the belt."

With a mischievous grin, Sharon set aside her plate, got out of her chair and turned the music on and the lights off. There was a nice blaze in the fireplace, and she stretched out on the floor in front of the hearth, letting the light and warmth wash over her.

When Tony joined her, she reached up and put her arms around his neck. "I've missed you so much," she said as the music swelled around them like an invisible river. Soon, it would lift them up and carry them away, and Sharon had no intention of swimming against the current. "I love you," she whispered, pulling Tony downward into her kiss.

Soon they were spinning and whirling in a torrent of sensation, and it ended with Sharon arching her back in a powerful spasm of release and crying out for Tony as she ran her hands feverishly over his flesh. He spoke tender, soothing words to her even as he tensed in the throes of his own gratification.

The big house was full of laughter and the scent of roasting turkey when Sharon and Tony arrived, and Vincent smiled when he saw them. It was Maria who took Sharon's hands in her own and thus noticed the wide golden band on her finger.

"When?" she asked, her eyes bright with joy.

Tony kissed her forehead. Before he could answer, though, Briana and Matt made their way through the crowd of cousins and aunts and uncles, approaching from different directions but arriving at the same moment.

"Something's happened," Bri said, assessing her father and then Sharon. "What is it?"

"They're married, metal-mouth," Matt told her with affectionate disdain. "Can't you see those rings they're wearing?"

Sharon nodded in answer to the hopeful question she saw shining in Bri's eyes, and the girl flung herself into her stepmother's arms with a cry of joy.

Michael, in the meantime, was shaking Tony's hand. "Does this mean you're going to be fit to work with again?" he asked, his voice gruff, his eyes shining.

Tony laughed and lifted an excited Matt into his arms.

"We're all going to live together in the same house now, right?" the little boy wanted to know.

"Right," Tony confirmed.

"How did you two manage to get a license so fast?" Tony's sister Rose demanded from somewhere in the throng of delighted relatives.

"We were married in Nevada this morning, and I chartered a plane to fly us here," he explained. "Is everybody satisfied, or do I have to call a press conference?"

Sharon got out of her coat with some help from Tony, and went into the kitchen with Maria. Bri and Rose followed.

The place was a giant cornucopia—there were pies, candied yams, special vegetable dishes, gelatin salads, cranberry sauce—all the traditional foods. Sharon wanted to help, to be a part of the festivities, and she went to the sink and started peeling the mountain of potatoes waiting there.

Maria was preparing a relish tray nearby, and Bri and Rose were arguing good-naturedly over the football game that would be played that afternoon. They weren't concerned with who would win or lose; the bone of contention was which team had the cuter players.

Within the next hour, dinner was ready to be served and Bea had arrived in her old car, proudly presenting her three-bean casserole as a contribution.

Sitting beside Tony, her hand resting in his on the tabletop, Sharon counted the men, women and children gathered to give thanks under the Morelli roof. There were forty-three smiling faces around the card tables and the oaken one that had been a part of Lucia's dowry.

A reverent prayer was said, and then Vincent began carving the first of three turkeys with great fanfare. Sharon felt the sting of happy tears in her eyes when she turned to look at Tony, then Briana, then Matt.

She offered a silent prayer of her own, one of true thanksgiving, and laughed and cheered Vincent's expertise as a turkey carver with the rest of the family.

Her family.

* * * * *

INTO HIS PRIVATE DOMAIN

Janice Maynard

For my siblings: Scotty, Kathy and Patti...
I love you all!

Chapter 1

Gareth stepped out of the shower and stared at himself in the mirror. The frigid water had done little to dampen his restlessness. Still nude, he began to shave, his toes curling reflexively against the cool stone floor beneath his bare feet.

When his chin was smooth, he grimaced at his reflection. His thick, wavy black hair almost touched his shoulders. He had always worn it longer than current fashion dictated, but now it had grown so much it was getting in his way when he worked.

He reached into a drawer and drew out a thin leather cord. When he ruthlessly pulled back the damp shanks of hair, they made no more than a stubby ponytail, but at least it was out of his eyes.

A sudden loud knocking at the front door made him groan. Neither of his brothers nor his father would bother to announce their presence. And Uncle Vincent and his cousins sympathized with Gareth's grumpiness too much to bother him. Deliveries always went to the main house. So who in the hell could it be?

He'd had his fill of being the brunt of tabloid stories over the years. Later, the communal nature of military life had given him a deep appreciation for solitude. With the exception of family, Gareth had little desire to interact with humanity if he could avoid it.

When a man had money, everyone with access to him had an angle to play. And Gareth was tired of the game. He grabbed a pair of jeans and thrust them on sans underwear. The single item of clothing would have to suffice. He wasn't in a mood to get dressed just yet. Maybe his dishabille would scare away whoever was demonstrating the temerity to bother a surly Wolff.

He strode through the house, cursing suddenly as the leather thong broke and his hair tumbled free. What in the devil did it matter? Whoever stood on his porch was going to get short shrift from him.

He flung open the door and stared at the diminutive redhead with the wildly corkscrewing, chin-length curls. His stomach plummeted to his feet, but his libido perked up. He inhaled sharply and ground out a few terse words. "Who are you and what do you want?"

The woman caught her breath and backed up half a step. Gareth framed himself in the doorway, bracing his long-fingered hands against the lintel. His barefoot stance deliberately bore no semblance of welcome.

The woman dragged her gaze from Gareth's chest with an effort that might have flattered him in other circumstances. She looked him straight in the eye, speaking slowly but distinctly as if she feared he was a wild animal in need of soothing. "I need to talk to you."

Gareth glared at his undeniably sexy intruder. "You're trespassing."

She was fair-skinned, slender and had a spine so straight a man could use it as a plumb line...or maybe trace his tongue from one end of it to the other until the woman cried out in—

He sucked in a ragged breath and shoveled his hands through his hair, his heart thumping in his chest. He couldn't afford to let down his guard for a second. Even if fire-lit curls and delicate cheekbones were his own personal Achilles' heel. His sex swelled with no more than a whiff of her subtle perfume to give him encouragement.

How long had it been since he'd had a woman? Weeks? Months? He clamped down on the yearning that gripped his body like a fever. "What do you want?"

Her eyelids fluttered nervously over irises that were the clear blue of the sky above. Her small chin was stubborn, her posture defiant. As she wiped her damp brow with her hand, she smiled winningly. "Could we go inside and sit down for a few minutes? I'd love something to drink, and I promise not to take too much of your time."

Gareth tensed, and rage flashed through him with the ferocity of the furious torrents that arose in these mountains during thunderstorms and decimated the low ground far below. A user. Like all the rest.

He ignored her outstretched hand, crowding her, relying on his size and temper to bully her. "Get the hell off my land."

The slight woman stumbled backward, her eyes huge, her face paper-white.

He pressed his advantage. "Go on," he snarled. "You're not wanted here."

She opened her mouth, perhaps to protest, but in that instant, one foot slid off the edge of the porch into thin air. She tumbled backward in graceful slow motion, her hip and head striking his steps with audible, dreadful thuds before her small body settled into an ungainly heap on the unforgiving ground.

Mary, Mother of God. He was at her side in the slice of a second, his hands shaking and his brain mush. He was an animal, no better than the coyotes who roamed the hills at night.

She was unconscious. Gently he stroked his palms down her extremities, searching for breaks. Growing up with male brothers and cousins, he had seen his fair share of broken limbs over the years, but he might be sick if he found a sharp bone protruding through her silky, fine-textured skin.

He heaved a sigh of relief when he found none. But the purplish bruise blooming near her temple and the blood trickling down her leg galvanized him into action.

He scooped her negligible weight into his arms and carried her into the house and to his room, his private sanctuary. He deposited her carefully on the unmade bed and went for ice and medical supplies.

The fact that she was still unconscious began to worry him even more than the deep cut on her leg. He grabbed for the phone and dialed his brother Jacob. "I need you. It's an emergency. Bring your bag."

Ten minutes later, his sibling joined him at the bedside. Both men looked down at the woman who was dwarfed by the bed's size and masculinity. Her red-gold hair glowed against the somber gray and navy of the cashmere blankets.

Jacob examined her rapidly from head to toe, his mien serious, his medical training as automatic as it was thorough. "I'll have to stitch the leg. The knot on her head is bad, but not life-threatening. Pupils seem okay." He frowned. "Is she a friend of yours?"

Gareth snorted, his gaze never leaving her face. "Hardly. She was here for all of two minutes when she fell. Said she wanted to talk to me about something. I'm guessing she could be a reporter."

Jacob's brow creased. "What happened?"

Gareth leaned forward and brushed the hair from her face. "I tried to scare her off and it worked."

Jacob sighed. "That hermit act you put on is going to bite you in the ass someday. Maybe today. Damn it, Gareth. She could sue the family to hell and back. What were you thinking?"

Gareth winced when Jacob stuck a needle in the woman's leg, deadening the small area around her cut. She never moved. "I wanted her gone," he muttered, irritated, brooding as he battled inward demons. He hoped this female was as innocent as the first pristine snows that fell in late autumn.

But she could just as easily be a viper in their midst.

Jacob finished the last stitch and covered the wound with a neat bandage. He checked his patient's pulse, gave her another shot in the arm for pain and frowned. "We'd better check for ID. Did she have anything with her?"

Gareth nodded. "It's on the chair over there." While Jacob rifled in the woman's long-handled tote, Gareth stared down at the intruder. She looked like an angel in his bed.

Jacob held up a billfold and sheet of paper, a troubled frown on his face. "Take a look at this photo. And her name is Gracie Darlington."

"Unless the ID is a fake."

"Don't jump to conclusions. You wear paranoia like a hair shirt, but this might be nothing sinister at all."

"And pigs could fly. Don't expect me to be gullible just because she's cute and cuddly. I've been down that road."

"Your ex-fiancée was overly ambitious. And cuddly wasn't in her vocabulary. It happened a long time ago, Gareth. Let it go."

"Not until I know the truth."

Jacob shook his head in disgust as he broke an ammonia caplet beneath Gracie's nose.

She moved restlessly and moaned as reality returned.

Gareth took her small hand in his. "Wake up."

She opened her eyes, blinking against the light. Her lips trembled. "There are two of you?" Her brow creased in confusion.

Jacob's chuckle was dry. "As long as you don't see four, I think we're okay. You probably have a concussion. You need to rest and drink plenty of fluids. I'll be nearby if you get worse. In the meantime, don't make any sudden moves."

His attempt at humor didn't register on Gracie's face. Her nose wrinkled in discomfort. "Where am I?"

Jacob patted her arm. "You're in my brother's bedroom. But don't worry. Gareth doesn't bite. And I'm Jacob, by the way." He glanced at Gareth. "Keep ice packs on her leg and the side of her head. I'm leaving a mild painkiller that should give her some relief as the shot wears off. I'll check back in the morning unless anything changes. Bring her to the clinic and I'll x-ray her to make sure I haven't missed something."

Gareth didn't bother to see his sibling out.

He sat down on the edge of the bed and winced inwardly when Gracie, damaged as she was, made the effort to move away from him. The simple exertion drained what little color she had left in her face, and she shuddered, leaned past him and emptied the contents of her stomach onto the floor.

Then she burst into tears.

Gareth was momentarily frozen with indecision. He'd never in his life felt such an urgent, desperate need to comfort anyone. Gracie might be a lying, cheating witch. And even worse, a woman who could cause untold trouble for his family.

But he was helpless in the face of her heartfelt misery. No one could fake such distress.

He went to the bathroom for a damp washcloth, handed it to her and proceeded to clean up the mess on the floor in silence. By the time he was done, her sobs had subsided into hiccupping, ragged sighs. Her eyes were closed, her body still as death. Probably because every little movement sent pain shooting through her skull.

Gareth had been thrown from a horse when he was twelve, and the resulting head injury had left him weak as a babe.

He knew how she felt.

He didn't risk sitting down again. Instead he went to the windows and opened both of them, letting the fresh spring breezes cleanse the room. He pulled the curtains together to dim the light, wanting to make her as comfortable as possible.

Afterward, he stood by the bed and stared down at her, wondering how a day that had begun so normally had rapidly skidded off track. He cleared his throat and gently pulled the bedding to cover her slight frame, tucking it to her chin. "We need to talk. But I'll wait until you've had a chance to rest. It's almost dinnertime. I'll fix something simple that won't aggravate your stomach, and I'll bring it in when it's ready." He hesitated, waiting for a reply.

Gracie tried to gather her composure, sure that any minute now she would get a handle on her scattered wits. This all seemed like such an odd dream. The glowering man tending to her with patent reluctance was huge.

His face was remarkable, wholly masculine, but striking rather than handsome. He had a crooked nose, a jaw carved from granite and cheekbones that drew attention to his deep-set, black-as-midnight eyes—eyes so dark, his pupils were indiscernible.

Equally dark hair framed his face aggressively, suggesting wildness and a lack of concern for polite conventions. The strands were thick and vibrant, and Gracie wanted to bury her hands in them and drag his head down to see if the tousled layers were as soft as they looked.

His broad, bare chest was golden-tan, its sleekly muscled beauty marred by three small scars over his rib cage. She frowned, her fingers itching to trace each imperfection. She refused to acknowledge that she was gob-smacked by his sheer magnificence. He left the room finally, closing the door behind him, and eventually, she dozed, rousing now and again to the awareness of pain and frightening loneliness. Shadows cast the room into near darkness by the time her host returned.

He carried a tray which he set on a wooden chest at the foot of the bed. She feared the sudden onslaught of bright light from the fixture overhead, but instead, he turned on a small antique table lamp with a cream silk shade. The diffused glow was bearable.

He stood beside her. "You need to sit up and eat something."

Questions clogged her throat. The smell wafting from a handmade earthenware container made her stomach growl loudly. He didn't comment, but helped her into a seated position. His manner was matter-of-fact. Everywhere his skin touched hers, she burned.

His expression was hard to read. When she was ready, he placed the tray across her lap. She sucked in a breath as she moved her leg beneath the covers. She hadn't even realized until that moment that she had injured more than her head.

He answered her unspoken question. "Jacob put six or seven stitches in your shin. You hit some sharp gravel when you…" His voice trailed off, and she saw discomfiture on his face. He pulled up a straight-back chair and watched her eat. If she hadn't been starving, his intense scrutiny would have made her nervous. But it must have been hours since she'd had any food, and she was hungry.

He, or someone, had prepared chicken soup, which required far more effort than simply opening a can. Large chunks of white meat mingled with carrots and celery in a fragrant broth. She tore off a hunk of the still-warm wheat bread and consumed it with unladylike haste.

Neither she nor her companion spoke a word until she had cleaned her plate, or in this case, her bowl.

Removing the trappings of the decidedly fine dinner, Gareth—was that his name?—sat back down and folded his arms across his chest.

He was dressed casually in old faded jeans and bare feet. But he had buttoned his top half into a rich burgundy poet's shirt made of an unusual handwoven fabric. Some men might have appeared ridiculous in such garb. On him, the shirt looked perfectly natural, enhancing his air of confidence and male superiority.

She struggled to conquer panic, postponing the moment of truth. "I need to go to the bathroom." It galled her that she required his help to stand up. Her injured leg threatened to crumple beneath her, but after a moment, she was able to shuffle to the facilities.

The bathroom was enormous, with a stone-lined, glass-enclosed shower. She caught a sudden mental picture of the mysterious male's huge body—nude—glistening beneath the spray of water and soap.

Her knees went weak. Despite her distress, she was stingingly aware of her host's blatant sexuality. She took care of necessities, washed up, and then made the mistake of glancing into the mirror. The image confused her. Good Lord. She was so white her freckles stood out in relief, and her hair was a bird's nest.

She rummaged without guilt through his drawers until she found a comb. But when she tried to run it through the worst of the tangles, she scraped against her injured skull and cried out at the pain.

He was beside her in an instant, not even making a pretense of knocking. "What is it?" he demanded, his gaze fierce. "Are you sick again?" In an instant he saw what she was trying to do. "Forget your hair," he muttered, scooping her into his arms and carrying her back to bed.

When she was settled, ice packs back in place, he handed her two pain pills and insisted she wash them down with milk. She felt like a child being soothed by a parent, but everything about her reaction to this strange man was entirely adult. He headed for the door. "Don't go," she blurted out, blushing as if he could see her inner turmoil. "I don't want to be alone."

He returned to the chair, swinging it around to straddle the seat, and folded his arms across the back. His expression was guarded. "You're perfectly safe," he said, his low voice rumbling across her shattered nerves with a tactile stroke. "Jacob says you'll recover rapidly."

Any bit of softness she sensed in him moments before had been replaced with almost palpable hostility and suspicion. What in the heck did he have to fear from her?

She picked at the edge of the blanket. "Does your brother live with you?"

He frowned. "Jacob has a house on the property. Why did you come here?"

Her tiny surge of energy abated rapidly, leaving her weak and sick again. She slid down in the bed and turned her head away from him toward the open window. "I don't know," she said dully.

"Look at me."

She did so reluctantly, feeling embarrassed and disoriented.

He frowned. "You're not making sense."

She bit her lower lip, feeling the hot sting of tears behind her eyes. "You seem angry. Is it because of me?"

If she hadn't been watching him so closely, she might have missed it. For the flicker of a second, alarm flashed in his eyes and his white-knuckled fingers gripped the back of the chair. But as quickly as it appeared, the expression went away.

He shrugged. "Not at all. You'll be on your way soon enough."

He was lying. She knew it with a certainty that filled her chest with indignation. Her presence in his house was a problem. A big one. She threw back the covers, panicked and agitated. "I'll go."

His frown blackened as he straightened the bedding. "Don't be ridiculous. You're in no shape to go anywhere tonight. Stay in my bed. But tomorrow, you're history."

The pain in her head bested her. That and a heart-pounding sense of foreboding. She clenched the edge of the sheet in her hands, fighting hysteria. "Please," she whispered.

"Please what?" Now his expression was confused.

"Please tell me who I am."

Chapter 2

Gareth narrowed his eyes, trying to disguise his shock. Here it was. The ploy. The act. Part one of whatever scam she was running. She couldn't be for real…*could she*?

He kept his expression bland. "Amnesia? Really? We're going to do the daytime soap opera thing?" He shrugged. "Okay. I'll play along. I'm Gareth. Your name is Gracie Darlington. You're from Savannah. Jacob and I checked your driver's license."

He watched her bottom lip quiver until she bit down on it…hard. She made an almost palpable effort to gather herself. A gifted actress could do as much. But the look of sheer terror in her painfully transparent gaze would be hard to manufacture. She sucked in a ragged breath. "How did I get here? Do I have a car outside?"

He shook his head. "As near as I can tell, you hiked up the mountain. Which is no small feat, by the way.

There are no cleared trails at the bottom. Your arms and legs are all scratched."

"Do I have a cell phone?"

He cocked his head, studying her face. "I'll check." The only item she'd had with her when she arrived was the pink carryall Jacob had examined earlier. Gareth rummaged in it without remorse and, in a zippered pocket, found a Droid phone. He turned it on and handed it to her, tossing the tote on the bed beside Gracie. Fortunately the battery seemed to be fully charged. Gracie pulled up the contact screen.

"Well, at least you remember how to do that." His thick sarcasm made her wince, but she didn't look at him. Instead she studied the list of names as if she were cramming for a test. Focused. Intent.

When she finally looked up, her beautiful eyes were shiny with tears. "None of these names mean a thing to me," she whispered. One drop spilled over. "I don't understand. Why can't I remember?"

He took the phone from her, squashing a reluctant sympathy. Gareth Wolff was no pushover. Not anymore. "You whacked your head when you fell off my porch. Jacob's a doctor. He says you'll be fine." But Jacob had left before the whole amnesia thing came to light. Damn it.

Gareth scrolled through the contact list himself, not sure what he was looking for. But then it hit him. There was an "I.C.E." entry. In case of emergency. Edward Darlington…and the word Daddy.

He hit the call key and waited. A man on the other end answered. Gareth spoke calmly. "This is Gareth Wolff. Your daughter took a fall and has been injured. She's been checked out by a doctor, and she's going to be fine. But she's suffering a temporary memory loss.

It would be helpful if you could reassure her. I'll put her on the line."

Without waiting for an answer, Gareth handed the phone to Gracie.

She eased up into a half-sitting position, resting her back against the headboard. "Hello?"

Gareth sat down beside her, close enough to hear that the voice on the other end was amused. Close enough to catch snatches of conversation.

"Hot damn, my little Gracie. I didn't think you had it in you. Faking an accident on Wolff property? Pretending to have amnesia? Good Lord, you've got him right where we want him. The whole family will be terrified we'll sue. Phenomenal idea. Nothing like going after what you want whole hog. Brilliant, my girl. Sheer brilliance."

Gracie interrupted the man's euphoria. "Father...I don't feel well at all. Can you please come pick me up and take me home?"

Darlington chortled. "He's standing in the room with you, isn't he? And you've got to play this out. Splendid. I'll do my part. Sorry, Gracie. I'm headed for Europe in half an hour. Won't be back for a week. And the house is a wreck. I told the contractor to go ahead with the remodel since we were both planning to be out of town. You'd have to stay in a hotel if you came back."

"This isn't funny," she muttered. "I'm serious. I can't stay here. They don't want me. I'm a stranger."

"Dredge up their guilt," he insisted. "They owe it to you to be hospitable. Flirt with Gareth a little. Play on his sympathies. Damsel in distress and all that. Get him to agree to our proposal. We'll talk next week. I've gotta run."

"No, wait," she said desperately. "At least tell me if

I have a husband or a boyfriend. Anyone who's missing me."

Her father's cackle of a laugh was so loud she had to hold the phone away from her ear. "Of course not. Lay it on thick. I'm loving this. Wish I could see his face. So long now."

The line went dead. Gracie stared down at the phone, her composure in shreds. What kind of father did she have? Who could be so callous? So blasé about her injuries? Embarrassment and humiliation washed over her in waves, adding to her feeling of abandonment.

She laid the phone aside and managed a weak grimace. "How much of that did you hear?"

Gareth stood up and crossed to the window, his back to her. "Enough," he said, disgusted with himself and with her. If he had any sense, he would boot her off the property ASAP.

Gracie's voice wobbled. "He can't come pick me up right now, because he's on his way out of the country for a week. But if you'll make travel arrangements for me, I'm sure he'll reimburse you."

Gareth Wolff turned to stare at her with a mixture of suspicion and pity. "He thinks you're faking amnesia."

Her cheeks flamed. "The whole conversation was confusing. I came to see you for a reason. But I don't know what that is. Though he seems to."

"And you really don't have a clue?"

She shook her head. "I'm sorry. I'll leave as soon as I can."

"You're not going anywhere at the moment." Gareth's jaw was clenched. "If you really do have memory loss, then I have to let Jacob know. The Wolff family doesn't make a habit of throwing the injured out on the street. And believe me, Gracie, we're not going to give you or your unbelievably unconcerned father any ammunition for a lawsuit."

"We're not going to sue you," she said quietly. Depression depleted her last reserve of spunk. "I don't believe in frivolous lawsuits."

"How do you know?" he shot back. "Maybe the woman you can't remember would do just that."

Gracie slid back down into the bed, her skull filled with pounding hammers. "Please leave me alone."

Gareth shook his head, his demeanor more drill sergeant than nurse. "Sorry, Gracie." His tone didn't sound sorry at all. "If we're playing the amnesia game, I have no choice but to let Jacob know. I'll drive you over there."

The thought of standing up was dreadful. "Can't he come back here? It's not that late, is it?"

"It's not a question of being late. Jacob has a fully outfitted clinic at his place. He'll be able to scan your head and x-ray your leg."

"I'm sure that's not necessary. All I want to do is rest. Tomorrow you can get rid of me."

Gareth strode to the door. "You're in Wolff territory now. And in no position to call the shots." He paused and glanced back at her, his expression grim. "I'll grab my keys and shoes. Don't move."

Gracie closed her eyes, breathing deeply, half convinced she was in the midst of a dark and disturbing nightmare. Surely she would wake up soon, and all of this would be a surreal fantasy. *Gareth Wolff.* She whispered the name aloud, searching for meaning. Why had she come to see him? What did her father want? And how did she get from Georgia to Virginia? Did she have luggage somewhere? A hotel room? A vehicle? Maybe even a laptop? Her tote held nothing but the phone, snacks and some tissues.

She froze, her brow furrowed in discomfort. How could she know what a laptop was and not even remember her own name?

Gareth strode back into the room, his feet shod in worn leather boots. Everything about the room she inhabited made Gracie feel at a disadvantage—the expensive bedding, the masculine decor, the large scale furniture…the total lack of anything familiar.

But something about those scarred boots eased the constriction in her chest. They struck her as normal. Human.

Gareth approached the bed, his face closed. "I've spoken to Jacob. He's expecting us. Let's go."

Gracie screeched in shock when he gathered her up, blankets and all, in his strong arms.

He froze. "Did I hurt you? Sorry." The gruff apology was instantaneous.

She shook her head, trembling as they traversed a wide hallway. "You startled me. That's all." Not for anything would she admit that being in his arms was exciting and comforting at the same time. His scent and the beat of his heart beneath her cheek aroused her and gave her the illusory sensation of security.

The earlier fleeting impressions she'd formed of wealth and privilege increased tenfold as they passed through the house. Gleaming hardwood floors. Westernthemed rugs. Intricate chandeliers of elk horn shedding warm yellow light.

But Gareth walked too quickly for her to carry out any deeper inspection. In minutes they were out the front door and stepping into the scented cool of a late spring evening.

And how did she know it was spring? The little blips of instinctual information that popped into her head gave hope that her memories were simply tucked away in hiding. Not permanently gone…merely obscured by her injury.

Gareth carried her carefully, but impersonally. It wasn't his fault if her hormones and heartbeat went haywire. He smelled of wood smoke and shampoo, a pleasing mélange of masculine odors. Despite his flashes of animosity, she felt safe in his embrace. He might not want her in his home, but he posed no threat to her well-being…at least not physically. The unseen dangers might prove to be more hazardous.

She *liked* being held by Gareth Wolff. What did that say about her?

Of course, her instinctive response could be attributed to something akin to Stockholm syndrome—the bonding between kidnapper and victim. Not that Gareth had done anything wrong. Quite the contrary. But at the moment, he was the only reality in her spinning world. He and his brother Jacob.

Most likely, her affinity for the surly Wolff brother was nothing more than an atavistic urge to seek protection from the unknown.

Gareth's Jeep was parked outside a large garage at the rear of the house. The building, roomy enough to house a fleet of vehicles, had been designed to blend into the landscape, much like the house. A cedar shake roof and rustic, carefully hewn logs seemed to match the edge in her host's personality. Gareth's home was enormous and clearly expensive, but it suited his gruff demeanor.

Once he had tucked her into the passenger seat, he loped around the side of the vehicle and slid behind the wheel. Thick fog blanketed their surroundings. Gracie peered into the darkness, shivering slightly, not from the temperature, but from the feeling of being so isolated. She'd seen horror movies that rolled the opening sequence in a similarly creepy fashion.

She clenched her fist in the blanket and pulled it closer to her chest. "Where are we?"

Gareth shot her a quick glance. "Wolff Mountain."

She cleared her throat. "I hope that's not as sinister as it sounds."

His quick snort of laughter ended as quickly as it began. She had a hunch he didn't want to show any signs of softening toward her.

He wrenched the wheel to avoid a tiny rabbit that scampered in front of them. "This is my home. I grew up here with my two brothers and three cousins. I'm sure all of this will come back to you," he snarled. "My family has no secrets."

She wanted to ask for more details, more explanations, anything to fill in the blanks. But her innocent question had clearly hit a nerve. She lapsed into silence, using her free hand to grip the door of the vehicle as Gareth sent them hurtling around the side of the mountain.

The trip was mercifully brief. Without warning, another house loomed out of the eerie fog. This one was more modern than Gareth's, all steel and glass. Almost antiseptic in design. Though in all fairness she wasn't getting a first look at it in the best of situations.

Jacob met them at the door and ushered them inside, his eyes sharp with concern as Gareth set her on her feet. "Any change?"

The terse question was aimed more at Gareth than Gracie, so she kept her silence.

Gareth tossed his keys onto a black lacquer credenza. "She doesn't remember details of her life. But functional knowledge appears to be unaffected. She knows how to use her phone, but the names are a mystery… or so she says."

Gracie flushed. She was embarrassed and exhausted. The last thing she needed was Gareth's mockery.

Jacob waved a hand toward a living room that looked like something out of a designer's catalog. "Make yourself comfortable, bro. The game's on channel fifty-two. Beer's in the fridge."

Gareth frowned. "I should come with you."

Jacob put a hand on his shoulder. "Not appropriate, Gareth. Trust me. She's in good hands."

He turned to Gracie, his smile gentle. "Let's get you checked out, little lady. I promise not to torture you too badly."

Unlike Gareth, Jacob trusted her to walk on her own. She abandoned her cocoon of blankets in the foyer and followed him down a hallway to the back of the house. Everything was in black and white—walls, flooring, artwork… A highly sophisticated color scheme, but oddly cold and sterile.

When she stepped through a door into the clinic proper, all became clear. Jacob Wolff had designed his house to mirror his professional domain.

Gracie's curiosity as she surveyed the state-of-the-art facility had nothing to do with her amnesia. She had never seen such equipment and facilities outside of a hospital. Even with her memory loss, she was sure of that.

As Jacob positioned the CT scanner, she cocked her head. "I may not remember much, but isn't this setup a little unusual?"

His quick glance reminded her of Gareth. "I have a number of high-profile patients who want to be able to get medical attention away from the eyes of the paparazzi."

She gaped. "Like movie stars?"

He shrugged, adjusting a dial. "Politicians, movie stars… Fortune 500 CEOs."

Something must have shown on her face, because his expression grew fierce. "Having wealth doesn't make a person's right to privacy any less important. I'm fortunate enough to have the means to give them anonymity and quality medical care."

She held up her hands. "I didn't say a word."

"You were thinking it." He motioned to the machine. "Have a seat. There's nothing to be afraid of. You won't be closed in."

She sat gingerly on the narrow bench and tensed as he slid rubber wedges on either side of her head, immobilizing her skull in a semicircle of metal. The camera thingy rotated around her upper body in several quick passes, and it was all over.

Jacob waved her into a chair. "Now I'll show you the inside of your head. Hopefully we won't see anything too alarming."

She sat down gingerly. "As long as you find a brain… that's all I ask."

He chuckled, but didn't speak as he brought up the 3-D images on the screen. Gracie waited, her heart pumping madly. Jacob examined the results with the occasional unintelligible murmur.

Gracie lost patience. "Well?"

He pushed back his chair and turned to face her. "I don't see anything alarming…no fractures…nothing to require further medical attention. You have swelling, of course, as a result of the blow to your head, but even that is in the normal range."

She bit her lip, disappointment roiling in her stomach. If there was nothing to substantiate her amnesia, Gareth would think, more than ever, that she was liar.

Jacob seemed to read her thoughts. "Absence of fractures doesn't discount your current situation. All jokes aside, temporary amnesia is more common than you might think. And we have every reason to think it will resolve itself naturally."

"But when?" she cried, springing to her feet. "How can I go to sleep tonight and not know who the hell I am?"

Jacob leaned back and linked his hands behind his head. "You do know who you are," he said gently. "You're Gracie Darlington. It may take a little while for your brain to accept that as fact. But it will happen. I promise."

Gracie stewed inwardly as he finished his exam. As expected, the X-ray of her leg showed no sign of any damage other than the bad cut.

After a quick check of temp, blood pressure and a few other markers, Jacob patted her shoulder. "You'll live," he teased.

They walked back through the house and found Gareth sprawled on an ivory leather sofa. The thick, onyx carpet underfoot was a sea of inky, lush luxury.

Gareth bounded to his feet. "Sit here," he commanded Gracie. "I want to talk to my brother."

Despite the fact that they lowered their voices, Gracie heard every word.

Gareth grilled her doctor. "Well…could you tell if the amnesia is for real?"

Jacob muttered a curse. "This isn't an exact science, Gareth. All her symptoms fit the profile. But I can't give you any hard-and-fast answers. My medical opinion is yes, she's very likely telling us the truth. That's the good news. The bad news is that amnesia is a tricky bastard. It might be tomorrow morning or next week before she gets it all back." He paused and grimaced. "It could be several months. We have no way of knowing."

"Bloody hell."

Gareth's heartfelt disgust lodged like a thorn in Gracie's heart.

Jacob walked back into the living room, giving Gracie a gentle smile. "Take her home and put her to bed," he said to his brother. "Things always look better in the morning."

Chapter 3

Put her to bed. Gareth tensed inwardly as images teased his brain. Him. Gracie. Tumbling with abandon between the sheets on his comfortable king-size mattress. He'd never brought a woman into his bedroom on Wolff Mountain. Whenever his physical needs overrode his phenomenal control, he sought out one of a handful of women who were as much loners as he was. Mature women who weren't interested in relationships.

But the last such encounter had been ages ago. And the Wolff was hungry. Put a red hood on Gracie, and she'd be in big trouble. Or maybe she was in trouble already. Taking advantage of a damsel in distress wasn't his style, but then again, he had never felt such a visceral and instantaneous response to a woman.

He wanted her desperately, and they had only met. At some anonymous bar in a big city he could have invited her back to his room. But this was Wolff Mountain, and different rules applied. Though he was a reluctant host, he had no business lusting after her.

She stood up, her expression half defiance, half vulnerability. "Couldn't I stay here, Jacob? You know...in case anything happens."

"No way." Gareth blurted it out, uncensored.

Jacob and Gracie stared at him.

He shrugged, refusing to admit he had a proprietary interest in the redhead. "Jacob's a soft touch." He directed his remarks to Gracie. "I want you where I can keep an eye on you."

Jacob frowned at his brother. "Gareth's bark is worse than his bite, Gracie. He'll take good care of you. But don't worry. I'll be around in the morning to see how you're doing." He put an arm around her shoulders and squeezed. "Try not to worry. Everything will be fine. I'd stake my license on it."

Gareth ushered Gracie back out to the Jeep, this time letting her walk on her own. He'd liked holding her too damn much. It was best to keep his distance.

The short ride back was silent. Temperatures had dropped, and out of the corner of his eye, he saw Gracie pull the blankets to her chin. When they arrived at the house, he realized that he was actually going to have to be hospitable. And since she swayed on her feet from exhaustion, he shouldn't waste any time.

He motioned for her to follow him. At the insistence of his architect brother Kieran, Gareth had agreed to a five-bedroom home. The square footage had seemed like a useless expenditure during construction...and now, four of the bedrooms sat unoccupied. But at least for tonight, Gracie would have a place to lay her head.

He showed her the suite that would be hers...for a *very* short time, he promised himself. Too long, and his iron control might snap. "The bathroom is through that door." Even now his hands trembled with the need to touch her.

He eyed her clothing. She was still wearing the simple cotton blouse and jeans she'd had on when she arrived. "I'll find something for you to sleep in. Tomorrow we'll work on getting you some clothes."

When he returned two minutes later with one of his old T-shirts, Gracie was still in the same spot, her expression stark, haunted. Unwillingly his heart contracted. If she was telling the truth about her amnesia, she must be scared as hell. But sweet and courageous, and so damned appealing in her determination not to break down. The reluctant admiration he felt had to be squashed.

When he brushed her arm, she jumped, as if she had been a million miles away. He offered the substitute sleepwear. "Sorry I can't do better. You'll find toiletries in the drawers and on the counter. I let my cousin do the decorating, and she promised me that no bathroom was complete without all sorts of smelly soaps and doodads. Help yourself."

Gracie took the shirt and held it, white-knuckled. "Will you be in your bedroom?"

God help him. He knew she meant nothing by her artless question, but it shook him. "Yeah. As soon as I lock up and turn out the lights." He paused, feeling uncustomarily conflicted, since he rarely second-guessed himself. "Remember...I'm just around the corner. Maybe if you leave a light on, things won't seem so strange."

She nodded her head slowly. "Okay."

Something about her posture was heartbreaking. She was doing nothing to deliberately manipulate his sympathies, but the bravery in her narrow shoulders set so straight and the uplifted tilt of her chin touched him in a way he hadn't thought possible.

He hardened his heart. "Good night, Gracie."

She heard the door shut quietly behind him and felt tears burn her eyes. It took great effort, but she held them at bay by virtue of biting down on her bottom lip and swallowing hard. She refused to let Gareth see her exhibit weakness. He was a hard, suspicious man, despite his physical appeal.

Even so, she wanted him. And the wanting scared her. She felt like the heroine of a dark, Gothic novel, left all alone with the brooding lord of a sprawling, mysterious house.

A glance at the clock sent her stumbling into the bathroom. No wonder she was so wiped out. It was late. Everything would look better in the morning. Darkness invariably bred bogeymen and unseen monsters. Her lack of memory fueled the fires of apprehension.

Gareth had told the truth about the facilities and accoutrements. The floor was inlaid with cream-colored marble veined in gold. An enormous mirror ran the entire length of one wall, showing Gracie reflection after reflection of a strange woman with unkempt hair and no makeup.

Jacob had covered her stitches with a waterproof bandage. Doggedly she stripped off her clothing and climbed into the enormous polished granite enclosure that boasted three showerheads and a steam valve. The hot water pelted her back and rained over her arms and legs. She bowed her head, braced her hands against the wall and cried.

When the tears finally ran out, she picked up a fluffy

sponge and squirted it with herbal soap from a fancy bottle inscribed in French. The aroma was heavenly.

Twenty minutes later she forced herself to get out and dry off. Gareth's T-shirt hung to her knees, half exposing one of her shoulders. The woman in the mirror appeared waifish and very much alone.

She took a few minutes to wash out her undies and hang them on a brass towel rod to dry before returning to the bedroom. In her absence, Gareth had left several items on the bedside table. A pair of thick woolen socks, a tumbler of water with two pain pills and a copy of *Newsweek*. She wasn't sure if the latter was for entertainment or edification.

She put on the socks, and for the first time all day, felt a glimmer of humor at how ridiculous she looked. Even with no memory, she knew that a man like Gareth had his pick of women. He might be surly and prickly, but he exuded a potent masculinity that any female from eighteen to eighty would have to be blind not to notice.

Though her accommodations were worthy of the finest resort, sleep didn't come easily. She tossed and turned, even when the medication dulled the ache in her leg and her head. Every time she closed her eyes, she remembered waking up in Gareth's bed and seeing two strange men staring down at her with varying degrees of suspicion.

Why had she come to Wolff Mountain? What did she hope to accomplish? Was her father involved in something dishonest? The questions tumbled in her brain faster and faster, erasing any hope of slumber.

Finally, when the crystal clock on the bedside table read two-thirty, Gracie climbed out of bed and tiptoed to the door. It wouldn't hurt to explore the house. She'd seen very little of it so far. Maybe there was something out there that would jog her memory.

And besides, she was hungry. With her heart beating like a runaway train, she eased open the door to the hall.

Gareth knew the moment she left her room. He'd always been a light sleeper, at least as an adult, and even the faint whisper of Gracie's soft footsteps was enough to wake him. His frequent insomnia was the penance he paid for defying his father's wishes and enlisting in the military. A five-year stint in the army had taught Gareth that deep sleep could be fatal. It served him right for giving his father such grief.

Gareth crept down the hallway, following the muffled trail of sounds. He found his houseguest in the kitchen. At first, her mission was prosaic. She poured a glass of milk and consumed it with a chunk of cheddar cheese and a slice of bread.

When she was finished, she carefully washed her glass and saucer and placed them back in the cabinet. Gareth grinned. Did she think she was erasing any record of her nocturnal wanderings?

His amusement faded when she approached the laptop on the built-in desk. All important files were password protected, but a knowledgeable hacker could cause mischief even still. Gracie sat in the swivel chair, tucked her feet on the rungs and began to hit keys with a sure touch.

He worked his way around the adjoining room until he was able to approach her from behind. Her head was bent. She was focused intently on the computer screen.

Gareth's temper surged. He stepped into the room, girded for battle. "What in the hell do you think you're doing?" he demanded.

Her gasp was audible. She whirled to face him, guilt etched on her face. "I couldn't sleep."

"So you decided to poke your nose into my business…is that it?" He glanced down at the laptop and his jaw dropped. Hell. He hated being wrong.

She shrugged, her expression wry. "Apparently I remember how to play Solitaire."

"So I see."

She cocked her head and frowned. "Why would I be poking into your business? Do you think that's the kind of woman I am?"

He refused to apologize for well-founded suspicion. "I don't *know* what kind of woman you are. Therein lies the problem."

She shut down the game and stood up. "I'll go back to my room," she said, every syllable drenched in offended dignity.

"Oh, for Pete's sake," he muttered. "Do whatever you want." She wore his T-shirt like a centerfold model striking a pose, but he was a hundred percent certain her seductive invitation was unintentional.

As he turned to leave, running from temptation if the truth were told, she stopped him with a beseeching look. "Please tell me about your family…this place. Maybe something you say will trigger a memory."

"That's a convenient excuse." He still wasn't convinced that Gracie wasn't a reporter looking for a story. His family had suffered terribly at the hands of the press, the Wolff tragedy and grief offered up for public consumption without remorse. Never again.

Dark smudges beneath her eyes emphasized her pallor. "Please," she said quietly. "Anything. Tell me anything. I've combed my cell phone and I did a Google search on myself and my father. But I didn't find out much except that we own a gallery."

In spite of himself, compassion surfaced. "You're on top of a mountain in the Blue Ridge. My family moved here in the eighties. My uncle and my father live in a huge house at the very peak. My siblings and cousins and I are in varying stages of building homes here as well."

She frowned. "You all live here together? Like a commune?"

"Not a commune," he grated. "It's over a thousand acres. We're hardly in each other's pockets."

"So, more like the Kennedys at Hyannis Port."

"I suppose. But none of us are in politics, thank God."

"You're wealthy."

He narrowed his eyes. "You could say that." It was damned hard to carry on a conversation when he kept getting distracted by the way her nipples pressed against the soft knit fabric. All he had to do was reach for her arm and pull her against him. The knowledge dried his mouth. He didn't think she would stop him. Though not any more vain than the next man, he had seen interest in her unguarded gaze earlier in the day.

But he was an honorable man. Damn it.

She frowned. "If I hiked through the woods, how did I know which house was yours?"

"You had an aerial photograph in your bag." He shrugged. "My place is circled in black marker."

Now, every last shred of color leached from her face. "So all we know for sure is that I was trespassing and that I wanted something from you."

"That's it in a nutshell. And based on the conversation you had with your father, he knows why you came and thinks you're faking amnesia to get what you want."

Her lips twisted. "Maybe I don't want to remember. It sounds like I'm not a very nice person." She paused. "Why didn't I simply drive up the road?"

"It's private. You wouldn't have gotten past the guard gate without an appointment."

"Hence my ill-advised hike."

"Apparently."

"I'm sorry," she said simply.

"For what?"

"For whatever I was going to do. I wish I could remember."

"When you came to my door, you said you needed to talk to me about something."

"And then what happened?"

He felt his neck redden. "I may have been a trifle unwelcoming."

Her mouth fell open, and a flicker of emotion akin to fear flashed in her eyes. "You *pushed* me off your porch?"

"Oh, for God's sake. No. Of course not. All I did was tell you to leave. Forcefully. You backed away from me, and..."

"I fell."

"Yes." He was uncomfortably aware that the family lawyer would be hyperventilating by now if he were here to track the conversation. Gareth had pretty much incriminated himself.

He rubbed a hand over the back of his neck. "It was an accident. And you were breaking the law. So don't go getting any ideas about draining us dry. We have a legal team that would chew you to pieces."

"Why do you need a legal team?"

This conversation had gone on long enough. "Go to

bed, Gracie. Get some sleep. Maybe when you wake up, all will be clear."

She hesitated, looking at him with need that went beyond simple survival. He wondered if she understood the feminine invitation she was unwittingly telegraphing. Deliberate or not, every bit of testosterone in him responded with a *hell, yeah*.

Groaning inwardly, he turned his back on her and left the room.

When Gracie woke up, the sun was high in the sky, the clock said it was noon and nothing was any clearer than it had been the night before. She leaped from the bed and then staggered when the pounding in her skull threatened to send her to her knees.

A hand to the wall and several long breaths finally steadied her. This time, the woman in the mirror looked more familiar. She brushed her teeth, put on her clean undies and her not-so-clean clothes and went in search of food. The house was quiet, too quiet. In the kitchen she found a note scrawled in bold masculine handwriting. *Plenty of food in the fridge. Help yourself. I'm working. Will check on you midafternoon.*

She crumpled the paper and tossed it in the trash. Working? What did that mean? A sandwich and a banana later, the front doorbell rang. Gracie waited a few seconds to see if Gareth would appear. But when the bell rang a second time, she walked quickly toward the front of the house, grimacing when she saw her reflection in a mirror. She was hardly fit for company.

The woman who stood on the porch was a surprise. She gave Gracie a blinding smile and muscled her way through the door, forcing a befuddled Gracie to step back.

"I'm Annalise," she said, holding out a hand after she dropped an armload of packages on the nearest chair. "Jacob had your height and weight, so we guessed at sizes. I've got all the basics, I hope. Enough to see you through at least a week. After that, we'll see."

"Well, I…"

Annalise was already pulling things out of packages. "My favorite boutique in Charlottesville couriered over everything I asked for. The manager there is really sweet."

Gracie quivered with alarm. She had no clue about her own finances. What if she couldn't afford all this? And heaven knew how much the delivery charges were. "Um, Annalise…" she said as she tried to slow down the mini tornado. "I really only need one change of clothing. I do appreciate all the trouble you've gone to, but I can't stay long. And until I begin to remember things, I don't know if I can repay you."

Annalise sat cross-legged on the rug and began removing price tags. "Don't be silly," she said happily. "Gareth is paying for all of this. It's the least he can do after you hurt yourself so badly."

An arrested look came over her face and she hopped back to her feet. "Speaking of which, Jacob wanted me to take a look at your head. He's only a phone call away if we need him."

Before Gracie could move or protest, Annalise was sifting through Gracie's curls, her fingers delicate as they parted the hair and brushed over the knot near her temple.

"Hmm," she said, "The swelling's not terrible, but you've got a nasty bruise." She fluffed Gracie's curls back into place and returned to her task of sorting through the new clothes. "That small bag over there has antibiotic ointment and more waterproof bandages. Jacob says you can take off the current dressing on your leg after you shower today and replace it."

"Annalise?"

She looked up with a winsome smile. "What?"

"Who are you?"

The beautiful woman with the waterfall of raven-black hair smacked her head and groaned. "Shoot. I'm always getting ahead of myself. I'm Gareth and Jacob's cousin, Annalise Wolff. The baby of the crew. Which is no picnic, let me tell you. Especially since I'm the only girl."

"You live here, too?"

"Well, not yet. But sometime soon. I'm only here for a quick visit with my dad and Uncle Vic. It was a good thing, though. Can you imagine a man trying to supply a woman with a new wardrobe? Lord knows what they would have chosen."

Gracie bent and picked up an item that still had a price tag attached. "A swimsuit? Really? Not entirely necessary, is it?"

The tall slender woman's eyes widened. "Gareth hasn't showed you yet?"

"Showed me what?"

"The indoor pool."

"Um, no. I haven't exactly been offered the guided tour. He doesn't want me here, you know."

"But you *are* here," Annalise said with a grin. "And it's about time someone bearded the grizzly old bear in his den. Gareth is a wonderful man, but he's let the past trip him up. His hermit ways aren't healthy."

"What about the past?"

Suddenly the other woman looked abashed. "It's not my place to say. I babble too much. Gareth can tell you what he wants you to know. C'mon," she said brightly. "Let's go to your room and try on all this booty."

Gracie participated more out of curiosity than from any urgent desire to play dress-up. Annalise fascinated her. She could be a runway model or a movie star. Gracie envied her the boundless confidence that radiated from her in almost physical waves.

What was Gracie's personality like? Here on the mountain, she felt wary, anxious and confused. But amnesia would probably have that effect on anyone. Maybe in *real* life Gracie was as self-possessed as Annalise. On the other hand, Gracie had a hunch that being wealthy and beautiful was the key. For someone like Annalise, the world was ready for the taking.

Gracie drew the line at modeling the wildly lavish lingerie. Petal-soft silk, handmade lace, confections of mauve, blush-pink and palest cream. It was the stuff of fantasy. But apparently Gracie was fairly modest when it came to exposing herself, even to another female.

At long last, Annalise glanced at her watch and screeched. "Lord have mercy. I'm going to miss my flight if I don't get crackin'. Daddy always wants me to use the private jet, but it's so damn pretentious. And do you have any idea how hard it is for a man to see the real you when he finds out about the seven-figure portfolio?"

"I can only imagine." Gracie's tone was wry. Annalise's artless comments weren't boastful. Her stream of consciousness conversation wasn't as practiced as that.

At the front door, Gracie put a hand on her benefactor's slim arm. "Thank you," she said simply. "I won't see you again, but I'm very grateful."

Annalise grabbed her in an enthusiastic embrace and

kissed her cheek. "Never say never. Remember…don't let Gareth bully you. And as for the shopping spree… the pleasure was all mine."

Chapter 4

With Annalise gone, the oppressive quiet settled over the house again. Gracie wanted to explore, but the possibility of being caught snooping deterred her. Instead she escaped outdoors, relishing the spring sunshine. It was a perfect day…the sky robin's-egg blue dotted with cotton-ball clouds, the sun warm but mild.

Her fingers itched for a paintbrush, wanting to capture the simplicity and lushness of burgeoning life. She stopped short, caught up in a memory…

I'm competent, Daddy, technically proficient, but I don't think I have that spark to take me to the next level. That's why I want so badly to be the gallery manager. I would be good at it, you know I would…

The snippet of conversation faded, and she clenched her fists in frustration. So she was an artist? But maybe not a very good one…and if that was true, what was the connection with her trip to Wolff Mountain?

Nothing. Nothing else materialized, no matter how hard she tried. And without something more concrete to go on, Gareth wasn't likely to be appeased by her efforts.

With a hiccuped breath, she fought back a sob. Patience. She would have patience if it killed her. She walked down the driveway, away from the copse of trees sheltering the house, and glanced upward. What she saw drew a gasp of admiration. The house at the top of the mountain defied description. It was part palace, part fortress, an amalgam of Cinderella's castle and George Vanderbilt's sprawling mansion in Asheville, North Carolina.

She stopped dead, this time seeing a vision of herself during a visit to the Biltmore House. The clarity of the memory sent a surge of hope rushing through her veins. She'd been wearing a red sundress. And she was laughing, happy. Someone stood beside her. Who was it?

Her head ached from the effort to concentrate. Moments later, the scene in her brain shimmered and faded. Tears of frustration wet her cheeks. The knowledge was so close, so damn close.

She took a deep breath and turned around to stare at Gareth's house. Yesterday she had stood on that porch. Had conversed with him. Why?

What had happened right before she fell? Was her mission in coming here sinister or innocent or somewhere in between?

No answers came her way. As hard as she tried, the earliest memory she was able to conjure up was waking in Gareth's bed. Now, in the light of day, feeling a hundred times better than she had twenty-four hours before, the knowledge that Gareth had cared for her in the moments after her accident gave her an odd feeling in the pit of her stomach.

She was sexually attracted to him. That much was clear. Even though she knew his Good Samaritan efforts were performed grudgingly. Despite his attitude, she had to be grateful that he hadn't called the police to cart her off the property.

She had trespassed. Knowingly. And in doing so, had paid a hefty price. A brain that was *tabula rasa*... the clean slate. Even if Gareth found her at all appealing, he would never act on that connection. Because she had broken the rules of polite society. She had invaded his privacy.

With a sigh, she headed back toward the house. Gareth was working. Where? Why? The man was a freaking millionaire. Joint heir to what appeared to be a sizable fortune. By all rights, he should be cruising on the Riviera. Playing the roulette wheel in Monte Carlo.

The image of taciturn Gareth Wolff as a jet-set playboy didn't quite come into focus. Some rich men enjoyed spreading their wealth around, flaunting their abundance. She had a hunch that the fiercely private Gareth would just as soon not be around people at all.

She wandered back toward the garage, stopping to stand on tiptoe and peer in the windows. Every pane of glass was spotless. She saw the Jeep, along with four other vehicles—a vintage Harley-Davidson motorcycle, a classic black Mercedes sedan, a steel-gray delivery van, and a small electric car.

The odd assortment intrigued her. Nothing about Gareth Wolff was easy to pin down.

She walked around the rear of the garage, and there, at the back of a large clearing, stood a third building. The exterior was fashioned to match the house and the garage. But this structure was smaller. A stone chimney, similar to the three on top of Gareth's house, emitted a curl of smoke. Feeling more like Goldilocks than she cared to admit, Gracie gave into the temptation to explore.

Instead of a traditional front door, the side of the building closest to Gracie was bisected by double garage doors, one of which was ajar. Feeling like the interloper she was, Gracie peeked inside.

Gareth stood opposite her, his big hands moving a scrap of sandpaper back and forth across an expanse of wood. He worked intently, all his focus on the project at hand.

The interior of the building was comprised of a single large room, partitioned here and there, but fully open to view. One quadrant stored lengths of lumber, another held shelves of small figures that appeared to be birds and animals. A large vat of some kind of liquid-soaked strips of wood. Other tables were laden with myriad hand tools.

The air smelled pleasantly of raw wood and tangy smoke from the open fireplace. An enormous skylight shed golden rays onto the floor below, catching dancing motes of dust along the way. Piled curls of wood shavings littered the floor at Gareth's feet.

Though she knew it was unwise, she moved forward into his line of sight. His head jerked up, and he stared at her, unsmiling.

She tucked her hands behind her back. "I take it this is your *work*?"

He put down the sandpaper and wiped his hands on his jeans. As he stepped from behind the workbench, she saw that the old, faded denim had worn in some very interesting places, emphasizing his masculinity in a throat-drying way.

"Did you eat?"

She nodded.

"And Annalise found you?"

A second nod.

"Do you remember anything?"

She swallowed hard. "No." Nothing concrete.

When he grimaced, she tried to squash an unreasonable feeling of guilt. He couldn't be any more frustrated than she was about her situation. "Sorry," she added, wondering why it was that women always seemed to feel the need to apologize and men seldom did.

He leaned against one of the rough-hewn posts that supported the vaulted ceiling, his hands in his pockets. The plain white T-shirt he wore was as sexy as any tux, and she had a gut feeling that he could wear either with ease.

As he surveyed her from head to toe, he frowned. "Why haven't you changed?"

"Is there a dress code?" Maybe she was a smart-ass in her previous life.

Finally…a small smile from the man with the stone face. "I thought you'd be eager to get out of those clothes."

Her stomach plunged at his suggestive words, but her brain wrestled with her libido. "I'll change later. Didn't seem to make sense to get all cleaned up when I was coming outside to explore. It's a beautiful day."

He nodded abruptly. "Glad you feel up to getting around. Does your head still hurt?"

"A little. I only took one pain pill. Didn't want to sleep the day away."

The conversation stalled. She worked her way closer. "What are you making?"

He paused, as if considering whether or not to answer. Then he shrugged. "A cradle."

"For someone in your family?"

"No."

Sheesh. It was like squeezing a stone to get water. "Then who?"

He rubbed a hand across the back of his neck, a gesture she was beginning to associate with his response to her. "A member of the British royal family."

She gaped. "Seriously?"

He cracked a smile, a small one, but definitely a tiny grin. "Seriously."

"Tell me. Spill the details."

He shook his head, his eyes dancing with humor. "If I told you, I'd have to kill you. That information is on a strictly need-to-know basis."

She pursed her lips, wondering why she could remember things she'd read in line at the grocery store while scanning the front page of a gossip rag, but not be able to visualize her own home. Rather than dwell on that unsettling fact, she put two and two together.

"Ohmigosh," she cried. "Are they pregnant? Is it—"

He put a hand over her mouth. "Uh, uh, uh… No questions. My lips are sealed."

They were so close together she could smell the soap he'd used in the shower…and the not unpleasant odor of healthy male sweat. For some weird reason, her tongue wanted to slip out and tease his slightly callused fingers. His eyes darkened and she could swear he was reading her mind at that very moment.

She gulped and backed up a step. A more lighthearted Gareth was definitely dangerous. "Does your improved mood mean that you believe me…about not remembering, I mean?"

His hand fell away. "I'll admit that deliberately falling to substantiate a claim of amnesia seems a bit far-fetched. I'm willing to give you the benefit of the doubt. For the moment, at least." His dark eyes seemed to see inside her soul.

She pretended to examine his workshop in order to give her ragged breathing time to return to a more normal cadence. "You must enjoy all this…the peace, the creativity." Her voice rasped at the end when she swallowed hard, caught suddenly by a memory of her own hands spreading paint across a canvas. Watercolors, maybe? The image left her.

He nodded, watching her with the intensity of a hawk stalking prey. "It keeps me off the streets," he deadpanned, seemingly relaxed.

But she had the notion that he was tense beneath his deliberately casual demeanor. She picked up a bottle of linseed oil and rubbed the label. "Why do you do it? Certainly not for the money."

"That's where you're wrong, Gracie."

She turned to face him, frowning. "What? Do you have some weird need to prove yourself and not lean on the family money?"

"You've been reading too many novels." He chuckled. "I'm quite happy to enjoy my share of the Wolff family coffers."

"And by the way," she said, "what *is* the family business?"

"Railroads originally, back in the 1800s. We've diversified since then. Most of the Wolff ancestors were good at making money from money."

"And now?"

"We took a hit, like everyone…when the economy tanked. But my father and my uncle are shrewd businessmen. We have interests in shipping, manufacturing, even agriculture to some extent."

"But you make furniture."

He nodded. "Indeed."

She put a hand on the piece of walnut he'd been sanding. Already, the finish was smooth to the touch. "Indulge me," she said, wondering if she was being far too nosy. "How much does a cradle for a royal cost?"

He shrugged, an enigmatic smile teasing the corner of his mouth. "Seventy-five thousand dollars…give or take. Depends on the exchange rate on any given day."

"Seventy-five…" Her mouth hung open. She didn't know what she, Gracie, did for a living, but it was a good bet she didn't make half that amount in a year. She didn't know why she was so sure, but she was. Maybe because hearing him say the number out loud was shocking.

He took pity on her. "I have a charity that I created a long time ago. My furniture pieces are one of a kind… and for whatever reason some people are willing to shell out big bucks for them. So I make the furniture, cash the checks and put all the money to good use."

"What's your charity?"

His face closed up. "You wouldn't have heard of it." Any good humor he'd exhibited had evaporated. "I need to get back to work."

"Tell me what else you make," she coaxed. "And for whom."

He let out an exaggerated, aggrieved sigh. "An armoire for a Middle Eastern sheikh. Windsor chairs for a Boston heiress. A desk for a former president…"

"That's amazing," she said simply. "You must be phenomenally talented. Is this what you studied in school?"

His expression darkened. "I earned a law degree at my father's urging. But I found out pretty quickly that I wasn't cut out for litigation. To show my dad what a badass I was, I enlisted in the army and did some time in Afghanistan."

"He must have been proud."

"He was terrified," Gareth said flatly. "And I regretted my rebellion almost from the beginning. Thank God nothing happened to me. I think it would have killed him."

Gracie saw the moment Gareth left her and went to some dark place. His eyes looked out across the room, unseeing. She struggled to find a new topic, one that didn't make her host look as if tragedy hovered far too close. A framed eight-by-ten photograph caught her eye. "Who's that?" she asked, moving closer.

Gareth's lips tightened. "Laura Wolff. My mother."

Again, a wisp of remembrance teased her. But it was gone before she could process what it meant. Gracie noted the resemblance in coloring between the woman and her son, but Gareth's strong profile must come from his father. His mother's features were delicate. She had an upturned nose and laughing eyes. "Does she live in the big house on top of the hill?"

"She'd dead."

He was trying to shock her into shutting up. She realized that. But she was hungry for information, anything to fill up the gray void that was her brain. "I don't suppose you want to tell me what happened."

"No," he said, his voice and expression harsh. "It's none of your damned business."

"I get that," she said quietly. "But you have to understand that if I don't ask questions…if I don't try to piece together the world around me, I'm scared to death I'll never remember anything." Her chin wobbled, and she swallowed the embarrassing tears that ambushed her at odd moments. It was easy enough to distract herself for a few minutes, but the truth was, she was as lacking in self-knowledge as a newborn babe.

Gareth made a visible effort to pull himself out of whatever funk her volley of questions had put him in. And she saw genuine sympathy in his gaze.

He returned to his task, his big hands moving over the wood with a lover's caress. His eyes focused downward. "It's barely been twenty-four hours, Gracie. Give it time."

"How much time?" she asked, feeling frustrated at her impotence. "A day? A week? I should go home to Georgia. Familiar territory may be the only thing that jogs my memory."

He paused, looking up at her with reluctant compassion. "You need to stay for now. I can't in good conscience let you go home, because your father is gone. Until we get more information about you, or until a friend or relative comes forward to care for you, you're stuck with us."

"You could take me to a hotel in Savannah. I could explore the town like a tourist...see if anything pops."

"I'm not dumping you in an impersonal hotel all alone. And if you're honest, I doubt you really want me to."

She wrapped her arms around her waist, rocking back and forth on her heels. "My father didn't sound like a very nice man," she said slowly. "I'm embarrassed to say that, but it's true. And when I think about leaving here, it panics me...because I only have twenty-four hours of life in my data bank, and Wolff Mountain is all I know. Does that sound stupid?"

"Not stupid. But perhaps naive. You don't really know anything about this place...or at least not much. You've seen part of my house and some of Jacob's. But nothing here is likely to stimulate the return of your memory."

"Which is why I should leave," she said flatly, feeling a sharp ache in the pit of her stomach.

He abandoned his work and closed the gap between them. "I think you should relax."

"Easy for you to say."

His brief but striking smile returned. He brushed his thumb over her cheekbone, the fleeting caress as shocking as it was tantalizing. "Lucky for you, I'm always right."

Gracie's stomach plunged and her heart went haywire in her chest. She had no defenses against a Gareth who chose to be tender and teasing. Backing away slowly, she tried to smile. Did he notice the flush of color that heated her cheeks?

"I'll let you get back to work," she said hoarsely.

He nodded, his gaze hooded.

For several long heartbeats, they simply looked at each other.

And when it seemed as if something cataclysmic might shatter the tense silence, she fled.

Chapter 5

Gareth climbed the side of the mountain behind his workshop, pushing the pace, making his lungs labor. But he was unable to outrun the problem that waited below. And unfortunately, Gracie Darlington was potentially *more* than a problem. At last he stopped, bent forward with his hands on his knees and cursed.

Once before in his life, a beautiful, seemingly guile-free woman had used a strong physical attraction to persuade Gareth to trust her. Back then he had not been able to see past his own testosterone-fueled hunger to the calculating bitch she really was. The resultant debacle cost Gareth dearly.

During a dinner party at the family home, his girl-friend had stolen a priceless piece of art, a small-enough-to-hide-in-a-purse Manet worth a quarter of a million dollars. The painting was eventually recovered, but the damage was done. On top of the tragedy in Gareth's childhood, this betrayal closed him off for good. He became cynical, antisocial and mistrustful of strangers. And he liked it that way.

His father had chastised him harshly in the aftermath of the unfortunate incident. Gareth's resultant humiliation led to his reckless run-away-from-home stint in the army. In all fairness, he'd only been twenty-four at the time. And his lack of judgment eight years ago had taught him valuable lessons about human nature. But even now, feeling an undeniable response to sexy Gracie, Gareth was on his guard.

He wiped his mouth, staring sightlessly at the ground, feeling the soft cushion of moss beneath his feet, listening to the quiet gurgle of the nearby creek.

His mind wrestled with frustration, both mental and physical. He'd awakened before dawn, his erection rigid and painful. Dreams, dark and hot, tormented his subconscious. And Gracie walked in those dreams. Smiled. Beckoned.

All around him, the early-spring abundance mocked Gareth's barren bed. The forest teemed with life. Gareth knew it well…had played in these same woods as a boy. It was a landscape as familiar to him as the small silver scar on the back of his right hand. For eighteen years he had lived and learned and grown, protected by geography and his father's phalanx of security guards from the dangerous outside world.

He wondered if Jacob and Kieran had resented the isolation as much as he had. The siblings were close, but in the way of men they seldom articulated feelings.

Even as adults they catered to their father's and uncle's paranoia in many ways, though they had each outgrown the fears the older men had bred in them as boys. And now, bit by bit, the cousins were all coming home.

Was it integrity or foolishness?

A bee buzzed gently around Gareth's ear. He batted gently at the insect then stretched. Losing himself in the forest was no way for a man to deal with the conundrum of a woman he wanted. But Gareth felt at home here, as much as in the elegant but oddly empty house he'd built and furnished in the last eighteen months.

He'd come home from the army, not a broken man, but a man who understood that it was possible to be lonely in a crowd. No one really understood what his life had been like growing up. His buddies on the front line didn't really care. Every day there was about survival. And that was Gareth's goal now…survival.

The furniture creation had begun on a whim, an extension of his boyhood love of carving. But in the grip of creative passion, he had gradually begun healing and had found a purpose for his life on the mountain.

Gracie could so easily destroy his newfound peace.

He firmed his jaw, took one last look at the budding green of tree and bush and turned his back on the bucolic scene. As he strode back down the mountain, his long legs made quick work of the journey despite the lack of a marked path.

He paused on the knoll above his house. Below him, framed in the deliberate swath he'd cut in the treetops, lay the valley floor. It seemed almost dreamlike, a fairy-tale place of warm hay, newly minted corn sprouts and the muted, busy hum of tractors. Normal people lived in the valley. Families with mortgages and financial worries and homes filled with noisy offspring.

Some days Gareth envied them. He was no longer a carefree, barefoot lad with stained, ripped shorts playing amidst blackberry thickets and flopping belly-first to watch salamanders in the creek. That boy had never hesitated to grab the world by the tail.

Thank God he had his workshop. At least when he was there, he could concentrate on the grain of fine wood, could smooth his hands over sleek curves, searching for any imperfections, forcing the oak or cherry or cedar to his own design.

As Gareth tromped with noisy footsteps onto the porch of his hideaway, the heavy basset hound dozing peacefully by the door shuffled suddenly into a new position, tucked his big head onto his paws and sighed deeply. His floppy ears were mottled with sawdust. It was enough to make Gareth smile despite his discontent. But only for a moment.

He was a man. Lonely. Frustrated. Torn between caution and desire. His entire body ached with the need to bury himself between a woman's soft thighs, to touch her breasts and ride her to oblivion. And not just any woman. Gracie. God, he could feel the moment of climax in his imagination.

As he picked up his handsaw, a hard-won measure of peace calmed him. The steps of his craft were familiar. Whenever he worked at his lathe with a lover's concentration, all else faded away. In his head there was always a vision of the finished piece. A beautiful chair, a sleek modern table, a sturdy chest. He'd tramped these hills in weeks past, locating materials, dragging them home. The art came from his Irish roots, the business sense a maternal genetic gift of Yankee drive and intuition.

But this afternoon, even the familiar routines of cut and turn, sand and polish, were not enough. After an hour and a half, he tossed his tools aside with a growl of displeasure. Nearly butchering a lovely length of chestnut told him it was time to stop. He poured a cup of coffee, and carried his mug outside.

The dog, Fenton, had scarcely moved. Gareth finished his drink, set the mug on the floor and clenched his hands on the split-log railing, heedless of splinters or rough shards of bark. He worked with such realities every day. His hands were a workingman's hands, callused, strong, not at all pretty.

A stinging discomfort pierced his introspection, and he realized his hand was bleeding. He'd gripped the railing so tightly that one thin sliver of wood had pierced his thumb. Absently he removed the piece and sucked at the tiny oozing wound.

He glanced up at the sky, feeling the warmth of the sun on his face. It had been a long, cold winter. And because of Gracie's advent into his life, he was, for the first time in a long time, questioning his self-imposed social exile. His father had forgiven him a long time ago. But Gareth had not been able to let go of the past. So many mistakes. So much pain for those he loved.

Was Gracie an arousing, fascinating gift, or a Trojan horse?

No divine intervention appeared from the fluffy clouds that resembled frolicking lambs. No jolt of understanding filled him with purpose.

He dropped his head forward, pressing it against a post, inhaling and exhaling, feeling on the precipice of disaster. He acknowledged what he'd been fighting to ignore all morning. Change was on the way. He could feel it in his bones, the sinews of his flesh.

Something was in the wind. He felt it brush his skin, smelled it in the air, tasted its unfamiliarity.

And her name was Gracie…

* * *

Gracie woke from a nap to find Jacob Wolff loitering in the kitchen, drinking a beer and reading email on his BlackBerry. He glanced up with a smile. "You look much better. How do you feel?"

She poured herself a glass of water. "Pretty good. The headache's almost gone."

"But your memory?"

She wrinkled her nose. "Still blank."

He stood and smoothed a hand over the front of his crisp white shirt. With his expensive haircut and knife-pleated black slacks, his appearance couldn't have been more different than Gareth's. But Jacob, handsome and sophisticated though he was, didn't stir Gracie's pulse in the least.

"Can I ask you something?" she said abruptly.

Jacob finished his drink and set the bottle on the counter. "Of course."

"This house is immaculate…and the fridge and freezer are stocked with food. But there's no one here except for Gareth."

Jacob chuckled. "We call it the silent army." At her upraised eyebrow, he explained. "My father and uncle employ a significant number of people at the big house… everything from gardeners to housekeepers, chefs, mechanics. And my cousins and I have access to those services as we choose."

"But Gareth isn't fond of people."

"So my father has set up an elaborate system whereby the various service employees sneak down here and take care of things either when Gareth is out of town or is working in his shop."

"Well, that explains it," she said smiling. "I was beginning to think he was Superman."

"He is, in many ways. Never underestimate him, Gracie. He's been through a hell of a lot in his lifetime. And yes, he's a bit of a curmudgeon on the outside. But he feels things deeply. Perhaps too deeply for his own good."

"I asked him about his mother...your mother. He wouldn't speak of her."

"That doesn't surprise me." He motioned toward the den. "Do you mind if I give you a quick exam? For my own piece of mind?"

"Of course not."

They sat side by side on the sofa as Jacob took her pulse, checked her blood pressure and examined her head. "The knot is smaller," he murmured. He took out a penlight and held her chin steady.

Gracie blinked as the strong beam hit her pupil. "Will you tell me?" she asked quietly. "About your mother?"

Jacob used his thumb to hold open her other eyelid. "Why is it so important to you?"

"I want to understand Gareth. There was some reason I showed up here in the beginning. Something that had to do with him. My father knows, but he doesn't seem inclined to communicate with me, especially now that he's left the country. I'm scared that my motives were questionable. And I don't want Gareth to be angry when the truth comes out. I'll go home as soon as I can, but in the meantime, surely you see that the more I learn about him, the better chance I have of remembering why I came."

Jacob's expression was skeptical, and suddenly, the resemblance between the two brothers was more pronounced. "We don't talk about our family to outsiders," he said bluntly. "We've had our fill of sensational news stories and would-be novelists trying to benefit from our misfortune."

"I don't want to hurt Gareth...or anyone."

"But you don't know who you really are. You might be a reporter looking for a story. And as such, that means Gareth may be sharing his home with the enemy."

"Ouch," she said, wincing. "Isn't that a bit harsh?"

"You have no idea the things that have been written about the Wolff family over the years."

"I wouldn't do that. Please, Jacob. I'm floundering in this huge sea of nothingness. Toss me a life raft. I won't do anything with the information, I swear. I just want to know how your mother died."

His face grayed, his eyes dull. "I may as well tell you. It's nothing you couldn't find on the internet with a little digging." He paused and took a ragged breath. "She and my aunt were murdered. In the eighties, when we were all children. Gareth is the only one of us who was really old enough to remember them clearly. They were kidnapped, held for ransom and killed anyway... even when the money was paid. Is that what you wanted, Gracie? Well, now you know."

He stormed out of the room and out of the house, leaving her feeling sick. Thank God she hadn't pressed Gareth for details. Given the way the calm, friendly Jacob reacted in the telling of that horrible tale, Gareth would likely have exploded.

Her heart bled for him. What an unimaginable tragedy. One that affected two families. And clearly, the pain lingered even after twenty-plus years. No wonder the two old men gathered their young around them like broody mother hens. Their experience would have changed them irrevocably.

She jerked when Gareth's voice sounded behind her.

"Was that Jacob I saw leaving?"

"He came to check on me." She stood up, feeling as if guilt was inscribed on her face.

"And?"

Had he overheard part of the conversation? "And what?" she said, playing for time.

"Your head? Your leg?"

"Oh." She gave an inward sigh of relief. "He says I'm recovering very well."

"Would you like to swim?"

The odd segue wrinkled her forehead. "Um, yes…I suppose."

"I told Annalise to get you a suit. Can you change in ten minutes?"

"Of course."

She made it in eight. Gareth was standing in the kitchen wearing nothing but navy boxer-style swim trunks that clung to his body and left little to the imagination.

Her throat dried and her tongue felt clumsy in her mouth. She was suddenly stingingly aware that her swimsuit left her mostly naked, though for the moment she was veiled in a terry cover-up.

"This way," he said abruptly, leaving her to follow along in his wake.

The house was built into the side of the mountain, with several staircases leading to various levels. Gareth led them down and down until they passed through a set of glass doors and into a steamy, scented enclosure big enough to hold six or eight of her luxurious bedrooms.

The centerpiece of the room was an inviting pool, irregularly shaped to resemble a natural lake. All around the edge, tropical plants and flowers thrived in the misty air. Somewhere in the distance, soothing music played, with lots of flutes and Native American overtones.

The decking was cobblestone. Lounge chairs covered in batik-print fabric were scattered about.

At the far end of the pool, draped by thick palm fronds, flowed a waterfall, an actual waterfall.

Gareth tossed his towel on a seat. "What do you think?"

She scanned the whole area, quite sure her mouth was hanging open. "It's amazing. I've never seen anything like it."

"How would you know?"

She looked at him curiously, finally returning his smile when she realized that the taciturn Gareth Wolff was actually teasing her. "That's just mean," she said, her lips twisting in a wry grin.

"C'mon," he said abruptly. "Let's see if you know how to swim."

Fortunately for Gracie's peace of mind, Gareth dove in without ceremony and began doing laps. She walked around to the shallow end, preparing to shed her cover-up. When she thought Gareth wasn't watching, she took it off. The haute couture bikini in lime-green and saffron was as tiny as it was undoubtedly expensive.

She felt painfully exposed.

Chapter 6

Gareth almost swallowed his tongue when he got a first glance at Gracie in the next-to-nothing swimsuit Annalise had picked out. Gracie was slim, but sweetly curved in all the right places. Her pale, creamy skin befitted a natural redhead. Trying to disguise his avid interest, he watched her slip carefully into the pool.

She took a few steps before tentatively launching out in a creditable backstroke. Apparently he wouldn't have to play lifeguard. Too bad.

Her long legs kicked lazily. Her pert breasts rose above the water as she moved. Already, he was painfully hard, his erection taunting him with the knowledge that he'd not had a woman in his bed in recent memory.

Now Gracie was here…available…and he wanted her desperately, but could he trust the woman whose past was obscured?

After twenty minutes of punishing laps, he permitted himself to approach her. At arm's length, he took note of the way the shiny fabric clung to her like a second skin. The room was plenty warm, but Gracie's nipples thrust against the triangles of her bikini top.

He tried not to stare. "Would you like to try out the waterfall?" The hoarseness in his voice could be attributed to exertion.

She licked her lips, her eyes big. "Of course."

He took her hand, feeling her start of surprise. They moved against the water, walking deeper and deeper into the pool. When Gracie's feet left the bottom, she protested.

"It's too deep. I can't touch."

He put his hands on her narrow waist, imagining those fabulous legs winding around him. "Get on my back," he said.

They eyed each other from a distance of eighteen inches. He could see her chest rise and fall with each breath…could count the water droplets clinging to her eyelashes.

Slowly, clenching his hand tightly, she moved around until she could rest her hands on his shoulders.

"You can put your legs around me," he said.

"This is fine."

Her prim response made him grin.

"Hang on." He forged into deeper water until the waterfall was directly in front of them. The formation looked amazingly natural. The pool architect had constructed a pile of rocks that was home to colorful orchids and tiny, jewel-toned parakeets.

Gareth pulled Gracie around to stand beside him on the step hidden beneath the water. "You okay on your own now?"

She found her footing and nodded, her face turned up to the spray. "Never better."

Her delighted laughter as the cascading water drenched both of them tightened something in his gut. He wanted to take her here…in this wild setting. The hunger was fierce and relentless. He had to look away from her radiant face to catch his breath.

No matter how much he tried to remind himself that he'd been a fool for a woman once before, he couldn't shake the notion that Gracie was his. Even without her memory, there was a sweetness about her…a strength and a zest for life. She had shown remarkable courage in a difficult situation.

He moved them just out of the main torrent and touched her hand. "It's not my habit to ask, but you've had a rough two days."

Her smile faded to confusion. "Ask what?"

"May I kiss you?"

The shock on her face was unmistakable. But moments later, he saw the dawn of something else. Interest. Arousal. Caution.

He understood the caution. Hell, this was probably the stupidest idea he'd had in a while. But he couldn't help himself. "Gracie?"

A long, pregnant pause ensued. Just when he thought she was going to shut him down, she lifted her arms. "Okay."

He knew there was a good chance she was experimenting with him, hoping something might jog her memory. According to her father, she had no husband or boyfriend. But even still…

When their lips touched, her arms linked behind his neck, all rational thought evaporating in the cloud of steam that engulfed them. The pool at this end was heated by underwater jets, more like a hot tub in temperature. But Gareth was pretty sure he and Gracie would have generated steam even in an ice bath.

Her mouth was hesitant beneath his, her lips soft and curious. He tried to be gentle. He really did. But the taste of her intoxicated him. Their bodies melded, skin to skin. His tongue slid between her teeth, probing gently, dueling with hers.

She wasn't exactly embracing him. Her hands rested on his shoulders as if she wasn't sure if she would pull him closer or push him away. He kissed her firmly, without apology. He had asked. She had answered. He had nothing to feel guilty about. But he did.

Gracie Darlington didn't know anything about her past. And Gareth didn't know anything about her.

Heaving a deep breath, acknowledging the tremor in his own limbs, he broke the connection and stepped back as much as the step beneath his feet would allow.

Gracie stared at him glassy-eyed. "Wow."

His broken chuckle surprised even him. "Yeah."

"I think I'm in over my head," she said softly. "Not such a good swimmer, after all."

"Can you make it to the side of the pool?"

"You think you made me weak in the knees?" Her teasing smile relaxed a bit of the tension in his gut. "Braggart."

He shifted restlessly. "I'm going to do some more laps. Can you find your way back through the house?"

She nodded slowly, her gaze locked on his. "Thanks for the swim."

Gracie climbed out of the pool, aware that Gareth's gaze tracked her every motion. Though he moved through the water with the ease and speed of an Olympic swimmer, she knew he had his eyes on her.

She toweled off and then shrugged into the cover-up, glad to use it as armor. With one last wistful glance at the man in the pool, she wandered back to her bedroom, taking note of the decor and design of the house along the way. Every inch of Gareth's home was stunningly beautiful. Yet he lived here all alone, like a wounded beast hiding from the world.

After a quick shower, she dried her hair and surveyed her new clothing. Annalise had been kind enough to include basic makeup, so Gracie brushed on some eye shadow, darkened her lashes with mascara and covered her lips in pink gloss.

Feeling a bit too much like Cinderella, she picked out a cherry-red sundress with white appliquéd flowers at the hem and slipped it on. The woman in the mirror looked relaxed and happy…as long as no one looked too closely at the lost expression in her eyes.

Gracie gnawed her lip with indecision. What exactly was she supposed to do with herself for the next few hours? Perhaps it wouldn't hurt to browse through Gareth's extensive collection of books and DVDs. Who knew what small detail might tug at a memory?

But when she made her way back to the enormous den/living room, the low table in front of the entertainment center had been set with china and silver and an assortment of mouthwatering dishes.

Gareth stood by the fireplace, staring into the flames. He had changed as well. His dark slacks and cream Irish fisherman's sweater suited his wild masculinity.

She paused on the threshold. "Something smells wonderful."

As he crossed the room to stand beside her, she realized that her words had a dual meaning. Gareth smelled like the crisp, clean fragrance of his shower soap, a combination of lime and fresh evergreen. Though he was covered from neck to toe, she had a vivid memory of what that large, hard body looked like.

Perhaps he would attribute her flushed cheeks to the warmth from the fire.

He held out a hand. "Will you eat with me?"

She was flustered to realize that he meant for them to sit on the floor. That seemed altogether too intimate. Hesitating only a moment, she slipped out of her crimson sandals and situated herself on a comfy, velvet-covered pillow. Gareth joined her at the opposite corner of the table.

They ate in silence for several minutes. Beef tenderloin…asparagus with hollandaise sauce and fluffy mashed potatoes.

Gracie sighed, swallowing a bite of heaven on a fork. "My potatoes never turn out this well." She froze, fork in the air. "I remember," she said, her heart thumping. "My kitchen is yellow and white. I think I'm a decent cook."

Gareth had quit eating as well, his gaze intense. "What else?" he asked. "Take your time. Don't stress."

She closed her eyes, reaching with all her might for what was just on the other side of a frustrating curtain. Bit by bit a scene materialized in her head. "I was standing beside the stove, laughing. Another woman was there."

"Tell me about her."

Try as she might, the face wouldn't come into focus. She put down her fork, the food a hard knot in her stomach. "I don't understand," she whispered. "Why won't it come back?"

"The brain's a funny thing," Gareth said, his matter-of-fact tone soothing her nerves. "It will come when it comes."

"I've wondered about hypnosis," she said, doodling her fork in burgundy sauce. "I need to do *something*."

Gareth snorted. "I hardly think hypnosis qualifies as *something*...unless of course you're hoping to find out that you were a Persian princess in a past life."

"You're so open-minded," she mocked. "How do you know it wouldn't work? Maybe I should talk to Jacob about it."

"If Jacob thought hypnosis would solve your problem, I assure you he'd have already mentioned it. My brother is brilliant when it comes to the human body. I told you to quit worrying about it." He uncovered the last dish. "Eat some cherry pie. Pie helps everything."

"Says the man who probably never gains an ounce."

His gaze lashed her with heat. "You're perfect," he said bluntly. "Eat the damned pie."

She chewed and swallowed, barely tasting the scrumptious dessert. Gareth exhibited all the signs of a man in the throes of sexual frustration. And she was right there with him. The temperature in the room was rising ten degrees at a time...

He shoved back from their makeshift table and stretched out his legs, ankles crossed, hands behind his head. "I have an idea," he said. "I need to make a quick trip to D.C. in a couple of days. You could come with me."

"Why?" She frowned.

"I'm not going to leave you here unattended."

"You still don't trust me."

He shrugged. "I trust what I know of you. But that's not much, is it?"

"Why are you going to D.C.?"

"Some hotshot senator purchased an enormous gun cabinet from me. He wants to show off his new chest—and the creator—at a fancy-ass party in Georgetown."

"I'm shocked that you would agree."

"I didn't want to do it, so I told him that a personal appearance would mean another hundred grand for my charity. I never dreamed he would take me up on it."

She laughed out loud at the look of chagrin on his face. "Poor Gareth. It must seem like a fate worse than death."

"It would be a hell of a lot more enjoyable if you go with me."

"So I'm just a warm body to keep you from getting bored?"

The deliberate flirting was a skill that surprised her.

Gareth's eyes narrowed, reading the underlying message. "Be careful, Gracie. Don't start something you can't finish."

A huge yawn caught her off guard. "Sorry," she said, blushing.

He stood and pulled her to her feet. "Say good-night, Gracie."

She tilted her head, studying his face. "That's funny. I think my father used to say that to me."

He brushed a kiss across her cheek, fleeting, tantalizing. "Get some rest. We'll talk about the trip in the morning."

She put a hand to his cheek. "Are you afraid of me?" she whispered teasingly, deliberately moving closer so their bodies touched.

His head bent and he covered her mouth with his. The kiss shook her to the bone. It mixed raw carnality and seeking hunger with a tenderness that took the starch out of her knees. Everywhere she was soft, he was hard. But it was over almost before it began.

Disappointment flooded her chest as she let him scoot her down the hall. "I could help with the dishes."

"Go to bed. And stay there."

She had the distinct impression that he was trying to keep the two of them from doing something ill-advised. Her common sense lauded his fortitude, but deep inside, she wouldn't have minded if he had dragged her down to the lavish carpeting and had his way with her.

Her beautiful bedroom was beginning to feel like a prison. She changed into a silky negligee that felt naughty against her bare skin, and brushed her teeth. Jacob had said it was okay to take a pill before bedtime, so she filled a tumbler with water and washed one down. The medication worked its magic, and she fell into a deep, exhausted slumber.

Chapter 7

Gareth awoke at the first scream. By the second, he was down the hall and into her room. She had left a light on in the bathroom, so he was immediately able to see, even in the dimly illumined bedroom, that Gracie was tangled in the covers, writhing as if she were fighting something or someone.

He sat down beside her, tugging back the blankets.

Before he could do more than that, she cried out, *"No!"*

The sheer terror in that one syllable made the hair stand up on his arms. She was sobbing, struggling with him as he tried to wake her. "You're okay, Gracie. Wake up. You're okay."

He repeated it over and over, his voice low but firm as he coaxed her out of her deep, tormented sleep. Finally, thank God, she took a shuddering breath and opened her eyes. Her pupils were dilated, and her entire body shook with tremors. When he was sure she was aware of her surroundings, he gathered her into his arms, warming her with his body heat.

"Shh," he said softly. "Everything's all right. It was a dream." He stroked her hair, twining a finger in a curl and rubbing the base of her skull. "Nothing can hurt you."

She wrapped her arms around his waist and buried her face in his chest. Only then did he realize what she was wearing. The feel of silk beneath his hand made his mouth go dry. *Damn Annalise.* His romantically minded cousin had tried to coax him out of his cave on many occasions—in the old days throwing her sorority sisters at him and more recently her coworkers.

He didn't need a woman to be happy. Sex...well, that was another story. But a man could take matters into his own hands if need be. Until Gareth found a woman he could trust, he wasn't interested in female companionship.

Liar. His libido jumped into the conversation, pointing out how soft Gracie was, how the smell of her hair made Gareth hard, even without her barely covered breasts mashed up against him. She had thrust herself into his life without compunction. He ought to be angry as hell. By all rights, he should send her packing.

But he wanted to keep her...just for a little while. She made his big house seem more like a home. Light and life shadowed her every step. And if she had any nefarious purpose in coming to Wolff Mountain, he'd yet to see any sign of it.

Finally she eased back, shoving the hair from her face with an unsteady hand. "Turn on the lamp," she pleaded, the words husky and quiet.

He did as she asked, relieved that the low-wattage

bulb cast little more than a rosy circle of light. "Do you want to tell me about it?" he asked, still holding her with one arm.

Her lower lip trembled until she bit down on it and took a deep breath. "I was running in the dark. Something was after me. I knew if I could find my way home, I'd be safe. But every time I opened a door, nothing was there."

He pulled her closer again, his chin on her head, his fingers twined with hers. "I don't think we have to look too far to figure that one out. You're trying so damn hard, Gracie. You know it doesn't happen by sheer force of will. God knows if it did, you would already remember. I've never seen anyone so determined to make something happen. But Jacob said it may come in bits and pieces so gradually it will slip up on you. Or some little thing may trigger a release that gives it back to you all at once. You can't do this to yourself."

"I'm so scared that you'll hate me when I find out why I came." The words tumbled out—bald, unadorned— her expression similarly stark.

Gareth acknowledged the truth of her statement in his brain, but his body shied away from the unpalatable possibility that Gracie was as sleazy a person as her father. She couldn't be. Not when she felt so damned perfect in his embrace. "You'll be going home in a few days. Until then, you need to focus on something else." And in the meantime he wouldn't tell her that investigators were even now checking out the truth about Edward Darlington.

She gave a hiccupping sob and laughed unsteadily. "Easy for you to say. You're not the one with a major brain malfunction." She winced. "Were you sleeping?"

"It's 2:00 a.m.," he muttered. "Yes, I was sleeping." And having better dreams than hers.

She shivered. He ran his hands up and down her arms, feeling the gooseflesh. "Will you be okay now?"

She looked up at him…vulnerable, lost. "No. Will you stay? Please."

Gracie heard the words come out of her mouth and felt her cheeks flame with embarrassment. Could she be any more needy? She was clinging to Gareth like a port in a storm. The fact that she wasn't imagining the attraction between them didn't excuse her artless invitation.

Was she the kind of woman who slept with a man on a whim? Or had losing her memory simply stripped away her inhibitions?

Gareth went slack-jawed for a split second before his expression closed up, leaving no clue as to his emotions. He couldn't hide the erection that pulsed between them, but then again, he wasn't jumping at her offer.

And it *was* an offer. She knew it, and he knew it.

He stood up and ran his hands through his hair. "I can sit in that chair until you fall back asleep."

"But I could still have another nightmare after you leave," she pointed out.

"I haven't had sex with a woman in eleven months," he said flatly, clearly trying to shock her.

"Why?"

Her question seemed to perplex him. "Lots of reasons. I don't bring women here so I have to go somewhere and seek it out. Do the dance. Stay at her place. It's not worth it anymore."

"I see. But I didn't ask for sex."

His eyes flashed. "Don't be coy. We both know where this is headed. A man would have to be a real bastard to take advantage of a woman in your situation. And if I stay in this room with you—all night—you won't be sleeping."

If she had been standing, her knees would have buckled at his declaration of intent. He was bare from the waist up, his broad chest rippled with muscle. A pair of cotton pajama pants hung low on his hips, but she had a sneaking suspicion that he had donned those on her behalf.

"What if I take advantage of *you*?" she asked quietly. "You're an amazing man, Gareth Wolff. Very soon I'll be gone. Can you blame me for wanting to have you in my bed?"

The fabric at his groin pulsed visibly. His jaw was granite. "I won't make you any heartfelt promises. If you finally remember why you came, it won't make any difference. I can't give you softness and romance. I'm not that guy. This will be nothing more than two people scratching an itch…satisfying their curiosity."

His words hurt, though they were no more than she had expected. If she had some far-fetched idea that she could change this man, she was deluding herself. He'd been molded by tragedy, shaped by a childhood of fear and secrecy. He was as inflexible as the wood he crafted into beautiful objects.

He was fair and considerate. And he had been remarkably generous in letting her stay. But Gareth Wolff was not the kind of guy to be manipulated by a pretty face or a night of raw, make-me-forget sex.

She rose up on her knees, her body trembling in anticipation now, rather than fear. "I understand. I accept your terms." She held out a hand. "And I still want you."

The night, already still and silent, seemed to freeze in time. Gareth could have been a statue were it not for the quick up-and-down bob of his Adam's apple. His entire body was rigid. His hands clenched at his hips. For one long, aching minute, she thought she had lost.

And then he exhaled visibly, his gaze stormy. "I'll be right back."

He was true to his word, returning in mere seconds with a handful of plastic packets that he tossed on the bedside table. She could feel her heart beating in her ears as he shed his pants without modesty and put a knee on the mattress.

His body was magnificent, beautifully sculpted…all the way from his broad shoulders, to his trim waist, to that most masculine part of him that thrust upward in either invitation or intent, or both.

She was still on her knees, and he matched her pose. "Take it off," he said gruffly. "Knowing Annalise, that damn bit of sin and silk probably cost a fortune."

Gracie lifted her arms as he pulled the wisp of fabric over her head, leaving her clad in nothing but a matching scrap of lace at the hips. His chest heaved, one deep breath, before he put his hands on her waist. His gaze was hooded, his cheekbones slashed with a flush of red.

Face to face and chest to chest, their lips met. Tentative nips and tastes segued into harder, longer, drugging kisses. He was masterful, in control, clearly experienced in the ways of pleasing a woman. Gracie gasped, buffeted by waves of longing, dragged under by a hunger so strong she felt light-headed.

Beneath her questing hands, his skin was hot to the touch…as if his big body was a furnace ready to consume her. He tasted of mint and coffee, and pressed against him, she could feel the thunder of his heartbeat. He took her down to the mattress, spreading her thighs and settling between them.

She tensed. "I don't know how to please you…what you want."

He toyed with the band of lace that rode high on her thigh. "Time enough for that later," he said, his words guttural. "The important question at the moment is do I know how to please you?"

Without ceremony or warning, he scooted down in the bed and used his hands to spread her legs even wider. She shoved at his shoulders. "I don't think so…"

He glanced up at her, a glint of amusement in his dark eyes. "Oh, but I do…"

When he removed her panties and tasted her center, her hips came off the bed. The sensation was indescribable, and for a split second, she acknowledged the certainty that she had never allowed any man this liberty.

But Gareth wasn't waiting for approval. He set about destroying her completely with long, slow passes of his tongue. She was embarrassingly damp, even before he began his assault. Soon, her body shuddered wildly, lost to sensation. She grabbed handfuls of his soft, thick hair and clung helplessly while Gareth sent her rocketing to a climax so intense, she saw stars and fell softly back to earth.

Though she was scarcely aware of it, he moved up in the bed and gathered her in his arms. She wanted to weep at the beauty of what he made her feel. But she couldn't. Tears were for sadness, and with Gareth she was happy, perhaps happier than she had ever been in her life.

He stroked her hair, her back, the curve of her bottom. When she shivered, he covered them both with the comforter. His voice was a low, sexy rumble. "You're beautiful," he said softly. "And I love the way you come for me."

"Stop," she groaned, burying her face in his shoulder. "I'm not used to *talking* about it."

He kissed her brow. "So you want me to just *do* it. Okay, Gracie. I can oblige."

"That's not what I—"

Her inarticulate protest was lost as he made quick work of donning a condom and then entered her with a forceful thrust. Her breath caught in her throat. He was big and powerfully aroused. Her body struggled to accept him.

He stilled, clearly feeling the same incredible connection. "You okay, little Gracie?"

She nodded, mute.

Slowly, so slowly she wanted to beg him to hurry, he began to move in her. Her legs wrapped around his waist, deepening the penetration. She heard him curse.

He withdrew and thrust again, sliding in and out with a lazy rhythm that stoked the fires of a hunger she had thought quenched. But rapidly, her body responded again, eager for a repeat of the singeing pleasure only he could give.

Their skin slicked with sweat. Breathing labored. He reared up suddenly and looked down at her. "Promise me you won't regret this. Tell me Jacob won't have my hide." He was panting, but his eyes sparked with mischief.

She gazed at him sleepily, feeling a twinge in the vicinity of her heart. He was too damned gorgeous for his own good. "No promises," she dared to taunt. "Remember?"

His eyes narrowed. "Witch. If that's the way you want to play it…" He manacled her wrists in a gentle grip and held them over her head. "Beg me," he growled.

Her eyes widened. "For what?" Her tongue moistened her lips as her heart thudded wildly.

"You know damned well." He flexed his hips. "You may not remember the past, but I'll make sure you remember this, Gracie Darlington."

His head came down and his mouth found hers.

In between strangled gasps, she obeyed. "Please, Gareth. Make love to me." Even as she said the words, her heart wept. Gareth didn't love her...he didn't even know her. The only reason he was in her bed was to satisfy a need.

The delicious friction as his body stroked into hers brought her to the edge again. She felt him stretch her almost painfully as he gave a hoarse shout, and then she went with him, falling, falling into a blissful, dizzying tumble.

Gareth rolled to his back, lungs burning, eyes gritty. Good God. What had he done?

Gracie lay quietly against his side, one of her slender arms curled across his chest and one of her legs tucked between his. He tried for humor. "Not bad for a first go..."

Her lag in response time told him she was as off balance as he was. She moved restlessly. "Any man can impress an amnesiac." The tart bite in her joking words bemused him. Gracie Darlington was no pushover. Even hampered as she was by her hopefully temporary condition, she seemed determined to hold her own with him. He nuzzled her hair. "Come to Washington with me. The cherry blossoms are in bloom."

"I don't have anything to wear. Annalise outfitted me with casual clothes, but nothing that would work for a fancy dinner."

"She can shop anywhere. I'll call her in the morning and get her to send what you need directly to the hotel. It will be fun. You can forget about your problem and we'll paint the town red."

"My problem?" She shook her head. "It's a little more than a problem. I have no life, Gareth."

"Potayto…potahto…"

"You're such a compassionate man."

"It's one of my best qualities." He pulled her on top of him and arranged her like a doll, ready for action, but not quite there yet.

She blew a curl out of her eye. "Can I ask you something?"

He tensed, and then forced himself to relax. "I suppose." It was difficult to deny a woman anything when she was fulfilling every fantasy he'd had in recent memory.

"Why do you wear your hair so long?"

Not what he expected…not at all. "You don't like it?"

"On you, it's sexy and gorgeous and you know it." She leaned forward to winnow the fingers of one hand across his scalp, coincidentally squishing her small but lovely breasts against his chest as she moved. "But you and Jacob are so different. The family resemblance is striking. So I'm guessing there's a reason he looks like a rich doctor and you—not so much."

Gareth chuckled. She had a point. "You remember I told you I enlisted in the military for less than stellar reasons?"

"To rebel against your dad?"

"Yeah, but the army was good for me. Turned me from a boy into a man, you know the cliché. I was a damned good soldier. In almost every way. But conformity is not my strong suit. I swore to myself that when I got out, I'd never again have a buzz cut."

"And there's no middle ground?"

"I get it cut occasionally."

"For D.C.?"

He shook his head, running his palms over her soft, perfect ass. "I'll be playing a role for the senator. The untamed Wolff in a tuxedo. His party will be the talk of the season."

"That's pretty cynical."

"I'm a pretty cynical guy. People love a good story. And when they don't have one, they'll make one up."

She was silent for too long, her cheek resting over the steady bump of his heartbeat. "I'll have to go home after we return from D.C. My father will be back by then, surely. Will you go with me? Take me, I mean?"

"Yes. But you don't have to be afraid, Gracie. I'm guessing everything will come flooding back as soon as you're on home turf."

"And if it doesn't?"

"One day at a time." He reached out to grab protection. "You haven't answered me yet. Will you come with me? I'll take you to this great boutique hotel near the Capitol. A million thread count sheets. Pillows so soft you'll never want to get out of bed. Fresh flowers every day. A view of the Washington Monument…"

"Have you taken other women there?"

The note in her voice was hard to decipher. Nothing as simple as jealousy. If he hadn't known better, he'd say it was pained resignation. He shifted her off him long enough to sheath his eager erection. No amount of pillow talk had deflated it. "Does it matter?"

He lifted her again, fitting the head of his straining penis to the warm heart of her. She braced her hands on his chest, looking down at him. Her lips curved in a wry half smile. "Apparently not," she muttered.

"So you'll go with me?"

She nodded slowly, crying out as he joined them with one sharp upward thrust of his hips.

"Is that a yes?" He gritted his teeth and squeezed shut his eyes, trying desperately not to come like a green kid. Being inside Gracie was the closest he'd come in recent memory to peace. To sheer, God Almighty, too-good-to-be-true physical nirvana.

"Yes," she whispered. She sat up straight, lodging him to an incredible depth. Slowly, with all the confidence of a siren, she rode him to heaven and back.

His hands gripped her hips. "Slower," he pleaded. He didn't want this to end. Not ever. The desperation he felt might have alarmed him in a less fraught situation. As it was, he ignored the flashing lights in his brain, attributing them instead to mere frustration.

Gracie shuddered when he slid a finger over the spot where their bodies joined. He nudged the tiny swollen nerve center and she went rigid, clenching him with inner muscles in such a way that his eyes rolled back in his head, his climax hit him like a Mack truck, and they both fell, sated, into a messy tumble of arms and legs and ragged breathing.

Chapter 8

"Are you insane?"

Gareth winced at the incredulity in his brother's voice. They were seated in Jacob's large office with its picture window that looked out at the forest. Rain droplets drizzled down the wide single pane. "What can it hurt?" he asked calmly. "She's making herself crazy trying to remember. A trip to D.C. will give her a break. A change of pace. Fresh scenery."

"If this is about you not trusting her, I'll let her stay here with me until you get back."

"It's not that," Gareth protested. "Or not entirely."

"You can't take someone with amnesia and let them loose in an uncontrolled environment. Anything could happen. She has no self-protection, Gareth. You might as well let a toddler play in traffic."

"Isn't that overstating things a bit? C'mon, Jacob. She can handle ordinary daily tasks. She's impaired, not stupid." He shot to his feet and paced.

"You're deliberately misunderstanding me." Jacob's face, so like Gareth's own, creased with concern. "Gracie is terribly vulnerable right now, as anyone in her condition would be. She doesn't have a framework for making rational decisions. Emotionally she's a wreck, even if she hides it well."

Jacob's words pricked Gareth's conscience. He moved restlessly. "You're too late with your advice. We…talked last night. I invited her and she accepted."

"Good Lord. You've slept with her." Jacob rose to his feet, his hands-on-hip stance combative. "How could you? She's a woman in your care, under your protection. I've never known you to be so cavalier about an innocent."

Jacob knew him far too well for subterfuge. Gareth's instinctive urge to defend himself mingled with the sick certainty that Jacob was right on all fronts. "It just happened," he muttered.

Though in truth he'd been imagining sex with Gracie almost from the first instant he laid eyes on her. She made him feel emotions he'd thought long dead and buried. The warmth in her smile and the admiration he felt for her poignant fortitude thawed the ice castle to which he'd condemned himself. Even if her reasons for coming were unacceptable, Gareth still wanted her. At least for now.

Jacob still glared at him.

Gareth didn't care. "She had a bad dream. I comforted her."

"Shit, Gareth. That's the lamest excuse I've ever heard. You could have walked away. You *should* have walked away. You didn't have to screw her."

"It was her idea."

"And you went along with it like the saint you are."

"I tried to say no. She's very persuasive."

Jacob threw up his hands in disgust. "I give up. You've obviously lost your mind. But swear to God… if taking her on the road makes things worse don't expect me to mop up the pieces."

"You're a doctor. You took an oath to help people."

"But I never promised to cover for your sorry ass."

Gareth rubbed his neck. "She has to go home. After D.C. And she wants me to take her."

"Did you agree?"

"Yeah."

"You know she's scared."

"I get that. But there's still the matter of why she came in the first place. And what her father had to do with it."

Jacob shrugged. "Clearly she's not a threat. Even if she's a reporter, what kind of story could she write? You've never even taken her up to the house to meet Father. Is that intentional?"

"Of course it's intentional." Gareth joined his brother at the wide, plate-glass expanse that turned a dry medical office into an inviting arboretum. "He's not been feeling well. Her tenure here is extremely temporary. It seemed pointless to involve him."

"Where is she right now?"

"I left her sleeping. But I suppose it's getting late. I should go check on her."

"If she wants to go with you to Washington, it's her prerogative. But be damned careful, Gareth."

"I have it all under control. Don't worry."

Gracie awoke midmorning to memories of an incredible night. She would have chalked the heated visions up to wild dreams, were it not for the unmistakable dent in the pillow beside hers.

"Gareth?"

No answer. Feeling embarrassed and bashful, she slid out of bed and wrapped herself in the sheet, tiptoeing to the bathroom. She couldn't decide if she was relieved or disappointed that it was empty.

She shook her head as she climbed into the shower. It was practically lunchtime. No wonder Gareth hadn't lingered. He'd been considerate enough to let her catch up on her rest, but that didn't mean he'd waste a day watching her sleep. That image should have made her laugh, but instead, it inspired a wistful, haunting regret.

Last night she and Gareth had sex. And it was amazing. But in the light of day he was still a Wolff, and she was still an interloper with a murky agenda.

When she was dry and dressed in one of the cute outfits Annalise had provided—navy capri pants, a white sleeveless eyelet tunic, and red paisley slides—she pondered her options. Going with Gareth to Washington was fine, but after that, playtime was over. She had to get her life back in order. And clearly, doing so meant reconnecting with her father.

After a quick mini-meal of yogurt and cereal, she found her cell phone and turned it on. Three bars and a partial battery. That would work. With trepidation, she scrolled through her contacts and found the one marked "Daddy." Her heart beat madly as she hit Send.

"You have reached Edward Darlington, owner and operator of Darlington Gallery in Savannah, Georgia. I'm out of the country at the moment, and the gallery is closed. Hope to be back in my office next week. Please leave a message. Oh, yes…and if this is Gracie, don't give up, baby girl. Make it happen. Make me proud."

Beeeeeppppp...

Gracie stared at her phone with a scowl of frustration. Damn it. What in the heck was going on? Why had her father sent her to confront a Wolff? And Gareth Wolff in particular?

Make it happen. What did that mean? Had she come willingly? Or been coerced...? Closing her eyes, she replayed the message and concentrated on her father's voice. She caught snatches of conversation, whispered fragments of memory. Pleasing her father. She wanted to please him. But why? Because she was a dutiful daughter? Or was there a more selfish reason?

She could see shadowy images of a gallery...of paintings. But was she inventing a memory?

She flipped through the entries, hoping one name... any name, would look familiar. But none jumped out at her. Even reading a sampling of emails was futile. Most of them seemed to be business-related. Back-and-forth chitchats with clients wanting this or that.

The ones that were personal came from user names that meant nothing to Gracie.

Relax. Gareth's deep, comforting voice rang in her ears. She needed him. Now.

He wasn't in the kitchen or in the living room and his bedroom was empty, the bedspread made up neatly, pillows plumped, carpet perfectly vacuumed. *The silent army strikes again,* she thought with a grin.

She slipped on a light cardigan and made her way outside. The sun had faded, blocked by turbulent clouds. Shivering, she hurried to Gareth's workshop, and then stopped short. The doors were firmly shut. Was Gareth too chilled to leave them open, or did that signal his need for privacy?

She sneaked closer, and cautiously took a quick

glance in the window. The large, mostly open room was completely empty of human inhabitants. A dog, curled up on a rag rug, raised his head, whined half-heartedly, and promptly went back to sleep. Clearly not a guard dog.

Clouds scudded more quickly now, and the smell of rain scented the air. It occurred to Gracie that she was in the middle of nowhere, with no one to turn to in an emergency, and with little true knowledge of the man whose home she had invaded.

Cowed by the gathering storm and her sensation of utter aloneness, she stumbled back to the house, slammed the heavy front door against the wind and stood with her back to it. Now what?

She prowled the halls of Gareth's house, studying paintings, sculptures, priceless wall hangings. For the first time, she noticed an eerie omission. Nowhere in the house could she find a single photograph, not even in Gareth's designer-perfect, strangely austere bedroom.

The homiest room in the entire dwelling, aside from the luxuriant solarium and pool, was the kitchen. Shiny pots with gleaming copper bottoms hung overhead along with ropes of garlic and dried tomatoes. Behind the stove and sink, handmade terra-cotta tiles with images of a dancing Kokopelli lent warmth and color.

But no refrigerator art…no framed photographs on the built-in desk, nothing.

And still no sign of Gareth.

Outside, the storm lashed the house with fury. She flinched once at a particularly synchronous bolt of lightning and thunder, but apparently she wasn't afraid of nature's pyrotechnics. In the quiet of empty rooms, she could hear the drumming of heavy rain on the roof.

With the right companion it would have been the perfect day to curl up in front of the massive fireplace and enjoy the flames while reading...or better still, making love.

She'd been trying to put last night out of her mind. Had she made a fool of herself? Begging Gareth to stay in her room...in her bed? Was that why he disappeared this morning? To give them both breathing space? Mortification heated her face, even though she was all alone with her painful thoughts.

At last, she landed in the library. It was a fabulous room, with three entire walls of built-in shelves running waist high to the ceiling and cabinets below. She scanned the titles, all neatly divided into categories. Gareth Wolff might give the appearance of wildness and lack of concern for convention, but in his workshop and in this book-filled room, she caught glimpses of his control.

For half an hour she flipped aimlessly through one volume and another. Too restless to read in earnest, she finally knelt and opened a cabinet door. She found nothing out of the ordinary: stacks of magazines, writing and mailing supplies, a collection of baseball cards.

But moving on to the next section, she hit pay dirt. The photographs for which she'd unconsciously been searching. Albums of them. Expensive leather volumes of archival paper...covers imprinted in gold with dates from the 1980s.

Curiosity trumped caution. Scooping three of the big books into her arms, she stood, kicked off her shoes and carried the heavy volumes to the sofa. Curled up with an afghan, she began flipping pages. Like Pandora, she soon wished she had left well enough alone. Someone had painstakingly documented every print story about the Wolff family's tragedy.

The publications ranged from the *New York Times* to the most lurid of tabloids. Some accounts were strictly journalistic, others were prurient and speculative. One picture in particular caught her eye. It was black and white, fairly grainy, but heartbreakingly poignant.

Perhaps the photographer had been surreptitious in his labors, because she couldn't imagine Gareth's family allowing press at a funeral. In the image, two men of similar height and bearing stood flanking a matched set of flower draped coffins. Between them, tiny in stature, wearing a dark suit, was a young boy. Each man held one of his hands.

The caption read, "Financial titans Victor and Vincent Wolff grieve the loss of their wives. With them is seven-year-old son and nephew, Gareth Wolff."

Tears rolled down her cheeks and her heart broke. How awful, how impossibly tragic. She read on…

In a kidnapping scenario that has state police and federal law enforcement baffled, the spouses of multimillionaires Victor and Vincent Wolff were snatched at gunpoint during a shopping trip on a busy street in downtown Charlottesville, Virginia. No word from the perpetrators for three days, and then a demand for money. Despite the fact that the Wolff brothers handed over the ransom (reputed to be in the neighborhood of three million dollars), the women were later killed execution-style, with single gunshots to the head. Their bodies were found in an abandoned warehouse in suburban D.C. A reward is being offered for any information regarding this crime.

Gracie trembled, wishing she had never read a word. Who had assembled this morbid collection? Why would Gareth hold on to something so clearly painful? The tragedy had altered life for his entire family of eight. They had withdrawn from society and built walls, both literal and metaphorical.

A few of the clippings described how the brothers sold fabulous homes in central Virginia, bought a remote mountain and built a fortress to lock their offspring away from a dangerous world. Private tutors, a guard gate and little contact with the public. Ever.

No wonder Gareth hadn't wanted her here.

She laid aside the albums, leaving one open to the picture of little Gareth, and pulled her legs to her chest, resting her chin on her knees. The fire couldn't warm the cold that seeped deep into her bones. Did Gracie have a mother? Somehow she didn't think so. She glanced at the newspaper photo again, and for the flash of an instant, she saw another funeral. And a young girl hand in hand with her daddy. Was the young girl Gracie? Did she have that in common with Gareth?

In an instant, the memory was gone. If indeed it *was* a memory. Maybe she was trying so hard to regain her past that she had begun *inventing* recollections that were nothing more than wishful fiction.

The rain slashing the window doubled in intensity, drumming painfully at Gracie's shattered nerves. Where in heaven's name was Gareth?

Gareth jumped out of the Jeep and made a dash for the porch, shaking like a dog before opening the front door and ducking inside. He was soaked through to the skin, and he still hadn't decided how to handle Gracie and what happened last night.

Should he go with nonchalant avoidance? Or did they confront what they had done?

In his bathroom, he stripped out of his sodden clothes and changed into a soft flannel shirt and old jeans. This afternoon he needed to make some arrangements for the D.C. trip, but making sure Gracie was okay had to take priority. The sizzle of excitement he felt at the thought of seeing her was disconcerting.

He needed to back off a little and make sure she understood the score. And given Jacob's dire warnings, perhaps he ought to give her an out on traveling with him. After last night, the trip took on a whole new significance. Him and Gracie. In a hotel. Together.

Shit. He hardened in his jeans, making the relaxed fit not so relaxed after all. Leaving her in bed this morning had been sheer torture, but also a matter of self-preservation. Getting in too deep with a female relationship hadn't been a problem for a long, long time.

But Gracie, with her mysterious entrée into his life and her total lack of self-knowledge didn't fit the mold. He wanted to protect her. And at the same time, protect himself *from* her. Damned stupid and probably mutually exclusive outcomes.

Pausing only to towel dry his hair and run his hands through it, he left the steamy bathroom and went on a hunt, finding his quarry ensconced in front of a cozy fire in one of his favorite rooms in the house.

He stopped short in the doorway, lead in his gut. "What in the hell do you think you're doing?"

Her head snapped up, her expression wary. Mascara smeared one cheekbone, evidence that she had been crying. "I shouldn't have," she whispered.

Fury shook him. Conflicting emotions shredded his control. He had been ready to scoop her into his arms and carry her back to bed. Now he could barely look at her. "No, you damn well shouldn't have." Again and again she broke through barriers he'd erected, opening him up to emotions he hated. He didn't *want* to feel anything.

His icy-cold voice made Gracie blanch. Her eyes welled with tears, distress written on her delicate features. "I'm so sorry," she whispered.

"For what? Snooping?"

Her lower lip quivered. She scooted out from under the cashmere afghan and stood to face him. "No... Well, yes...for being nosy. But I meant I was sorry about your mother. So sorry. Gareth, you were only a baby."

"I won't discuss my mother with you." Gracie's simple compassion picked at the scab of a wound that was raw despite the passage of time. He couldn't allow her to expose the lack of healing. Not now. Not ever.

"But it was so long ago, and you're still hurting."

"And you're an authority on grief now? You and all your wonderful memories?"

She flinched, making him feel like a heel, but he was so angry he shook with it. No one else dared push at the walls that isolated him.

"Who made the albums?" she asked, her eyes raking his face with a sympathy he didn't want...didn't need.

"I did." He kicked the leg of the sofa with his toe. "None of the adults around me seemed to realize that I was the only one of the kids old enough to read. And newspapers were all over the house. I cut out the articles and saved them. I thought every word was true. And believe me, some of the worst stories made my stomach hurt."

"How do you mean?"

"I saw pictures of the bodies. My mother. My aunt.

Eyes closed. Blood oozing from gaping holes in their heads."

"Dear God."

Gracie looked on the point of a breakdown, and he didn't care. Couldn't care. "A few of the tabloids hinted at drug deals and secret affairs…anything to sell papers. I was too young to know they were inventing things at random."

She took a step in his direction, but he held up his hand, his stomach twisting with nausea. "I didn't sleep for months. I'd wake up screaming, and my father never came. It was always a nanny. My dad was sedated in his bedroom, unable to deal with the grief, the guilt."

"The guilt?"

"He felt as if he'd failed in his duty as a husband. That he hadn't been proactive in protecting her."

Gracie held out her hands. "They were shopping, like a million women in America every day. People can't live in a bubble, Gareth."

"Oh, but you're wrong," he sneered. "With enough money you can hide indefinitely. He and my uncle did that to us. No Little League. No pizza parties at Chuck E. Cheese's. No trips to the zoo. Our entire world became this mountain. And it was years before we realized what we were missing…before we rebelled."

He hated rehashing this, hated that Gracie had seen the nasty underbelly of his life. But something in those big solemn eyes made him spill his guts uncensored as if hoping against hope that she could take away the agony of remembering.

He poured himself a shot of whiskey from a crystal decanter, enjoying the burn as it hit his throat. "Are you happy now?" he asked, seeing the sarcasm hit its mark on her expressive face. In her stocking feet she was so small, so slight, so defenseless.

Jacob was right. Anything could happen to her. And Gareth wouldn't be able to protect her. Evil lurked on every corner, even more so now than in 1985. He couldn't afford to fall in love with her. He wouldn't allow it.

She shrugged helplessly. "I'm not happy, Gareth. How could I be? I wish I could make those terrible memories all go away."

"That's just it," he muttered, downing a second reckless shot, though he seldom drank. "You've been making such a big damn deal about having amnesia, but there have been too many nights when I would have given anything to be able to forget."

"It must have been unbearable." Her compassion rolled over him in waves, and he hated the way it made him feel. Stripped raw. Completely naked.

He hurled the glass into the fireplace, hearing the gratifying sound as it shattered, enjoying the wide-mouthed shock on Gracie's face. "Get out of my sight," he said, jaw clenched. "I don't want to look at you."

Chapter 9

Gracie sobbed, half crazed, as she blundered through the forest. She didn't even remember which way she came in the beginning, but she was leaving. There would be help at the bottom. A police station. Kind townspeople. Whatever...it didn't matter.

She couldn't stay here.

Briars scraped her legs. Sweat rolled down her temples. A fleeting sense of déjà vu tweaked her memory, but she was too distraught to care. The rain had stopped, and now that the sun was back out, the humidity turned the spring forest into an itchy, moist sauna.

The ground was soggy. She slipped time and again, falling on her butt, leaving mudslides as she tumbled down the mountain. In the midst of one headlong plunge, a thick root caught her foot and twisted her ankle painfully.

She cried out and fell to her hip, curling into a fetal

ball. Even above the harsh sound of her breathing, she could hear crashing and cursing above her. It was impossible to outrun a wolf.

Gareth burst through a thicket of rhododendron and stopped dead, his face ashen. "I'm sorry, Gracie. Hell, I'm sorry." He knelt beside her, eyes aghast. "You're barefoot. Holy God."

Her feet were a mess…cut, bleeding. And her ankle had already swollen to alarming proportions. She buried her face in her arms, embarrassed, hurt. "I wasn't thinking straight. And I know what you're going to say. *Stupid, irrational woman.*"

He lifted her carefully and started the trek back up the mountain. His arms were strong as tree trunks, his mighty legs covering the uneven ground with ease. "You're wrong," he muttered. "I was thinking what an ass I am."

This time, Jacob was not quite so welcoming when they showed up at his house. He glared at his brother. "Christ, you're hardheaded."

The two men faced off in a visual battle of wills. Gareth held Gracie tightly. She smelled his sweat, felt the faint tremor in his arms. "I don't need a lecture, Jacob. Take care of her…please."

Gracie knew that the final word had been dragged out of him. He was not in a conciliatory mood. She touched his arm. "I'm fine." The last thing she wanted was to cause discord between the two siblings.

Jacob cursed beneath his breath as he led them back to an examining room. Gareth deposited Gracie gently on the table. He touched her hair. "Should I stay?"

Before she could answer, Jacob held open the door. "No. We don't need you for this."

Again the two men bristled, but amazingly, Gareth bowed out and left the room.

Jacob turned to Gracie, his gaze a mix of professional assessment and personal concern. "Are you okay?"

Tears clogged her throat, but she was damned if she'd let them fall. "I did something stupid. It wasn't Gareth's fault."

"Yeah, right." The wry twist of his mouth said he didn't believe a word of her defense. "I know my brother, Gracie. He's hard as glass, not to mention stubborn. Let me look at you."

Even the gentle probe of his fingers was painful. Her ankle looked dreadful, but fortunately the X-rays showed no sign of a break. After cleansing the cuts and abrasions, Jacob wrapped her foot and lower leg tightly in an ACE bandage. He worked in silence, his expression grave. "You can walk short distances without hurting anything, but ice it today while you're resting. Ibuprofen will help." He covered her feet in soft cotton socks.

When he was done, he sat down on a rolling stool and crossed his arms over his chest.

In that moment his resemblance to his brother was uncanny. He sighed. "I think you should let me take you home, Gracie."

"Not yet," she whispered. "My father's out of the country, and I can't exactly call someone in my list of phone contacts and tell them the truth. I have no way of knowing which ones are personal and which ones are business related. They would think I'm insane. Besides…" She paused and fumbled for an explanation. "Gareth—"

"If you're hoping for something from him, you'll never find it. Gareth doesn't have much capacity for love or for trust. He was the only one of the six of us kids really old enough to remember our mother and our aunt. He was the only one they deemed able to go to the funeral."

She bowed her head. "It makes me sick to think about it." She didn't mention the albums. Jacob might not know about them, and it wasn't her place to reveal that secret.

"Gareth endured what no child should ever have to face. Not only the loss of a parent, but the violence of it…the public forum. Kieran and I were only four and five. We were protected from the worst of it."

"But obviously you knew your mother wasn't coming back."

He shrugged. "Yeah. We got the speech about heaven and how much she loved us. I remember some bad dreams and feeling confused. But in the end, I was a kid…I got past it. Gareth wasn't so lucky."

"He's still hurting, Jacob. A lot."

"I know. And if you're not careful, his pain will damage you as well."

"He's kind when he wants to be. And gentle."

"Don't go to Washington with him," Jacob urged. "Don't fall in love with him."

"I don't plan to," she said, raising her head and meeting his gaze, hers bleak. "Fall in love, I mean. What would be the point?"

Jacob stood and put a hand on her shoulder. "Be strong, little Gracie. Concentrate on regaining your memory. You have a life waiting for you. I love my brother. He's a complicated, wonderful man. But he's no Prince Charming, despite the castle vibe around here."

He kissed her cheek just as Gareth knocked impatiently and entered the room.

Jacob held up his hands when his brother's eyes flashed with displeasure. "Doctor-patient privilege."

Gareth scowled until his eyes landed on Gracie's bandaged foot. His face softened, and he went to her, absentmindedly stroking her hair. "Did Jacob get you all fixed up?"

She nodded, her throat tight. "I could get used to having my own private physician on call." Her attempt at a joke fell flat, none of the three of them in a mood for levity.

Gareth scooped her up for the return trip to the Jeep. "I owe you one, Jacob."

Jacob followed them out. "Remember the ice. And elevate the ankle if you can. That will help with the swelling."

It was warm outside. And Gareth had taken the cover off the Jeep while he waited. He tucked Gracie into her seat. She smiled at her physician. "Thank you, Jacob. You're a wonderful doctor."

Gareth snorted as he got in and started the engine. "If he was that good, he'd have cured your amnesia."

"Gareth!" She punched his arm.

"Jacob knows I'm kidding."

The brothers stared at one another over Gracie's head. "He's my big brother," Jacob said. "I'm used to it."

Back at the house, Gareth carried her again, despite her protests. He bypassed his room and took her straight to hers, depositing her gently on the bed. "I'll get you some lunch."

She lay still, studying patterns in the wooden raftered ceiling. Her brain didn't want to think about anything more complicated than counting knotholes at the moment.

Gareth returned in short order with a tray set for two.

The turkey and provolone sandwiches wouldn't have passed muster for a Martha Stewart photo shoot, but the single pink rose he'd tucked into a tiny crystal pitcher drew attention away from the efforts of a clumsy chef.

He set the tray on the bedside table and perched beside her, taking a linen napkin and laying it across her lap. She accepted the glass of lemonade he offered and downed a thirsty gulp. "I'm not hungry," she protested when he picked up a plate.

"You need to eat. Doctor's orders."

It was clear from his dogged expression that he would brook no protest. She tried to chew a few bites, but the food stuck in her throat. She dropped the half-eaten sandwich on her plate. "I really am sorry, Gareth. So sorry. I've intruded upon your life in so many ways, it appalls me. If you would rather I not go to Washington, Jacob will take me home."

He leaned forward and rescued a crumb from her chin. "Did he put you up to that?"

She bit her lip, shifting restlessly. "He's protective of you."

"And you, I think."

"Only in a professional capacity. You're his major concern."

"I'm a big boy. I can take care of myself. We'll stick with the original plan. A couple of days in the Capitol and then we'll see if your father has returned. I'm not taking you to Savannah until I know he'll be there to look after you." He sighed deeply and turned away from her, resting his elbows on his knees and dropping his head into his hands. "I owe you an explanation."

She touched his shoulder, felt the rigid muscles. "You owe me nothing."

He jumped to his feet and paced her elegant bedroom. "You're the only person who has ever seen those albums." She couldn't see his face, but his body language shouted his unease.

"How is that possible? They weren't exactly hidden."

He shoved his hands in the back pocket of his jeans, his brooding masculine beauty threatening to take her breath away. "For years, I kept the newspaper and magazine clippings concealed in boxes under my bed. When I was fourteen, I persuaded my tutor to help me order the special albums. He was a nice guy. One of my favorite teachers ever, actually. But he got married and moved away…"

She remained silent, reluctant to halt the flow of his painful introspection.

Gareth continued. "Bit by bit…in secret…I started arranging all the papers by date and securing them in the books. I'm sure it was unhealthy…this obsession I had with the kidnapping and murder. But I couldn't seem to let it go. One day my father caught me looking through my macabre collection and went practically apoplectic with rage. He ordered me to destroy the albums…called in one of the servants to take them away."

"Oh, Gareth…"

"I begged, pleaded… He didn't understand that those scraps of paper were all I had left of my mother. They were a connection, albeit a terrible one. A link that kept her alive in my memory."

"What happened then?"

"Our housekeeper saved the albums, secretly. Bless her dear old heart. Years later, when I was twenty-one, she produced them and said that I was old enough to decide their fate."

"So you kept them."

"I didn't *not* keep them. I had changed, matured. I

thought about destroying them…for my own mental health. But I was caught between the past and the present. It felt disloyal to wipe away my mother's memory entirely."

"But that's not exactly what you would have been doing."

"I understood that intellectually. But for whatever reason, I couldn't do it…couldn't get rid of them. My solution and the proof of my sanity was that I never once opened them…not even that first day. I've kept them the way a recovering alcoholic tucks away a bottle of gin. As a test."

She felt sick. "And when you walked into the library today…"

"I saw that you had one of the albums spread on the sofa. I could see the picture from across the room. I overreacted. I'm sorry."

She clambered from the bed, wincing as her abused feet made contact with the floor. His body was stiff, but she embraced him anyway, arms around his waist, her cheek tucked to his chest. "If you apologize again, I'll smack you."

That coaxed a grin from him. "You're mighty fierce." He hugged her tightly, releasing some of her tension. "You don't have to be afraid of me. I'm not crazy, Gracie. Honest to God."

She smiled, releasing him. "No one ever said you were."

"I'll get rid of them if you think I should."

The import of that single sentence jangled in her brain. This was too intense, especially for someone who couldn't remember what she ate for breakfast last week. "I think they can go back into the cabinet for the moment. No harm, no foul. Do you want me to take care of it?"

"Already did," he said gruffly. "And no...I didn't look at them."

"It would have been okay if you had."

"Not to me. I'm done with that part of my life. My brothers and my cousins and I have moved on."

And it was time for her to do the same. She reached for her cell, and put it on speaker phone. "Listen to this."

"You have reached Edward Darlington, owner and operator of Darlington Gallery in Savannah, Georgia. I'm out of the country at the moment, and the gallery is closed. Hope to be back in my office next week. Please leave a message. Oh, yes and if this is Gracie, don't give up, baby girl. Make it happen. Make me proud."

Gareth's face darkened. "No offense, but I'm not a big fan of your dad. And I've never even met the guy."

"What do you think he wants? Do you by any chance paint in addition to making furniture?"

"No." His lashes flickered as if he had thought of something she hadn't. "And I don't have a clue what he wants. He owns a gallery. Maybe he's like the senator. Thinks that having me do a public appearance will help his bottom line."

"But that doesn't make sense. I don't even know you. And I approached you under less than ideal circumstances. Surely he knew the answer to any request like that would be a resounding *no*."

"Maybe he thought your charm would win me over. You are kind of cute and cuddly."

"Kind of?" She pretended to scowl.

He surprised her with a hungry kiss. "Men are weak," he mumbled, kissing his way along her neck. "Maybe your dad is smarter than we think."

She wriggled free, suddenly less amused. "I have old messages from clients on my phone. Maybe he wanted to sell you something."

Exasperation marked his features. "I don't know. I wish the hell I did. But we'll find out. I promise you."

Chapter 10

Gracie improved rapidly. Seventy-two hours later, her ankle was sore but in working order. Her head barely ached at all. Cuts and bruises had begun to fade, and Jacob was able to remove the handful of stitches from her leg.

Gareth disappeared for the most part. He holed up in his workshop, avoiding Gracie much of the day. When they *were* together, he seemed ill at ease, lending credence to her theory that he was not happy that he had shared so many intimate details of his life with her.

The evening meal was their only contact of any length, and even then he ate his food, drank his wine and conversed only at a bare minimum. After the first awkward day, Gracie gave up, retreating into silence herself and pretending that she had never seen Gareth Wolff naked.

She put the hours she was alone to good use, combing newspapers and magazines, as well as scouring the internet for information about the world in general and her place in it in particular. Her father's gallery had a website, but her name wasn't listed anywhere. She studied the photos, and though it all seemed vaguely familiar, even looking at the head shot of Edward Darlington produced nothing more than a nagging sense of anxiety.

Articles about Savannah caught her eye. She studied photographs of the old Southern city...read stories about its history. Little flashes, snippets of recollections, reassured her that the entire picture would soon slip into focus. Her life *wasn't* a blank slate. It was there, waiting. All she had to do was be patient.

Easier said than done when she lay in bed at night, her body yearning for Gareth's possession. She was poised on the blade of a two-edged sword. If she remembered everything, her time with Gareth would come to a messy end. But if the amnesia continued, she still had only a short window to savor his protectiveness and his sensual attentions. Very soon, she would go home and try to *find* her past, bit by bit.

Gareth sought her out on the fourth morning after the photo album contretemps. She was in the library searching for any book that might spark a memory. He braced his hands in the doorway as if not trusting himself to go in. "We're leaving at noon. Does that work for you?" His eyes were hooded. The dark smudges beneath them indicated restless sleep.

She wanted to help, but she didn't know how. Moving toward him with the caution afforded an unpredictable animal, she smiled hesitantly. "Will Jacob be taking us to the airport?"

A glint of humor danced across his face. "No."

"We're driving?" Several hours in the confined intimacy of a car seemed dangerous.

"No."

Hands on hips, she shot him a threatening stare. "Then how are we getting there?"

Gracie Darlington was about as threatening as a kitten. "You'll see." He loved teasing her. The pink in her cheeks and the flustered look in her eyes made him want to devour her one sensual inch at a time. He cleared his throat. "Your suitcase was delivered a little while ago. Annalise didn't want to send it to the hotel and risk anything getting lost. She assures me that you'll be covered for any fashion emergency…with the possible exception of a White House state dinner."

"What should I wear for travel?" The suspicion on her face hadn't abated.

He shrugged. "Comfortable. Smart casual. She sent a garment bag, too. You'll probably find what you need in there."

For a moment, the combative kitten appeared unusually upset. "I don't even know if I can afford to repay you," she fretted. "Your sister must have spent thousands of dollars."

He muttered a curse. "For God's sake. I have enough money to outfit you in something new every day from now until we both keel over dead. Forget about it." He reached for her hand, dragged her out into the hall, closed the library door and backed her up against it, crowding her deliberately with his considerable size advantage.

When she opened her mouth to continue the argument, he shut her up the quickest way he knew how.

"Shh, Gracie." He loved the way her body went lax when his mouth captured hers. "I've missed you."

She nipped his bottom lip with sharp teeth. "I'm not the one who's been hiding out."

"I've been working," he said, setting the record straight. Wolff men didn't hide from anything. "I'm sorry if you felt neglected. I'll make it up to you this weekend."

She closed her eyes, a dreamy smile tilting lush, pink lips. "I may not know much, but I'm pretty sure some-one must have warned me about men like you."

"I'm harmless." Her quick gurgle of laughter eased into a sigh of pleasure that hardened his shaft painfully and quickly. Staying away from her for several days had seemed the smart thing to do. Hearing her father's sleazy voice on the phone recording had reminded Ga-reth of all the reasons he shouldn't trust her.

So he went cold turkey. No Gracie. Period.

But he had ached, God, how he ached. Already his body knew hers, remembered the jolt of pleasure that threatened to pull him under when he entered her. Soft skin, soft breasts, soft everything. A softness so beau-tiful a man could bury himself in it willingly and never surface again.

He cupped her ass. "You need to know something, though."

Her pelvis was pressed to his with predictable re-sults. "What?"

"I've booked two rooms at the hotel in D.C. You don't have to go there as my lover. We can be friends if that's what you want."

She pulled back and searched his face. "You're seri-ous." It was a statement, not a question.

He tucked a silky curl behind her shell-like ear.

"Jacob has been on my case. And I feel a certain need to protect you from myself."

"Is that even possible?"

"Hell if I know." He kissed her again. "I don't want you to think badly of me when this all ends."

The happiness on her face dimmed. "You haven't done anything wrong. Why would I think that?"

"I should never have made love to you."

She stiffened in his embrace. "That was my fault. And I've already apologized."

The strangled hurt in her voice made him swear again. "I don't want your regrets *or* your apology. All I want is you." He picked her up, pressing his erection against her in a move that made them both gasp.

She circled his waist with her legs. "I want you, too. And the trip to D.C. is *not* going to be platonic. You know it and I know it. But it would be nice if you could act a little happier about it."

"I don't feel happy," he admitted grudgingly. He lifted her up and down, rubbing his considerably aroused shaft against the spot he so badly wanted to feel, to see, to fill. "You've messed up my life, Gracie. Made me question things I've never questioned before."

She dropped her head back against the wood, baring her slender, delicate neck to his mouth. Skin that tasted like strawberries. "You'll be fine when I'm gone," she whispered.

The regret in her words hurt something deep inside his chest. He pushed the pain away. He knew how to do that…had been doing it for twenty-five years. "I'm not fine now." The words ripped from a throat raw with suppressed emotion. He dropped her to her feet and unzipped her jeans, dragging them and her panties down her legs.

"*Gareth.*" She had her hands behind her, braced on the door. Nothing about her posture suggested that he stop what he was doing.

"Lift your arms."

She obeyed instantly, but protested. "Somebody could walk in…"

"Not today. I swear. Relax. We're alone." He was having trouble stringing words together coherently. When he had her naked, he stopped breathing and just looked at her. Narrow waist. Flaring feminine hips. Small but perfect breasts. A neat fluff of red-gold hair between her slender thighs.

She folded her arms across her chest, gnawing her lower lip. "It's embarrassing that only one of us is wearing clothes." Clearly she was trying for sophisticated humor, but her cheeks were fiery red.

He moved her arm and touched one breast, circled the pale pink nipple, watching in fascination as it tightened. "I'll catch up. But first, let me enjoy the view." He bent his head and tasted her there, sucking gently until Gracie cried out.

Her hands tangled in his hair, pulling him closer. "Shouldn't we go to your bedroom…or mine…?"

He unfastened his pants and freed himself, hardly able to touch the tight, sensitive skin. "No time," he groaned, desperately glad he had stuffed a condom in his pocket. He couldn't fool himself. This was what he'd had in mind since he awoke hard and hungry that morning.

He rolled on the protection, wincing when Gracie brushed her hand over him intimately.

She touched his cheek with gentle affection, almost unmanning him. "I want you so much," she said softly.

"You make me shake with it. I look at you and I melt inside."

He lifted her a second time, aligning their bodies, probing at her slick entrance with the head of his shaft. "I need you, Gracie." The confession was wrung from him…and he regretted it almost immediately. But in the bliss of burying himself deep inside her, he ignored the thought.

He forged the physical connection, meeting no resistance, relishing the snug, tight fit. All the way to the head of her womb, heartbeat to heartbeat. He resented the condom that separated them. Wanted to fill her with his seed, mark her at the most primitive level.

Her forehead rested on his, her breathing ragged. "I won't ever forget this," she whispered. "I won't ever forget you."

Again, the understanding of deferred pain hovered just out of reach. He shook his head, refusing to think beyond this moment. "Don't talk, Gracie. Let me make you come."

He thrust hard, banging her bottom against the unforgiving door in a reckless rhythm. She chanted his name. "Gareth. Gareth. Gareth." Her arms tightened around his neck in a stranglehold. "Don't stop," she panted. "Please don't stop."

As if he could. Blinded now, eyes closed, he felt the end barreling toward him. His hips flexed. He felt Gracie's inner muscles clench in orgasm as he shouted his release. All the oxygen departed his lungs. His brain exploded.

Afterward, staggering, he shuffled them down the hall toward his room, her body clinging to his like a limpet, his legs trembling as he tried to find a handhold on reality.

* * *

Gracie had amnesia. Even after an interlude that left her reeling with weepy joy. But she was pretty sure no one had ever banged her against a door, pardon the pun.

For a moment, when Gareth entered her, a flash of some sweet memory tangled with the present urgency. She was no virgin. There had been at least someone in her life before. She was sure of it. But memory or no memory, she was positive no one had ever made her feel the way Gareth did. No one had ever made her *want* with such intensity.

She was torn between wanting to giggle and battling a barrage of inexplicable, hot-behind-the-eyes tears. They didn't fall. She blinked them back with dogged ferocity. She had Gareth. For this moment in time, he was hers.

When he dumped her on the bed and dropped face-down beside her, she rolled to look at the clock. "We're going to be late."

He half lifted his head, blinked in the direction she pointed and groaned. "They'll wait…"

"They who?"

His muffled answer segued into a gentle snore. Allowing herself sixty seconds to snuggle against him, she heaved a deep sigh, slid out of bed and scuttled into the hall.

The unmistakable evidence of their spontaneous combustion met her gaze. Panties here, bra there… No one could mistake what had happened. She retrieved her clothing and ran for her room, locking the door and leaning against it with a frantically beating heart.

No one was around to witness her chagrin. She was all alone. But she shivered nonetheless. Gareth continued to surprise her.

She made quick work of a shower and dug into the new bounty Annalise had provided. A navy pantsuit in silk shantung struck her as appropriate travel wear. The matching silk camisole was cream with navy piping.

This time, Annalise had also provided a carry-on stocked with expensive cosmetics. Gracie dressed, applied makeup with a light touch, and packed up her things. The only items of any value she'd had with her when she first arrived on Wolff Mountain were her wallet and cell phone. She tucked those in a bag and went to meet Gareth.

She wasn't about to invade his personal domain, so she perched on a chair in the den and waited for him to show up. It wasn't long. But when he appeared, she couldn't hold back a blush.

Gareth eyed her with a grumpy stare. "You left."

"You said we were leaving at noon. I had to get ready."

He surveyed her from head to toe. "Annalise has great taste, but I like you better naked."

She gaped at him, but shut her mouth sharply and refused to rise to the bait.

Gareth grinned. "No comment?"

She shook her head. "My big suitcase is in the bedroom. Everything else is right here."

In a matter of moments Gareth had loaded their bags into the Jeep and they were on their way. He looked strong and handsome in a crisp white dress shirt and dark slacks. The open collar and rolled up sleeves suited him.

They took a different route this time, bypassing the cutoff to Jacob's place and instead, climbing higher up the mountain. This was the closest she had come to the

magnificent home where Gareth had spent his forma-
tive years. The enormous house was amazing.

She knew why Gareth had not taken her there. He
didn't trust her to be around his family. And knowing
that hurt. Still, she would love to see inside the massive
structure. It demanded respect because of its sheer size,
but it was beautiful as well.

She could come right out and ask him to give her a
tour when they got back. But given her father's cryp-
tic words, she didn't want Gareth to think she had any
mischief in mind. Surely her father didn't expect her to
steal the family silver or to try her hand at safe-breaking.

It was a measure of her good mood that she could
joke about it, even with herself.

The Jeep angled sharply, and she grabbed on to the
door. "You can't tell me there's an airstrip up here."

Gareth shot her an amused glance. "Of course not.
Don't be ridiculous."

They shot through an opening in the trees. Gracie's
eyes widened even as instinctive apprehension made her
muscles tense. No airstrip, but instead, a helipad. The
chopper itself was black and yellow. The body was sleek
and shiny, with lots of glass, and on the side, the words
Wolff and Sons, Inc. painted in sharp relief.

"Um, Gareth?"

He didn't give her time to freak out. "C'mon."

A uniformed attendant greeted Gareth respectfully
and made short work of stowing their bags. The pilot,
who had been standing nearby smoking a cigarette, gave
a salute and climbed into the vehicle, starting up the ro-
tors with a *whoosh* of sound.

Gareth grabbed Gracie's hand and helped her board,
tucking her into a seat and fastening her seat belt. "Wear
these," he said, placing large noise-deadening head-

phones over her ears. Instantly she could hear the radio-transmitted conversation between the pilot, his copilot/attendant and Gareth.

It was crystal clear who was boss. Though Gareth's manner with his employees was joking and relaxed, they treated him deferentially.

Without warning, the chopper lifted straight up into the air, hovered just long enough for Gracie to get to an incredible vantage point from which to see the house and then they were off, headed northeast and covering ground rapidly.

Gracie was either fascinated or terrified or both. She felt like a bird, streaking high above the earth. Below her, Virginia's fertile farm fields lay like patchwork quilts on the land. Cars were no more than ants scurrying along twisted silver highways. Lakes and rivers marked the landscape. Once she got past her initial frozen fear, she loved it.

The copilot passed back two boxed lunches. Gareth dug into his, polishing off the chicken salad sandwich quickly and swigging a root beer. Gracie's meal was similar, but it included her favorite lemon/lime soda and one large chocolate chip cookie. Clearly someone had studied her preferences.

She ate a few bites and waited to see if her stomach could handle eating and flying at the same time.

Gareth touched her hand. "You okay?" He mimed the words instead of speaking into the headset.

She nodded. Their seats were close, their hips practically touching. He took a small blanket and tucked it around her shoulders. She appreciated the gesture, because the air was definitely cold.

In record time, it seemed, she began to recognize what she knew as Washington landmarks. The pilot made a wide sweep over the Potomac, and soon they were descending slowly and at last settling gently as a cloud onto the rooftop of a multistory building.

Another trio of helpful young men gathered the luggage and spirited it away. As Gareth bid farewell to the crew, Gracie frowned at the chopper. When he joined her, she waved at the lettering. "Why does it say *and sons*? What about your cousin? She's a girl."

He chuckled, putting his arm around her waist and ushering her toward a nearby door. "Annalise is terrified of helicopters. Hates that we use one at all. She doesn't want to have any part of it…thinks it would be bad luck to have her name or sex included."

Suddenly, Gracie recalled Annalise bemoaning the need for a private jet. Wow. This family could give Bill Gates a run for his money.

Inside the hotel, the air was lightly scented, the thickly carpeted hallways silent but beautifully decorated with sconces and sparkling chandeliers. The cordial manager, a sophisticated blonde with eyes for no one but Gareth, met them in the lobby.

She held out a hand, immaculate nails painted scarlet. "We're delighted to see you again, Mr. Wolff. Your suite is ready for you."

Chapter 11

Gracie disliked the woman on sight. The tall, leggy female was a little *too* friendly, and if Gracie had been someone important in Gareth's life, the woman's total lack of acknowledgment would have been insulting.

Gareth didn't seem to notice. He shook the woman's hand briefly, his arm still wrapped protectively around Gracie's waist. "Hello, Chandra. The place looks welcoming, as always."

She practically gushed. "How nice of you to say so. We're always delighted to get your reservation." She afforded Gracie a single dismissive glance. "As you requested, we've given you the Jefferson suite. I think you'll find the amenities extremely comfortable. And your *companion*—" a little dig there "—will be equally pampered."

Gareth smiled lazily. "Gracie and I will be very happy, I'm sure."

The other woman blanched and visibly lost several degrees of confidence. Did the lovely Chandra have designs on Gareth Wolff?

The manager grimaced slightly. "Shall I escort you upstairs? Help you get settled in?"

Gareth nuzzled Gracie's cheek, making no bones about his intentions. "I can handle it from here." He took the two key cards. "Thanks, Chandra."

Gracie allowed herself to be propelled across the marble foyer to the small, elegant elevator. As they rode up to the penthouse floor, she studied the crimson paisley wallpaper in the enclosed space. One wall was mirrored, and in its reflection, she saw Gareth's eyes on her. Recognized the sensual intent on his face.

"Quit staring," she muttered.

"I like the view." His lazy smile sent bubbles of anticipation sparkling through her veins.

When the brief ride ended in a smooth stop, he stood back and waited for her to exit. For some reason, she was as nervous as a virgin bride. Their door—the only one in the hallway—was directly opposite the elevator. Gareth used the key card and opened it.

Soft classical music drifted into the foyer from the spacious living room directly in front of them. Lavish flower arrangements, massive bouquets of everything from roses to freesias to tiny Dutch iris, graced the entrance hall cabinet, the coffee table and a duo of marble and cherry pedestals.

Gareth put out the Do Not Disturb sign and locked the dead bolt. He tossed his wallet, phone and keys on the escritoire. "Alone at last." His mocking half smile was perhaps self-directed, but it made Gracie's toes curl in her Italian calfskin pumps.

She licked her lips. "I'm impressed. Though I can't

say for sure at this point, I have a feeling that I'm a Holiday Inn Express kind of girl. You know…mass-produced artwork, breakfast in the lobby, that kind of thing. You may have spoiled me forever."

. He took her hand. "Come look."

French doors opened out onto a small, private balcony hedged in with black wrought-iron grille work. To their right, the mall, decked out in spring green, stretched from the Capitol building to the Washington Monument, with all the iconic museums in between. The afternoon sun hung low in the sky, shedding warm light over tourists with cameras and joggers enjoying the gentle breeze.

Gracie braced her hands on the railing, peeking down to the street below. "I wish I could remember if I've ever been here," she said, overcome with a pensive melancholy. "It all seems so wonderfully familiar, but I suppose that might simply be the sum total of movies and television programs I've seen."

Gareth massaged her shoulders, his big body trapping hers against the metal that still held the warmth of the day's heat. "Why does it matter either way?" he asked, his tone matter-of-fact. "Embrace the experience. Soak in the sights and sounds. Enjoy being here with me…"

His breath was warm on her nape as he kissed the sensitive spot behind her ear. Gripping the bar at her waist, she tipped her head to one side, offering access, offering an invitation.

Gareth wasn't slow to accept. But his actions were circumspect at first…given their public venue. His hands grasped her hips as he nibbled a course from her ear to her collarbone. With tantalizing slowness, he reached around to unbutton her jacket and slip it from her shoulders, tossing it carelessly on a nearby patio chair.

The spaghetti-strap chemise she wore was thin, as was the delicate ivory bra beneath. There was no hiding her excitement as he brushed the tip of first one breast and then the other. He didn't linger. To the casual observer, they were no more than a man and a woman enjoying the fresh air.

She felt the heat of him, the intensity. The scent of expensive aftershave—something new she hadn't noticed before—teased her nostrils. It was a potent aphrodisiac. Mingled with the essence of the man himself, it hit her at a most basic level. Speaking of abandoned pleasures and pheromones and wicked temptation…

"When do we have to be at the senator's home?" she croaked, trying desperately for common sense, for self-preservation. They'd had sex only a few hours before, and yet between them shimmered a need so intense she felt it as a physical pain.

"Eight o'clock," he murmured, caressing her bottom. "Hours from now. We have all the time we want."

Her body went boneless, slumping backward, moving unconsciously into his embrace. "I don't have much time left," she whispered. "Don't make me wait."

He growled. He actually growled. The masculine sound sent gooseflesh all over her body. His chest heaved. "Inside, Gracie Darlington. Let me have my way with you."

Stunning her into an awed silence, he scooped her into his arms and carried her back to the luxurious room with the antique settee and the thick Persian rug. Hesitating only momentarily, he strode through the door to the right and found his own quarters, his set of bags stowed in the enormous, open armoire.

He flipped back the chocolate duvet, slipped off her shoes and deposited her carefully on a nest of pillows.

"We've done hard and fast," he said, already stripping out of his clothes. "Now I'm going to make you ache, make you yearn." He paused, magnificently naked. "Imagine that we're all alone in the world. Nothing exists outside this suite. No phones. No meddlesome relatives. Only you and me."

And no memories that, when recovered, would almost surely come between them.

The sight of Gareth's nude body literally took her breath away. Muscle and bone and sinew combined to create a man who emanated confidence and beauty in equal measure. He was fully erect, and her mouth dried, imagining the moment when all that power would penetrate her, fill her, claim her.

She sat up on her elbows. "I'll pretend I have amnesia," she teased. "The only memories I want are the ones of you and me in this room."

"I like how you think." He chuckled, coming down on the bed beside her and unzipping her elegant slacks. "Close your eyes," he murmured. "Relax. Let me give you pleasure."

Her eyelids fluttered shut, even as the butterflies in her stomach increased tenfold. She wasn't by nature a passive person, and ceding control didn't come naturally. Some things a person never forgot.

Gareth's hands were warm and slightly rough as he bared her legs, removing her lace panties in the process. She was still partially dressed from the waist up, but he seemed intent on exploration.

His breath tickled her thigh. Moments later she felt his lips and tongue at the heart of her, teasing her with an intimate caress that arched her back in shocked reaction. "Be still," he commanded.

The words were stern, but his hands on her body were

infinitely gentle. She gripped fistfuls of the sheet and cried out when he brought her close to the brink, only to change his course and kiss his way down to her ankle.

She trembled all over, her breathing choppy.

Again he issued an order. "Raise your arms."

It never occurred to her to disobey. She felt him move up and over her, his weight straddling her thighs, but not crushing her. He took the camisole and slithered it up her arms and over her head, pausing to kiss her hard on the lips. Before she could respond, he was dealing with her bra, spiriting it away so easily she might have been perturbed if her brain had been working clearly.

She felt his hands on her waist, her rib cage, her breasts. Breathing became difficult, almost impossible. Every cell in her body was wondering…anticipating. Where would he go next?

A light brush of his thumbs on her nipples furled them tightly. The similar caress he bestowed on her collarbone made her move restlessly. With her eyes closed, every response intensified. She felt deliciously helpless, though he had not restrained her in any way.

"Open your mouth," he whispered, tracing the curve of her ear with a fingertip. His lips moved over hers… teasing, seductive. He slipped his tongue inside to taste, to tangle with hers. She tried to hold him, but he pulled back. "No touching, no talking." The silky insistence in his words made her shiver.

The life she couldn't remember was hazy, unimportant. With Gareth on his mountaintop and Gracie in Savannah, all the light would disappear from her days. She didn't need her memories to know that. Despite her body's demands, the sexual mood faded. Tears stung her eyes, and she wanted to curl into the

covers and sob out her frustration, her confusion…
her premonition of dread.

Gareth was no fool. He sensed her emotional disen-
gagement almost instantly. "What's wrong?" he asked.
The words were husky with alarm. "Tell me, Gracie.
Whatever I did, I'm sorry."

Her lashes lifted, and he saw such pain in her beautiful eyes it made his gut hurt. He smoothed a hand over
her pale cheek. "I shouldn't have assumed…and after
I told you we could come here as friends. God, I'm a
fool. Forgive me, Gracie."

She shook her head, a single tear spilling over and
marking a wet path to her chin. "It's not that. I want
you. I do…"

"But…?" He was a man who fixed things, who solved
problems, and he hadn't a clue what to do. He missed
her smile desperately.

Her lower lip trembled badly, and he saw her bite
down hard to stop the quiver. "I don't think I'm the kind
of woman who can do light and easy. I want to. I've
tried. But I think I'm falling in love with you."

The words hit him like a sledgehammer. The swift
jolt of joy was immediately obscured by suspicion. He
was vulnerable when it came to Gracie Darlington. And
a vulnerable man was a weak man.

He rolled to his side and leaned on his elbow facing
her, head propped on his hand. "That's impossible. Your
situation is making you—"

She stopped him with a hand on his lips. Even that
was enough to harden his flagging erection. "Don't discount what I feel," she said, her eyes bleak. "This is my
problem, not yours. I have no business getting close to
you…to any man, until I regain my memory."

The *any man* reference lit a fury in him that was as fierce as it was unexpected. "Your father told you there's no husband or boyfriend. You don't believe him?"

She pulled a corner of the comforter over her shoulder. "Yes, of course I believe him. But I have this gigantic void that scares me to death. I want to know, but I'm afraid of what I'll find out." Her gaze beseeched him to understand, but damned if he did.

"How is enjoying sex with me a threat?"

"You have everything, Gareth. Family, wealth, an ego the size of Texas. And all that adds up to your incredible confidence. Not a bad thing, but pretty intimidating for a woman who has nothing but a few phone messages from a man who will never deserve a father-of-the-year prize."

"Intimidated?" That word jumped out at him. "Bullshit. You've held your own with me every step of the way. And I want to believe that you came to my mountain without any intent to do wrong. You're a darling, Gracie. By nature and by name. Everything about you is sweet and innocent and untainted by greed."

"You *want* to believe it, but you're not willing to make that last step. Because maybe I'm a darned good actress. And you can't bear the idea that I might play you for a fool and cause you to betray your family."

"No one is that good an actor."

She needed to believe he'd had a change of heart, he could tell. But the moment was lost. Gracie was smart enough to sense that his tiny slivers of doubt that still remained could prick the bubble of their happiness. And he needed to give her some space. With his body protesting every step of the way, he rolled out of bed and pulled on his pants. In the bathroom he found a thick terry robe and took it to her. "Here. Go settle in. Take a bath if you want to…or a nap. Order room service."

She sat up, exchanging the comforter for the robe. With the collar turned up and her hair tousled, she looked far too young to be the object of his baser instincts. Her slim hands tugged the sash into a solid knot. "What will *you* do?" The words were husky.

He shrugged. "I have some phone calls to make. Email to check. If you feel up to it, we'll leave about seven-fifteen. I've ordered a car. The senator's home is in Maclean, Virginia."

She scooted out of bed and bent to gather her things. As she knelt, the robe tightened across her bottom. Gareth swallowed and had to turn away. He was appalled to realize how close he was to an attempt to talk her back into bed.

He pretended to study a pamphlet about hotel room security while Gracie found each piece of the clothing Gareth had removed from her body. When she was done, she hovered in the doorway. "I'm sorry, Gareth."

"Go," he said, his throat tight. "We'll talk later."

As soon as he heard the door to her bedroom close, he jotted a quick note, placed it prominently on the table in the foyer and escaped. The walls were closing in on him, and this time he couldn't disappear into his workshop to find peace.

He strode out the front door of the hotel, ignoring Chandra's attempt to waylay him. Pressure built in his chest like a geyser. Somewhere deep inside him a fault line vibrated. *I think I'm falling in love with you.* Good God. What did a man say to that? She wasn't thinking clearly…that's all. Amnesia was a scary thing. Gracie was deluding herself.

He wasn't the kind of man she needed for the long

haul. He was selfish and cynical. No woman in her right mind would want a guy who still battled demons from the past. Gracie was soft…trusting. And she should have a partner to cherish her and make her the center of his world.

Gareth wanted her body. And he enjoyed her quick wit and her sharp tongue. But *love*? No. Not now. Maybe not ever. Especially not when he had yet to determine why she came to Wolff Mountain and what she wanted from him.

Once upon a time, he'd been a naive, horny young man. He'd fancied himself falling in love. Even after all that had happened to him as a child, he'd been willing to lay his heart on the line. To open himself up to the possibility of a future.

The resultant debacle had ripped a jagged hole in his ability to trust. Intimacy. Love. Those two words were babble in a foreign tongue. He liked women. Liked Gracie even more. But if what he offered wasn't enough for her, it was too damn bad.

He'd take her home as promised. Let her find her roots, her life. And then he'd return to his mountain and remind himself that he liked solitude and an empty bed at night.

He didn't need Gracie Darlington to be happy. Not at all.

Chapter 12

Gracie ran water into the lovely Jacuzzi tub and added a handful of scented bath salts. The resulting aroma fogged up the gilt-edged mirrors that hung over matching marble sinks. She was glad to have her image obscured. Every time she looked at her reflection, the woman in the glass shook a disapproving head.

Coward. Tease. There weren't enough pejorative adjectives to cover the way she felt about herself at this moment. She had told Gareth she was falling in love with him, and then had put on the brakes. Her behavior looked manipulative at best. She wanted to embrace the opportunity life had tossed in her lap. She wanted to embrace the big, hardheaded, fascinating Gareth Wolff.

But she was scared. She had a hunch that a broken heart was even harder to mend than a broken brain.

As she took off her robe and slipped into the deliciously warm water, she felt her face burn. Not from the temperature, but from the remembrance of Gareth's slightly panicked expression when she mentioned the "L" word. Had she subconsciously been testing the waters? Hoping at some pathetic level that he would fall at her feet and proclaim his reciprocal pledge of adoration?

She snorted, blowing a clump of bubbles across the tub. Surely the real Gracie Darlington wasn't so needy. Grabbing a razor, she extended one leg and started turning the skin into a smooth expanse ready for a lover's questing touch.

It was possible that she had spooked him badly enough to make *him* be the one to back away. She'd heard the door to their suite close only moments after she fled his bedroom. No doubt, he was putting physical distance between them.

Commitment-phobic guys were famous for nipping relationships in the bud, rather than getting trapped into situations that made them uncomfortable. Judging from Gareth's expression when she dropped her little bomb, he'd been *very* uncomfortable.

It hurt. No two ways about it. The physical intimacies they had shared in the last week seemed like so much more than sex. But even with a few synapses misfiring, she knew enough to realize that men were contrary animals. They saw the world through a different lens. And she'd be wise to remember that.

So, the question was: did she have enough guts to see this thing through to the end, when the truth about Gracie Darlington was revealed? And could she bear to see hatred in Gareth's eyes if that truth was unpalatable or even worse, hurtful?

She had promised to spend the evening with him. Even in a crowd, the connection that sizzled between them would be difficult to ignore. It wasn't fair to Gareth to send out mixed messages. Either she wanted him, or she didn't. It was that simple.

Tonight, when they returned to the hotel, she had to advance or retreat. Once and for all.

When the water cooled, she jumped into the shower to wash her hair, then stepped out and dried off with a velvety towel. Annalise had provided more than one choice for the evening. All three gowns, with familiar names on the sewn-in labels, were sultry, vivid, and skin-baring. They ranged the gamut from red satin to emerald chiffon to a basic black jersey with a halter neck. Black seemed the safest choice. It looked like nothing on the hanger, but surprisingly, morphed drastically when Gracie slid it over her head.

She stared into the mirror, turning this way and that. It would be impossible to wear a bra. In fact, other than a thong panty, anything between her skin and the dress would show. The V-neckline plunged modestly in front, but the reverse side of the dress was nonexistent, nothing but a cowl fold at her lower back.

A smattering of sequins and bugle beads drew attention to her breasts. The expensive fabric clung to her waist and hips, flaring out only slightly as it made its way to the floor.

She thought about changing, but vanity won out. The woman in the mirror was beautiful…confident…sexy. Gracie wanted badly to be that woman.

Her hair was almost dry. She finger combed the loose curls into a deliberately tousled array, stepped into black stilettos, and pirouetted. Not bad for a woman who couldn't remember if she'd ever worn a designer label.

Moments later she grimaced when her stomach growled on cue. She'd been nervous in the helicopter and hadn't finished her sandwich. Dinner would be late.

Though she didn't want to cross paths with Gareth, at least not just yet, she dialed room service and ordered soup and crackers. The mini meal arrived with stunning swiftness, making her wonder if Gareth's presence in the hotel was the equivalent of a red alert.

It wasn't the smartest idea she'd ever had…getting dressed and then trying to eat soup. But she managed not to ruin anything. Afterward, she paced her beautiful room restlessly, torn between wanting to confront Gareth and get it over with and hiding out until the last possible second.

He took the decision out of her hands. The in-house phone on the bureau rang. It was him.

"Hello?"

"It's time, Gracie."

The ominous words sent her stomach into a free fall until she realized he was talking about the senator's party. She smoothed a hand over her stomach. "I'll be right there."

When she opened the door into the living room, her heart stuttered and skipped a couple of beats. Gareth's back was toward her, his wide shoulders straining the fabric of a crisp, obviously tailor-made tux. He'd gotten his hair trimmed while he was out. It still brushed his collar, full and wavy and dark, but she doubted he could put it into his customary stubby ponytail at the moment.

He turned around, and she saw his eyes widen. But she was too dumbstruck to give it much thought. He was magnificent. The white shirt drew attention to his sun-browned skin. Knife-pleated slacks molded to his powerful thighs, and the requisite bow tie and cummerbund almost made him appear civilized.

But she only had to look at his hawklike features

and piercing eyes to see the predatory male animal he really was.

Her thighs tightened in instinctive, feminine reaction. Gripping her tiny evening bag, she forced herself to walk forward instead of beating a hasty retreat. "You look wonderful," she said quietly. "I'm sure the senator will be impressed."

Gareth found himself unable to speak for a full ten seconds. What had happened to his pretty, girl-next-door, memory-challenged Gracie? The woman in front of him was a goddess. Confident, sensual, serene in her infinite beauty.

He cleared his throat. "The senator is known as a womanizer. Perhaps taking you tonight is a bad idea. He probably gobbles up sweet young things like you for breakfast."

"I read my driver's license. Thirty doesn't sound all that young." She approached him, one long, toned, slender leg appearing briefly through the mile-high slit in her narrow skirt. "But it's a good thing I have you to protect me." As she slid an arm through his, he almost groaned. His erection was heavy…painful. Every muscle in his body clenched in helpless desire. Appearing at some fancy society dinner and being paraded around like a damned lapdog was so far down the list of things he wanted to do tonight, it was criminal. Reminding himself of the charitable payoff was the only way he could follow through with what promised to be torture… in more ways than one.

He clasped her fingers with his. "The car is waiting." His conversation had been reduced to banalities. But damned if he could do better. All the blood in his body had rushed south. It was a miracle he could walk upright.

In the elevator her reflection in the mirror taunted him. Narrow white shoulders, shapely breasts, a flat belly and just the hint of a dip in the fabric that covered her most vulnerable femininity. Was she naked beneath that man-killer dress?

He noticed the omission of a wrap. "Won't you be cold?" he asked hoarsely. Still no more than a four-word sentence.

"You can keep me warm." Her smile was dauntingly close to making him come with no more than a look.

"You're not playing fair, Gracie Darlington."

She sobered. "You're right. I'm not. My only excuse is extreme confusion. But things are clearer to me now than they were this afternoon."

He resisted the urge to slide a finger inside his collar and loosen his tie. "How so?"

She leaned into him and slid her silly little purse into his pocket. Her slim arms encircled his neck. "I was scared."

"And now?"

Her hips brushed his. He wondered if she felt his urgency.

Apparently so. Her eyes widened. She looked up at him. No artifice. No coquettish invitation. Nothing but unveiled, completely vulnerable feminine need. "Forget what I said about love," she whispered. "To hell with who I am, who I was. All I want is to enjoy this thing between us for as long as we can. No looking forward. No looking back. No regrets."

He cursed long and low. "You're killing me, woman. Do you really expect me to walk around with a boner all night?"

Her lips caressed his chin. "Suffering builds character."

"Then you might as well nominate me for sainthood," he said gruffly. "Because if I make it through the evening without shoving you into a coat closet and taking you hard and fast, it will be a miracle."

She didn't have a chance to respond. The elevator slid to a halt in the lobby with a muffled *ding*, and the door slid open. For once, Chandra was not in sight. Gareth was glad.

The limo waited out front. Gareth gave the chauffeur the address, helped Gracie into the car and followed right behind her. He made no pretense at polite, socially acceptable behavior. With one quick flick of a button, he raised the privacy screen. Seconds later, he hauled Gracie into his lap and kissed her urgently. Tinted windows kept the world at bay.

It was almost like holding her naked. Every hill and valley of her body was his to explore, the thin fabric more of an enhancement than an impediment. The skirt of her dress succumbed to gravity, baring her legs. He slid a hand up her thigh and found only a tiny excuse for panties. His handkerchiefs were bigger.

The satin between her legs was damp. He rubbed gently, dangerously close to losing control. "You want me." He needed to hear the admission, needed to know that he wasn't the only one going crazy with lust...with hunger so intense it obscured all other realities.

"Yes." Her voice was little more than a reedy breath of air.

He stroked a pert nipple, now sure that nothing stood between him and her bare skin but the dress. "God, you are beautiful." He tangled a hand in her loose curls, wrapping one around his finger and seeing how it clung to his skin. Tugging gently, he half lifted her and helped her straddle his lap. The dress had to be shoved higher. He couldn't risk tearing it. Not now. With the skirt rucked up to her waist, he could see that the panties were hot pink, his new favorite color.

The naughty position made her vulnerable to his touch. His thighs stretched hers deliberately, opening her to him completely. He could have removed the panties…thought about it. But certain boundaries had to remain if he was to fulfill his role tonight.

Deliberately he stroked his thumb over her clitoris. She moaned and writhed as if trying to get away. No way in hell. He had her right where he wanted her. Again, he repeated the caress.

"Gareth…"

"Hmm?" He probed with two fingers at the opening of her channel, hampered by the cloth, wishing this erotic play was going to lead directly to the intimate contact he craved.

She didn't say anything else. Her eyes were closed. She was wrapped up in the pleasure he was giving her. That knowledge filled him with fierce satisfaction. The evocative bouquet of her perfume mingled with the scent of feminine arousal.

"Look at me." As her eyelashes fluttered open, he locked his gaze on hers, demanding obedience. "Put your hands on my shoulders."

She did as he asked…immediately. Without a word.

"See how long you can hold out," he urged. "Show me your strength, your power."

He moved his thumb back and forth, changing things up with quick strokes of his fingers. Gracie whimpered and begged, coming nearer every second to completion. But as soon as he knew she was close, he cupped her with his palm, petting her and lulling her body into submission.

She fought him. She called him names. And finally, when he was close to the breaking point himself, he nudged firmly and sent her shooting into a climax that was beautiful and humbling to watch.

He'd long since resigned himself to an evening of agony. Now the night would be layered with sexual suffering as well.

Holding her close, he stroked her bare back, traced the delicate spine, buried his face in her hair. The city streets swept by unnoticed. Gareth had the means to keep the car going indefinitely—all the way to L.A. if he chose—but the journey had an end. And Gareth had made a commitment he was forced to honor.

Reluctantly he sat her up straight. Wincing at the sight of her sprawled legs, he turned her, straightened her dress and pulled her to his chest. "You okay?"

She nuzzled her cheek against his starched shirt, right over the spot where his heartbeat thundered. "Yeah."

They rode in silence, just like that, for miles. The Welcome to Virginia sign made him curse inwardly. He didn't want to let her go. Not now. Maybe not ever.

By the time the limo rolled to a smooth stop, Gracie had returned to her seat, fixed her makeup and hair and huddled in her own corner, staring out the window.

The senator's mansion was impressive by any standards; white columns, softly weathered brick, a curved driveway filled with cars and guests. Gareth felt his gut tighten. He'd been in social settings as upscale or more than this one since he'd been a child. But the thought of being trotted out like a dancing monkey filled him with loathing.

And the worst part was it was his own damn fault. He

hoped that three hours would cover drinks and dinner and the obligatory mingling. All else aside, he wanted to take Gracie back to the hotel as quickly as possible.

He reached across the seat and touched her hand. "I don't know what your background is..." He chuckled ruefully. "And neither do you. But in my experience, the super elite are pretty much like anyone else. You'll meet the vain, the cocksure and the genuinely charming. I'll do my best to stay by your side, but the senator can be pretty bullheaded when he wants something. So if we get separated and you're at all uncomfortable, grab a glass of wine, hide in a corner and I swear I'll rescue you."

"And if I embarrass myself with a devastating faux pas?"

He grinned, already focused on thoughts of having her tonight. "Don't worry. After a few rounds of drinks, I guarantee you no one will notice."

Chapter 13

Gracie decided that the best way to handle the evening was to approach it as a movie. Her role was a tiny bit part that might end up on the cutting-room floor. Gareth was the star. And her job, at least for tonight, was to trail in his wake and be there if he needed her.

As she placed her hand in his to be helped out of the car, their fingers clung. When she was standing on the flagstone driveway, he lifted her hand to his mouth and kissed the back of it, lingering long enough to make her knees weak. Though she tried hard not to show it, she was still reeling from Gareth's drive-time entertainment. She had let him reduce her to a mass of quivering need, begged him with no thought for pride and then collapsed in his arms, sated…wrung out…head over heels in love.

A love he didn't want. A love she would keep to herself from now on.

But sadly, there was no time for a post mortem, inward or otherwise. Their car was already pulling away. Gareth ushered her up a flight of steps flanked by topiaries sculpted in the shape of eagles. Tiny white lights entwined in the branches sparkled in the amazingly balmy night.

The senator and his two-decades-younger wife received guests in the elegant foyer. "Mr. Wolff. I'm delighted to finally meet you." The suave politician was tanning-bed bronze, twenty pounds overweight and had a smile that didn't quite reach his calculating eyes. "This is my wife, Darla. And your lovely guest is…?"

Gracie shuddered. This man gave her the creeps.

Gareth squeezed her hand unobtrusively. "Gracie Darlington. A very good friend of mine."

"We're so happy to have you visit our home." The simpering Darla sized up Gareth with an experienced eye, her avid expression as she looked him over disturbingly akin to Chandra's. Definitely a *fresh meat* nuance in her gaze.

Fortunately guests were bottlenecking on the steps, so Gareth and Gracie were allowed to shuttle back through the hallway to the formal salon where hors d'oeuvres were being served. She found herself tucked close to his side to keep from getting crushed in the melee. Where was a fire marshal when you needed one?

They snagged a table tucked to the side of a strangely out-of-place palm tree, and Gareth shook his head in bemusement. "Want some champagne?" he asked.

Gracie nodded. "I have a feeling we'll need more than one glass apiece."

He kissed her cheek. "You are so right. But we'll start with one."

In a surprisingly short time given the crush around the food table, he returned with a duo of expensive crystal flutes and a single plate of food piled high. Scallops wrapped in prosciutto, wedges of baked brie, skewers of fat boiled shrimp and grilled eggplant.

They stood elbow to elbow at the tall linen-covered table and demolished the bounty, Gareth consuming two-thirds of it. He smiled sheepishly as he filched the last shrimp. "Forgot to order room service. I'm starving."

Her lips quirked. "We could have snacked in the car," she said demurely, feeling her chest flush with remembrance.

His eyes darkened. Patting his mouth with a thick napkin, he cocked his head and stared at her. "Some of us did. You're awfully cheeky for a woman who was screaming my name thirty minutes ago."

"Gareth!" She glanced around to see if anyone was close enough to hear. "Behave yourself," she said, pinching his muscular forearm through the fabric of his jacket.

"That's no fun."

She watched as his eyes scanned the room. The monstrous cabinet he had created for the senator held a position of honor on the far wall. It still amazed her to think of the talent hidden in Gareth's large, masculine hands. But then again, she probably shouldn't be surprised at all. He played her body like a maestro.

Uniformed staff unobtrusively moved the crowd in the direction of the dining room. The long, narrow space held a magnificent dinner table surrounded by antique chairs, the seats covered in crimson-and-cream-striped damask. Handwritten place cards mingled with heavy silver and exquisite china.

Gracie found herself seated between a charming ambassador and a famous baseball player. The fact that she knew the pitcher's name told her she was a sports fan.

Just one more piece in the puzzle. She was nervous, though she understood the functions of the place setting pieces and the flow of a formal dinner. Perhaps her father's gallery hosted the occasional soiree, though on a far less exalted level.

Gareth's assigned spot was across the table from her, just far enough away to make conversation difficult. He, on the other hand, was surrounded by a pair of Botoxed socialites who hung on his every word. Though he conversed easily through at least five interminable courses, Gracie already knew him well enough to see the tension in his big frame…and his distaste for the way his dinner companions continued to touch him with seemingly innocent motions.

It was a distinct relief when the senator rose to his feet and quieted his guests with the clink of a fork against his wineglass.

He smiled expansively, clearly in his element as the cynosure of all eyes. "It gives me great pleasure tonight to introduce you to the incomparable Gareth Wolff." He paused for the muted smattering of applause. "Gareth… if I may call him that?"

The raised eyebrows and jovial urbanity directed at his reluctant star demanded a positive response.

Gareth nodded stiffly.

The senator continued "Gareth, in addition to being part of the well-known Wolff financial empire, is a master craftsman in wood. He creates only special order pieces, and has a waiting list of several years. After much cajoling on my part—" polite laughter on cue "—Gareth agreed to build the gun cabinet you have all seen tonight, one that is a close replica of a piece once owned by the incomparable Teddy Roosevelt. I couldn't be more pleased with the result, and it is my distinct honor to introduce to you tonight…Mr. Gareth Wolff."

Gareth rose to his feet, and for the first time, Gracie understood that Gareth Wolff was part of this world, despite his proclivity for seclusion. He was born to it, bred to be a mover and shaker. His stance was relaxed but compelling, his personality dominant in the hushed silence. His dark coloring made him seem like an exotic predator in a room full of colorful, insubstantial social animals.

With one hand in the pocket of his tux, he swept his arm out in a motion that encompassed the senator's largesse. "It's an honor to be here tonight in the senator's lovely home. And many thanks to our hostess, Darla."

The woman actually tittered nervously.

Gareth smiled at her. "Not only has the senator met my outrageous purchase price, all of which, as you know, goes to charity, but he has also donated an equally large check for my delivery fee." That last, self-deprecating, tongue-in-cheek remark amused the crowd.

Gracie watched them, noted the way all eyes were on Gareth, the women with sexual appreciation, the men with respectful admiration. Even the senator didn't appear to mind that Gareth's sheer charisma had hijacked center stage.

Gareth continued. "Most of the major fundraising in this country is financed by the generosity of men and women like yourselves. You make a difference in so many ways, and I respect your willingness to share with those in need, those less fortunate. Tonight, I'm especially grateful to the senator and his wife. I'll look forward to meeting more of you as the evening progresses."

Gareth sat down to uproarious applause. Gracie was impressed and humbled. If there had been any doubt in her mind before, now there was none. She had no permanent place in the life of a man like Gareth Wolff. Though her own past was still an unknown, she sensed that her calendar was not studded with such evenings, and that hobnobbing with the social elite was not something she did on a regular basis.

When dinner drew to a close, the crowd moved en masse to an actual ballroom. It was impossible to gauge the square footage of the senator's home, but Gracie had seen enough of it to know that the man in question clearly had a private fortune to supplement his earnings as a public servant.

Gareth joined her, an arm around her waist. He stood out in the crowded room. "You having fun?"

His droll question made her smile. "It's been an educational evening. I'll give you that." She leaned her head against his shoulder briefly. "You were very charming. I won't be surprised if several of these women slip checks into your pocket."

"Not the men?" His eyes danced.

"Perhaps. But you have every female in this house panting after you. And if they have to give money to get close to you, I'm sure that's what they'll do."

He turned her to face him, his hands on her shoulders, warming her bare skin. "Jealous, Gracie Darlington?"

The question was teasing. He clearly expected a riposte from her in return. But the truth was—yes she was jealous. Not because of any specific woman's attentions to Gareth, but because she knew that the females gathered here tonight were the sort of pool from which a man in Gareth's position would select a wife…if he ever did. She shifted slightly, forcing his hands to fall away. "Just making an observation," she said lightly.

"I'm not in a position to be jealous. And besides, that's why we're here, isn't it?"

Gareth frowned. Opened his mouth to say something. But in that instant, Darla appeared by his side, her face alight with enthusiasm. "I'd like to share the first dance with our guest of honor… Hostess's prerogative, you know." She barely glanced at Gracie. "What do you say, Mr. Wolff? And may I call you Gareth? By the way, a half dozen of my girlfriends are planning to make donations tonight. I'm sure you won't mind a few turns around the dance floor in return. Right?"

As her high-pitched prattle continued, she drew Gareth out into the throng of dancers. Gracie watched them go, heartsick…alone. But when an older man with a bad hairpiece moved zealously in her direction, she hastily slid out a side door and found the ladies' room.

After using the restroom and checking her makeup, she sat on an ornate ottoman for a long time, giving Gareth a chance to make his obligatory rounds. Finally she sucked up her courage and returned, like a weary Cinderella, to the ball.

Gareth saw her as soon as she entered the room. The knot in his stomach eased. He'd known the instant she vanished, had fretted like an old woman until she reappeared.

If he had his way, he would make a beeline for her right now. But the fact that he now had a sheaf of checks in his pocket, which at first glance totaled well over two hundred thousand dollars for his charity, kept him on the job. Reluctant. Frustrated. But resigned. Probably less than five percent of the crowd gave a damn about what was important to Gareth. But if they were willing to toss cash around like confetti, he wasn't going to stop them.

As he watched, Gracie found a seat on the side-lines and waved at him, her face serene, her expression amused at his expense. He grinned at her wryly over the shoulder of his current dance partner. Gracie knew how much he hated this. What she probably didn't under-stand was how much her presence made it all bearable.

During every interminable song, in the midst of every cloying conversation, he subverted his impatience with the knowledge that tonight he'd have Gracie in his bed, wrapped naked in his arms.

Another woman cut in, her determined gaze brook-ing no opposition as she elbowed her predecessor out of the way. Gareth sighed inwardly, ground his teeth and manufactured a smile that was beginning to fray at the edges. "Tell me your name," he said, consigning the woman to hell and back. "It's a pleasure to meet you."

It was after eleven when Gracie visited the bar for one last glass of wine. During the course of the evening she had exchanged banalities with a host of people whose names she would never remember. She was ready to find a chair and hide out until Gareth cut loose and decided it was time for them to leave.

A half dozen times he had moved in her direction, clearly expecting to dance with her, only to be waylaid at the last moment by one of the senator's guests.

Not all of Gareth's admirers were female. Almost as many men approached him, not to dance of course, but to pull him aside, offer a cigar out on the terrace, or merely to engage him in conversation.

Gracie was disappointed, but not hurt. She wanted to dance with Gareth, but this evening was not about romance. That would come later. Just the thought of being alone with him in their fancy hotel room made her breath catch. These glitzy people might have dibs on him for the evening, but when it was time to go, she had him for the whole night.

As she sipped her wine and contemplated how much her feet hurt in her beautiful shoes, a pleasant-faced older woman approached her.

"Hello, my dear. I'm Genevieve Grayson. My husband works as a lobbyist for the beef industry." She paused, smiled diffidently and continued: "You seem a bit lost, and I know how that feels. I've passed many an hour at these kinds of functions, waiting patiently as my spouse does his job. I just wanted to say hello."

Gracie was touched. "Hello, Genevieve. How kind of you." Perhaps that last glass of wine had been a mistake. The room seemed to be spinning slightly. "You must be a very patient woman. I can't imagine doing this on a regular basis. Not that the senator's dinner party isn't lovely, but I confess I'm more of a *curl-up-with-a-book* kind of gal."

Genevieve asked the bartender for a gin and tonic and sipped it slowly. "He's thinking about retiring soon…my husband, that is. We have our eye on a beautiful horse farm out in rural Virginia. I have visions of the two of us sitting in rocking chairs watching the sun set."

"Sounds lovely."

Genevieve's absent gaze was wistful. "Perhaps only a fantasy, unfortunately. He thrives on the high-octane energy in Washington. I'm not sure how he'll take to being put out to pasture."

"I hope everything works out for you."

They stood in silence for several moments. Gracie appreciated the woman's kindness to a stranger, but even this minimal conversation was tiring after a long day, a long week. Her stomach rolled. Perhaps she should eat something.

Genevieve seemed to call herself back to the present. "So, Gracie. Are you and Gareth Wolff an item?"

"Just friends." Gracie grimaced inwardly. How many women this evening had wondered the same thing? Obviously Genevieve's motive in asking was no more than simple curiosity, but Gracie felt self-conscious nevertheless.

"He's a very impressive man."

"Yes, he is. I admire him very much."

"Tell me, Gracie. What do you do when you're not socializing with one of the East Coast's most eligible bachelors? Are you an artist like Gareth?" Genevieve's gentle interrogation was nothing out of the ordinary. Simple dinner party conversation. Queries a six-year-old could answer.

Gracie froze. Deer-in-the-headlights froze. She and Gareth should have come up with a plan for this eventuality. But they had been too busy indulging their hunger for each other. "Well, I…"

Her face must have shown distress, because Genevieve backed off immediately. "I'm sorry, my dear. My husband always accuses me of being nosy. If you'd rather not say, I certainly understand. All of us inside the beltway certainly understand secrecy."

"Oh, no," Gracie said, legs trembling. "It's not that at all. I have nothing to hide. It's just that…"

Her throat closed up. Nausea rose and crested in her belly. Embarrassment rolled over her head like a suffocating shroud. How had she not prepared for this eventuality? She could have lied. Pretended to be a lawyer, a teacher…anything.

Genevieve took her arm. "It's okay," she said in a

soothing voice. "I didn't mean to upset you. Let me take your glass so it doesn't spill."

Gracie's hands were ice-cold. Her vision tunneled. She must have looked like hell, because Genevieve's placid expression went from cordial to panicked.

Gracie tried to breathe through the constriction in her chest. "Gareth," she whispered. "I need Gareth."

Her world went black.

Chapter 14

He saw her go down. For a split second his brain couldn't process what was happening. "Sorry," he muttered, thrusting the woman in his arms away and sprinting across the dance floor.

The older woman who had been conversing with Gracie had managed to catch her somewhat, supporting Gracie's dead weight long enough to keep her from hitting her head as she collapsed to the floor.

Gareth scooped up the unconscious Gracie in his arms, cursing his stupidity. "Help me find a bedroom," he demanded, his tone harsh.

The woman never missed a beat. They walked quickly down a hallway into a quiet wing, ending up in a beautifully appointed guest room that was thankfully empty.

Gareth laid Gracie carefully on the bed. Put his hand on her chest momentarily. She was breathing. One small part of his brain had wondered if Jacob missed something…if the previous head injury had resulted in death. *Dear God…*

He closed his eyes for a split second, his composure in shreds.

As he turned around, the woman held out her hand. "I'm Genevieve," she said.

Shaking her hand briefly, he turned back to where Gracie lay so still and lovely in her black dress, the color emphasizing her pallor. "What happened?"

"I don't really know." Genevieve shrugged, her face unhappy. "We were having a nice conversation when she suddenly became overwrought."

"In what way?"

"I asked her about herself…you know…what she does for a living, and she became very agitated before passing out."

Gareth cursed furiously.

Genevieve blanched. "I'm sorry. Is this my fault somehow?"

He fisted his hands, wondering if he should call 911. "No," he muttered. Gracie wouldn't want her personal business to end up the source of gossip. "She's been through a very difficult time lately. I thought an evening out would be good for her. Apparently I was wrong."

Gracie stirred on the bed, her colorless lips moving silently as she began to wake up.

"What can I do to help?" Genevieve asked.

He rummaged in his pocket for a card. "Please call the car service. This is my driver. Ask him to come to the back door ASAP." He paused, knowing he owed this woman a debt and an apology. "Thank you for being kind to her. I'm sorry if I was rude."

Genevieve touched his arm gently. "I saw your face,

young man. This woman is your life." With no more than that, she exited the room.

Gareth sat down on the bed and pulled Gracie into his arms, holding her tightly. "I've got you," he said, his eyes stinging. "I've got you."

Her lashes lifted, revealing a cloudy, confused gaze. "Gareth?"

"You're fine. Everything's fine. We're going home."

"But I wanted to dance with you."

He hadn't thought he could feel any worse. "Maybe another time," he said, the words torn from his throat. "Let's get you home."

Genevieve was as good as her word. As soon as Gareth spirited Gracie to the back of the house, carrying her with utmost care, the car appeared at the back door. Genevieve waved them off and promised to give Gareth's goodbyes to the senator.

Gareth would have taken Gracie away under any conditions, but the hour was late, and Gareth had certainly fulfilled his obligation.

In the limo he reached into the mini fridge for a bottle of water and unscrewed the cap. "Drink this," he said softly, holding her across his lap and wondering if he'd ever be able to let go. "You scared the hell out of me."

Her blue eyes met his. "I'm so sorry if I embarrassed you in front of the senator," she said miserably. "I never should have come."

"Correction," he said tersely. "I never should have brought you."

Her tiny gasp and the wounded look on her face reduced him to cursing again. "Hell, Gracie. You know that's not what I meant. I'm worried about you, damn it. Clearly neither of us has taken the consequences of this amnesia thing seriously enough. What happened in there? Why did you faint?"

She insisted on leaving his lap, her shoulders bowed in defeat. "It was nothing," she murmured, her face turned toward the window as they streaked along through the night, cocooned in intimacy. "A stupid nothing."

He caressed her arm. "Tell me. Please."

"She asked me what I did…when I wasn't dating the East Coast's most eligible bachelor. All I had to do was make up something, but for some reason, her simple question caught me off guard. I'd probably had too much wine…and I didn't eat enough of my dinner. What can I say? I was an idiot."

"Stop that," he said firmly. "You're not to blame. I brought you here. Took you out of a safe environment. Exactly what Jacob warned me not to do."

"But I *wanted* to come," she insisted. "I wanted this one special time with you before I have to leave."

"Not so special anymore, is it?" He brooded quietly in his corner, wishing he could turn back the clock.

At the hotel, she battled him, insisting on going inside under her own steam. The only reason he didn't over-rule her was that the argument took what little strength she had left and winnowed it away.

In their living room, he hesitated, unsure of the appropriate course of action. He wouldn't make love to her, not tonight. She needed to rest. But would she rather be alone?

She swayed on her feet, her skin paper-white, her eyes haunted. Not a trace of his spunky, combative house-guest remained.

"Maybe you'd be more comfortable in your own bed," he muttered. "No need to set an alarm. All I had planned for tomorrow was some touristy stuff. Or we can go home if you'd rather."

Her gaze was uncomprehending, her eyes bleak.

"Come here." He picked her up. She didn't protest as her head lolled against his shoulder.

In her room, he stood her on her feet only long enough to slide the dress from her body and tuck her between the sheets wearing nothing but those sinful panties. Seeing her almost-nude beauty shook him.

Earlier in the limo, a wanton and fabulous Gracie had dazzled him with her strength, her fiery femininity. Now she was a broken doll. And it was his fault.

Gracie woke in the dark, struggling to break free from the tentacles of a bad dream. She bit her lip, refusing to cry out and wake Gareth. She'd done enough damage as it was. He didn't need her to lean on him, to suffocate him with her neediness.

And if she was going to enjoy his lovemaking in whatever short time they had left, she surely didn't want a man who felt sorry for her.

After donning a thigh-length silk robe, she crept stealthily into the living room and opened the armoire that hid a small fridge. Taking out a bottle of sparkling water, she unscrewed the lid and sipped it slowly, wondering if her life would ever get back to normal.

She was trapped in a strange limbo. Too broken and confused to recognize the past, too distraught to contemplate the future.

She crossed the room, eased open the glass doors and stepped out onto the small balcony. It was cold now, the flagstones icy beneath her feet. She welcomed the discomfort, needing to shake off the lingering effects of the nightmare.

Traffic noise, even at this hour, hummed in the distance. This beautiful historic city had seen its fair share of heartache and pain. With equal measures of hope and triumph in between. Gracie intended to emulate that pattern. Life had dealt her a dual blow...erasing her memory and filling the resultant void with an intense yearning for a man who would not, could not be hers.

She had to trust that whatever followed, wherever the path led her, she would survive, both literally and emotionally. She was strong; she felt that in the marrow of her bones. And she was never going to admit defeat when it came to retrieving her memories, even if some of them were gone for good.

And as for Gareth...

Well, Shakespeare had it right. It was better to have loved and lost than never to have loved at all.

She shivered violently, her numb fingers clenched around the glass bottle. The thought of returning to her solitary bed held little allure. But she dared not risk adding pneumonia to her list of physical ailments.

As quietly as she had exited, she padded back inside, locking the French doors and pulling the diaphanous fabric panels into place. When she turned around, her heartbeat spiked in alarm. A man loomed in the shadows of the room. Gareth.

She set the water bottle on a table and wrapped her arms around her middle. "You scared me," she said softly.

"Then we're even. What are you doing out of bed?"

"I'm sorry I woke you." It wasn't an answer to his question, but she didn't mention the dream. If a woman planned to stand on her own two feet, she had to start somewhere.

Gareth closed the distance between them. For the

first time, she realized he was wearing nothing but a pair of navy silk boxers. His broad chest looked even more impressive au naturel than it had in a designer tuxedo. With rumpled hair and the dark shadow of a beard marking his roughly sculpted jawline, he looked nothing like the senator's honored guest. He stopped mere inches from her, their bodies almost touching.

"Come to bed with me," he said, the words a low rumble that stroked her nerves and weakened her knees.

"I can't, Gareth." She wanted to. She craved the oblivion that she would find in his arms, the soul-searing relief of climax, the physical bliss his claiming would bring. But she hadn't slept well the past few nights without Gareth in her bed. And she ached with a fatigue that was as much mental as physical.

"Not for that. You need to let me hold you." He stopped, backed up verbally. "I need to hold you," he said, dropping his forehead to hers as he slid his arms around her waist. "Good God," he exclaimed. "You're freezing."

She wanted to cry when he picked her up, his strength effortless as he carried her back to his bed. He tucked her beneath the covers and slid in beside her. The sheets still held the heat from his body. She curled into a ball, her head pillowed on her hand. Gareth spooned her from behind, his natural warmth so comforting she wanted to purr.

"Thank you," she whispered.

"For what?"

His unmistakable erection pulsed between them, but he neither acknowledged his physical state nor made any attempt to coax her into a more intimate embrace.

She yawned, sleep slurring her words. "For rescuing me tonight."

He chuckled, holding her close, his hard, hair-covered arm tucked firmly beneath her breasts. "A woman as strong as you are is more than capable of rescuing herself." He played with a curl behind her ear, his fingers sending shivers of sensation down her neck. "Go to sleep, Gracie." He kissed the back of her neck. "Go to sleep."

She obeyed him instantly, her body going lax, her breathing slowing to a calm, steady cadence. Holding her like this was both pleasure and pain. His body recognized the opportunity for what it was. His better instincts reminded him that she was fragile, in need of healing.

As the clock marked off the hours, he pondered his options. The life he'd built for himself had no permanent place for a woman. And even if he managed to rewrite his own hard-and-fast rules, Gracie might not need him anymore once she returned to her home turf.

He could love her if he allowed himself that leeway. But he hadn't. Not yet. Caution still held the reins. He knew what it was like to love and to lose, and he was in no hurry to experience that pain again.

He cupped one of her small, firm breasts. She fit into his arms perfectly. But into his life? That was another story.

Who *was* Gracie Darlington? And did it really matter if she had amnesia? The world was full of couples who married only to realize that they didn't know the other person at all. Was it ever possible to really know someone?

He loved the qualities Gracie had shown him. Her sweet spirit. Her compassion. Her refusal to whine or complain in the face of adversity. Surely nothing sinister lurked in the wings.

Marriage? He lifted a mental eyebrow, stunned that the word had popped into his head, even obliquely.

Resting his cheek against her shoulder, he tried to let sleep claim him. Hard as a pike, hungry as a lion, he forced himself to relax, to be lulled by the rhythm of her breathing.

The world outside their room ceased to exist as he closed his eyes and breathed in the scent of her hair.

Chapter 15

Gracie had disappeared when he woke up. But the pillow beside him still bore the imprint of her head. He yawned and stretched. She couldn't have been gone long.

After showering rapidly, he went in search of her... and found her standing on the balcony again, this time dressed in crisp white slacks and an off-the-shoulder turquoise peasant blouse. She looked fresh and beautiful, and he wanted her so badly, he shook with it.

He scowled, unused to being at the mercy of his body. Enduring periods of celibacy had always been his choice. But with Gracie, his self-control ceased to exist. If he had his way, they would never leave the suite. Spending the day in bed held a raw, seductive appeal.

She smiled at him when he stepped outside. "Good morning." Her eyes were clear, the shadows gone.

He gave her a hard kiss, one that left her flustered and rosy cheeked. "Good morning, yourself. Are you ready to hit the town? I thought we'd take in some of the museums."

"Sounds fun."

"Do you have any feel for whether you've ever explored the Smithsonian?"

"Not a clue. So I'm ready to be entertained."

He would have liked to interpret her words on a carnal level, but he'd promised himself to give her an uncomplicated, enjoyable day. Tomorrow they would head back to the mountain…and soon, on to Savannah. He shoved the thought aside. "Grab what you need. I have a driver picking us up in fifteen minutes."

Gracie managed to shut out all memories of the previous night's debacle. For a few short hours, she intended to have nothing on her mind but a handsome man, a fun day and a chance to spread her wings.

Gareth had hired a driver for their outing, insisting that Gracie was not up to walking the distances required to go from museum to museum. It was patently untrue. She felt full of energy and ready to tackle the world. But if Gareth insisted on pampering her, who was she to quibble?

After breakfast at a street-side café, they made their way via a maze of one-way streets to their first stop. The Museum of American History. Gracie recognized items in many of the exhibits: Dorothy's ruby-red slippers, Julia Child's kitchen, the Star-Spangled Banner, Michelle Obama's inaugural gown. But she had no clue if she had stood in these exact same spots before, or if she knew the cultural icons in other contexts.

Later, they picnicked on the mall, seated side by side on a park bench, the sun beaming down with benevolent warmth. The driver had picked up a preordered basket filled with all sorts of goodies. As they ate, Gracie smiled, enjoying the feeling of normalcy. All around them, life ebbed and flowed. "I like it here," she said, sipping a Coke and stretching her legs to admire the espadrilles Annalise had picked out.

Gareth extended an arm behind her along the back of the seat. "I'm glad," he said simply. "I thought we'd take in one more stop and then get you back to the hotel to rest."

"I'm not an invalid."

His expression was stubborn. "We're not having a repeat of last night. Jacob can't be here, and I take my medical responsibilities very seriously."

"If it makes you feel better. But I'm okay, I swear." Drumming up her courage, she spoke quietly, looking straight ahead, not at him. "May I ask you something?"

She was close enough to feel the tension that gripped his body. "If you must."

The half-joking tone was probably more truthful than he wanted her to realize. "Will you tell me about your charity?"

The silent pause that lingered between them could have spanned the length of the grassy mall. "What do you want to know?"

"Did you start it on your own? What does it do? Why didn't you talk about it directly last night?"

"Are you sure you're not a reporter?"

Again, the quasi-humor didn't quite ring true. "I'm curious about you," she said. "I'll admit it." Perhaps she shouldn't have pushed, but she really did want to know.

He exhaled, rolling his shoulders and grimacing. "It's called *W.O.L.F.*"

"An acronym?"

He nodded. "*Working Out Loss and Fear.* It's a

foundation that provides counseling opportunities for children who have lost a parent in violent or tragic circumstances—war, cancer, automobile accidents…"

"Kidnapping? Murder?"

She saw him flinch. The terrible words seemed out of place on such a beautiful day.

"That, too," he said, the words tight. "I started it when I turned eighteen. On that birthday, I inherited a bequest from my maternal grandmother. It had been held in trust for me, and there was also an amount from my mother, as well. With the help of the family lawyers, I fleshed out what I wanted and they made the legalities work."

"And you run it?"

He shook his head. "Not anymore. I have an excellent board who oversees the process of reviewing applicants and dispersing funds."

"Couldn't you have collected even more money last night if you had given a sales pitch for the charity?"

"Probably. But I swore when I started W.O.L.F. that I would never exploit my mother's death, even for good. I don't want her to be remembered for the way she died. In life she was happy and upbeat and incredibly giving. That's the image I try to carry in my head."

But clearly, such intent was not always successful. Gareth held within him a remnant of the young boy who had stared in horror at grisly crime scene photos he should never have witnessed.

She allowed the conversation to lapse. Gareth's willingness to answer her questions truthfully marked a milestone.

They tossed their trash and walked across the grass to the National Gallery of Art. Gareth took her arm as they climbed the broad, wide steps. "You clearly know something about the art world," he said, "since your father owns a gallery. So I thought this might shake something loose."

She stopped dead, halting his progress as well. "Can't we just have fun?" she pleaded. "Please don't look for miracles at this point. I can't take the pressure of you always wondering if I'm getting better. It makes me crazy."

He raked a hand through his hair, remorse flickering in his eyes. "Sorry. Of course we can. Once we go through that door, I'll follow your lead. I want this to be a day you'll always remember."

"Is that a joke?"

He actually reddened, his foot-in-mouth comment hanging in the air between them. "No," he muttered. "And I'm not saying another word."

The museum fascinated Gracie. She wandered from gallery to gallery, Gareth trailing in her wake. He kept his vow, remaining silent as she absorbed the centuries of artistic genius housed within the massive walls.

When they came to the impressionists, Gracie halted, struck by a yearning that caught her off guard. She knew these works…knew them well. One in particular caught her eye… *Girl With a Watering Can*. She moved closer, studying the brush strokes, the smears of color that added up to a masterpiece.

Suddenly a dam inside her brain breached, letting in a rush of certainty. "I've been here," she whispered. "I know it."

Gareth didn't comment. But he stood at her shoulder, bolstering her confidence with his quiet presence. She wanted to run her hand over the canvas, but the uniformed guard stationed in the doorway of the room was a deterrent.

Fascinated…scared…hopeful, she examined the

painting. "I think I have a copy of this in my bedroom… over my dresser."

"What else?" he prompted.

She bit her lip, concentrating so hard, her head ached. "The dresser is oak. And the drawer pulls are antique glass."

His arms went around her from behind. "Take your time. Don't force it."

She closed her eyes, the better to concentrate on a fuzzy image that threatened to dissolve like smoke in the wind. "I have a picture of my mother on my dresser. I don't think she's alive. There's no sense of immediacy in my memory of her."

Gareth's big frame surrounded hers, protective…supportive. "It will come, Gracie. Even if you have to go back to Savannah to complete the picture, it will come."

Long moments passed in silence as she reached for what could not be touched. "That's all," she said, frustrated, but no longer despairing. The clarity of this most recent memory convinced her that it was only a matter of time until she had everything back that she had lost.

Disheartened, but philosophical, she turned in his arms to face him, her hands at his waist. "I want you to know," she said slowly, "that I'm sorry. Sorry to have invaded your privacy. Sorry to have arrived on your mountain with some agenda of my father's in hand. It pains me to know that he convinced me to do it. Even if I don't know what 'it' is."

He kissed her softly, unconcerned with the groups of people milling around them. "I wouldn't have missed the chance to know you, Gracie Darlington. So I say to hell with your apologies. We'll deal with the truth, whatever it is."

"What if I'm more like my father than we know? What if I'm manipulative and nosy and self-serving?"

"You're not. Don't be ridiculous." He tugged her hand and led her out into the enormous rotunda. "Let's go back to the hotel. You don't realize what a toll these bits and pieces of memory take on you. This is supposed to be a fun day. Not stressful. Let it go for now."

She allowed herself to be persuaded, though the instinct to prowl through the museum again was strong.

In the limo, Gareth leaned back, his gaze focused outside the window. Gracie wanted to know what he was thinking, but she was afraid to ask. The unknown hung between them, an impenetrable curtain that might or might not mask an unpalatable truth.

His profile had become as familiar to her as the image of her own features in the mirror. She sensed a restlessness in him and wondered if he was missing his mountain.

In their suite, he confronted her, stone-faced, hands stuffed in his pockets. "I have some calls to make," he said abruptly. "I thought you might want to shower and freshen up. Later, I'd like to take you out for the evening if you feel up to it."

She waved a hand impatiently. "Of course I do. What's wrong, Gareth? You've been brooding ever since we left the museum. Did you think I'd remember more than I did? I tried. Honestly I did."

"It's not that."

"Then what?"

He shrugged, dark eyes turbulent with emotion. "I don't have a good feeling about taking you home to Savannah. I'm hardly in a position to throw stones when it comes to sensitivity, but your father appears to be an ass. I'm not at all sure he'll give you the support you need until you have your memory in place."

"We don't really have a choice," she said, the tight knot of dread and regret in her stomach something she couldn't control. "I have to go home. Familiar territory will bring it all back. I have to believe that, and I have to pick up the pieces of my life. You know it's the only way."

She wanted him to fight for her. To say he couldn't bear for her to leave.

But Gareth was not the kind of man to spill his emotions in a messy declaration. "I don't have to like it," he muttered. Without warning, he slid a hand beneath the hair at her nape and dragged her toward him. His lips settled over hers in a rough, seeking kiss.

"Gareth…" She felt the violence in him, the mixture of frustration and sexual hunger. Though he held her gently as he ravaged her mouth, his body thrummed with tension.

Finally he broke free and pushed her away. "Seven o'clock. Be ready."

She stepped into her lavish shower stall, wishing she had the guts to invite Gareth to share it. Instead she washed quickly and got out, her skin tingling, her blood pumping, her breath choppy and shallow.

Though the bedroom was warm, she had gooseflesh as she dressed for her lover. Coffee-colored lingerie accented with pink rosettes. Thigh-high nylons in a lighter shade of mocha. And the dress. The one she'd not had the guts to wear the night before.

Red satin. The kind of dress worn by a courtesan. A temptress. A dangerous woman.

The mandarin collar was modest. But any propriety

ended there. The sleeveless sheath fit her as if it had been sewn onto her where she stood. Wearing a bra was impossible. The sumptuous fabric clung to her body like a second skin. The unapologetic scarlet should have clashed horribly with her hair, but instead, it warmed her coloring and made her skin glow.

With a shaky hand, she applied eyeliner and shadow, making her eyes mysterious and dark. A dab of perfume, wrist to wrist, earlobe to earlobe. Soon, she was ready. A ragged laugh escaped her as she realized there would be no limousine high jinks in this ensemble. She'd be lucky if she was able to sit down at all.

In another time, she would have carried a black lacquer cigarette holder...or a painted fan. Perhaps if Gracie emulated those women of the past, the outrageous females who dared not to conform to society's expectations, she might be able to enjoy the evening without heartbreak.

Before leaving her room, she dialed her father's number one more time and got the same message. Anger burned in her gut, along with hurt and suspicion. He was avoiding her. No question about it. But the day of reckoning was fast approaching, and if necessary, she would force him to apologize for whatever stupidity he had tried to perpetrate on the Wolff family in general and Gareth Wolff in particular.

She didn't wait to be summoned. A full twenty minutes early she stepped into the living room and scanned the space. Gareth wasn't there. A bottle of Perrier gave her something to hold on to and at the same time soothed her nerves along with a dry throat.

When Gareth appeared, she was prepared. "I'm ready," she said, conscious of her double meaning and wondering if he heard her not-so-subtle invitation.

This time she was able to look at him in his tux without swooning. He was every bit as handsome and charismatic as he had been the evening before, but she was not going to let him see how desperately she wanted him. At least not yet.

"You look lovely, Gracie." Something about the pole-axed expression on his face filled her with simultaneous satisfaction and amusement. With the right dress, a woman held the power to topple kingdoms.

Chandra was present in the lobby, tracking their departure with a jaundiced eye. Gracie called out a cheery, deliberate greeting and tucked her hand through Gareth's arm, proof that she was not above a little petty grandstanding.

The limo driver held open the car door, his face a respectful, expressionless mask.

Gareth looked down at Gracie, humor vying with sensual intent in his beautiful, dark brown, almost-black eyes. "Can you actually bend in that thing?"

She went up on tiptoe and kissed his chin. "Guess we'll see."

With as much grace as possible, she eased inside, settling onto the smooth leather seat and tucking her legs to one side. Gareth followed her in, his gaze not missing the way the skirt molded to her thighs and left little to the imagination.

They politely ignored each other for several miles. Finally she caved. "Where are we going?"

He stretched out his long legs, ankles crossed, and tucked his hands behind his head. "Dinner and dancing."

Her heart skipped a beat. "Seriously?"

"We didn't get our shot at the ball last night. Seemed a shame. So I called around to find a hotel that has live music and a dance floor."

Her eyes misted. "That's very sweet."

"Or very manipulative."

Her eyebrows lifted. "Meaning?"

"Dancing is little more than a civilized man's public foreplay."

"I might buy that if I were going out tonight with a civilized man."

"Touché." His lips twitched, and she was ridiculously glad she'd managed to coax him out of his earlier somber mood.

As they pulled up in front of an old, established hotel with a burgundy awning, Gareth slid out of the car and extended a hand to draw her to her feet. He paused for a moment to brush a soft kiss across her cheek. The innocent caress lit a fire deep inside her.

Without speaking, he led her inside where the ambiance was old Washington. Lavish decor with the slightly faded appeal of a genteel lady past her prime.

Every employee bowed and scraped in Gareth's wake. Soon he and Gracie were seated at a table near the crackling fire. Over salads and what she suspected was horribly expensive wine, he studied her face, his own unsmiling.

Finally she protested. "What? Do I have crumbs on my chin?"

He leaned his head on his hand, sober, speculative. "I can't figure out how a woman so innocent-looking can turn a man inside out without even trying."

"Do I really do that to you?" she asked boldly. He was speaking of carnality when she craved something far different. But even still, she was gratified to know he could admit weakness in her presence.

"That and more. Let's dance."

Chapter 16

Gareth hovered on the cusp of a blinding revelation. His brain tried to make sense of what he felt for the slender, strong-willed woman in his arms, but it was all he could do to keep from dragging her into the nearest dark corner and pressing his aching erection into her until oblivion claimed them both.

In her heels, she stood tall enough to rest her head against his shoulder. They swayed together, the music a faint counterpoint to the thudding of his heartbeat. His hands roved her back, tormented by the layer of slick fabric that separated him from her bare skin. Every man in the room stared at him with envy and at Gracie with barely concealed lust.

He couldn't blame them.

She was a burning in his veins, a sweet torment he would gladly endure. It came to him in that moment that he could never let her go. No matter the reason she

had to come to him in the beginning, she was his now…
body and soul.

Caution rang a warning bell in his subconscious. But
with Gracie pressed against him, chest to chest, thigh to
thigh, all he could think about was taking her. Claiming her. Proving to her that new memories were all she
needed.

One song ended, then another. Reluctantly he es-
corted her back to the table. The filet mignon and lob-
ster tails he had ordered for both of them were no more
than cardboard in his mouth. He watched her eat…saw
the way her small white teeth bit delicately into a crust
of bread, the gut-wrenching way her tongue ran across
her bottom lip to catch a drip of clarified butter.

They barely spoke. Words seemed unnecessary. Gracie glowed as if lit from within. Close. He came so close
to saying the words that would make him vulnerable to
her…promises that couldn't be withdrawn. But something held him back.

He had time. All the way to Savannah, in fact. Instead of taking the chopper, he would drive her. Just the
two of them…for hours. Making her laugh. Binding her
to him in every way he knew how. So that whatever secrets she was hiding couldn't tear them apart.

The truth washed over him, making his eyes burn.
He loved her. The walls he had built to protect his heart
had fallen brick by brick. Gracie was warmth and light
and happiness. He would tell her. Soon. When he'd had
a chance to get used to the idea.

Surely the words were superfluous tonight. Surely
she could see what she did to him.

Dinner dragged on with the agonizing gait of a snail.
After key lime tarts and rich coffee, he dragged her out
onto the dance floor one last time, his control fraying.

With little compunction, he slid his hands over her ass, cupping those curves and dragging her as close as was humanly possible.

Gracie came willingly it seemed, as unconcerned as he was with anything or anyone around them.

They moved together in drugged silence, perfectly in sync until the band had the temerity to take a break.

At last the waiter produced a check, signaling the end to Gareth's time upon the rack of impossible desire. Barely concealing the shaking in his hands, he scrawled his name on the signature line, included a large tip, and scooted his chair from the table with unconcealed impatience.

He tugged her hand, drawing her to her feet. "Time to go, Gracie."

In the car, he was unable to touch her. His fuse was so short as to be nonexistent. He drummed his fingers on his knees, his skin too tight, his collar strangling him.

Getting from the car to their suite took an eternity.

When at last the door closed behind them, sealing her with him in undisturbed intimacy, he stripped off his jacket, ripped away his tie and cummerbund and kicked off his shoes.

Gracie watched him, big-eyed, her hands clenched around a silly little evening bag.

He tugged it from her grasp and tossed it aside. "Tell me you want me," he whispered, twining his hands in her curls and massaging her scalp.

"I do," she said.

Her simply phrased response sounded a bit too weddinglike for his peace of mind. He ignored the odd shiver her words produced and kissed her roughly. He tried to wedge a leg between her thighs, but the siren's dress was too damned tight.

Reaching around her for the zipper, he lowered it without waiting for permission. The rasp of the teeth in a downward slide sounded abnormally loud in the stark silence. The fabric gaped, but Gracie clutched it with her hands, apprehension shadowing the cornflower-blue of her eyes.

He unfolded her fingers one by one. "Don't be afraid of me, Gracie. Not now. Not ever."

With one smooth slide of his hand, she was all but naked, standing in a pool of crimson fabric, her pert nipples a paler shade of ruby. Fiery hair, high breasts, long shapely thighs.

He held her hand as she stepped free of the gown and came to him eagerly, her arms sliding around his neck. Her shocked cry as his heavy shaft prodded her belly echoed inside his head.

Slowly, carefully, he backed her toward his room. *Her* room tonight, as well. And along the way, he kissed her. Long, slow, intimate kisses that tested his control.

Gracie's lips mated with his, her enthusiasm increasing his own ardor exponentially. Heated whispers. Soft sheets and scented pillowcases. A curved breast gripped by hard fingers. Pale, slender thighs parting instinctively.

His passion consumed him, threatened to tear away the veneer of polite society and rage unchecked in this room filled with shocked gasps, quiet sighs and muttered curses.

Everywhere she was soft, he was there. The inside of an elbow. A delicate earlobe. The moist petals at her center. He wanted it all…ached to claim every inch of her for his own.

Shuddering…shaking…he hooked her legs over his forearms. He saw on her face the moment she realized how the new position increased her vulnerability… opened her to him without reservation.

The condom was a frustrating but necessary stop on the road to heaven. Hovering over her, the head of his shaft nudging impatiently for entrance, he sucked in a gulp of oxygen and tried to formulate the words. Words she deserved to hear. But his throat closed up and his ability to speak was incinerated in the rush of ravenous hunger that drove him to the brink of insanity.

Gracie's eyes were closed. Her breasts rose and fell with the rhythm of her breathing. Against the pure white of the sheet, her hair glowed like fire. And that sweetly curved mouth, those perfect lips, parted in a whimper of pleasure as he fingered her deliberately.

She was swollen, wet and more than ready for his possession. And still he waited. Was he testing her or himself? Or was he simply relishing a night that was waning with reckless speed?

He positioned his shaft…rubbed her intimately. "Watch us, Gracie."

Her lashes lifted in slow motion, the glaze of need in her eyes telling him that the time for play was over. In deadly earnest, he lunged forward, drawing a shout from him and a faint cry from her. The sensation was indescribable. Her body received him with the tight squeeze of a too-small glove.

Heat rocketed down his spine, pooled in his loins. He withdrew and drove in again, losing himself in sheer bliss. How long had it been since he felt this raw, unshakable need? Maybe never.

Again and again he rocked into her, going so deep he felt the mouth of her womb. He would give his entire fortune, gladly, to be able to love her like this all night, never pausing, never falling off the edge.

But only a robot could withstand the intense pleasure. Only a eunuch could be immune to the way her tight passage milked him, her inner muscles caressing his shaft, giving him an excruciating pleasure he hadn't known existed until now. In a faraway corner of his mind he acknowledged that such perfect union was far more than physical. That the mating of two souls was as integral a part of this cataclysm as damp flesh and aching lungs.

He felt the end stalking him…fought it off with slow strokes that tormented them both. Gracie's legs were on his shoulders now, giving him compete access, total trust.

When he snapped, his vision blurred, his heart stopped. And then he could do no more than hang on as he shot to the stars and then fell helplessly into her arms.

Dimly, uncomprehending, he sensed her completion as it sparked from his. He held her tightly as darkness claimed him.

Gracie slipped from the bed in the wee hours to use the bathroom and sponge the evidence of their lovemaking from her body. She felt used and abused in the best possible way, her muscles lax with remembered pleasure, but at the same time sore and spent.

In her absence, Gareth had rolled onto his back, but he never stirred when she climbed back under the covers. His big body radiated heat. She snuggled into his embrace, one leg resting across his hard thigh.

Suddenly wide-awake, she moved her hand bravely across his abdomen and found his groin. His shaft, already partially erect, flexed and grew. He murmured in his sleep. As she held him in a loose grasp, he hardened to steel wrapped in velvety skin. The drop of moisture that wet the head of his erection signaled his eagerness.

"Gareth?"

Her whispered invitation bore no fruit other than the pulsing, rigid length of him.

Filled with a dangerous mixture of bravado and desperation, she scooted around and over him, taking him in her hand once again and guiding him into her body. She needed him so badly. The hourglass was almost empty. And who knew what moment would be their last?

Rising and falling on her knees, she pleasured herself on his erection. Eventually Gareth rose from the depths of sleep and moved with surety, surging upward and filling her beyond the realms of possibility.

Despite their earlier excess, the climax was near painful…drawn out…shiveringly intense.

She was half-asleep already when she felt him draw the covers over both of them, warming chilled skin and cocooning them in down-filled layers.

When she finally surfaced from a deep, restful sleep, she sensed someone watching her. Cracking one eye open, she witnessed Gareth's grin. He was lying on his side, leaning on an elbow, head in his hand. "I had the most *amazing* dream," he drawled.

She licked her lips, wondering what to say that would perhaps not implicate her. "I don't know what you mean."

"Liar." How a single word could convey amusement, affection and lust in equal measures baffled her. He grinned. "I'm not complaining, mind you. A guy can never have too many good dreams."

She smiled lazily, recognizing the dual gifts of happiness and contentment as they took up residence in her heart. No words could convey her mood.

His smile faded into something less lighthearted while his hand, hidden beneath the covers, parted her legs. "Feel like dreaming again?" he asked huskily, his breath warm at her throat as he moved over her.

Her stomach growled audibly. "I need breakfast," she complained, giggling when he groaned in protest. Already she felt him pushing deep.

"Later, darling Gracie."

His unexpected transposition of her names caught her off guard. A man like Gareth Wolff didn't make free with careless endearments. So she savored the unexpected sweetness and tucked it away in her heart.

Surely by now his determined possession should not have been as shocking, his take-no-prisoners approach to lovemaking less overwhelming.

But nothing about this barely blossoming relationship was predictable. Moments later when she arched in stunned pleasure and found her release, it was as shiningly perfect as the first time he'd taken her and as sweetly sensuous as the last.

They were late for checkout. Fortunately for Gracie, such mundane concerns were not on Gareth's radar. When they made their way to the rooftop, the helicopter and pilot awaited them despite their tardiness.

Gracie was more able to enjoy the return trip to Wolff Mountain than on the first leg of their journey. Any nerves borne of a new experience had settled in the interim. As the pilot and Gareth chatted via their radio headsets, Gracie was content to take in the spectacular view. Like a bird on a mission, the chopper flew a steady, swift path south and west. In no time, they were settling onto the helipad and disembarking.

The Jeep, keys inside, awaited them. Gareth stowed

their bags and after seeing that Gracie was tucked in, jumped behind the wheel and slung gravel as he turned and headed back through the forest at a fast clip.

As they broke through a gap in the woods, the magnificent Wolff fortress came into view. Gareth, face carved in mysterious lines, slowed the vehicle to a stop. With the engine still running, he half turned to face her. His hand covered hers, fingers linking with hers.

She was shocked to see his teeth worry his lower lip. All around them nature burst forth in a panoply of spring exuberance. Gracie's heart followed suit. Gareth felt *something* for her. She knew it. Without false modesty or brain-addled, amnesia-created, pie-in-the-sky dreams, she sensed his caring at a most basic level.

He played with a lock of her hair, his eyes trained on the house above them, the home where he had grown up so harshly, so quickly. "I want you to meet my father tonight," he said. "I think the two of you will like each other."

Her heart bounced and swelled, dancing with amazement and joy. "I'd love to," she said softly, trying not to let him see how much this significant gesture of trust gave her hope for the future—their future. Was it possible that she and Gareth were more than lovers passing in the night? She hoped so…dear God, she hoped so.

He held her hand the rest of the way to his house. With the sun beating down on her head and the breeze tossing her hair in her eyes, she was momentarily blinded. Gareth was her lodestone, her anchor.

Jacob's car was parked in front of the house when they pulled up. Gareth hopped out. "I see we have a welcoming committee. Hopefully he's brought lunch. I'm starving."

But when they entered the cool, dimly lit foyer and

then made their way to the living room, Gracie knew that Jacob was not here to provide a picnic. His face was somber, his eyes hooded.

He never even glanced at Gracie. Instead he went to his brother and wrapped his arms around him, holding tight. Gareth returned the embrace and then broke away to stare at his sibling in puzzlement. "What's wrong?"

Jacob swallowed, his Adam's apple bobbing visibly as he strove for control.

Fear like she had never known crashed over Gracie, threatening to swallow her whole.

Gareth paled, his gaze locked on his brother's face. "Tell me, damn it."

"I thought about not showing you," Jacob said, his voice harsh with suppressed emotion. "You're not going to like it." He half turned and gestured to what Gracie had not been able to see until this moment. Strewn across the surface of the coffee table was a series of tabloids, Gareth's unmistakable face plastered on the cover of each one.

But even more shocking were the small, square insets on all of the papers. Blurry, grainy head shots of Gracie. Her stomach clenched.

Gareth's mouth opened and snapped shut. He reached for the worst of the gossip rags, one where Jacob had folded back the page to reveal the article inside. With no one to stop her, Gracie stood at his elbow and read with shocked dismay.

Edward Darlington, owner of Darlington Gallery in Savannah, Georgia, spoke to our reporter at a charity golf tournament in Cannes this past weekend. It seems that Mr. Darlington is on the verge of scoring a coup for his modest gallery. Darling-

ton's daughter, Gracie, has recently become intimately involved with the reclusive eldest son of
the renowned Wolff family, whose considerable
fortune has suffered very little at the hands of the
American economy. Mr. Darlington hints that he
will soon be allowed to exhibit the small but remarkable collection of oil paintings completed by
Gareth's Wolff's mother, Laura, prior to her violent and untimely death in the mid-1980s…

The story went on for another sentence or two, but
Gracie turned away, unable to read another word. Sick
to her stomach, she cringed when Gareth turned on her
and stared through eyes that chilled her with black ice.
"How did he find out about the paintings?" His voice
shook. At his sides, his hands clenched, as though he
wanted to strike her. "And was this your intent from the
beginning? To fake amnesia…worm your way into my
bed… God, you're self-serving…both of you."

Jacob touched his arm. "Give yourself a minute. I
know this stings."

"Stings?" Gareth's expression was incredulous. "It
doesn't sting. It makes me want to put my hands around
Edward Darlington's neck and squeeze until he's a dead
man."

He stared at Gracie, his expression fierce as a thun-
derstorm waiting to strike. "And you. You *know* I don't
exploit my mother. I told you that. You've been playing
me from the beginning, haven't you? And God knows
I fell for it."

Chapter 17

Gracie backed up to the wall, her arms wrapped around her waist. "I didn't know," she whispered hoarsely. "I'm so sorry."

Jacob still barely looked at her. All his attention was focused on his big brother, the man who was in so much pain it was terrible to watch. Jacob spoke soothingly. "Clearly the man's an ass. He's using this as a publicity stunt to draw business to his gallery. No one will take him seriously. We've never exhibited Mother's work, and we won't start now. He's trying to pressure you into agreeing to a gallery showing, but little does he know you're a stubborn bastard."

Gareth stalked Gracie, grabbing her shoulders in a bruising grip and shaking her. "Get out of here," he yelled. "Now."

She clung to him, her heart shattering at his feet. "I didn't know. I swear I didn't know."

The rage melted from his face to be replaced by something far more frightening. He thrust her away. "But that's just it, Gracie Darlington."

It hurt unbearably to hear him say her name with such loathing.

He bit out the words. "You *did* know at one time. And how *convenient* that you forgot."

Tears streamed down her face. "It's not really such a bad thing, is it? He went about it the wrong way, trying to bully you, but the showing could be a beautiful tribute to your mother. I never meant to hurt you. I wouldn't. I couldn't."

"I thought I knew how low a woman could sink. But you're a bitch of the first water. It was lies from the very beginning, every bit of it."

She fell to her knees, willing to beg, to humble herself on behalf of her idiot father. "I love you," she cried. "Why would I hurt you?"

But it was too late. The wolf had gnawed off his own foot to spring free of the trap. Whatever tender feelings he might have had for her were cauterized in an instant.

He stared downward, disgust and fury shriveling her where she knelt. "Don't make me call the authorities," he said coldly, every inch the firstborn of the manor.

Sensing the utter futility of any appeal, she stumbled to her feet and fled. The keys were still in the Jeep. She could barely see through the burning wash of tears. Cranking the engine, she threw the vehicle into Reverse, turned and shot down the road, hysteria dictating every motion.

The driveway was kinked with twists and turns that negotiated the mountainside. At the third switchback, she lost control and slammed into a tree.

* * *

"Gracie. Wake up. You're okay. Open your eyes."

Sluggishly, wrapped in a cloud of dread, she complied. Jacob sat beside her in the passenger seat, his gaze watchful. He took her wrist in an impersonal grip and checked her pulse. "That was a stupid thing to do. The Jeep is a mess, and you're lucky you didn't get hurt."

"Where's Gareth?" Just saying his name out loud was like scraping her throat with razor blades.

Jacob shrugged. "He headed up the mountain. I've known him to disappear for days at a time. He won't come back until you're long gone. I've been charged with escorting you off the property and taking you to the airport. I'll pay for a first-class ticket and arrange for one of our employees to meet you at the other end and stay with you until your father returns."

"But I…"

He got out and motioned for her to follow. "We need to collect your things. Get in my car."

At Gareth's house, she held her breath, hoping he had relented, but knowing in her heart that he would never forgive her.

Jacob stood in the doorway of her bedroom while she packed. It didn't take long. Gracie took nothing of Annalise's bounty except for a couple of casual outfits. She didn't know what to expect during the journey home, and it seemed prudent to have a change of clothing. When she had added her few personal items, the things she had brought with her when she first arrived, she zipped shut the small carry-on and stood quietly. "I'm ready."

Jacob nodded tersely.

The forty-five-minute drive to the airport was accomplished in dead silence. Nothing looked familiar to Gracie. And she no longer cared.

At the departure gate, Jacob pulled to the curb, engine idling. With his face set in grim lines, the resemblance to his brother was striking. He scowled at Gracie, not a shred of the compassionate doctor in evidence. "Don't contact him," he said bluntly. "No phone calls. No texts. No emails. If you ever try to approach our property again, you'll be charged with trespassing. Do you understand?"

A dagger of unbearable pain lodged beneath her heart, making it difficult to breathe. "I understand." Her voice was dull. Every scrap of life had been beaten out of her. No memory. No future. No Gareth.

As soon as she stepped out of the car with her bag, Jacob drove away without a backward glance.

She wandered the airport terminal in a fog of agony, feeling as if she had lost a limb. To have something to hide behind, she purchased a copy of *People* magazine. All the faces on the cover were familiar. It was too damn bad that the rich and famous were more accessible in her memory bank than her family and friends.

When the flight boarded, she huddled in her first-class window seat and tried to block out the world. After one abortive attempt at conversation, her travel companion, a balding middle-aged man, left her alone.

Gracie rested her head against the glass, eyes closed. If she could have ended her life at that moment, she might have considered it. The yawning chasm of emptiness inside her chest threatened to swallow her whole.

Perhaps she dozed. Or perhaps the pain simply became too much to bear and she lapsed into a stupor of grief.

But when the plane touched down and the flight attendant insisted Gracie leave the plane, she managed to get to her feet and shuffle in the wake of the other passengers.

As she exited the concourse, a tall man with a deep artificial tan and a cautious smile waved at her. "Over here, Gracie."

And just like that, it all came flooding back. Every bit of her lost memory. In an instant. He was her father.

Twenty-four hours ago such a development would have elated her. Now all she felt was a dull acceptance. If Gareth had been standing beside her, he would undoubtedly have been skeptical in the extreme.

Fortunately she didn't have to explain herself to anyone. Her father thought she was pretending to have amnesia while on Wolff Mountain, so as far as he was concerned, nothing had changed.

He took her arm as they made their way outside. "I'm glad you're home, baby girl. Those Wolff men are scary. I've had to hire a lawyer…can you believe it? They made all kinds of threats…just because I joked with some sleazy reporter."

"I thought you were gone."

He pulled out into traffic and glanced at her. "Came in on a flight half an hour ago. When I saw a woman holding a sign with your name on it, we had a little chat and I sent her on her way. You want to stop for lunch? My treat?"

Gracie turned away from him, too desolate to be indignant. Her father was shallow, ego-driven and about as thick-skinned as a rhino. If he picked up on her distress, he showed no sign.

Even with no response from her, he stopped at the restaurant anyway. While her father polished off a substantial meal, Gracie pushed around several bites of syrup-soaked pancake on her plate and waited for the interminable stop on her journey home to be over.

Suddenly she was struck by a revelation. "You never had any intention of letting me manage the gallery, did you?" Only now did she remember that he had promised the job as an incentive to get her to invade Wolff Mountain and coax Gareth Wolff into giving them his mother's paintings for the gallery. "You knew I would fail," she accused. "This was all nothing more than a futile goose chase. Why, Daddy? Why would you do that to me?"

He set down his coffee cup and sighed, his put-upon expression designed to make *her* feel guilty instead of the other way around. "Misty's the new manager, sweetheart. And if you think about it, it makes perfect sense. She needs the job…you don't."

Misty was her father's less-than-brilliant girlfriend. "And *why* don't I need the job?" Gracie asked. She'd worked at the gallery in one capacity or another for years. Knew the business inside and out. Becoming manager was something she had wanted for a long time. So she had acceded to her father's audacious request that she track down Gareth Wolff and ask about Laura's paintings. Gracie had actually been the one to stumble across the mention of them in an old art journal she'd picked up at a flea market.

Edward took her hand in his, surprising her with the open affection. Her father rarely made the effort to play his parental role. "You're a gifted artist, Gracie. You should be creating art…not selling it. Every penny of the money your mother left you is still sitting in the bank. Take some of it. Go away. Find your muse. And when you come home, I'll be begging *you* to let me exhibit your work."

She took the flattery with a grain of salt. Edward knew he had screwed up, and he knew she would not be easily appeased. What he didn't know was that she was too heartsick to work up a head of steam over his transgressions. Fighting with him was simply more than she could endure right now.

An hour later, she was alone in her bedroom. The air was stale and musty, so she threw open the windows and curled up on one of the cushioned gable seats searching for solace.

Everything surrounding her was comfortable and familiar. And she had never felt so alone in all her life.

Two weeks of grieving were all she could tolerate. Nothing was going to change unless she took the reins and quit letting the days wash past her...unnoticed, unappreciated.

She wasn't the first woman to lose a man she loved. And she wouldn't be the last. Life moved on.

But what hurt the most—the regret that was hardest to shake—was that Gareth thought she had been willing to use his mother's art for personal gain. And it was true. Not knowing Gareth or his personal history, she hadn't thought the idea so terrible at its inception. In fact, Gracie had gone to the Blue Ridge sure she could persuade Gareth Wolff to share his mother's talent with the world. Thinking of him alone and hurting in his mountain hideaway made her ill. Knowing that she had added to his pain was almost more than she could bear.

When she could stand it no more, she took her father's advice. Loading up her yellow VW bug, the one that had been returned to her from a small town in Virginia with no note, no acknowledgment at all, she fled the city.

With her she had a month's stash of food and several boxes of art supplies. She had rented a small, isolated cabin in the north Georgia mountains, and for the next thirty days, she planned to do nothing but paint, sleep and paint again.

Halfway up the state, she came close to a crisis. A huge part of her wanted to drive northward, not stopping until she reached a certain mountain in Virginia. She actually pulled over in a rest stop and folded out a map to see how long it would take her.

But at the last minute, she acknowledged the futility of such a plan. Not only would she face the very real possibility of being arrested, but even worse, the likelihood that Gareth might throw her out himself. The God's honest truth was, she couldn't bear to see hate in those beautiful, dark eyes that had shown her such tenderness and care.

She had cried enough tears to fill a small lake. There were none left. Only a dull acceptance of what could not be changed.

The sun was almost gone when she spotted a turnoff on the narrow two-lane road. Now she traversed a rough, hard-packed dirt lane. Forty-five minutes later, when it seemed as if she might drive off the end of the world, she found her lodging, a small, unimpressive house in the heart of the forest.

Peeling paint, a leaning porch and ill-kempt landscaping made her wonder if she had been scammed. Fortunately the inside was more prepossessing. Though had she not been so bone tired, she might have spared a moment's amusement for the mental juxtaposition of Gareth's incredible home with this dump.

The first night in the cabin was unsettling. She was a city girl, used to the sounds of sirens and traffic and quarreling neighbors. Here the solitude was oppressive, the deep, impenetrable night threatening.

On Wolff Mountain, the conditions were similar. But there she'd had Gareth to share her bed, to keep her safe and warm. Now she was on her own.

She slept little, choosing instead to curl up on the screened-in porch in a cushioned wicker chair and listen to the chirp of crickets and the rustle of nocturnal animals. Occasionally she dozed, but it was not until the faint light of morning dawned that she was finally able to crawl back into her bed and fall into a deep, exhausted slumber.

The pattern continued over the next week. Sleeping much of the day…eating a single meal in the evening, and working as the night hours waned. Sometimes she dragged a small lamp out onto the porch. At other moments she labored by candlelight.

Her water colors remained untouched. Instead she used pen and ink, filling page after page of heavy paper with black slashes, most of which translated into the same subject.

As her hands flew over the pages, her mind was unfortunately free to wander. Her world was topsy-turvy, changed beyond recognition. She couldn't continue with the life she had known for so many years. The potential for a future with Gareth was obliterated. Where did she go from here?

On the eighth day of her walkabout, it rained. Not a gentle sprinkle, but a raging, stormy deluge. In the wake of her usual nighttime insomnia, she slid into bed, pulled the covers over her head and fell asleep to the drumming of the storm on the tin roof overhead.

Dreams swirled in her subconscious, memories of Gareth making love to her. Vivid images of the two of them talking, laughing, wanting, taking. Hunger and heat.

She moaned, restless and aching. The dream was sweet at first, but then terrifying and wretched. Gareth turned his back on her, walking away until he was no more than a speck on the horizon.

Thunder rumbled again, but with an oddly insistent beat. It took her long minutes to shake off the vestiges of sleep and recognize that someone was beating on her door.

Heartsick…exhausted…she contemplated not answering the summons. But perhaps there was a neighbor with an emergency…someone who needed her help.

Cautiously she peeped around the edge of the front window draperies and felt her limbs go numb as her heart ceased to beat. It was Gareth. Wasn't it? She hardly recognized him.

Swinging open the door with an unsteady hand, she stared at him. "Why are you here?" she demanded.

Chapter 18

Gareth considered himself an intelligent man, but the lessons he had learned since Gracie left the mountain were hard-won. Giving up his grief and bitterness was no easy task. But in Gracie's absence, he had seen a man in the mirror who was a ruthless bastard. A man who suffered.

He'd walked miles in the mountains, trying in vain to outrun his demons. And at night he'd tossed and turned in restless dreams, aching for Gracie as if he had lost a limb.

His current quest was half closure, half penance. First to Savannah for a heated conversation with Edward Darlington, then on north and west to track through an obscure area with few directional signs and many roads that didn't show up on his GPS.

He was exhausted, frustrated and frankly, miserable. He drank in the sight of Gracie like a tonic. He felt dizzy, disoriented. None of his recollections of her came close to the real thing. Though she was thinner perhaps, and pale, too pale, she was so beautiful it hurt to look at her. He leaned against the door frame, his knees embarrassingly weak. "May I come in?"

She debated saying no. He saw the refusal form in her eyes, and yet at the last minute, he was granted a reprieve. But instead of answering him, she merely stepped back and allowed him to brush past her. He inhaled her familiar scent and his gut clenched. Another part of him tightened, as well, but he knew such a craving would not likely be appeased. Not when he had acted like a complete and total jackass.

"Nice cabin," he said, running his hand over a questionable support beam. With an inward wince, he admitted to himself that sarcasm probably wasn't the best approach.

"Why are you here?" She reiterated the question bluntly.

In her face he could see no sign of welcome. He had hoped… God, he had hoped that she would still feel at least an iota of the love she had professed. But he'd done a damned good job of riding roughshod over her tender heart, and he couldn't blame her if she hated him.

He paced the small living room, noting the bunch of wildflowers in a milk-glass vase, the remnants of a snack on a rickety end table. "I had your father investigated," he said bluntly.

Some strong reaction flashed in her eyes before she recovered and presented him with an impassive gaze. "And?"

"He's not a criminal. I suppose you would say his worst sin is an overabundance of ego."

"You're hardly one to throw stones in the arena."

"A fair point," he acknowledged. "Do you have anything to drink? I'm parched."

He followed her into the kitchen, waiting as she poured a cup of lukewarm coffee and handed it to him… black…the way he liked it. He downed half the cup and grimaced. The sludge tasted as if it had been brewed hours ago.

He set the unfinished drink on the scarred Formica counter and scowled. "Why didn't you just ask to see my mother's paintings?"

Her glare was incredulous. "I had amnesia."

"So that part was true?" In the aftermath of her leaving, he'd had a hell of a time deciding which aspects of Gracie Darlington were gold and which were dross.

"Yes," she muttered. "It was all true. Believe me, if I had remembered why I was there, I would have told you. You would have kicked me out and the two of us would have remained strangers."

"But instead, you became my lover."

She went white, her eyes agonized. And then just as quickly, the expression vanished. With a shrug, she nodded. "Apparently so."

"Did you ever get your memory back?" He had vacillated between wondering if she had regained her past and doubting that she had ever lost it in the first place.

Gracie perched on a stool, dark smudges beneath her eyes. After a wide-mouthed yawn, she rubbed her hands on the knees of her flannel sleep pants. They were cotton-candy pink with little bunnies hopping across the fabric. "As soon as I saw my father, I remembered everything. Not that it mattered at that point."

"I'm glad." He stopped short, the words he had come to say bottled up in his chest. "I had a serious girlfriend once."

His abrupt change in topic left her visibly confused. "Okay…"

"She used me to get to my father and steal a priceless painting during a family dinner."

Though he didn't deserve it, her eyes softened. "I'm sorry."

"I was afraid of making the same mistake with you." The admission hurt his chest.

"What mistake?"

"Confusing lust with love. Opening my family to harm."

Her pretty face, usually so open and easy to read, baffled him with its lack of expression. She shrugged. "I'm sorry my father was such an idiot. And I regret the fact that I let him coax me into doing something as stupid as infiltrating your privacy. I've apologized before. I don't know what else I can do."

"Why *did* you come to Wolff Mountain, especially knowing how unlikely it was that I would agree to your proposal?"

"My father promised me that if I could get you to place your mother's work in the gallery, he would appoint me manager."

"And he wouldn't have done that anyway?"

"No. Not even if I had succeeded in my mission with you. When I got back, he had already installed his bimbo girlfriend as manager. Apparently she needs the job more than I do."

"I'm sorry."

"For once, he was probably right. I have an MFA degree. But I convinced myself that the percentage of artists who make a full-time career from painting was so small, there was no point in trying. As manager of the gallery, I would still be using my degree, but without the personal risk. Essentially I wanted my father to give me the job so I could settle down and move on with my life."

"You're awfully young to settle down. Are you any good?"

His blunt question dragged a laugh from her. "You be the judge." She left him only long enough to retrieve a sketch pad from another room. "I've done all these since I've been here."

Gareth flipped the pages slowly, at once impressed and humbled. She was damned good. The only real surprise was that in every one of the admittedly outstanding sketches, the subject was him. Gareth.

He studied each of them, noting how she had captured his expressions so succinctly. Arrogance. Humor. Anger. Hostility. It didn't escape his notice that very few of the pages revealed any softer nuance in him. Perhaps if she had drawn his face during lovemaking, she could have seen what was in his eyes. As it was…no wonder she had greeted him today with such a marked lack of emotion. The man in the images was certainly not lovable as far as Gareth could see.

A blank page came next, and when he flicked at it, preparing to close the pad, he realized that here was another sketch still unseen. He turned the page. And his heart stopped. *Dear God.*

His mother's eyes gazed back at him with amusement and compassion.

Gareth looked up, shock flooding his belly. "How did you…"

Gracie moved past him and perched on the arm of the sofa, her feet tucked beneath her. "The photo in your workshop. I recreated it from memory…at least the portion that was your mother. The more I sketched, the more I realized how much you look like her. She must have loved you very much. Her first child. A precious boy."

With a fingertip, he traced the features of a woman who had once meant the world to him. But in an instant, unbidden, another picture, a newspaper photo, momentarily threatened to replace his current nostalgic mood. With all his mental acuity, he forced it back.

He refused to let those old images hurt or define him. Not anymore. The likeness Gracie had created of his beloved mother warmed his heart and further cracked the shell he had built around himself. "It's perfect," he said, his throat tight and painful. "The spittin' image…" He paused. "Is it for sale?"

Gracie nodded.

"How much?"

"Seventy-five thousand dollars. A check made out to my charity."

He managed a grin, the first time he had really felt like smiling since he'd chased Gracie out of his life. "And what charity would that be?"

"I'll think of one."

He sobered, laying aside the collection of Gracie's art. "I'll never be able to make it up to you for the way I reacted that day. I'm ashamed, Gracie. And so damned sorry."

She picked up a snack plate and carried it to the kitchen, ensuring that it was impossible for him to see her face, though the two rooms were connected. "I think we've both spent far too much time on apologies."

He followed, taking her arm and forcing her to confront him. Without shoes, she was small, defenseless. Her big blue eyes looked up at him with wary calm.

She seemed cool as ice. He was the one whose hands trembled. He swallowed his pride along with the lump in his throat. "I understand loyalty to a parent, Gracie. Believe me. I've made decisions over the years, choices to please my father that anyone looking in would have questioned…and often did. I no longer fault you for coming to Wolff Mountain. You had to try."

"And the newspaper interview?"

"It felt like betrayal," he said simply, reliving for a moment that terrible afternoon. "I'd planned to tell you that night that I loved you. But instead, it seemed as if I had made the same mistake all over again…that I had been ruled by my libido at the expense of my family."

"Were there any follow-up stories?"

"No. It was a nonarticle in the first place. Just one stupid guy shooting off his mouth and saying asinine things."

"He is my father and will always be my father. No matter how badly he screwed up or will screw up in the future, I can never abandon him."

"Does that same level of forgiveness and acceptance extend to me, as well?"

He held his breath, the balance of his life in the palms of her small, feminine hands.

The fact that she couldn't meet his gaze gave him his answer. "I'll go," he said curtly, almost beyond social niceties. The agony of his chest being torn in two as he left his heart in those same small hands almost crippled him. He made it to the door before she stopped him.

"I don't want you to leave," she said, breathless as she wrapped her arms around him from behind and hung on. "Of course I forgive you."

He stopped, whirled and grabbed her up in his arms. "I love you, Gracie," he said hoarsely. "God knows you have no cause to believe it, but it's true."

Her arms were around his waist, her cheek to his

chest. Frustrated with her silence and his inability to read her face, he scooped her up and carried her to the sofa. With her in his lap, he began to think the world might once again make sense.

He tipped up her chin, the better to see her crystal-clear eyes. But the blue was muted today, veiled in a way that made him afraid.

She grimaced faintly, pressing a kiss to his chin and curling into his embrace. "I love you, too."

"Come back with me," he urged. "The house is empty now. You stole the life away from it."

"No." Her answer was simple. Quiet. "You're welcome to stay here for a few days. In my bed." She seemed to realize that her invitation needed clarification.

"And after that?" Anger clenched his muscles.

"You have a life and I have mine. Parallel lines, Gareth. No intersection."

"That's where you're wrong." He could outstubborn her any day. "I'm not letting you go."

"You never had me…not really. We were playing a game, that's all. The scullery maid and the prince. Can you imagine my father and yours if they ever met? It's a ludicrous thought. We live in totally different worlds."

"But you're willing to have sex with me for old times' sake? Is that it?"

"You needn't make it sound so tawdry. There's no reason we can't maintain a physical relationship until you find the right woman to marry."

"And then you'll let me go…just like that?" He thrust her away and stood to pace, ridiculously hurt. Did she think so little of him?

Her bullheaded attitude convinced him he had to take another tack. "Let's go to bed then. Right now."

"I…uh…"

He took her hand and dragged her to her feet. "Where's your room? Through here?" It wasn't too hard to locate his target in such a tiny cabin.

The covers on her bed were tumbled. Either she was a little on the messy side or she had still been asleep when he arrived.

Without waiting for an engraved invitation, he stripped her out of her practical sleepwear, divested himself of his own clothing and bent her over the bed, hands at her hips. He almost forgot the condom, remembering only at the last second to bend down and pull one from his jeans pocket.

When he was sheathed in latex, he surged into her from behind, feeling the long, slow slide home on a million different levels. Her body accepted him easily now, warm and moist and slick with welcome.

He touched the back of her head, ruffling her curls. "Is this what you had in mind, Gracie? Friends with benefits?"

She was mute, her sharp gasps as he rammed into her repeatedly the only response. From this angle, the view was unbearably erotic.

"Look at us in the mirror," he urged. His tanned hands on the white skin of her ass made a memorable picture. "This will never be enough," he muttered, almost beyond speech. "You're wrong. Dead wrong."

He reached beneath her to cup her breasts and play with them, slowing his drive to completion only by exerting every inch of his iron will. Her nipples budded at his touch. He used his other hand to pinch lightly at her labia. She cried out and came, squeezing his shaft so tightly at the peak of her climax that he shuddered and saw stars.

"Gracie. God, Gracie." Gripping her ass once again,

he moved desperately in her, stroke after steady stroke. The tempo increased, his body tensed. Without warning, his world exploded as release snatched him up and tumbled him onto a rich, blissful, panting shore.

He had collapsed on top of her at the end. Boneless with pleasure, he shifted her all the way onto the bed and climbed in with her. Gracie was already asleep, which struck him as odd since it was morning, but he'd not had much rest in the last week, so he succumbed to postcoital fatigue and joined her.

Chapter 19

Gracie awoke at noon, completely disoriented, but feeling as if something momentous had happened. The broad hair-roughened chest to which she was currently plastered gave her the first clue.

Gareth had found her. She reprimanded her silly, nonsensical heart for its cartwheel of jubilation and told herself to enjoy his apology visit without regret for the future.

Her movements wakened him. He rubbed his eyes and sat up, the sheet barely protecting his modesty. "I'm starving," he said, running a hand over her hip and caressing her butt.

She managed a smile. "I can feed you. Give me a minute to get dressed."

He rolled over her, trapping her with his thighs and resting his weight on his arms. "Do you understand what just happened?" His expression was sober as he looked down at her.

She chewed her lip, wondering why he was not putting a truly magnificent erection to good use. "Makeup sex?"

He bit her neck, sending shivers in wild seismic patterns all over her body. "Beyond that."

"No."

"I showed you how wrong you are."

"Not following." How could a woman concentrate when a man had his *you-know-what* pressed tantalizingly close to her most needy spot.

"I love you. You love me. We're not going to skulk around having some Romeo and Juliet affair. We're going to get married."

Like a beached fish, Gracie struggled to breathe. "Excuse me?"

"You heard me." He used his swollen penis to nudge her gently.

"Not gonna happen. Now that I have all my memories back, I get the full picture. I'm firmly middle-class and you're stinkin' rich. Your father would have apoplexy if you brought me up to the castle. Admit it. That's why you never introduced us to start with."

"Wrong again. I wanted him to meet you, but I was afraid you were up to no good. Now that I know the truth, I can tell you that he'll welcome you with open arms."

"I still have an unpredictable, not always clear-thinking father."

"Let me tell you a secret, Gracie Darlington." He entered her half an inch or so and withdrew. "As we speak, UPS is delivering a dozen of my mother's painting to the Darlington Gallery in Savannah…in preparation for an exhibition entitled *For Those We Love*. Dear old Edward is free to show them however long he likes…as long as the foundation gets the requested fee."

She searched his face, stunned to see he was telling the truth. "But you were so angry with him. He was insensitive about your mother's death, her life, your memories."

Gareth sank deep, his mouth finding hers in a deep carnal kiss as he claimed her. "He created you, my love. And for that, I'll forgive him almost anything."

Gracie couldn't stem the tears that wet her cheeks. "Thank you," she whispered.

He moved with a power that left no question as to his passion, his adoration. "You're mine," he muttered, the muscles in his arms straining as he supported his upper body. His hips flexed. "Mine."

Gracie gave herself up to the moment, overwhelmed not only by his incredibly generous gesture to her father, but by the openness she sensed in him, the lack of bitterness, the almost palpable contentment.

The end sparked at one instant this time, both of them groaning with pleasure as they came together, perfectly in sync, exquisitely attuned to one other.

Lazily, feeling like the luckiest woman in the world, she ran a hand over his shorn head. The hair was no more than a half an inch long all over. "Why did you cut it?" she asked. "When I looked out the window, I wasn't sure at first that it was you." Though he was still incredibly handsome, his new appearance was more hero and protector than wild man and dangerous predator.

Gareth dragged them both to a seated position against the headboard, Gracie's back to his chest. In the mirror opposite the bed, she could see his expression clearly.

He ran a hand over his head, his smile rueful. "In ancient days, men sometimes cut off their hair as a sign of penitence and devotion. I hurt you badly, Gracie. The very person to whom I owed the greatest debt… for bringing me back to life. For loving me. This was the only way I knew how to make you see what was in my heart."

"Oh, Gareth…"

Their gazes met in the mirror, hers tremulous, his amazingly tender as he rubbed the wetness from her cheeks with a gentle touch.

He grinned suddenly. "Well, the haircut wasn't the *only* thing I thought of. Wait here. Don't move."

He left the room; she heard the front door open and close, which made her laugh out loud, because he was buck naked. Moments later he was back, this time scooting up beside her so they faced each other.

She leaned toward him and used both hands to caress his head. "I'm getting used to it already. It makes you look like even more of a badass than you did before."

He hugged her tightly, his arms bands of steel that made it hard to breathe. "I'll never hurt you again, Gracie Darlington."

Reluctantly he released her, handing over a small parcel clumsily wrapped in tissue, but without tape or bow. She took it with a quizzical smile and peeled back the paper.

"Oh, Gareth." That was her new refrain. But what else was there to say when he had given her the most exquisite box. The wood was cherry, the dimensions two inches by three inches and barely an inch deep. The lid was inlaid with an intricate pattern of turquoise and silver and onyx. "You made this?"

He nodded. "Open it."

She slid the lid to one side, revealing a small compartment and an even smaller wad of tissue. Inside the tissue was a diamond ring, the square cut center stone flanked by two perfect emeralds. She was speechless.

"It was my mother's," he said hurriedly. "And if it makes you feel bad to wear it, we'll find something else. But I've already talked to Kieran and Jacob. They gave me their blessing to pass this on to you…since I was the one who remembered her best."

She gulped as he slid the lovely ring on to her finger.

Gareth's expression was more open and vulnerable than she had ever seen it, his heart laid out for her to see. "Marry me, Gracie. Bring light and life and children to our mountain."

She rested her head against his shoulder, already contemplating the memories they would create together. "Yes, my dear wolf," she said. "Always and forever, yes."

* * * * *